Tales From South America

Traditional tales, fables and sagas

from South America.

Compiled, Adapted & Edited by Clive Gilson

Tales from the World's Firesides

Tales From South America,

edited by Clive Gilson, Solitude, Bath, UK

www.clivegilson.com

Printed by IngramSpark

ISBN: 978-1-915081-40-7

- I have edited Clive Gilson's books for over a decade now – he's prolific and can turn his hand to many genres. poetry, short fiction, contemporary novels, folklore, and science fiction – and the common theme is that none of them ever fails to take my breath away. There's something in each story that is either memorably poignant, hauntingly unnerving, or sidesplittingly funny - *Lorna Howarth, The Write Factor*

- *Ragged A**** Ruffian reviewed on Amazon in the United Kingdom on 27 January 2021* - A truly heartwarming, interesting, story with a wonderful narrative. Unquestionably a splendid read

- A Solitude of Stars: With deft turns of phrase and an imagination that would make Philip K. Dick jealous, Gilson foresees a dystopian future, the seeds of which are definitely being sown right now. The story is a chilling glimpse of what may come to pass, warmed by a thread of love that raises the narrative beyond despair. I found the stories disturbing and breath-taking in equal measure. The Apparat and Dirigiste tribes are ranging across our solar system seeking peace by waging war, raising the question; is humanity actually capable of peace? A riveting read. - *Rob Swan, The Write Factor*

- Songs of Bliss gripped me from the start - I had to read right to the end. Loved the humour. Impressed by the surprising empathy that I felt for rather - on the face of it - unlikeable characters. Look forward to seeing it in print. - *Maighdean-Mhara, commenting on Authonomy*

- I just wanted to thank you once more for your help acquiring this beautiful collection. It's found a new home at the top of my library. I've already stumbled onto some wonderful stories in a couple of the collections, and I can't wait to get more. Have a wonderful holiday and a great new year... - *Richer Daniel Laporte, California, December 2021*

Interior image: Silke Schäfer from Pixabay

Cover image: by Image by Vicki Hamilton from Pixabay

CONTENTS

Preface

How Night Came

The Cursed Admiral and the Goblins' Revenge

Coniraya Viracocha

A Boy Of The Andes

How the Rabbit Lost His Tail

The Miracle of the Countess and the Magic Tree

The Llama's Warning

How the Toad Got His Bruises

The Bad Light

The Curse of the Silver Viceroy

The Myth of Huathiacuri

Paricaca

How the Tiger Got His Stripes

Why the Lamb Is Meek

The Mummy Miner

The Miser's Curse

The Soldier

Why the Tiger and the Stag Fear Each Other

How the Speckled Hen Got Her Speckles

Delgadina And The Soap Opera

Doña Feliciana and the Jealousy Curse

Andrés, the Arriero

How the Monkey Became a Trickster

The Tale of Little Tenquita

How the Monkey and the Goat Earned Their Reputations

El Pombero

How the Monkey Got a Drink When He Was Thirsty

The King Has A Piece

How the Monkey Got Food When He Was Hungry

Why the Bananas Belong to the Monkey

The Huachita Lamb

Rere's Bell

How the Monkey Escaped Being Eaten

The Little One

Why the Monkey Still Has a Tail

The Fortune Parrot

The Curse of Luison

How the Pigeon Became a Tame Bird

The Ship Of The Three Axe Blows

Tale of a Tortoise and of a Mischievous Monkey

The City of the Caesars

Why the Sea Moans

The Compadrito Leon, Burnt Potato

How the Brazilian Beetles Got Their Gorgeous Coats

The People From Stone

Chilindrín, And Chilindrón

The Legend of Imaybé and Iniguazu Chiriguana

The Story of the Yara

The Princess Of The Springs

The Myth of Manco Capac and Mama Ocllo

Juan the Brave and the Stolen Heifer

The Fountain Of Giant Land

Go Out With Your Sunday Seven

The Boy And The Violin

The Devil And The Peasant

The Most Beautiful Princess

The Mystery of the Burnt Skeleton

The Little Sister Of The Giants

The Forest Lad And The Wicked Giant

The Three Brothers Who Went Out To Learn To Speak

How The Giantess Guimara Became Small

The Vision of Yupanqui

The Adventures Of A Fisherman's Son

The Legend of Viracocha

The Beast Slayer

The Bird Bride

The Quest Of Cleverness

The Myth of Alicanto

The Giant's Pupil

Thonapa

The Poet Viceroy and the Pirate's Curse

Domingo's Cat

Historical Notes

About The Editor

Preface

I've been collecting and telling stories for a couple of decades now, having had several of my own fictional works published in recent years. My particular focus is on short story writing in the realms of magical realities and science fiction fantasies.

I've always drawn heavily on traditional folk and fairy tales, and in so doing have amassed a digital collection of many thousands of these tales from around the world. It has been one of my long-standing ambitions to gather these stories together and to create a library of tales that tell the stories of places and peoples from all corners of our world.

One of the main motivations for me in undertaking the project is to collect and tell stories that otherwise might be lost or, at best, be forgotten by predominantly English-speaking readers. Given that a lot of my sources are from early collectors, particularly covering works produced in the late eighteenth century, throughout the nineteenth century, and in the early years of the twentieth century, I do make every effort to adapt stories for a modern reader. Early collectors had a different world view to many of us today, and often expressed views about race and gender, for example, that we find difficult to reconcile in the early years of the twenty-first century. I try, although with varying degrees of success, to update these stories with sensitivity while trying to stay as true to the original spirit of each story as I can.

I also want to assure readers that I try hard not to comment on or appropriate originating cultures. It is almost certainly true that the early collectors of these tales, with their then prevalent world views, have made assumptions about the originating cultures that have given us these tales. I hope that you'll accept my mission to preserve these tales, however and wherever I find them, as just that. I have, therefore, made sure that every story has a full attribution, covering both the original collector / writer and the collection title that this version has been adapted from, as well as having notes about publishers and other relevant and, I hope, interesting source data. Wherever possible I have added a cultural or indigenous attribution as well, although for some of the titles, the country-based theme is obvious.

This volume, *Tales From South America*, is a collection covering settler and indigenous tales from South America, an area that actually covers a whole host of nations and storytelling traditions.

South American legends, folk tales, and fairy tales are rich with cultural diversity and draw from a wide range of influences, making them unique in several ways. South America is a culturally diverse country with a rich tapestry of indigenous, African, European, and other influences. South American legends and folk tales often reflect this diversity, incorporating elements from various cultural traditions.

Brazil, for example, has a significant Afro-Brazilian population, and African cultural influences are prominent in Brazilian folklore.

Many folk tales and legends feature characters and themes from African mythology and folklore.

South American legends and folk tales often reflect a country's history, including colonialism, slavery, and the struggle for independence. These stories may contain elements of resistance, resilience, and cultural adaptation.

South America's diverse ecosystems, including the Amazon rainforest, the Pantanal wetlands, and the Atlantic Forest, provide a rich backdrop for many folk tales and legends. These stories often incorporate elements of the natural environment and the animals that inhabit it.

Like Central American folklore, South American folklore exhibits syncretism, with indigenous, African, and European cultural elements blending together. This syncretism is particularly evident in religious practices and festivals but also influences folk tales and legends.

South America is vast with distinct regions, each with its own unique folklore and traditions. Stories may vary from one region to another, reflecting local customs, landscapes, and historical events.

Overall, South American legends, folk tales, and fairy tales offer a fascinating glimpse into the country's cultural heritage, history, and natural environment, making them unique and diverse expressions of national and tribal identity.

As for the fireside project, these collections will grow over coming years to tell lost and forgotten tales from every continent, and even then, I'll just be scratching the surface of the world's lore and love. That's the great gift in storytelling. Since the first of our ancestors sat around in a cave, contemplating an ape's place in the world, we have, as a species, continued to tell each other stories of magic and cunning and caution and love. All those years ago, when I began to read through tales from the Celts, tales from Indonesia, tales from Africa and the Far East, tales from everywhere, one of the things that struck me clearly was just how similar are our roots. We share characters and characteristics. The nature of these tales is so similar underneath the local camouflage. Human beings clearly share a storytelling heritage so much deeper than the world that we see superficially as always having been just as it is now.

These tales were originally told by firelight as a way of preserving histories and educating both adult and child. These tales form part of our shared heritage, witches, warts, fantastic beasts, and all. They can be dark and violent. They can be sweet and loving. They are we and we are they in so many ways. I've loved reading and re-reading these stories. I hope that you do too.

Clive

Bath 2025

How Night Came

This story has been adapted from a tale originally told by Elsie Spicer Eells in Fairy Tales from Brazil, published in 1917 by E. M. Hale and Company, Chicago. The book contains a selection of fairy tales and folk stories from Brazil, each brimming with vibrant characters, magical creatures, and moral lessons. These tales offer readers a glimpse into Brazilian culture, traditions, and beliefs, as well as the country's diverse landscapes and wildlife.

Years and years ago at the very beginning of time, when the world had just been made, there was no night. It was day all the time. No one had ever heard of sunrise or sunset, starlight or moonbeams. There were no night birds, nor night beasts, nor night flowers. There were no lengthening shadows, nor soft night air, heavy with perfume.

In those days the daughter of the Great Sea Serpent, who dwelt in the depths of the seas, married one of the sons of the great earth race known as Man. She left her home among the shades of the deep seas and came to dwell with her husband in the land of daylight. Her eyes grew weary of the bright sunlight and her beauty faded. Her husband watched her with sad eyes, but he did not know what to do to help her.

"Oh, if night would only come," she moaned as she tossed about wearily on her couch. "Here it is always day, but in my father's kingdom there are many shadows. Oh, for a little of the darkness of night."

Her husband listened to her moaning. "What is night?" he asked her. "Tell me about it and perhaps I can get a little of it for you."

"Night," said the daughter of the Great Sea Serpent, "is the name we give to the heavy shadows which darken my father's kingdom in the depths of the seas. I love the sunlight of your earth land, but I grow very weary of it. If we could have only a little of the darkness of my father's kingdom to rest our eyes part of the time."

Her husband at once called his three most faithful slaves. "I am about to send you on a journey," he told them. "You are to go to the kingdom of the Great Sea Serpent who dwells in the depths of the seas and ask him to give you some of the darkness of night so that his daughter may not die here amid the sunlight of our earth land."

The three slaves set forth for the kingdom of the Great Sea Serpent. After a long and dangerous journey they arrived at his home in the depths of the seas and asked him to give them some of the shadows of night to carry back to the earth land. The Great Sea Serpent gave them a big bag full at once. It was securely fastened and the Great Sea Serpent warned them not to open it until they were once more in the presence of his daughter, their mistress.

The three slaves started out, bearing the big bag full of night upon their heads. Soon they heard strange sounds within the bag. It was the sound of the voices of all the night beasts, all the night birds, and all the night insects. If you have ever heard the night chorus from the jungles on the banks of the rivers you will know how it sounded. The three slaves had never heard sounds like those in all their lives. They were terribly frightened.

"Let us drop the bag full of night right here where we are and run away as fast as we can," said the first slave.

"We shall perish. We shall perish, anyway, whatever we do," cried the second slave.

"Whether we perish or not I am going to open the bag and see what makes all those terrible sounds," said the third slave.

Accordingly they laid the bag on the ground and opened it. Out rushed all the night beasts and all the night birds and all the night insects and out rushed the great black cloud of night. The slaves were more frightened than ever at the darkness and escaped to the jungle.

Meanwhile, the daughter of the Great Sea Serpent was waiting anxiously for the return of the slaves with the bag full of night. Ever since they had started out on their journey she had looked for their return, shading her eyes with her hand and gazing away off at the horizon, hoping with all her heart that they would hasten to bring the night. In that position she was standing under a royal palm tree, when the three slaves opened the bag and let night escape.

"Night comes. Night comes at last," she cried, as she saw the clouds of night upon the horizon. Then she closed her eyes and went to sleep there under the royal palm tree.

When she awoke she felt greatly refreshed. She was once more the happy princess who had left her father's kingdom in the depths of the great seas to come to the earth land. She was now ready to see the day again. She looked up at the bright star shining above the royal palm tree and said, "Oh, bright beautiful star, henceforth you shall be called the morning star and you shall herald the approach of day. You shall reign as queen of the sky at this hour."

Then she called all the birds about her and said to them, "Oh, wonderful, sweet singing birds, henceforth I command you to sing your sweetest songs at this hour to herald the approach of day." The cock was standing by her side. "You," she said to him, "shall be appointed the watchman of the night. Your voice shall mark the watches of the night and shall warn the others that the madrugada comes." To this very day in Brazil we call the early morning the madrugada. The cock announces its approach to the waiting birds. The birds sing their sweetest songs at that hour and the morning star reigns in the sky as queen of the madrugada.

When it was daylight again the three slaves crept home through the forests and jungles with their empty bag.

"Oh, faithless slaves," said their master, "why did you not obey the voice of the Great Sea Serpent and open the bag only in the presence of his daughter, your mistress? Because of your disobedience I shall change you into monkeys. Henceforth you shall live in the trees. Your lips shall always bear the mark of the sealing wax which sealed the bag full of night."

To this very day one sees the mark upon the monkeys' lips, where they bit off the wax which sealed the bag; and in Brazil night leaps out quickly upon the earth just as it leapt quickly out of the bag in those days at the beginning of time. And all the night beasts and night birds and night insects give a sunset chorus in the jungles at nightfall.

The Cursed Admiral and the Goblins' Revenge

This story has been adapted from a tale originally told by Ricardo Palma in Peruvian Traditions, A Spanish language book originally, and published in 1872 by Imprenta del Estado, Lima.

Once upon a time, in a grand house with towering stone walls and a magnificent fountain in its courtyard, there lived an admiral as proud as a peacock and as cold-hearted as winter itself. This man strutted about like he was carved from stone, his ruffled collar starched so stiff it could cut the wind. He loved his noble titles more than he loved his people and relished in the respect that fear, not kindness, demanded.

Now, the fountain in his courtyard was no ordinary one. It was the finest in the city, its waters so pure and clear that people from all over the neighbourhood would come to fill their jugs, as was their right. After all, as the old saying goes, water and fire should be denied to no one.

But one morning, the admiral awoke in a foul temper, stormier than the sea after a tempest. With a voice like thunder, he bellowed orders to his servants, "Beat any wretch who dares cross the threshold for my water. Let them know that my kindness is not for beggars."

The first to suffer his wrath was a frail old woman, bent with age, who had come merely to fill her jar. The servants, eager to please their cruel master, pushed her to the ground and struck her with sticks. The news spread like wildfire through the town, and outrage filled the air.

The very next day, a young man arrived, his eyes burning with fury. He was a cleric from the parish of San Jerónimo, a few leagues from Cuzco, and he was none other than the old woman's son. Seeing the bruises on his mother's arms, he wasted no time. He stormed to the admiral's grand house and demanded justice.

But the admiral, proud and wicked, merely sneered. "Son of a goat and a green candle." he spat, hurling insults that dripped with venom. And before the young cleric could protest, the admiral's fists flew, delivering a savage beating that left him sprawled in the dust.

The city was in uproar. The common folk cursed the admiral's name, but the nobles and officials, fearing his power, turned a blind eye. The magistrates stalled, hoping that, in time, anger would fade. But the Church and the people did not forget. The admiral had dared to lay hands on a man of God, and for this, they declared him excommunicated.

The injured cleric, bruised and bloodied, dragged himself to the great Cathedral of Cuzco. There, beneath the towering image of Christ, one gifted to the city by the mighty Emperor Charles V, he knelt in prayer.

"If men will not deliver justice," he whispered, "then let Heaven itself take vengeance."

When his prayers were done, he placed before the Supreme Court a written complaint, demanding divine retribution upon the wicked admiral. Then he left, resigned to his fate, and awaited an answer, not from men, but from powers far greater.

The next day, as if in answer to his plea, he returned to the court and found his petition marked with a chilling decree:

"As requested, justice will be done."

Three months passed. The admiral continued his days as if he was untouchable, laughing at those who muttered against him, while the cleric went about his priestly duties, waiting.

Then, one dark and moonless night, a woman passing by the great gallows in the town square stopped in her tracks. She let out a shriek, for there, swinging in the cold wind, hung the admiral, his body lifeless. No one had seen or heard a thing. No footprints were found. No witnesses stepped forward. Justice had come in the dead of night, swift and silent.

The city was now gripped with terror. Who had done it? The magistrates launched an investigation, and rumours filled the air. Suspicion fell upon the cleric, but when questioned, he provided witness after witness who swore he had never left the parish that night.

And so, the mystery deepened.

Then, two women came forward, their faces pale as ghosts. "We saw them," they whispered. "The ones who built the gallows."

The magistrates leaned in, eager for their testimony.

"They were not men," one woman stammered. "They were goblins. Small creatures, round-headed and tiny, scuttling like shadows. They appeared out of nowhere, working with unnatural speed. And when they were done, they knocked on the admiral's door, three times."

The courtroom fell silent.

"And then?" the judge prompted.

The women exchanged glances, their hands shaking. "On the third knock, the door opened. The admiral stepped out, dressed in full finery, as if answering a summons. The goblins surrounded him, and without a word, they dragged him to the gallows and strung him up like a bundle of sticks."

The judges sat in stunned silence. What could they say? The law had no answer for magic, no prison for goblins.

The case was closed.

For years to come, the people of Cuzco swore that it had been the goblins, the spirits of the night, who had taken vengeance upon the excommunicated admiral. They whispered that the priest's prayer had been heard, and that the old woman's suffering had not gone unanswered.

But others, those who did not believe in fairy tales, pondered on a different theory. "It was the Jesuits," they murmured in hushed voices. "They planned it all, to remind the world that no man may strike a priest and walk away unpunished."

Yet whether it was goblins or men who delivered justice that night, one thing was certain. The admiral had wronged the people, and the people had not forgotten.

And so, beneath the shadows of the Andes, the legend of the Cursed Admiral was passed from father to son, from grandmother to grandchild. And even today, when the wind howls through the ancient streets of Cuzco, some say they hear the echo of a knocking, three times, at a door long since abandoned.

Coniraya Viracocha

This story has been adapted from a tale originally told by Lewis Spence in The Myths of Mexico & Peru, published in 1913 by Thomas Y. Crowell of New York..

Long ago, in the highlands of the Andes, where the mountains touched the sky, there lived a cunning spirit named Coniraya Viracocha. He claimed to be a great creator, the one who shaped the land itself, but he rarely appeared as a mighty god. Instead, he walked among mortals dressed as a ragged beggar, his clever eyes twinkling with mischief. No one ever suspected that this scruffy wanderer held the power of the heavens.

Now, in a village by a great tree, there lived a maiden of extraordinary beauty, Cavillaca, the most admired woman in all the land. Many noblemen longed to win her heart, but she had sworn to remain untouched, weaving her finest garments beneath the shade of a great lucma tree.

Coniraya, ever the trickster, transformed himself into a shimmering bird, his feathers dazzling in the sunlight. He perched in the tree, watching the lovely maiden below, and in that moment, he devised a plan. Using his magic, he took a drop of his divine essence, placed it inside a ripe lucma fruit, and let it fall gently near Cavillaca. Curious, she picked up the golden fruit and ate it without a second thought.

Seasons passed, and soon, a child was born to the maiden. She knew not how it had happened, for no man had ever touched her. But the boy grew strong, and when he reached an age where he could crawl, Cavillaca demanded an answer.

She summoned all the huacas and gods, the spirits of mountains, rivers, and stars, to gather before her. "Let the father of my child step forward," she declared.

Every noble god dressed in their finest robes, was hoping to be chosen. Gold glimmered, jewels shone, and feathers swayed in the wind. But Coniraya, still in his disguise as a ragged wanderer, stood quietly among them. Cavillaca did not even glance at him.

When no one answered her call, she placed the child upon the ground and said, "Go to your father, little one."

Without hesitation, the boy crawled straight to Coniraya, laughing with delight as he reached him. Gasps echoed through the crowd. The mighty gods watched in shock.

Cavillaca, however, was horrified. "A filthy beggar?" she cried, her face twisting in disgust. "This cannot be!"

Without another word, she gathered her child in her arms and fled, running as fast as she could towards the distant sea.

Coniraya watched her go, then laughed to himself. He threw off his tattered rags, revealing a form as radiant as the sun, clad in garments woven from stardust and moonlight. His hair gleamed like gold, and his eyes shone with the power of the heavens. Surely, if Cavillaca saw him now, she would regret her scorn!

He sped after her, his footsteps as light as the wind. But Cavillaca never looked back, not once. On and on she ran, her feet barely touching the earth, until she reached the waves of Pachacamac. And just as she reached the water, she and her child transformed into stone, forever frozen where the land meets the sea.

Coniraya stood upon the shore, his divine beauty wasted upon the rocks. But his journey was not yet over.

As he wandered, searching for a sign of his lost love, he met a great condor soaring in the sky. "Have you seen a woman pass this way?" he asked.

"Yes," the condor replied. "She was very near."

Pleased, Coniraya blessed the condor, declaring that no man who killed one would ever go unpunished. Then he met a fox, slinking along the rocky path.

"Have you seen Cavillaca?"

"You will never find her," the fox sneered.

Angered by the fox's answer, Coniraya cursed him, saying, "You will carry a stench so foul that no creature will ever seek your company, and you shall only roam in the darkness of night."

Then came a lion, noble and fierce.

"Have you seen Cavillaca?"

"She is close," the lion answered.

Pleased once more, Coniraya granted the lion the power to punish the wicked and declared that whoever slew a lion must wear its skin, head, teeth, and all, so that it might forever be honoured in death.

He met another fox, which mocked him, and so he cursed that one as well.

When he met a falcon, which spoke of Cavillaca's presence nearby, he blessed it, saying it would be admired above all birds. But the parrots, who shrieked lies in his ears, he punished, "You shall scream so loudly that all your enemies will know where to find you!"

And so, Coniraya blessed those who spoke kindly and cursed those who did not.

At last, he arrived at the shore, where Cavillaca and the child stood, now nothing but stone. His heart sank, but he did not weep. Instead, his eyes fell upon two beautiful sisters, daughters of the sea god Pachacamac. They guarded a great serpent, its body as long as the rivers and its fangs as sharp as lightning.

Ever the lover of mischief, Coniraya wooed the elder sister, but the younger one, suspicious of his ways, transformed into a wild pigeon and fled into the sky.

At that time, the sea was empty, home to no fish, no life. But a certain goddess had kept a small pond of fish, hidden away. Coniraya found it, and with a single motion, he released the fish into the ocean, and in doing so, he gave the sea its first creatures.

The goddess, furious that he had stolen her sacred fish, tried to trap him, to destroy him, but Coniraya outwitted her, slipping away like a shadow in the wind.

And so, the great trickster returned to the mountains of Huarochirí, where he played tricks on the villagers once more, forever laughing, forever weaving mischief into the world.

A Boy Of The Andes

This story has been adapted from a tale originally told by Charles F. Lummis in The Enchanted Burro And Other Stories As I Have Known Them From Maine To Chile And California, published in 1912 by A. C. McClurg & Co., Chicago. The Enchanted Burro and Other Stories features a collection of folktales, legends, and anecdotes gathered by Lummis during his travels from Maine to Chile and California. The stories reflect the rich cultural diversity of the regions he visited, encompassing Native American, Hispanic, and Anglo-American traditions.

They probably wouldn't have noticed Ramón Ynga at all, if not for the llamas. There was plenty else to look at. The towering mountain walls on either side seemed to steer their gaze, just as they channelled the foaming Rimac, into an inescapable path. At the far end of the ravine was a sight no man could ignore for long, the black peak of Chin-chán, bowed under the weight of its eternal winter. There is something unsettling about snow that never melts, vast, blank expanses, wrinkled glaciers, savage ice cornices, and the black rocks jutting out hopelessly here and there. It is nothing like the familiar, friendly snow of home, with its sledging, snowmen, and playful snowball fights.

They were high up in the Peruvian Cordillera, at the very base of the last wild peaks that soared 18,000 feet into the sky. The mules, panting with effort, trudged along 3,000 feet below the summits, where there was still some low, green vegetation. Another 500 feet down, a torrent, white as the snow it was born from, alternately roared and chuckled with the shifting wind. But up there, all was white and still. Their eyes kept drifting upwards, captivated, forgetting the treacherous trail beneath them. The mules could manage that on their own. The poor creatures seemed uneasy, breathing in short, laboured gasps, stopping every forty feet or so to rest, unmoved by the spur. Then, when ready, they would sigh heavily and start again. At this rate, they wouldn't last much longer.

"I think I'll get off and walk for a bit," said the younger of the two, a bronzed, sinewy man of twenty-five. "Even this scenery doesn't make up for seeing the mules suffer. You wouldn't think they'd struggle so much on such a good path."

"It's not the incline," remarked the Professor calmly, "as you may soon find out. I feel sorry for the mules too, but it's better to risk them than something more important."

"You talk as if there's some real danger," said the younger man, now striding confidently along, letting his mule follow. He had climbed Pike's Peak and its brother giants in Colorado many times, and had even stood atop Popocatépetl once. A peak was nothing to him, and this excellent path, well, it was child's play.

The Professor watched him silently, his expression a mixture of amusement and seriousness. After a hundred yards, he spoke. "You don't seem quite as sprightly, Barton. I've never seen you so heavy-footed before."

"Well, to be honest, Professor," gasped Barton, somewhat sheepishly, "I feel incredibly strange. My knees ache like never before, not that I'd mind that too much. But I can't seem to breathe properly. My heart and lungs are pounding away as if I've just sprinted a 220-yard dash. It's embarrassing."

"There's no shame in it, my boy. You're simply experiencing what everyone does at high altitudes. Now, get back on your mule."

"No, I'll push through it," Barton insisted impatiently. "I'm no weakling, giving up just because I feel a bit off. I'll keep going and overcome it."

"Barton," the older man said, his tone more commanding than Barton had ever heard before, "get on that mule and stop this nonsense. I admire your determination, and it's precisely because you have more grit than any young man I know that I chose you for this journey. But courage is dangerous unless you temper it with intelligence. There are some things that sheer willpower can't overcome, and this is one of them. Now, mount."

Barton obeyed, though grudgingly, and was immediately frustrated with himself when he realised how much of a relief it was to be back in the absurdly comfortable Peruvian saddle. He couldn't shake the sense of shame that muscles, which had withstood the toughest trials of the frontier, had now "acted like a child," as he put it. He rode on in sullen silence.

It was here that Ramon Ynga stumbled into their lives, all because of the llamas. As the travellers rounded a sharp bend in the trail, the mules suddenly stopped, coming almost face to face with the strangest creatures Barton had ever seen. They were shabby, grotesque figures, with splayed feet, long, awkward legs, and bodies resembling clumps of dry grass. But their necks were the worst, tall and ungainly, like hairy stovepipes. Their backs barely reached the height of the undersized mules, but their absurdly long necks brought their heads level with Barton's. And what heads they were. Disproportionately small and ludicrously narrow, with pointed ears, mean little faces, and lips curled back in a wicked grimace.

"Why, I've never seen anything look so spiteful, except a rattlesnake." Barton exclaimed. "What on earth are they?"

"That," said the Professor with a mischievous glint, "is the national bird of Peru. We'll see plenty more of them up here. In fact, if we'd had daylight in Casapalca, you'd have spotted hundreds. They transport ore to the stamp mills and handle most of the freight. You won't find them below 10,000 feet; llamas are mountain animals and perish if taken to the coast."

"So that's a llama. But I thought they were called 'Peruvian sheep', and these look no more like sheep than my mule does."

"That foolish name comes from armchair naturalists. No one who's ever seen a llama could mistake it for anything but a camel, smaller and shaggier than the eastern variety, and without a hump, but still a true camel."

"What a comical-looking beast," Barton laughed. "It looks like it spends its days brooding on a personal vendetta. Oi. Shift, you walking grievances."

The Professor and the young frontiersman had, until now, enjoyed their forced stop, but the need to press on returned to their minds, and Barton's outburst was intended as a signal to move forward. However, the llamas remained stubbornly in place, blocking the trail. He nudged his mule with his spurs, prompting it to take two steps before halting again, legs braced, utterly indifferent to the prodding. The llamas didn't move an inch, only lowering their bodies slightly on those long legs.

"They're not as foolish as they look." Barton cried, his sharp eye catching the subtle shift. "See? They're going to force us onto the edge."

The trail was barely two feet wide, a thin ledge carved into the mountainside. To the right, the great dark slope stretched skywards into the clouds; to the left, a single pebble flicked over the edge would tumble straight into the raging white torrent, 500 feet below.

"I've heard they always take the inside," the Professor mused. "When two llama trains meet on these trails, passing can be nearly impossible. Sometimes, they even push each other off the cliff."

"I'd rather not test my right of way, taking a dive into the Rimac isn't on my itinerary." Barton said, dismounting and striding towards the blockaders, waving his arms in an attempt to shoo them off.

"Careful." the Professor warned, but before he could finish, the leading llama bared its teeth and spat at Barton with surprising ferocity. He recoiled at once.

"That's their defence mechanism," the Professor noted. "And their saliva is remarkably caustic. Lucky you didn't get it in the face. But I do wish they'd clear off, we've no time to waste."

At that moment, an even stranger sight appeared. From the steep hillside above, a small figure suddenly slid down and landed in the path, staring at the startled travellers. It was a child, barely four feet tall, with a large, round head, a sturdy torso, and oddly short legs, bundled up in unfamiliar clothing. A boy, but what on earth was he doing on such an impossible slope? He must be part mountain goat.

"Well, hullo there." Barton called, finding his voice at last.

"God grant you a good day, sirs," the boy answered solemnly in thick Spanish. "Wait just a moment, and I'll get you through."

With that, he called "U-pa." to the llamas, raising a finger as if to direct them up the path. Normally, they would have obeyed, but Barton's aggressive approach had only made them more obstinate. They stood their ground. The boy pressed his shoulder against one of them, heaving with all his might, but the creature refused to budge.

"Well, then, we wait." he declared.

He scurried about, gathering small pebbles until his shabby hat was full. Then, settling himself on a protruding rock as if prepared for a long sit, he gently lobbed a pebble at each llama. The animals turned their heads slightly, wrinkling their unpleasant noses. He paused, then tossed two more. The reaction was the same. And so he sat, slowly and methodically pelting the beasts with his harmless missiles. Clearly, he was in no hurry, and the travellers, impatient though they were, knew better than to rush him. They remained in their saddles, watching the ridiculous scene unfold. It was absurd, being held up by two stubborn creatures and relying on this odd little figure to free them.

The boy's ragged clothes were made of thick, coarse cloth. On his feet were crude yanquis, the rawhide sandals of the Peruvian mountains, worn over thick stockings that reached his knees. Over his trousers, he wore a strange garment, part apron, part leggings, while a similar pair of oversleeves, attached to a cord around his neck, covered his elbows. Both pieces were knitted with peculiar designs, featuring tiny, brown llamas wandering across a grey background. Around his waist, he wore a beautifully woven belt, now frayed with age. And his face, what a round, brown mystery.

"What's your name, friend?" the Professor asked in Spanish. "And are you ten years old, or a hundred?"

"Ramon Ynga, Señor. As for my age, I do not know. I've been here a long time, since they built the mill at Casapalca."

"Then you must be about fifteen. And where do you live?"

"Up there," Ramon answered, flicking another pebble.

"A curious habit of the mountain folk," the Professor remarked. "These native folk, rather than settling in the valleys, climb to the very peaks and build their stone huts there. They think nothing of the endless clambering up and down."

An hour dragged by, and the stones in Ramón's hat were running low. Suddenly, the brown llama snorted in disgust and strode off up the trail. The white one hesitated for a moment, snorted, and then followed.

"That way, they tire themselves out, sirs," said the boy, emptying his hat before pulling it back over his thatch of black hair.

"I'd give them a good thrashing with a club." Barton growled, placing great faith in the Saxon way of forcing things.

"No, the boy is quite right. This is another case where you mustn't try to outwit nature. The llama is the most stubborn creature alive. A mule is downright indecisive in comparison. Load it with even a pound too much, and it will simply lie down. You could beat it senseless or even light a fire beside it, and it still wouldn't budge. Only a Peruvian knows how to handle a Peruvian camel, and Ramón has just demonstrated the correct approach. If you hurt the animal, it only becomes more obstinate, but the pebbles merely irritate it until it can bear it no longer. And, in the end, patience pays off; after all, llamas are the only creatures that can work efficiently at these altitudes, where horses and mules are practically useless. But enough talk, adelante."

"Is your Excellency going to Cerro de Pasco?" the young Peruvian asked, running alongside the mule and looking up at the Professor with unusual animation in his otherwise impassive face. He had never spoken to "Yankees" before, and, in truth, it was rare for any outsider to take notice of him kindly. He rather liked these pale men, and a small, unfamiliar desire to please them stirred within him.

That big young man, why, he was taller than any Serrano in the Cordillera., seemed kind. Ramón had seen money before, but the round, gleaming sol the stranger had tossed him when the llamas moved was the first he had ever held in his own hands. It was almost unsettling to be so rich. But the other man, the one with a touch of grey above his ears, who looked at him like that and spoke as if he truly knew him, he was surely someone great. It was to him that the ragged boy had addressed the honourable title "Excelencia." His face was kind, with little smiles at the corners of his mouth, even though he did not laugh.

"No, little one," the Professor replied, "we are not bound for the mines. We are going to climb the Chin-Chán to examine the ice cornices and take measurements."

Even Ramón looked astonished at this. If a Serrano had said such a thing, everyone would assume he was mad. If it were the young man, well, what else could one expect from someone who would give away an entire sol? But this man, whatever he did, it must be right. He certainly wasn't mad. And yet...

"But the Soroche, Your Excellency," the boy ventured. "All outsiders suffer from it, and many die just crossing the slopes. Only those of us born here can go so high."

"We have no choice, my boy," the Professor said kindly. "I must study the snowfields and the ice cliffs, and take my measurements. I know all about altitude sickness, and we will be very careful. Besides, we are both very strong."

"It is not always the strong who survive," Ramón persisted. "Sometimes, the sick cross in safety, while those who are large and red-faced, even bigger than Your Excellency's friend, suddenly collapse and never rise again. The Soroche is stronger than any man."

"You are quite right, my wise friend. It is a terrible thing. But not all fall victim to it, and we must take the risk."

"At the very least, Excellency, let me come too. I know these hills well, and perhaps I could be of help. As for the llamas, my brother Sancho is already on his way, and he will take care of them."

"You're not really thinking of taking that little rat up there, are you, Professor?" Barton interjected. "It'd be the death of him."

"Hmm. I can only hope we'll be as safe as I know he will be. Está bien, my boy. Vamos."

*

At nine o'clock the following morning, the three of them reached the edge of the snowfields. They had spent the night in an abandoned hut at the head of the valley, where their mules could still be seen grazing, pulling as far down the slope as their ropes would allow. The hut was less than a mile behind them, yet they had been travelling since daybreak to get this far. The Professor looked aged,

23

and Barton's broad chest was rising and falling heavily. As for Ramón, he climbed steadily and calmly, stopping only when he saw the others had paused.

By midday, they arrived at the base of the final ridge, in a vast, rounded bay flanked by two spurs of the upper peak. Far above them, the curving crest was a fierce wall of ice, rising 1,500 feet sheer. At the summit, a great white overhang jutted out over the bluish precipice.

"It is… a… magnificent… cornice," the Professor gasped, as they sank onto the snow to rest for what felt like the hundredth time since morning. "But I fear… we… made a mistake. We… should not… have attempted this… without waiting… a few weeks… in Casa…palca… to acclimatise."

"It's unbearable." groaned Barton. "My head… feels… like it's going to… explode. But I'll be damned… if I… give up."

With sheer determination, the young man forced himself upright and staggered towards the spur. However, after just three steps, his tall frame twisted sideways, swayed for an instant, then collapsed like a dead tree in the wind. He landed heavily in the snow, his face dark with suffocation. A bright red trickle seeped from each nostril as the Professor dropped to his knees beside him, crying hoarsely, "My… poor boy. I've… killed you."

The Professor's face had taken on a strange look, too. His eyes were swollen and bloodshot, partly from the relentless glare of the snow, but his cheeks bore an unnatural greyish tinge that battled with the deep purple flush of exertion. He was so unlike the man he had been yesterday. He seemed dull, almost stupefied.

"Come, Excellency." Ramón was shouting in his ear. "It's the Soroche, the mountain sickness, no one can fight it. We must leave this place, or soon, both of you will be dead. Come."

The small brown hand tugged insistently at the old man's shoulder, and in the boy's usually quiet voice, there was a peculiar urgency. The Professor understood. Despite his dizziness, the way Ramón had spoken that single word, "Come, ", roused him, lifting his spirits like the distant sound of a bugle call announcing reinforcements to the besieged. He was not alone. He had help, the help of a small, wiry boy of fifteen. And sometimes, that was exactly the kind of help needed, not sheer strength, but the steady support of a loyal heart.

"But... Barton?" the Professor stammered. His thoughts were sluggish, and instinctively, he looked to Ramón for guidance. "Barton? We... can't... leave... Barton."

Ramón studied the unconscious figure, then glanced back at the Professor. Even in those bloodshot eyes, he saw something that made up his mind. It would be difficult, more dangerous this way, but the old man cared for his companion. And that meant he had to try.

Ramón unfastened his long woven belt and looped it under Barton's back. He pulled the ends up under Barton's arms, crossing them behind his neck. One end he handed to the Professor, keeping the other himself. When they pulled apart, the tension of the belt supported Barton's head.

"Now." cried Ramón. Together, they hauled the heavy, lifeless body across the snow towards the slope's edge. The Professor's face darkened further, beads of blood forming at his fingertips.

"Let me, Señor." the boy urged. Taking both ends of the belt over his shoulder, he plunged downhill, dragging Barton's limp body behind him. Barton's head bumped against Ramón's legs, while his body and heels carved a shallow track in the soft snow, acting as a brake. The Professor stumbled after them as best he could, his vision blurred, veins throbbing, legs unsteady. Several times, he collapsed face-first, ploughing through the snow. Once, he began to roll uncontrollably, but Ramón leapt to stop him just in time.

At last, they reached the end of the snowfield. Ramón laid Barton carefully on the matted grass, placing his head uphill and piling a small drift of snow around it.

"Do the same for your head," he advised the Professor. "I will fetch the mules."

With that, he sprinted down the slope, zigzagging expertly despite the treacherous incline, which seemed too steep even for a goat.

Half an hour later, an utterly exhausted Ramón was struggling to hoist two nearly unconscious men onto two barely-conscious mules. Had the animals been any stronger, they might have resisted; but weakened as they were, Ramón managed, using the downhill slope and his belt, to heave them into place. He tied Barton's feet beneath the mule's belly and fastened his hands around its neck. The Professor, though dazed, could remain upright, so Ramón only secured his feet.

"Hold tight." he commanded firmly, his voice still carrying that faint tremor of emotion. Seizing both reins in one hand, he forced his weight forward onto the bits, compelling the reluctant mules to follow him down the mountain.

Of that grim descent, only Ramón remembered much, and as he was not one for storytelling, no one truly knew what he thought of it. The Professor's next clear memory was waking aboard a train in Casapalca, a train on the world's most remarkable railway, the one that climbs above the clouds and tunnels through the Cordillera of Peru. Before that, there were only blurred impressions: a towering mountain wall leaning towards him; a twisting path suspended in empty space; and a boy's voice, warm and encouraging, speaking softly in Spanish.

Now, opposite him, a round, brown face watched him intently. The Professor imagined, perhaps fancifully, that there was tenderness in the gaze.

Meanwhile, the burly conductor was saying, "I've never seen it come so close. How that boy got you down, I'll never know. And I could see he hated to leave you, so I said to him, 'Just get in, son, come down to Lima with us, and I'll bring you back even if it costs me my job." He's a good lad, that one. You'll be right as rain as soon as you get to lower altitude, that's the only cure for the Soroche."

And indeed, the next day, in Lima, they were well again. Even Barton managed to sit up, nodding weakly as the Professor turned to Ramón. "My boy, I'd like you to stay with us. We still have much travelling to do in Peru, and if you come with us, you will earn a good wage. More than that, you will be as my son. For neither of us would be alive now, were it not for a little hero. Will you join us?"

A bright light of joy flickered across Ramón's face, then just as quickly faded. His eyes filled with tears.

"You are kind, Excellency. I would follow you anywhere. But in the Chin-Chán, my mother waits, with the little ones. Since my father died, I must be the man of the family, Sancho is still too young."

And with that, he turned and ran, so they would not see him cry.

How the Rabbit Lost His Tail

This story has been adapted from a tale originally told by Elsie Spicer Eells in Fairy Tales from Brazil, published in 1917 by E. M. Hale and Company, Chicago.

Once upon a time, many, many years ago, the rabbit had a long tail, while the cat had none. She gazed enviously at the rabbit's tail, for it was exactly the kind she longed to have.

The rabbit was a thoughtless and careless little creature. One day, he fell asleep with his beautiful long tail stretched out behind him. Along came Mistress Puss, carrying a sharp knife, and with a single swift motion, she cut off Mr Rabbit's tail. Being quick and nimble, she had nearly sewn it onto her own body before Mr Rabbit even realised what had happened.

"Don't you think it looks better on me than it did on you?" asked Mistress Puss.

"It certainly suits you very well," replied the generous and selfless rabbit. "It was a little too long for me anyway. I'll tell you what, why don't you keep it, and in exchange, give me that sharp knife?"

The cat agreed, handing over the knife, and Mr Rabbit set off into the deep forest. "I've lost my tail, but I've gained a knife," he mused. "I'll find myself a new tail, or something just as good."

Mr Rabbit hopped through the forest for a long time until he came across a little old man who was busy making baskets. He was weaving them from rushes and biting them off with his teeth. When he noticed the knife in Mr Rabbit's mouth, he looked up eagerly.

"Oh, please, Mr Rabbit," he said, "would you be so kind as to lend me that sharp knife? Biting through these rushes is such hard work."

Mr Rabbit let him borrow the knife. The old man began cutting the rushes, but snap, the knife broke in half.

"Oh dear. Oh dear." cried Mr Rabbit. "What shall I do? What shall I do? You've broken my nice new knife."

The little old man was very apologetic and assured Mr Rabbit that he had not meant to break it.

"Well," said Mr Rabbit, "a broken knife is no use to me, but perhaps you can still make use of it. I'll tell you what, I'll let you keep it if you give me one of your baskets in exchange."

The old man agreed, handing over a basket, and Mr Rabbit continued on his way through the deep forest. "I lost my tail, but I gained a knife. I lost my knife, but I gained a basket," he said to himself. "I'll find a new tail, or something just as good."

Mr Rabbit hopped along for ages until he reached a clearing. There, an old woman was busily picking lettuce, gathering it in her apron. She looked up and saw Mr Rabbit carrying the basket.

"Oh, please, Mr Rabbit," she said, "would you be so kind as to lend me that lovely basket?"

Mr Rabbit let her take the basket. She began placing her lettuce inside, but plop, the bottom of the basket fell out.

"Oh dear. Oh dear." cried Mr Rabbit. "What shall I do? What shall I do? You've broken the bottom of my lovely new basket."

The old woman was very sorry and assured him that she had not meant to damage it.

"Well," said Mr Rabbit, "I'll tell you what, I'll let you keep that broken basket if you give me some of your lettuce."

The old woman agreed, handing over some lettuce, and Mr Rabbit hopped away with it. "I lost my tail, but I gained a knife. I lost my knife, but I gained a basket. I lost my basket, but I gained some lettuce."

By now, Mr Rabbit was feeling very hungry, and the smell of the lettuce was delightful. He took a bite and realised it was the most delicious thing he had ever tasted. "I don't mind losing my tail," he said, "because I've found something I like even better."

From that day to this, no rabbit has ever had a tail. And never since then has a rabbit cared about not having one. From that time onwards, every rabbit has loved eating lettuce and has been perfectly happy and content as long as there is plenty of it.

The Miracle of the Countess and the Magic Tree

This story has been adapted from a tale originally told by Ricardo Palma in Peruvian Traditions, A Spanish language book originally, and published in 1872 by Imprenta del Estado, Lima.

Long ago, in the golden city of Lima, where the sun kissed the mountains and the ocean whispered secrets to the shore, the bells of every church tolled in mourning. Priests and monks from every order gathered in solemn prayer, their voices rising in sorrowful psalms.

The people of Lima flocked to the great palace, standing in hushed clusters before its grand side doors. The streets, which would one day host the bustling markets of Escribanos and Botoneros, now held only silence and worry. Something grave had happened, something that sent rumours fluttering like restless ghosts through the city.

Inside the palace, all was turmoil. Messengers darted in and out, their faces drawn with concern. It was as though a great galleon had arrived at the port of Callao, bringing dire news from Spain. Or perhaps, as in darker days, a great reckoning was unfolding, one that no earthly power could stop.

To understand the cause of such distress, we must slip past the guards, who stand rigid, muskets in hand, and enter a dimly lit chamber deep within the palace walls.

In that chamber stood two noblemen, Luis Jerónimo Fernández de Cabrera Bobadilla y Mendoza, the Count of Chinchón and Viceroy of Peru, and his closest friend, the Marquis of Corpa. They watched a door anxiously, their hands clenched, their breath held, as though awaiting a verdict upon which their souls depended.

The door creaked open, and in stepped a man unlike the rest of the bustling courtiers. He was old, his dark eyes sharp with knowledge. He wore breeches of fine black cloth, fastened at the knee, with sturdy buckled shoes. A velvet waistcoat adorned his chest, from which hung a thick silver chain with ornate charms, and gloves of soft suede covered his hands. This man was Doctor Juan de Vega, a scholar from Catalonia, newly arrived in Peru to serve as the viceroy's personal physician.

The count stepped forward, his voice nearly breaking. "Well, Don Juan?" he asked, though his eyes already knew the answer.

The doctor shook his head gravely. "There is no hope, my lord. Only a miracle can save the countess now."

And with that, he turned and left, his footfalls heavy with failure.

The news spread swiftly. The beautiful young Countess of Chinchón, who had come to Peru only a few months before, lay dying.

The viceroy had done all he could to protect her. Knowing that pirates prowled the seas, he had made her disembark in Paita, sparing her the dangers of a naval battle. But neither steel nor strategy could guard against the invisible enemy that now gripped her, a terrible fever, a relentless illness that the people called the tertian, and which the Incas had long known as the scourge of the Rimac Valley.

Even the great Inca warrior Pachacutec had lost thousands of men to this sickness when he marched upon Pachacámac. The Spanish settlers, too, had fallen to its cruel grasp, and though many survived through sheer luck, others were carried away, their names fading like footprints in the sand. Now, it seemed, the countess was to be among them.

The viceroy, a man of great power but helpless against death, sat beside his beloved wife. He whispered to her, though she no longer heard him. He touched her cold hands and thought of the Spanish skies she would never see again, the gardens of Granada where she had once laughed among the roses. Tears welled in his eyes. "My God," he whispered. "A miracle, Lord, a miracle…."

As he said this he heard a strange voice. "The countess will be saved, Your Excellency."

The viceroy turned, startled. Standing at the door was a priest, clothed in the robes of Ignatius of Loyola, his gaze filled with quiet certainty.

The count rose. "Father?"

"Have faith," the Jesuit said. "And God will do the rest."

Without hesitation, the viceroy led him to his wife's bedside.

A month later, the bells of Lima rang again, but this time, they sang of joy. A grand celebration was held in the palace, for the countess had recovered. But how?

The answer lay in a discovery as wondrous as it was unexpected.

Far away, in the lush forests of Loja, there lived a humble native man named Pedro de Leyva. One day, stricken with fever, he stumbled upon a quiet riverbank. His throat burned with thirst, and without thinking, he drank from the water, never realising that its roots stretched deep beneath the bark of a mysterious tree.

By dawn, his fever had vanished. Amazed, he shared his discovery with others, giving them water in which he had soaked the bark of the tree. One by one, they, too, were healed.

Realising the power of what he had found, Pedro de Leyva journeyed to Lima, where he told his tale to the very same Jesuit priest who had stood at the viceroy's door. The priest, trusting in both faith and wisdom, prepared a tonic from the bark and gave it to the ailing countess. And the countess, who had been at death's door, rose from her bed, saved by the miraculous tree.

For years, the Jesuits kept the secret of the tree, curing all who came to them. The magical bark, ground into a fine powder, was known only as "the Jesuits' powder."

But secrets have a way of spreading. In time, the knowledge reached Europe, where it stirred a mix of awe and suspicion. Some praised it as a divine gift. Others, jealous, fearful, or stubborn, called it a devil's trick. In Salamanca, whispers grew into warnings. Those who used the powder, they claimed, committed a mortal sin, for surely such a cure could only come from a pact with dark forces.

And yet, the truth would not be denied. In France, an English physician named Mr. Talbot used the powder to cure noblemen of high rank, the Prince of Condé, the Dauphin, and even the great Colbert. The secret was sold to the French government for a king's ransom, ensuring that none could claim it for themselves.

In the end, the great scientist Linnaeus settled the matter once and for all. In honour of the countess who had first been saved by its power, he gave the tree a name that would echo through the halls of science:

Cinchona.

Years passed, but the people of Lima never forgot. Even though the rest of the world called this miracle quinine, in the city where the miracle first took place, it was known by a different name. When a fever struck, when chills rattled the bones of the sick, mothers whispered to their children, "Fetch the powders of the Countess."

And in the forests of Peru, where the ancient trees stood tall and silent, their roots still reached deep into the earth, holding the same magic that once saved a young woman from death and gave the world a cure for one of its oldest plagues.

And so, dear traveller, should you ever find yourself in a place where the fever winds blow, remember this tale. For it is not only a story of sickness and healing, but of miracles, courage, and the whispered secrets of the trees.

And perhaps, just perhaps, the spirit of the countess still lingers in the forests of Loja, among the leaves of the magic tree.

The Llama's Warning

This story has been adapted from a tale originally told by Lewis Spence in The Myths of Mexico & Peru, published in 1913 by Thomas Y. Crowell of New York..

Once upon a time, in the vast and rolling highlands of an ancient land, there lived a humble herdsman who spent his days tending to his flock of llamas. Among them was a wise and noble beast, its fur as soft as the clouds that kissed the mountain peaks, and its eyes dark as the depths of a hidden lake. This particular llama was unlike the others; it was old and knowing, carrying in its heart the wisdom of many generations.

One fateful afternoon, as the herdsman led his animals to a lush pasture, he noticed that the wise llama stood apart from the others, its head bowed low, its spirit heavy. It did not graze upon the fresh, green grass, nor did it move with the usual ease of its kin. Concerned, the herdsman approached and gently laid a hand upon its neck.

"My friend," he said softly, "why do you stand so sorrowful while your brethren feast?"

The llama let out a mournful sigh before turning its deep and knowing gaze upon its master. "Oh, kind herdsman," it said, "how can I eat when I know what is to come? In five days' time, the sea will rise in anger and sweep across the land, drowning all beneath its mighty waves. Not a soul will remain unless they heed this warning."

The herdsman, his heart gripped by fear, knelt before his loyal companion. "Is there no way to escape this terrible fate?" he pleaded.

"There is but one hope," the llama told him. "Gather what food you can carry and climb to the highest peak of Villa-Coto. There you must wait, for the waters will rise and seek to claim the earth, but they shall not reach that sacred summit."

With no time to lose, the herdsman gathered what supplies he could and, trusting the wisdom of his faithful llama, began the arduous journey up the towering mountain. As they climbed, they passed many creatures fleeing the lowlands, birds of every colour, deer swift and nimble, even the sly fox, its golden coat flashing in the fading light. All knew of the coming doom and sought refuge upon the peak.

On the fifth day, just as the wise llama had foretold, the waters began to surge. From the distant horizon, a wall of sea roared forth, swallowing valleys, forests, and villages in its relentless tide. Higher and higher the floodwaters climbed, lapping at the slopes of Villa-Coto, until the great wave reached so near that it brushed the tail of a fox standing at the very edge of the summit. From that day forth, the tip of the fox's tail remained black as a mark of the sea's touch.

For five long days and nights, the herdsman and the gathered creatures remained upon the mountain, their eyes wide with sorrow as they watched the world below vanish beneath the waves. But just as the wise llama had promised, the waters eventually began to recede. Rivers carved new paths, and the land was reshaped by the flood's fury. When at last the earth dried, the herdsman stepped down from the heights, the only human left to tread upon the land.

And so, from that lone survivor, a new people came to be, carrying with them the memory of the great flood and the wisdom of the noble llama who had foreseen it. And to this day, those who know the ancient tales speak of the warning that saved the world, passed down from a creature whose heart held more knowledge than any man.

How the Toad Got His Bruises

This story has been adapted from a tale originally told by Elsie Spicer Eells in Fairy Tales from Brazil, published in 1917 by E. M. Hale and Company, Chicago.

Once upon a time, ages and ages ago, the toad had a smooth skin. In those days he was a great gad about. He never could be found in his own house. If anyone had a party he was sure to go, no matter how far away from home it was held, or how long it took to get there.

One day the toad received an invitation to attend a party in the sky. "You never can get to this party," said his friend, the armadillo. "You know how slowly you travel here upon earth."

"Wait and see whether or not I go to the party," said the toad.

Not far from the toad's house there lived a big black buzzard. No one liked the buzzard. He was very unpopular with all the birds and beasts. The toad hopped over to the buzzard's house. The buzzard was outside the door making music on his violin.

"Good morning, Friend Buzzard," said the toad. "Are you going to attend the party in the sky?"

The buzzard replied that he was planning to go.

"That is good," said the toad. "May I have the pleasure of your company for the trip?"

The buzzard was delighted to have the toad seek his company. It was a new experience.

"I'll be charmed to go to the party with you," replied the buzzard. "What time shall we start?"

"We'll start at four o'clock," said the toad. "Come to my house and we'll go on from there. Be sure to bring your violin with you."

Promptly at four o'clock the buzzard arrived at the toad's house. He had his violin with him, of course, because the toad had asked him to bring it.

"I'm not quite ready to go," the toad called out. "Just leave your violin there by the door and step inside. It will only take me a minute to finish getting ready."

The buzzard laid his violin carefully outside the door and went inside the toad's house. The toad jumped through the window and hid himself inside the violin.

The buzzard waited and waited for the toad to get ready but he did not hear a word from the toad. Finally he got tired of waiting. He picked up his violin and started.

When he arrived at the party he was a trifle late but he explained how he had waited for the toad.

"How foolish to wait a minute for the toad," said his hosts. "How could the toad ever get to a party in the sky? We just asked him as a joke because he is such a great gad about. Lay down your violin and come to the feast."

The buzzard laid down his violin. As soon as there was no one looking, out hopped the toad. He was laughing from ear to ear. "So they thought I would not come to the party. What a joke. How surprised they will be to see me here." he said.

There was nobody at the feast who was as happy as the toad. When the buzzard asked how he arrived he said, "I'll tell you some other day." Then he went on eating and dancing.

The buzzard did not have a very good time at the party. He decided that he would go home early. He went away without saying good-bye to his hosts and without taking his violin with him.

At the end of the party the toad hopped inside the violin and waited and waited for the buzzard to take him home. Nobody picked up the violin and the toad began to be very much worried. He almost wished he had not come.

After a while the falcon noticed the violin. "That violin belongs to the buzzard. He must have forgotten to take it home. I'll carry it back for him," he said.

The falcon flew towards earth with the violin. The toad shook about terribly inside of the violin. He got very tired. The falcon got tired, too.

"I'm not going to carry this heavy old violin of the buzzard's another minute," said the falcon. "I was foolish to offer to carry it in the first place. The buzzard is no friend of mine."

He let the violin fall. Down, down toward earth it fell.

"Oh, little stones, Oh, little stones, get out of my way," called the toad as he fell. The little stones had deaf ears. They did not get out of the way.

When the toad crawled out of the wrecked violin he was so covered with bruises that he could hardly hop home.

The buzzard never knew what became of his violin or why the toad had lost his good looks. To this very day the toad shows his bruises. And he is entirely cured of being a gad about.

The Bad Light

This story is my own telling of a traditional Argentinian folk tale based on various sources.

Once upon a time, in the vast and windswept pampas of Argentina, there existed a peculiar phenomenon known as "The Bad Light." This eerie occurrence took place when the sun dipped below the horizon, leaving the land shrouded in darkness. But unlike ordinary nightfall, during The Bad Light, strange and unsettling things would happen.

Legend had it that The Bad Light was caused by the mischievous antics of a wicked spirit who roamed the plains under the cover of darkness. This spirit, known as El Maligno, delighted in causing chaos and fear among the unsuspecting inhabitants of the pampas.

It was said that during The Bad Light, shadows would twist and contort into grotesque shapes, and eerie whispers would fill the air. Livestock would become restless, and even the bravest of gauchos would feel a chill creeping down their spine.

The people of the pampas knew better than to venture out during The Bad Light. They would huddle together in their homes, clutching rosary beads and praying for the sun to rise once more.

But despite their precautions, El Maligno would still find ways to wreak havoc. He would steal into homes and stir up trouble, causing arguments and sowing seeds of distrust among families.

One particularly chilling tale told of a young couple who became lost on the plains during The Bad Light. As they stumbled through the darkness, they heard sinister laughter echoing all around them. Terrified, they clung to each other, praying for dawn to break and banish the darkness.

Finally, after what felt like an eternity, the first faint light of dawn began to creep over the horizon. With a sigh of relief, the couple found their way back home, vowing never to venture out during The Bad Light again.

From that day forward, the people of the pampas remained ever vigilant, knowing that as long as El Maligno roamed the plains, The Bad Light would continue to cast its shadow over their land. And though they could not banish the darkness entirely, they took comfort in the knowledge that as long as they stood together, they could face whatever horrors lurked in the night.

The Curse of the Silver Viceroy

This story has been adapted from a tale originally told by Ricardo Palma in Peruvian Traditions, A Spanish language book originally, and published in 1872 by Imprenta del Estado, Lima.

Long, long ago a mighty procession entered the grand city of Lima. At its head rode Don Melchor Portocarrero Lazo de la Vega, Count of Monclova, newly appointed Viceroy of Peru. His presence alone commanded awe, for though he was a man of wisdom and grace, for he wore a gleaming silver arm where once flesh and bone had been. It was said that in battle, he had lost his right arm, and rather than surrender to fate, he had replaced it with silver, earning him the name Brazo de Plata, the Silver Arm.

With him from Mexico came his noble daughter, Doña Josefa, his household, and his finest soldiers. Among them rode Don Fernando de Vergara, a warrior of great renown, famed not only for his skill in battle but also for his reckless heart.

In Mexico, women whispered his name in both adoration and despair. He was a gambler, a duellist, a breaker of hearts. No woman could tame him, and no challenge could deter him. Yet the Silver Viceroy, who loved him as a son, believed that even the wildest stallion could be broken.

"A wife shall be his tether," Don Melchor declared. "Lima will give him a woman strong enough to bind him to honour."

In Lima, Evangelina Zamora was the jewel of the city. Not only was she beautiful, but she was also richer than kings. Her ancestors had once stood beside the great conqueror Pizarro, and their wealth had only grown through the years. She had been orphaned young, left in the care of a guardian, but there was no protection against the envious eyes that watched her fortune.

When she walked through the city, people whispered. Not of her beauty, though that was enough to bring men to their knees, but of the power she held. A woman so wealthy could choose any suitor, yet she had given her heart to none.

But then came Don Fernando de Vergara.

The fearless knight pursued, and Evangelina let herself be caught. Though she never admitted her love aloud, it shone in her eyes, in the way she listened to his voice, in the way her heart raced at his presence.

The match was made. And when the Silver Viceroy himself stepped forward as their matchmaker, who could refuse?

The bells of Lima rang for their wedding, and the people rejoiced. The wild warrior had been tamed.

For five years, their marriage was a tale of bliss. Fernando forgot the call of the dice, the thrill of the duel, the temptation of the chase. He became a man of honour, devoted to his wife and their children. But the curse of a gambler is never truly broken.

One night, at a grand festival, fate set its trap. Beyond the music and the dancing lay a hidden room, a place where fortunes were won and lost, where men whispered over a table of green velvet.

Fernando should have turned away. But he didn't.

The dice called to him. The hunger returned. He rolled, and with each turn, he fell deeper into ruin. By dawn, he had lost twenty thousand pesos. And so, the beast of addiction awoke once more.

Evangelina pleaded with him, wept for him, fought for him, but nothing could pull him from the abyss. His fortune vanished. His wife's riches began to fade. He wagered everything, chasing the cursed hope of redemption, the ever-elusive dream of winning it all back. But luck never favoured the desperate.

Among the gamblers of Lima was a Marquis, blessed, or cursed, with unnatural luck. No matter how much Fernando played, he always lost to this man. And so, in his despair, Don Fernando made a terrible mistake. Late one night, he woke Evangelina.

"Give me your wedding ring," he whispered.

She sat up, her heart pounding. Her wedding ring? The symbol of his promise, his love?

Fernando smiled, his voice silken with lies. "My friends doubt its worth. I only wish to prove them wrong."

Blinded by love, she slid the brilliant diamond from her finger.

Later that night the Marquis's laughter filled the gambling hall as he slipped the stolen ring onto his own hand. Fernando had traded love for luck, and he lost both.

The shame was too great. As Fernando stumbled home, he saw Evangelina, through a crack in the door, kneeling before an image of the Virgin, weeping.

And then, the fury consumed him. A shadow crept behind him. It was the Marquis, smug with victory, approaching to mock him, to gloat over his ruined soul. Fernando saw red. With the speed of a panther, he struck. A dagger flashed in the moonlight, and three deep wounds cut through the Marquis's back.

The man staggered, bleeding, and fell at Evangelina's feet, his last breath escaping in a choked whisper.

Fernando had won his revenge, but at what cost?

The city cried for justice. The Silver Viceroy, ever a man of law, could not protect him. Fernando was sentenced to death.

Evangelina pleaded, but the decree had been made.

On the day of his execution, she made a choice that would shape history. Dressed in black, she entered the palace hall, where the Silver Viceroy met with the judges. She stood before them with steady eyes and a breaking heart. And she spoke a single lie to save the man she loved.

"I was unfaithful," she declared. "Fernando caught me in betrayal. The Marquis was my lover. My husband had the right to strike him down."

A gasp filled the hall.

The Silver Viceroy listened. The ring on the Marquis's corpse, the secret meetings, the murder at her bedside, all seemed to confirm her story.

And so, Fernando was spared. But his mind had shattered. When the judge read Evangelina's confession to him in prison, he laughed, a hollow, broken sound. His sanity had been lost to the darkness.

Years passed. Evangelina, her heart heavy with sorrow, grew ill. On her deathbed, she called her children to her side, and with trembling lips, she spoke her final truth.

"The world will forget my name, but I gave my soul to save you. Had I not lied, you would have lived as the children of a condemned man. Let history judge me as it will, but let no shame fall upon you."

And with those words, she was gone.

A wind swept through the city, carrying with it the name of a woman who had given everything for love. And so, in the annals of time, her name was lost…but in the whispering draughts s of Lima, the legend of the woman who gave away her honour, so her children might keep theirs, remains.

The Myth of Huathiacuri

This story has been adapted from a tale originally told by Lewis Spence in The Myths of Mexico & Peru, published in 1913 by Thomas Y. Crowell of New York..

Long ago, in the days when the world had been reshaped by a great flood, the people of the land, now without a ruler, sought the bravest and wealthiest among them to lead. This era was known as Purunpacha, the time without a king.

Upon a high and sacred mountaintop, five enormous eggs appeared, gleaming beneath the sun. From one of these eggs emerged Paricaca, a divine being, destined to change the fate of men. In time, he fathered a son, Huathiacuri, who lived in wretched poverty, so destitute that he could barely cook his food. Yet, despite his hardships, his father imparted to him great wisdom, which in time would prove invaluable.

One day, Huathiacuri heard tale of a man who had built a house more marvellous than any other. Its roof was woven from the iridescent feathers of red and golden birds, shimmering like fire in the sunlight.

This man was immensely wealthy, for he possessed countless llamas and was honoured by all who knew him. Yet his heart swelled with such pride that he declared himself a creator of worlds. But fate, ever fickle, struck him down with a terrible illness, one which none could cure, casting doubt upon his divine claim.

It so happened that Huathiacuri, wandering the land in his travels, overheard the conversation of two foxes. They spoke of the rich man's sickness and the hidden cause of his suffering. Filled with determination, Huathiacuri set out to find this man.

Upon reaching the splendid house, he was greeted by a maiden of rare beauty, the daughter of the ailing lord. When he inquired about her father, she confirmed his affliction. Huathiacuri, enamoured by her kindness and charm, offered to heal the man, if only she would grant him her love. But the maiden, seeing the raggedness of his clothes and the dirt upon his skin, refused him.

Still, she led him to her father, who, in his desperation, allowed Huathiacuri a chance to cure him. Huathiacuri knelt before the sick man and declared, "Your suffering is born not of mortal ailment, but of betrayal. Your wife has been unfaithful, and because of this, two great serpents lurk above your home, waiting to devour it. Beneath your grinding stone dwells a monstrous toad with two heads, a beast of dark omens."

At first, the wife vehemently denied such accusations. But when Huathiacuri recounted hidden details of her misdeeds, and when the household uncovered the toad and the serpents just as he had foretold, she fell to her knees and confessed her guilt. The creatures were swiftly slain, and with their death, the rich man was restored to health. In gratitude, he gave his daughter's hand to Huathiacuri.

Yet not all rejoiced at this union. The husband of the bride's elder sister, a man of great arrogance, was displeased by Huathiacuri's lowly status. He challenged him to a contest of dancing and drinking, hoping to shame him before all. Seeking his father's counsel, Huathiacuri found Paricaca, who advised him to accept the challenge.

That night, Paricaca sent him to a distant mountain, where he was transformed into a lifeless llama. At dawn, a fox and its vixen arrived, bearing a jug of chicha and a flute of many pipes. Upon seeing the dead llama, they laid down their burdens to feast. But at that moment, Huathiacuri resumed his human form and let out a great cry, scaring the foxes away. He seized their jug and flute, which were imbued with magic, and used them to outdance and outdrink his rival with ease.

Still unwilling to accept defeat, the brother-in-law demanded another trial, this time, to see who could appear most splendid in festive attire. Once more, Paricaca came to Huathiacuri's aid, gifting him a lion's pelt so red that it shimmered like a rainbow about his head. Dressed thus, Huathiacuri stood unmatched in beauty, winning the contest once again.

Seething, the brother-in-law devised yet another challenge to see who could construct the grandest house in the shortest time. He gathered all his men, and by dusk, his house was nearly complete. Meanwhile, Huathiacuri had only begun his foundations. But as night fell, Paricaca summoned the creatures of the land, birds, beasts, and all manner of insects, to labour through the dark hours. By morning, Huathiacuri's house stood finished, save for the roof.

In a final effort, the brother-in-law summoned llamas laden with straw to complete his roof. But Paricaca placed a fearsome creature near the path, whose piercing cries scattered the llamas in terror. The straw was lost, and Huathiacuri triumphed yet again.

At last, Paricaca, weary of this ceaseless competition, whispered to his son a final challenge. Huathiacuri proposed that they see who could dance best in a blue shirt, tied at the waist with white cotton. The brother-in-law, confident as ever, went first, twirling and leaping in elegant steps. But when Huathiacuri took his turn, he let out a deafening cry, so sudden and terrifying that his rival turned to flee.

In his cowardice, the man was transformed into a deer, bounding away into the wilderness. His wife, who had ever whispered wicked counsel into his ear, was turned to stone, her head buried in the earth and her feet pointing skyward, a fitting punishment for her treacherous heart.

As the echoes of the final challenge faded, the remaining four eggs atop the sacred mountain cracked open. From each emerged a falcon, which in the blink of an eye took the form of mighty warriors. These warriors, filled with the power of the divine, summoned a storm so fierce that it swept away the rich man's house, washing it to the sea, never to be seen again.

Thus, through wisdom and courage, Huathiacuri overcame every trial, earning the love of his bride and the respect of his people. And so, the tale of the poor wanderer who bested the proud lives on, a legend whispered by foxes and sung by the winds of the high mountains.

Paricaca

This story has been adapted from a tale originally told by Lewis Spence in The Myths of Mexico & Peru, published in 1913 by Thomas Y. Crowell of New York..

Once upon a time there lived a mighty spirit named Paricaca. He had once been a humble mortal, but through the grace of the gods and the force of his own will, he had risen to great power. Having performed many miracles, he set forth on a journey, determined to carve his name into legend with deeds of might and wonder.

His travels led him to a village that lay trembling beneath the shadow of Caruyuchu Huayallo, a fearsome entity to whom the people sacrificed their children. Paricaca arrived on the eve of a grand festival. Music filled the air, and the villagers feasted beneath the star-dusted sky. Yet no one paid him any mind, for he was clad in tattered robes, his face streaked with dust from the road. He was offered neither food nor drink, nor a kind word.

At last, a young maiden, moved by his weary appearance, stepped forward. She placed a cup of chicha into his hands, her eyes filled with kindness. Paricaca took the drink gratefully and, as he set the cup aside, he spoke in a hushed voice.

"Kind girl, your heart is pure, and for that, I grant you a warning. Flee this village and seek shelter, for in five days, it shall be no more. But speak not a word of this to anyone."

The girl's heart trembled at his words, but she heeded them well. And as the fifth day dawned, Paricaca ascended a great hill and called forth the fury of the heavens. A storm of immense power swept across the land, sending torrents of water crashing through the streets. The village, with all its inhospitality and cold-heartedness, was swallowed whole, leaving naught but silence in its wake.

Paricaca continued on his way, and soon he came to another village, where the land lay parched and cracked beneath the cruel sun. It was here that he saw Choque Suso, a maiden of breathtaking beauty, weeping beside her withering maize fields. Her sorrow was like a shadow upon the earth.

"Why do you weep, fair one?" he asked, his voice as gentle as the breeze before a storm.

She lifted her tear-streaked face. "The crops are dying. There is no water to nourish them. If the drought continues, we shall all starve."

Paricaca's heart stirred at the sight of her grief, and love took root within him. "I shall bring you water," he declared, "but only if you agree to love me in return."

Choque Suso met his gaze with steady defiance. "Not for myself alone must you bring water, but for every farmer in this valley. Only then shall I consider your proposal."

Paricaca nodded, for he admired her selflessness. He cast his gaze upon the land and saw a trickling rill, its waters held back by a dam.

He knew that if the channel were widened, the water could flow freely and quench the thirst of the fields.

Summoning the creatures of the mountains, he called forth the birds to survey the land and find the best path for the canal. He beckoned the serpents and the lizards to burrow through the earth, and the beasts of the wild to clear the debris in their wake. Among them, the cunning fox appointed himself as the chief engineer, his keen eyes and wily mind directing the course of the waters. With great care and labour, they carved a mighty channel, and at last, the water rushed forth, weaving like a silver ribbon through the valley and bringing life where once there had been only dust.

At the heart of the village the water came to rest, and the crops flourished once more. The people rejoiced, and Choque Suso, true to her word, agreed to be Paricaca's love. But she had one request. "Take me to the summit of Yanacaca, where the winds are free and the sky stretches wide. Let us dwell there."

And so they did. Atop the rocks of Yanacaca, they lived in bliss, watching over the valley they had saved. But as time passed, Choque Suso spoke a wish from the depths of her soul. "I want to remain here forever, to watch over this land for all eternity."

Paricaca, though filled with love, knew that mortal flesh was fleeting. And so, with a whisper of magic, he turned her into stone, her form standing proudly at the head of the great canal, a guardian of the waters and the land she had fought to save.

And so, the tale of Paricaca and Choque Suso was woven into the whispers of the wind, carried from lips to ears through the ages, a story of love, sacrifice, and the power of a pure heart.

How the Tiger Got His Stripes

This story has been adapted from a tale originally told by Elsie Spicer Eells in Fairy Tales from Brazil, published in 1917 by E. M. Hale and Company, Chicago.

A long, long time ago, so long ago that the tiger had no stripes and the rabbit still had his tail, there was a tiger who owned a farm. But the land was overgrown with thick underbrush, and he needed someone to clear it so he could plant his crops.

So, the tiger gathered all the animals and declared, "I need a worker to clear my farm. Whoever does the job will be rewarded with a fine, strong ox."

The monkey was the first to step forward. He seemed eager, but it quickly became clear that he was too restless to get anything done. He swung from tree to tree, chattering away, but barely cleared a patch of land. The tiger soon lost patience and sent him away without a single payment.

Next, the goat had a go. He was diligent, but oh, was he hopeless. He'd clear a little here, then wander off and start on another spot, never finishing a single area properly. Frustrated, the tiger dismissed him as well, unpaid.

Then came the armadillo, strong and determined. He got to work with gusto, but there was a problem with his insatiable hunger. The place was crawling with ants, and the armadillo could never resist stopping to snack. It was a never-ending feast. Exasperated, the tiger sent him packing.

Finally, the rabbit stepped forward. The tiger burst out laughing. "You? A tiny thing like you? If the monkey, the goat, and the armadillo couldn't manage, what chance do you have?"

But there were no other volunteers, so the tiger sighed and agreed to give the rabbit a chance.

To his surprise, the rabbit worked tirelessly, clearing large sections of land faster than any of the others. The next day, he worked just as well. Pleased with himself, the tiger left his son in charge and went on a hunting trip.

The rabbit saw his opportunity. He turned to the tiger's son and casually asked, "The ox your father promised me, it's the one with the white patch on its left ear and a mark on its right side, isn't it?"

"No," said the tiger's son, "he's completely red, except for a small white spot on his right ear."

A little later, the rabbit asked again, "The ox is kept by the river, right?"

"Yes," the tiger's son confirmed.

That was all the rabbit needed. He ran off, planning to take the ox right away. But just as he reached the river, he spotted the tiger returning. Realising he couldn't get away with his trick, he went back to work.

The tiger noticed the rabbit hadn't worked as hard in his absence, so he decided to stay and keep an eye on him. Eventually, the entire farm was cleared, and the tiger, true to his word, handed over the ox.

"You must kill the ox," he told the rabbit, "in a place where there are neither flies nor mosquitoes."

The rabbit set off with the ox, searching for the perfect spot. At one place, he heard a rooster crow and thought, "A farm must be nearby, too many flies." He moved on. Further ahead, the ground was damp. "Mosquitoes here," he muttered, shaking his head.

Finally, he reached a high, breezy hill. "Perfect. No flies, no mosquitoes." He prepared to feast.

Just as he was about to eat, along came the tiger. "Oh, my dear friend Rabbit." he groaned. "I'm starving, just look at my ribs. Won't you share a bit of your ox with me?"

Reluctantly, the rabbit gave him a small piece. In the blink of an eye, the tiger devoured it. "Is that all?" he demanded, his hungry eyes gleaming.

The rabbit hesitated, but the tiger looked big and dangerous. What choice did he have?

The tiger ate. And ate. And ate.

Before long, the entire ox was gone. The rabbit barely got a bite. Furious but powerless, he swore to get his revenge.

A few days later, the rabbit started chopping thick, sharp branches near the tiger's home. The tiger, passing by, stopped and asked, "What are you doing?"

"Building a stockade to protect myself," the rabbit replied, looking serious. "Haven't you heard? All animals are fortifying themselves."

The tiger's eyes widened in alarm. "What? No. I didn't hear anything. Oh, rabbit, my good, wise friend, please, will you build mine first?"

The rabbit pretended to think. "Hmm, I really should build my own first… but, well, alright. Since we're such good friends, I'll help you."

The tiger sighed with relief.

The rabbit worked quickly, driving strong wooden stakes deep into the ground, forming a thick barrier around the tiger. He reinforced the top with more branches until the tiger was completely trapped inside.

"There you go." the rabbit said cheerfully. "Now you're safe." Then he skipped away, laughing to himself.

The tiger waited. And waited. But nothing happened. No disaster. No enemy attack. No need for a stockade at all. But now, he was stuck, and worse, he was starving.

Along came the monkey. "Oh, Monkey. Has the danger passed?"

The monkey, clueless, shrugged. "I suppose so."

"Then please, let me out." the tiger begged.

The monkey laughed. "Let the one who put you in there get you out." and swung away.

Next, the goat came by. "Oh, Goat. Has the danger passed?"

"I guess so," said the goat.

"Then free me."

"Let the one who trapped you set you free," the goat bleated, trotting off.

Then the armadillo arrived. "Oh, Armadillo. Is it safe now?"

"Seems like it," said the armadillo.

"Help me out."

The armadillo chuckled. "Not my problem." and scurried away.

Desperate, the tiger jumped at the top of the stockade, but it was too strong. He rammed against the sides, but nothing happened.

Then he took a deep breath. He thought about the warm sun, the jungle full of prey, the cool, refreshing water at the spring. With all his might, he threw himself against the back wall of the stockade.

CRACK.

The barrier splintered. He forced his way through, but as he squeezed out, the sharp sticks scraped deep across his sides.

The tiger was free, but from that day on, he bore the scars of his foolishness. And that, they say, is how the tiger got his stripes.

Why the Lamb Is Meek

This story has been adapted from a tale originally told by Elsie Spicer Eells in Fairy Tales from Brazil, published in 1917 by E. M. Hale and Company, Chicago.

Once upon a time there was a little lamb frisking gaily about the pasture. The bright sunshine and the soft breezes made him very happy. He had just finished a hearty meal and that made him happy too. He was the very happiest little lamb in all the world and he thought that he was the most wonderful little lamb.

A big toad sat on the ground and watched him. After a while the toad said, "Oh, little lamb, how are you feeling today?"

The lamb replied that he had never felt better in all his life.

"Even though you are feeling very strong I can pull you into the sea," said the toad.

The little lamb laughed and laughed until he rolled over on the ground.

"Just take hold of this rope and I'll show you how easy it is to pull you into the sea," said the toad.

The lamb took hold of the rope. Then the toad said, "Please wait a minute while I get a good long distance away from you. I can pull better when I'm not too near you."

The lamb waited and the toad hopped down to the sea. He hopped up into a tree which hung over the water's edge and from there he hopped on to the whale's back. He fastened the end of the rope around the whale and then he called out to the lamb, "All ready. Now we'll see how hard you can pull."

When the whale felt the lamb pulling at the rope he swam away from the shore. No matter how hard the lamb pulled or how much force he exerted it did not do one bit of good. He was dragged down to the water's edge as easily as could be.

"I give up," said the lamb as he reached the water's edge.

After that, although the sunshine was just as bright as ever, anyone who watched that little lamb could see that he was a little meeker.

One day not long afterwards the sunshine was again very bright and the little lamb was again feeling frisky. He was so happy and happy that he had forgotten all about how the toad had pulled him down to the water until the toad spoke to him. Then he remembered.

"Oh, little lamb, how are you feeling today?" asked the toad. The little lamb replied that he was very well.

"Let us run a race," said the toad, "I think I can beat you."

"You may be strong enough to pull me into the sea," said the lamb, "but surely I can run faster than you. I've watched you hopping about my pasture. You can't run fast at all. However, I'll gladly run a race with you to prove what I say."

The toad set a goal and told the lamb to call out every little while during the race so he could see how much farther ahead the lamb was. Then the toad and the lamb started.

The toad had assembled all his brothers and his sisters and his cousins and his uncles and his aunts before the race and had stationed them at various points along the path of the race. He had told them that whenever any of them should hear the lamb calling out, "Laculay, laculay, laculay," the toad which was nearest should answer, "Gulugubango, bango lay."

The lamb ran and ran as fast as he could. Then he remembered his promise and called out, "Laculay, laculay, laculay." He expected to hear the toad answer from a long, long distance behind him. He was much surprised to hear someone near him answer, "Gulugubango, bango lay." After that he ran faster than ever.

After running on for some distance farther the lamb again called out, "Laculay, laculay, laculay." Again he heard the answer at only a short distance away, "Gulugubango, bango lay." He ran and ran until his little heart was beating so fast that it seemed as if it would burst. At last he arrived at the goal of the race which the toad had set and there sat the toad's brother who looked so much like him that the lamb couldn't tell them apart. The lamb went back to his pasture very meekly and quietly. He acknowledged that he had been beaten in the race.

The next morning the toad said to him, "Even though you did not run fast enough to win the race, still you are a very fast runner. I have told the daughter of the king about you and I have said to her that someday she shall see me riding on your back with a bridle in your mouth as if you were my horse."

The lamb was very angry. "Perhaps you are strong enough to pull me into the sea, and perhaps you can beat me when we run a race," said the lamb, "but never, never in the world will I be your horse."

Time passed and the sunshine was very bright and the soft, gentle breezes were very sweet. The lamb was so happy again that he forgot all about how the toad had pulled him into the sea, and how the toad had beaten him at running the race. He was very sorry for the toad when he saw him all humped up in a disconsolate little heap one day. "Oh, poor toad, are you sick?" he asked. "Isn't there something I can do to help you?"

The toad told him how very sick he was. "There is something you could do to help me," he said, "but I don't believe that you are quite strong enough or can travel quite fast enough."

The lamb took a deep breath and blew out his chest. "I'll show you," he said. "Just tell me what it is."

The toad replied that he had promised to be at a party that afternoon at the house of the king's daughter and he did not see how he could possibly get there unless someone would carry him.

"Jump on my back," said the lamb. "I'll carry you."

The toad shook about on the lamb's back after they had started so that it seemed as if he would surely fall off. After a little he said, "I cannot possibly stand riding like this. It jars all my sore spots. I'll have to get off." He tried it a little while longer and shook about worse than ever. Then he said, "Do you know, I think I could endure this painful ride a little better if only I had something to hold myself by? Do you mind if I take a piece of grass and put it in your mouth? I can hold on to that when I shake about and my sore spots will not hurt so much."

The lamb let the toad put a piece of grass in his mouth.

After a while the toad asked for a little stick. "The flies and mosquitoes annoy me terribly," he said. "If only I had a little stick I could wave it about over my head and frighten them away. It is very bad for anyone in my weak, nervous condition to be bothered by flies and mosquitoes." The lamb let the toad have a little stick to wave over his head.

At last the lamb and the toad drew near to the King's palace. The king's daughter was leaning out of the window watching for them. The toad dug his feet into the lamb's sides, pulled hard on the piece of the grass in the lamb's mouth and waved the little stick about over the lamb's head. "Go on, horse," he said and the king's daughter heard him. She laughed and laughed, and when all the rest of the people in the palace saw the toad arriving mounted on the lamb's back and driving him like a horse they laughed too. The lamb went meekly home to his pasture and from that day to this when one wishes to speak of meekness one says, "as meek as a lamb."

The Mummy Miner

This story has been adapted from a tale originally told by Charles F. Lummis in The Enchanted Burro And Other Stories As I Have Known Them From Maine To Chile And California, published in 1912 by A. C. McClurg & Co., Chicago.

There was certainly nothing ancient about Faquito's appearance. His mischievous brown face, stocky boyish frame, and the alarming tatters of his scant clothing were as undignified as his nickname. His real name, Francisco, had once been stately, worthy of a great Peruvian, even sharing its grandeur with the legendary conquistador Pizarro himself. But names have a way of shrinking over time. Francisco softened into Francisquito, which was affectionate, then shortened to Franco, which was friendly, and finally crumpled into Faquito, which was downright cheeky.

It probably never occurred to the lad that the mighty Pizarro had once been a humble Faquito too, herding pigs in Trujillo before carving his name into history. And even if it had, such philosophical comforts never seem to arrive when we actually need them, only when we're too old to care.

But perhaps you're wondering, Why should a twelve-year-old cholo boy look ancient? Surely boys in Peru aren't expected to appear any older than their counterparts in New York or London?

Well, not exactly. Though in the rapid-growing heat of the tropics, a boy of twelve is already bigger, stronger, and more mature than one in the cooler north. But it wasn't Faquito's age that made him seem out of place, it was his job. There was something almost surreal about his twinkling, boyish face set against one of the most ancient backdrops on earth.

To see this half-Spanish, half-Indigenous boy of today unearthing lives and thoughts buried and forgotten for five hundred years, or perhaps even since before the Old World had dreamt of a New, was enough to make any explorer rub his eyes in disbelief, especially when they found out that Faquito was a Mummy Miner.

Faquito's life was no easy one. It should have been his father Pedro's job to provide for his family, but Pedro much preferred lounging around the big sugar plantation in the next valley, beyond the stretch of desert, keeping his dark skin soaked in the cheap rum, the worst and final gift of the sugar cane. He only ever came back to the little hut in Lurín, a fragile quincha shack of wattle and adobe, when he needed money.

Poor, Maria would have struggled terribly to look after her brood if not for Faquito. She toiled away in the cane fields of the nearest hacienda, scrubbing clothes for the priest in between, but the meagre reales she earned wouldn't have been enough to feed all those mouths, let alone clothe them. Mariquita, at just ten, was a perfect little mother, but her hands were full with the babies, a task far too big even for an older girl. So, it was a huge relief when Faquito grew old enough to bring in something himself, and even luckier that just two miles away, perched on the sandy cliffs, lay the great ruins of Pachacámac.

Every day, except Sundays and fiestas, Faquito would trudge along the dusty road to the ruins, spade slung over his shoulder, his plump face twisted in concentration, sometimes whistling a doleful yaravi, the only tune he knew, sometimes just busy chewing on a stick of sugar cane. The roadside was lined with cane stalks, a convenient sweet shop for a boy with no pennies. All he had to do was climb over the crumbling adobe wall, cut a thick stalk from among the bristling sword-like leaves, and hop back to the road, chewing at his leisure. More often than not, there was a fibrous culm clutched in Faquito's grubby fist, and when his jaws tired of gnawing the stubborn pulp, he would whistle instead.

After crossing the flats and wading through the shallow Lurín stream, Faquito faced the real challenge, the steep, breath-stealing scramble up the desert's jagged edge. Even he was gasping for breath by the time he reached the top. There, he would flop down in the shadow of an ancient wall, not just for a rest, but because he loved to take in the strange sight before him.

Behind him, the lush valley sprawled, a sea of sugar cane, banana trees, and whispering palms. But ahead, stretched out under the burning sun, was the great grey desert, lifeless, endless. Before him lay a wild, crumbling maze of towering walls, weathered and broken, their deep black shadows lurking in the corners. To his left, a colossal fortress loomed on its rocky headland, boxed in by tier upon tier of thirty-foot-high walls. And straight ahead, at the heart of it all, rose the central hill, crowned with an enormous, ancient ruin.

At the base of the fortress, the land was pockmarked with holes, as if the earth had been gnawed away. The remains of the dead, thousands of gleaming white bones, littered the sand. Small clouds of dust puffed into the air where Castro, Juan, and Pancho, the grown-up huaqueros from Lima, were already at work, hunched at the bottom of their makeshift shafts, hoping to uncover a tomb filled with treasure. Maybe even the legendary "Big Fish", the Pez Grande, of Peruvian folklore.

Faquito dreamed of it too. He had heard the stories a hundred times of how the Yuncas buried man-loads of gold in Pachacámac when Hernando Pizarro and his men came thundering down from the mountains, their horses shod with silver. If only he could find the Pez Grande. Or even just a piece of its glittering tail.

With a sigh, he dusted himself off and headed down the sandy trail toward the dig site. His own little "mine, " was there too, where he had spent the last week digging up nothing but bones and scraps.

But just then, something fluttered in the dust at his feet. A little brown desert owl. It landed on a nearby wall, dazed by the sun. Mariquita would love this as a pet. Faquito thought, heart racing.

Creeping up behind the wall, he reached out, ready to trap the bird under his hat, but just as his fingers closed, the owl flapped lazily a few feet further. Determined, Faquito crept up again. The owl, sluggish in the heat, seemed easy prey. Again, he reached and again, the owl fluttered just beyond his grasp. It became a game. Step by step, chase by chase, the owl led him up the central hill, through the ruins of the great temple, and down the other side. Finally, at the base of a sixty-foot adobe wall, the bird perched on the edge of a deep, crumbling pit.

Got you now. Faquito scrambled down a gap, inching closer along the parapet, then shot his hand up. Success. The startled owl flapped wildly in his grasp, its sharp claws hooking into his skin. But Faquito had made a mistake.

Pain shot through his hand as the bird's beak and talons sank deep. He yelped, jerking backwards, going too far. The ledge beneath him crumbled. He tumbled, arms flailing, twenty feet into the pit below.

For a few moments, he lay stunned, eyes swimming. Luckily, the only thing to break his fall was the soft desert sand. Dazed but not badly hurt, he groaned and sat up, blinking in confusion. The owl was still in his hand, its claws locked stubbornly onto his skin. Faquito prised them off, hissing at the sharp jabs of pain. He tore a strip from his ragged shirt and bound the bird's feet tightly.

"That should keep you from scratching me again", he muttered

A stubborn boy, Faquito. Once he set his mind to something, he never let go. So, at last, with his prize safely tethered to a lump of adobe, Faquito was free to focus on more pressing matters.

¡Pues. He had fallen straight into a trap. There were no doors, no windows, nothing but sun-baked adobe walls stretching twenty feet above him. The ancient builders had clearly used ladders to descend into these cellar-like chambers, but those had long since rotted away. And now, how was he supposed to climb out? He could carve steps into the adobe or even tunnel through the base of that eight-foot wall, but his spade was up there on the ledge, propped against the parapet where he had left it.

"¡Castro. Cas-tro-o." he bellowed at the top of his lungs. But his voice seemed swallowed by the chamber, trapped beneath the earth. No one would hear him. He screamed until his throat was raw, but the huaqueros, the treasure hunters, were too far away, still digging away on the other side of the hill. They wouldn't find him in time.

A wave of panic rose in his chest. In this maze of ruins, they might not realise where he was until it was too late. Maria would come looking for him when he didn't return by dark, of course, she would. But how could she possibly guess where to find him, so far from where he usually worked?

He knew all too well, this desert-born boy, that a man doesn't last long under the searing sun of the tropics. You can survive days without food. But without water? Under this heat? His tongue already felt thick and dry in his mouth.

And that damned owl. It was his fault. Faquito grabbed a lump of adobe, ready to hurl it at the bird, but then his arm dropped.

Nana always says that birds are children of Taita Dios too, and He loves those who are kind to them. Maybe I'm being punished for trapping it. Poor thing. Now we're both caught.

The owl, for its part, didn't seem bothered. It sat calmly, its talons curled around the tether, blinking at Faquito with an expression of quiet wisdom. It looked so serious, so knowing. Maybe, just maybe, it understood more about these ruins than he did. After all, it had lived here for generations. Perhaps it even knew where the Big Fish was.

As Faquito considered this, the owl tilted its head to one side, peering at him over its shoulder. Some people might have laughed at such a gesture, but not Faquito. He had too much respect for those who spoke without words.

With sudden solemnity, he asked, "You do know something, don't you, owl?"

At this, the owl turned its head the other way, looking wiser than ever.

"But where?" Faquito cried. "Tell me, friend owl."

The bird said nothing. It simply gazed at him, then twisted its head round again and began preening its feathers, as if to say, That's for you to figure out.

Such a clever bird. Faquito thought. How useful it must be to turn one's head all the way round like that. He can probably even see that strange patch of adobe right behind me, the one that's yellower than the rest. A repair job, most likely. A crack in the wall patched up long ago.

Faquito got to his feet, carefully set the owl to one side, and ran his fingers over the spot. It was about the size of his head, a circular patch of adobe, centuries old, but clearly newer than the rest. Curious, he picked at the edge. A small pebble came loose, revealing a tiny gap behind it. Not just a crack in the plaster, this was deeper, as if a hole had been deliberately filled in.

Faquito's eyes sharpened. A focused, professional look settled over his face.

"It must be a wall niche," he murmured. "Sometimes they sealed them up to change the wall. But why did the owl sit beside this one, if that's all it was?" He dug at it with his fingers until they were sore. He pounded the patch with his fists. But the adobe was stubborn, hardened by centuries. How infuriating to have his spade sitting uselessly up there. If only he could knock it down.

He grabbed a fallen chunk of adobe and hurled it at the spade. It struck the sandy ledge, sending down a little trickle of dust. Faquito's eyes narrowed. He picked up another clod and threw it again. And again. Each time, a little more sand trickled down. Soon, the shifting grains took over, pouring down in a miniature landslide. The spade wobbled, slid forward, then, at last, clattered down at his feet.

He jabbed the blade into the adobe, hacking away at the patch. Hard lumps showered down onto his bare toes. In minutes, he had uncovered a smooth-rimmed opening. He reached inside. It was nothing like the open niches he had seen before, the ones left untouched since the days of the Pachacámac people, where ancient trinkets and ornaments still lay on their stone shelves. This one was different. Like the hidden nest of a Dios-te-da bird, small on the outside, but deep within.

Something soft met his fingers. He pulled out the golden, silky fibres of vicuña wool. Faquito frowned. "Just wool? That's not worth much." But why seal it up? Maybe there was cloth inside too.

He plunged his hand back in, rummaging through the fleece. His fingers met something firm. Carefully, he pulled it free. It was a bundle, tightly wrapped in cloth. Not just any cloth, for this was ancient Peruvian weaving, the kind worth more than gold. The soft, durable fabric was woven with intricate patterns of gods, men, and beasts, a relic of lost artistry.

Faquito's eyes gleamed. "Ay. This must be worth at least twenty soles. But it's so heavy… maybe they wrapped it around a stone?"

Gingerly, he unwrapped the bundle. He worked slowly, so the centuries-old threads wouldn't snap under careless hands. And then, when the last fold fell away, Faquito stared. Then he dropped to his knees in the sand and cried, because it wasn't a stone at all.

*

If you ever visit the Exposición in Lima, among the dazzling collections of Peruvian antiquities, you'll find two priceless idols, each as large as a well-made doll. These figures, exquisitely sculpted to resemble human forms, are remarkable not just for their craftsmanship but for the alternating bands of gold and silver that run from their feet to their heads, reminiscent of the great image described in Revelations.

That was the closest Faquito ever came to discovering the Pez Grande, and, for one poor boy, it was close enough. It left me breathless when I woke up and, using my reata, hauled up the little, ragged cholo I had spotted by chance, fast asleep in the trap where he had wept himself into slumber, clutching something tightly in his arms.

Once he had placed the precious idols and the spade on the broad top of the wall and told me his story, he insisted on being lowered down again to rescue the owl. He freed it and watched it fly away before turning to me with the wisdom of someone far older than his years.

"Taita Dios, God our Father, sends us friends in ways we do not expect. The owl brought me here and led me to this place, so now we are rich. And yet, without you, I might have died there. So, I believe your grace may be just as wise as the owl, who knows where the Pez Grande is hidden."

A note on Mummy Miners:

The word huaco doesn't appear in Spanish dictionaries because it belongs solely to Peru. It comes from Quechua, the language of the Incas, a people about whom you've likely heard many extraordinary (and not always accurate) stories. In Peruvian Spanish, huaco refers specifically to an ancient relic from the pre-Hispanic civilisations that once flourished here. From this comes huaquero, a treasure hunter of such relics. Or, to put it bluntly, a mummy miner.

Mummy mining was a legitimate profession in Peru, as much as gold or silver mining. A skilled huaquero could earn as much as a labourer working the fabulous silver mountain of Cerro de Pasco. And if he works for himself? Well, the rewards could be far greater.

Peru is littered with the ruins of ancient cities, some built by the Incas, others by lesser-known tribes. For centuries, we were taught to think of these rulers as "kings," but in reality, many of them were closer to the Pueblo Indians of New Mexico, remarkably advanced in some ways, but still fundamentally Indigenous in their social, political, and intellectual structures. Some of these cities have been abandoned for so long that no one remembers who built them or why they were left behind. Peru is, in many ways, the Egypt of the Americas, except richer.

At its peak, Peru was the wealthiest land in the world. Even before the Spanish arrived to exploit its mountains of silver and valleys of gold, the ancient Peruvians had mastered metalwork. Gold and silver weren't just currency to them; they adorned themselves, their homes, and their temples with it.

Like all Indigenous peoples, they held a deep belief in an afterlife. And so, when they buried their dead, they wrapped them in fine textiles, placed exquisite pottery beside them, and left them with their most prized possessions, gold, silver, and all they might need for the journey beyond the grave.

And thanks to the bone-dry deserts of Peru, these mummies have been perfectly preserved for centuries, which is why mummy mining became one of Peru's most lucrative underground industries.

There are mummies everywhere. And where there are mummies, there is treasure. Golden ornaments, delicate woven fabrics, beautifully crafted pottery, all relics of a forgotten world, now worth a fortune to collectors and museums alike. And that is how Faquito, mischievous, grinning, twelve-year-old Faquito, found himself in the most ancient business of all.

The Miser's Curse

This story has been adapted from a tale originally told by Ricardo Palma in Peruvian Traditions, A Spanish language book originally, and published in 1872 by Imprenta del Estado, Lima.

In a year foretold by omens, the year of three sevens, a weary traveller arrived at the San Andrés Hospital in Lima. He was a man of forty summers, with no kin, no past, and nothing to his name but a hundred golden ounces strapped around his waist.

With a solemn nod, the physicians examined him and gave him their judgment. "Prepare yourself, good sir, for you have only a short time left in this world."

The stranger did not flinch. Instead, he called for Gil Paz, the hospital bursar, and made his final request. "I have no family, no heirs. This gold I leave to you. In return, dress me in the robes of Saint Francis, lay me to rest with dignity, and offer prayers for my soul."

Gil Paz, with a hand on his heart and a glint in his eye, swore by all the saints to honour the dying man's wish.

And so, with peace in his heart, the stranger closed his eyes that night and was gone by dawn.

But gold is a terrible thing, and Gil Paz, was a wretched miser, even though his name meant "Peace, ". He knew no peace, for he was not a man of honour. With greedy hands, he claimed the golden ounces, stuffing them into his purse with a laugh as cold as the grave. As for the dead man? No shroud. No prayers. No funeral.

"Why waste riches on the dead?" he muttered, tossing the body into a shallow pit behind the hospital.

And there, the stranger should have stayed. But fate had other plans.

At that time, the land was ruled by Don Manuel Guirior, a noble viceroy of silver arm and golden heart, a man of justice and wisdom. He had come to Lima with his wife and a vision for the kingdom, bringing light to the streets, breaking the chains of corruption, and shielding the people from the heavy hand of cruelty.

But not all men in power shared his virtues. One day, from the distant court of King Charles III, there came a new master, a man named Don José de Areche, sent to squeeze every last drop of gold from the people of Peru. He raised taxes, crushed merchants, and bled the poor, caring only for the treasure ships bound for Spain.

When the viceroy spoke against him, he was betrayed.

"Guirior is a weakling," Areche whispered into the king's ear. "He protects the people when he should be plundering them."

And so, after four years of noble rule, the Silver Viceroy was cast aside, exiled from his kingdom, and replaced by a man as cruel as Areche himself. Dark days fell upon Lima.

But even as tyranny spread, something unnatural stirred in the graveyard behind San Andrés Hospital. For as the gravedigger's shovel struck the earth, a fresh breeze stirred the dust. The corpse within twitched, its limbs stiff but moving. Then, with a shuddering gasp, the dead man's eyes snapped open. For a moment, he lay there, staring at the sky, confusion flickering in his gaze. Then, with slow, unsteady steps, he rose.

The gravedigger, whistling to himself, turned just in time to see the dead man climbing out of the grave. A scream tore through the silence. The cemetery owl shrieked, flapping into the night. And then, chaos.

The gravedigger fled, knocking over candles and shrines in his panic. People wailed in terror, for in their eyes, this was no miracle.

"The dead walk. The dead walk."

And in the hospital, Gil Paz counted his stolen coins with greedy delight, unaware that vengeance was coming for him.

In the flickering candlelight of the San Ignacio ward, Gil Paz hummed as he measured out sugar for the hospital's tea, though, being a wretched miser, he used as little as possible.

But then, a hand fell upon his shoulder. Cold. Heavy. Unmistakably real.

"Miser." rasped a hollow voice. "Where is my shroud?"

Gil Paz turned, and froze. There, standing pale and unearthly, was the man he had buried with nothing but rags. His face was gaunt, his lips ashen, but his eyes burned with the fire of the grave. Gil Paz tried to scream, tried to run, but his voice failed him. The room spun. The coins spilled from his hands, clattering to the ground like cursed relics. And in that moment, his greed turned to madness.

Fifteen days later, the stranger, fully healed, left the hospital, his past abandoned, his fortune given away to the poor. He sought no revenge, for fate had already delivered justice.

Gil Paz, once a man of calculated cunning, now wandered the streets of Lima, his mind broken, muttering of shrouds and dead men walking.

As for the stranger? He took the robes of a humble friar, devoting his life to prayer and service, until he vanished into history, his name fading into legend. But some say, in the quiet corners of Lima, in the shadow of old churches and forgotten graves, a lesson remains.

Beware the greedy, for gold can buy much in life, but in death, it may call you back.

The Soldier

This story has been adapted from a tale originally told by Ramón A. Laval in Folk Tales in Chile, originally a Spanish language title, and, published in 1923 by Cervantes Printing House, Santiago De Chile.

Once upon a time, there was a brave and restless soldier named John Sordaíllo. Tired of staying at home, he decided to seek adventure across distant lands. With a sturdy knife at his waist and well-packed saddlebags, he set off, eager to test his strength and courage.

After walking for hours, he came upon a noble-looking young man, dressed in fine silks and gleaming boots. The Soldier, ever respectful, removed his cap and greeted him.

"Good day, my lord. If I can be of any service, I am at your command."

The young man, who was none other than a Prince, smiled. "If you wish to accompany me, I will pay you well. I seek a lost enchanted princess, but I warn you, this journey is filled with great dangers."

The Soldier's eyes lit up. "My lord, I have fought in all the great battles of His Majesty the King, your father, and I have never fled from an enemy. No one has yet been born who would dare lay a finger on me."

The Prince, pleased with his boldness, hired him on the spot.

And so, the two set off as companions, walking side by side, speaking as friends. The Prince spoke of the princess whose portrait had stolen his heart, a woman so beautiful that no one in the world could compare. Yet she was trapped, enchanted, and no one knew where.

The Soldier swore to help him find her.

As they travelled, they met a man who was jumping enormous distances, leaping across the landscape with ease.

"What's your name?" called the Soldier.

"My name is Saltín, Saltón, son of the great Jumper." the man boasted.

"And what is your trade?"

"I jump, my good sir, higher and farther than anyone in the world."

The Prince turned to the Soldier. "This man would be a great help to us."

So the Soldier said, "Would you like to join us?"

"If the pay is good, I'll follow you anywhere."

And so Saltín, Saltón joined the company.

Later, they met a man striding endlessly, never stopping for rest.

"And you?" asked the Soldier.

"My name is Andín, Andón, son of the great Walker."

"And what do you do?"

"I walk, my lord. I never tire, and I am as strong as a hundred men. I can carry you all upon my shoulders and run as fast as the wind."

"This man is useful," said the Prince.

And so Andín, Andón joined them.

Soon after, they found a man cupping his ear to the ground, listening intently.

"What are you doing, my friend?" asked the Soldier.

"I am listening," the man said. "Far, far below, I hear a young woman weeping. She is trapped seven levels underground, crying for the father and mother she fears she will never see again."

The Prince's heart pounded. Could this be the very princess he sought? "What is your name?"

"I am Oidín, Oidón, son of the great Listener."

The Prince did not hesitate. "Come with us, and you shall be well rewarded."

And so Oidín, Oidón joined their quest.

Guided by Oidín's sharp ears, they travelled for seven days through a dark and tangled forest, until they stood before a towering castle. They circled it six times, finding no door, only a row of windows, all glowing with light, each one fortified by thick iron bars. On the seventh circuit, they finally found a great iron door, but no matter how hard they knocked, no one answered.

"This is no ordinary place," said the Soldier.

"Then let me try," said Saltín, Saltón, son of the great Jumper. With a mighty leap, he soared over the walls, landing gracefully inside. But just as he did, a thunderous voice roared from the depths of the castle, yelling, "I SMELL HUMAN FLESH."

Terrified, Saltín, Saltón leapt right back out again.

But the Soldier, unfazed, stepped forward into the castle alone. There, he came face to face with a monstrous giant.

"I've come to fight," the Soldier said, drawing his knife. "And don't shout at me so loud, or I'll cut out your tongue."

The giant lunged, but the Soldier dodged with ease. With a quick slash, he severed the giant's right hamstring, then the left. The beast crashed to the floor, roaring in pain.

Outside, the others trembled at the sound of his howls, but soon, the castle doors swung open wide. The Soldier, his blade dripping with blood, grinned. "The castle is ours."

But greater dangers still lurked within.

They moved cautiously through the grand dining halls, ignoring the tempting feasts that lined the tables. Their mission was clear, find the princess first, and celebrate later. Guided by Oidín, they reached a deep well.

"I'll go down alone," the Soldier declared. He tied a rope to his waist and descended.

As soon as his feet touched the first underground level, a giant serpent with seven heads lunged at him. Without hesitation, the Soldier swung his blade, and one head fell. The creature hissed and slithered deeper into the earth, and the Soldier pursued it.

At the second level, he struck again, and another head fell. At the third level, another. With each strike, the beast fled lower, until at last, at the seventh and final level, the Soldier severed the last of its heads. The beast collapsed, lifeless, and at last, the Soldier heard the princess's cries.

He kicked open a golden door and stepped into a chamber more magnificent than anything he had ever seen. Silver walls. Chandeliers of crystal. A floor of pure gold. And in the centre, lying unconscious, was the most beautiful princess in the world.

He scooped her up in his arms and carried her to the surface. As soon as she saw the Prince, she wept with joy.

"I was cursed," she whispered. "Only a brave Prince and his companions could free me."

The Prince's heart soared, for his quest was complete.

After a great celebration in the castle, Andín, Andón carried them all back to the royal city. There, the Prince and the Princess were married in a grand festival, with feasts, music, and joy beyond measure.

After the wedding, the Soldier and his companions prepared to depart. But the Prince and Princess, forever grateful, presented them each with a bag of silver and fine clothes fit for kings.

"For without Andín, Andón, we would have never reached the castle."

"For without Oidín, Oidón, we would have never found the princess."

"For without Saltín, Saltón, we would have never entered the castle."

"And without the Soldier, the princess would still be enchanted."

And so, the heroes set forth once more, seeking new lands, new adventures, and new stories to tell. And they lived, as heroes do, forever in legend.

Why the Tiger and the Stag Fear Each Other

This story has been adapted from a tale originally told by Elsie Spicer Eells in Fairy Tales from Brazil, published in 1917 by E. M. Hale and Company, Chicago.

Once upon a time there was a large handsome stag with great branching horns. One day he said to himself, "I am tired of having no home of my own, and of just living anywhere. I shall build me a house."

He searched on every hill, in every valley, by every stream, and under all the trees for a suitable place. At last he found one that was just right. It was not too high, nor too low, not too near a stream and not too far away from one, not under too thick trees and not away from the trees out under the hot sun.

"I am going to build my house here," he said, and he began to clear a place for it at once. He worked all day and did not go away until night.

Now in that same country there lived a large handsome tiger, with sharp, sharp teeth and bright, cruel eyes. One day the tiger said to himself, "I am tired of having no home of my own, of just living around anywhere. I shall build me a house."

Accordingly the tiger searched for a place to build his house. He searched on every hill, in every valley, by every stream, and under all the trees. At last he found a place which was just right. It was not too high nor too low, not too near a stream and not too far away from one, not under too thick trees and yet not away from the trees out in the hot sun.

The tiger said to himself, "I am going to build my house here. The place is all ready for me for there isn't very much underbrush here." He began at once and finished clearing the place. Then it became daylight and he went away.

At daylight the stag came back to do more work on his new house. "H'm," he said when he looked at the clearing. "Somebody is helping me. The place is cleared and ready for me to build the foundation."

He began to work at once and worked all day. At night when the foundation was laid, he went away.

At night the tiger came to work at his new house. "H'm," he said when he looked at it. "Somebody is helping me. The foundations of my house are all laid." He began to work at once and built the sides of the house. He worked all night and went away at daybreak, leaving the house with the sides completed. There was a big door and a funny little window in the side.

At daybreak the stag came back to work on his house. When he saw it he rubbed his eyes for he thought that he must be dreaming. The sides of the house were completed with a big door and a funny little window. "Somebody must surely be helping me," he said to himself as he began to work to put on the roof. He worked hard all day and when the sun went down, there was a roof of dried grass on the house. "I can sleep in my own house tonight," he said. He made his bed in the corner and soon was sound asleep.

At night the tiger came back to work on his new house. When he saw it he rubbed his eyes for he thought that he must be dreaming. There was a roof of dried grass on the house.

"Somebody must surely be helping me," he said to himself as he entered the door. The first thing he saw when he entered the door was the stag sound asleep in his bed in the corner. "Who are you and what are you doing in my house?" he said in his deepest voice.

The stag woke up with a start. "Who are you and what are you doing in my house?" said the stag in his deepest voice.

"It is not your house. It is mine. I built it myself," said the tiger.

"It is my house," said the stag. "I built it myself."

"I made the clearing for the house," said the tiger, "I built the sides and made the door and window."

"I started the clearing," said the stag. "I laid the foundations and put on the roof of dried grass."

The stag and the tiger quarrelled all night about whose house it was. At daybreak they decided that they would live together there.

The next night the tiger said to the stag, "I'm going hunting. Get the water and have the wood ready for the fire. I shall be almost famished when I return."

The stag got the wood and water ready. After a while the tiger came back. He brought home for dinner a great handsome stag. The stag had no appetite at all and he didn't sleep a wink that night.

The next day the stag said that he was going hunting. He told the tiger to have the wood and water ready when he got back. The tiger got the wood and water ready. By and by the stag came back bringing with him the body of a great tiger.

"I am nearly famished," said the stag. "Let's have dinner right away." The tiger hadn't any appetite at all and he could not eat a mouthful.

That night neither the tiger nor the stag could sleep a wink. The tiger was afraid the stag would kill him if he shut his eyes for a minute, and the stag was afraid the tiger would kill him if he slept or even pretended to be asleep. Accordingly he kept wide awake too.

Toward morning the stag got very cramped from keeping in one position so long. He moved his head slightly. In doing this his horns struck against the roof of the house. It made a terrible noise. The tiger thought that the stag was about to spring upon him and kill him. He made a leap for the door and ran out of it as fast as he could. He ran until he was far away from the house with the roof of dried grass.

The stag thought that the tiger was about to spring upon him and kill him. He, too, made a leap for the door and ran until he was far away from the house with the roof of dried grass. The tiger and the stag are still running away from each other until this very day.

How the Speckled Hen Got Her Speckles

This story has been adapted from a tale originally told by Elsie Spicer Eells in Fairy Tales from Brazil, published in 1917 by E. M. Hale and Company, Chicago.

Once upon a time, ages and ages ago, there was a little white hen. One day she was busily engaged in scratching the soil to find worms and insects for her breakfast. As she worked she sang over and over again her little crooning song, "Quirrichi, quirrichi, quirrichi."

Suddenly she noticed a tiny piece of paper lying on the ground. "Quirrichi, quirrichi, what luck." she said to herself. "This must be a letter. One time when the king, the great ruler of our country, held his court in the meadow close by, many people brought him letters and laid them at his feet. Now I, too, even I, the little white hen, have a letter. I am going to carry my letter to the king."

The next morning the little white hen started bravely out on her long journey. She carried the letter very carefully in her little brown basket. It was a long distance to the royal palace where the king lived. The little white hen had never been so far from home in all her life.

After a while she met a friendly fox. Foxes and little white hens are not usually very good friends, you know, but this fox was a friend of the little white hen. Once upon a time she had helped the fox to escape from a trap and the fox had never forgotten her kindness to him.

"Oh, little white hen, where are you going?" asked the fox.

"Quirrichi, quirrichi," replied the little white hen, "I am going to the royal palace to carry a letter to the king."

"Indeed, little white hen," said the fox, "I should like to go with you. Give me your permission to accompany you on your journey."

"I shall be glad to have you go with me," said the little white hen. "It is a very long journey to the royal palace where the king lives. Wouldn't you like me to carry you in my little brown basket?"

The fox climbed into the little brown basket. After the little white hen had gone on for some distance farther she met a river. Once upon a time the little white hen had done the river a kindness. He had, with great difficulty, thrown some ugly worms upon the bank and he was afraid they would crawl back in again. The little white hen had eaten them for him. Always after that the river had been her friend.

"Oh, little white hen, where are you going?" the river called out as soon as he saw her.

"Quirrichi, quirrichi, I am going to the royal palace to carry a letter to the king," replied the little white hen.

"Oh, little white hen, may I go with you?" asked the river.

The little white hen told the river that he might go with her and asked him to ride in the little brown basket. So the river climbed into the little brown basket.

After the little white hen had journeyed along for a time she came to a fire. Once upon a time, when the fire had been dying the little white hen had brought some dried grass. The grass had given the fire new life and always after that he had been the friend of the little white hen.

"Oh, little white hen, where are you going?" the fire asked.

"Quirrichi, quirrichi, I am going to the royal palace to carry a letter to the king," replied the little white hen.

"Oh, little white hen, may I go with you?" asked the fire. "I have never been to the royal palace and I have never had even a peep at the king."

The little white hen told the fire that he might go with her and asked him to climb into the little brown basket. By this time the little brown basket was so full, that, try as they might, they couldn't make room for the fire. At last they thought of a plan. The fire changed himself into ashes and then there was room for him to get into the basket.

The little white hen journeyed on and on, and finally she arrived at the royal palace.

"Who are you and what are you carrying in your little brown basket?" asked the royal doorkeeper when he opened the door.

"I am the little white hen and I am carrying a letter to the king," replied the little white hen. She didn't say a word about the fox and the river and the fire which she had in her little brown basket. She was so frightened before the great royal doorkeeper that she could hardly find her voice at all.

The royal doorkeeper invited the little white hen to enter the palace and he led her to the royal throne where the king was sitting. The little white hen bowed very low before the king, so low, in fact, that it mussed up all her feathers.

"Who are you and what is your business?" asked the king in his big, deep, kingly voice.

"Quirrichi, quirrichi, I am the little white hen," replied the little white hen in her low, frightened, little voice. "I have come to bring my letter to your royal majesty."

She handed the king the piece of paper which had remained all this time at the bottom of the little brown basket. There were marks of dirt upon it where the friendly fox's feet had rested. It was damp where the river had lain. It had tiny holes in it where the fire had sat after he had turned himself into hot ashes.

"What do you mean by bringing me this dirty piece of paper?" shouted the king in his biggest, deepest, gruffest voice. "I am highly offended. I always knew that hens were stupid little creatures but you are quite the stupidest little hen I ever saw in all my life."

"Here," and he turned to one of the attendants standing by the throne, "take this stupid, little white hen and throw her out into the royal poultry yard. I think we will have her for dinner tomorrow."

The little white hen was roughly seized by the tallest royal attendant and carried down the back stairs, through the back gate, out into the royal poultry yard. She still clung to the little brown basket which she had brought with her on her long journey to the royal palace and through all the sad experiences she had met there.

When the little white hen reached the royal poultry yard all the royal fowls flew at her. Some plucked at her rumpled white feathers.

Others tried to pick out her eyes. One pulled off the cover of the little brown basket.

Out sprang the fox from the little brown basket and in the twinkling of an eye he fell upon the fowls of the royal poultry yard. Not a single fowl was left alive.

There was such a great commotion that the king, the queen, the royal attendants and all the royal servants of the palace came rushing out to see what the matter was. The fox had already taken to his heels and the little white hen lost no time in running away too. She did not, however, forget to take her little brown basket with her.

The royal household all ran after her in swift pursuit. They had almost caught her when the river suddenly sprang out of the little brown basket and flowed between the little white hen and her royal pursuers. They couldn't get across without canoes.

While they were getting the canoes and climbing into them the little white hen had time to run a long way. She had almost reached a thick forest where she could easily hide herself when the royal pursuers again drew near. Then the fire which had changed itself into hot ashes jumped out of the little brown basket. It immediately became dark, so dark that the royal household could not even see each other's faces and, of course, they could not see in which direction the little white hen was running. There was nothing for them to do but to return to the royal palace and live on beef and mutton.

The fire which had turned itself into ashes sprang out of the little brown basket so suddenly that it scattered ashes all over the little white hen. From that day she was always speckled where the ashes fell upon her. The chicks of the little white hen (who was now a little speckled hen) were all speckled too. So were their chicks and their chicks and their chicks' chicks, even down to this very day.

Whenever you see a speckled hen you may know that she is descended from the little white hen who carried a letter to the king, and who, in her adventures, became the first speckled hen.

97

Delgadina And The Soap Opera

This story has been adapted from a tale originally told by Ramón A. Laval in Folk Tales in Chile, originally a Spanish language title, and, published in 1923 by Cervantes Printing House, Santiago De Chile.

Long ago, in a land of golden suns and whispering rivers, there lived a nobleman and his beloved wife. Their joy was complete when they were blessed with a daughter, Delgadina, a child of rare beauty and kindness. But fate is often cruel, and before the girl could even walk, her mother passed away.

The grieving nobleman, unable to care for his infant daughter, sent her away to be raised in safety, far from sorrow and hardship.

Years passed. Delgadina grew into a young woman, graceful, clever, and as innocent as a spring bloom. When she turned fifteen, she was returned to her father's home, unaware of the world's cruelties.

But misfortune had not been idle in her absence. The nobleman had lost everything to gambling. Now, with not even a loaf of bread left for the next day, he remembered an old, rusting rifle in the corner of his house. "I will go hunting," he decided. "If luck will not favour me at the cards, perhaps it will in the woods."

That morning, Delgadina's father brought home a bundle of small birds, which she prepared for supper. Taking them to the nearby stream, she washed them in the cool water. As she turned to leave, she noticed something strange beside a stone. A small serpent, barely moving, lay coiled in the frost, its scales stiff with cold.

Delgadina was a girl of great kindness. Without hesitation, she scooped up the little creature, placed it in her bosom to warm, and carried it home. From that day, the serpent became her dearest friend. She fed it, played with it, and kept it nestled in a basket lined with soft wool. As time passed, the creature grew and grew, moving from a basket to a tub, from a tub to a barrel, until it could fit nowhere else.

Then, one day, the serpent spoke. "Climb onto a chair, Delgadina," it said. "Place your hands upon the rim of the barrel, and I will grant you a gift."

She obeyed, and the serpent licked her hands with its cool tongue. The moment she pulled them away, something astonishing happened, golden coins fell from her fingers as though spun from the air.

"Whenever you wash your hands," the serpent whispered, "shake them gently, and gold will flow."

Delgadina was awed but saddened, for that same day, the serpent told her it could stay no longer. "Do not grieve," it said. "Though I leave, I will always watch over you."

And with that, the great barrel burst apart, and the serpent vanished.

The next morning, Delgadina went to the stream and washed her hands. As she shook them dry, a shower of golden coins fell into the water, glittering like stars. A passing stranger saw this miracle and, full of cunning, promised her beautiful dresses and fine shoes in exchange for her golden 'buttons." Not knowing their worth, Delgadina gladly gave them away.

That day, when she returned home in fine silk and lace, her beauty shone brighter than ever. But there were those who watched her with jealous eyes. Her godmother, a wicked old witch, burned with envy. With her equally vile daughter, she plotted against Delgadina.

"Go home, child," the old woman said sweetly. "Wait for your father. He will be so pleased."

Yet even as Delgadina left, the witch and her daughter hurried away to meet her father first.

Delgadina's father, weary from hunting, was invited into the old woman's house. "We have prepared your favourite dessert," the witch crooned. "Milk with rice."

As he ate, she whispered her poison into his ear, "Your daughter wears fine dresses, but tell me, noble sir... what man has bought them for her?"

At these words, her father froze. Fury blazed in his heart. Without even thanking his hosts, he grabbed his rifle and stormed home.

Delgadina, seeing him from afar, ran to greet him with open arms. But instead of an embrace, he raised his gun and fired. Yet an invisible force knocked his aim aside, and the bullet struck the earth, missing his daughter by mere inches.

Tears filling her eyes, Delgadina fled to the stream, dipped her hands into the water, and shook them. Golden coins poured from her fingers.

"Father," she wept, "these are the buttons that paid for my dress."

Seeing this, his anger melted into regret. He fell to his knees, gathering the coins in his trembling hands. Delgadina, innocent as always, forgave him at once.

Soon, word of Delgadina's golden gift spread throughout the land, and even the King himself heard of it. He summoned her father to the palace.

"Bring me your daughter," the King commanded. "If you fail, your life is forfeit."

Terrified, the father wept bitterly, for he did not wish to lose his child. But when he told Delgadina of the King's demand, she only smiled gently.

"Fear not, Father," she said. "We have nothing to hide."

The wicked godmother, overhearing their conversation, seized her chance.

"Let me take her," she offered, her voice like honey. "You could not bear the pain if the King kept her."

And so, Delgadina set sail with the old witch and her daughter, bound for the royal palace. But treachery was afoot. Three days out to sea, the old woman whispered to her daughter, "Let us rid ourselves of her."

"Let us not kill her," the daughter said. "Let us only take her eyes."

And so, as Delgadina slept under the stars, they stole her sight and cast her into the sea.

By fate's mercy, a poor fisherman's boat drifted nearby, and Delgadina, instead of sinking into the waves, fell into his arms. With his family, she found kindness and love, though the world now knew her only as Delgadino, believing her a blind boy.

But the serpent had not forgotten her. One day, when tragedy struck and the fisherman's child was stolen by a monstrous Culebrón, Delgadina demanded to be taken to the beast's lair.

The serpent appeared, and with a voice like thunder, it decreed, "I will return your son, but in exchange, his eyes must be given to Delgadina."

The desperate father agreed. The child was saved, and Delgadina's sight was restored.

Now, dressed in the richest silks, she went to the palace where the wicked godmother and her daughter had deceived the King. At first, they did not recognise her. But when she washed her hands, and the golden coins spilled onto the floor, their faces turned to stone.

Then, from the shadows, the serpent reappeared, but no longer as a beast. Instead, he was a child with golden wings. "I was your guardian all along," he told Delgadina. "For your kindness, you shall know happiness forever."

The King, realising the truth, had the wicked witches burned.

And as for Delgadina? She married a Prince, and they lived in peace, wealth, and kindness for the rest of their days. And thus, the wicked were punished, and the good lived happily ever after.

Doña Feliciana and the Jealousy Curse

This story has been adapted from a tale originally told by Ricardo Palma in Peruvian Traditions, A Spanish language book originally, and published in 1872 by Imprenta del Estado, Lima.

Once upon a time, in the grand city of Lima, there lived a woman unlike any other. Doña Feliciana was not known for her beauty, nor for the softness of her heart. No, she was known for something far more fearsome, her iron will and her endless silver.

With a fortune so vast that she laid silver plates out in the sun, and bags of gold stacked in her warehouses, she cared little for silken dresses or fluttering fans. Instead, her days were spent tending to her vast estates and running the most famous bakery and merchant house in Lima.

Her husband, Señor Mesías, had left three years earlier for Ica, supposedly to expand their business. And while Feliciana worked tirelessly, stacking flour, sugar, and oil in her great storehouses, she believed her husband was doing the same, growing their wealth and keeping to his vows.

But all fairy tales have a villain, and in this one, the villain arrived in the form of a letter.

One day, an anonymous message was slipped beneath her door. It was filled with poisonous rumours, of how Señor Mesías had found himself a new love in Ica, of how gold and jewels flowed from his hands into hers, and worst of all, how this "subject" was not even fit to polish Doña Feliciana's boots.

The letter burned in her hands. A buzzing rage filled her mind like a swarm of bees, and she decided then and there, she would catch him in the act.

But travel to Ica was not a simple matter. It took days on horseback, and her great warehouses could not be left unguarded. So, she turned to a trusted friend, a Spaniard named Vilches, and ordered him to sell off the business.

Vilches, a man of swift dealings, returned within two days with bags of money, each one worth a king's ransom. Feliciana, pleased with his efficiency, rewarded him handsomely and set off for Ica, vowing that her husband's betrayal would not go unanswered.

That night, as Feliciana lay awake, she counted her riches and planned her journey. But her heart would not let her rest. She tossed and turned, tormented by visions of betrayal, until suddenly, she heard an unfamiliar sound. It was faint at first. It was a careful, measured footstep in the courtyard below. Feliciana froze. She strained her ears, and then she heard another sound. This time it was a soft, scraping noise, coming from the wooden door that led to her chamber.

Then she smelt it, burning wood. Her blood ran cold. Thieves.

Someone was using a suction cup, an old trick among Lima's criminals, where a slow fire was used to bore a hole into a door without a sound.

Without hesitation, Feliciana sprang from her bed. From the corner of the room, she grabbed her weapon, a long wooden pole tipped with a sharp iron point. This was no ordinary woman's tool, but one used by landowners to defend their fields from bandits. And tonight, she would use it to defend her home.

She waited behind the door, her grip firm, her breathing slow. The scraping stopped. Then, she caught a hint of movement. A shadow appeared in the hole, and slowly, a head pushed through the opening. With the speed of a striking serpent, Feliciana lunged forward and drove the iron tip into the intruder's skull. scream of agony pierced the night. Footsteps scattered like frightened rats, and the thief collapsed, writhing in pain.

Feliciana threw open the doors and shouted for the guards. Within moments, the entire neighbourhood was awake, and the city patrol arrived. When they lifted the wounded thief, a gasp rippled through the crowd. It was Vilches, her trusted friend. The man she had rewarded now lay bleeding at her feet.

Before he died, Vilches confessed everything, naming his accomplices, revealing their plan to rob her blind before she left for Ica.

But Feliciana had outwitted them all.

By the time Feliciana arrived in Ica, her reputation had already galloped ahead of her. She had become a legend, the woman who speared a traitor and stood unshaken.

And when she found her husband, lounging in a lavish house, basking in his stolen riches, she stormed through the doors, carrying her iron-tipped spear like a queen of war.

"Get up."

Her voice was like thunder in a storm, shaking the very walls. Señor Mesías paled.

"We are leaving. Now. Or I will do to you exactly what I did to Vilches, and you will not even be good for radish seeds."

Fear struck him down like lightning. He leapt to his feet, stammering, shaking, nodding wildly. Within minutes, his bags were packed, his mule saddled, and he was following his fearsome wife back to Lima, without a single protest.

And from that day forward, he never dared stray again.

In the years that followed these events, Doña Feliciana ruled her home as a queen rules her kingdom. Her husband, once so bold, became the most faithful of men, for he knew one misstep would be his last. And whenever men whispered of power, of courage, of vengeance, they spoke of her, the woman who wore no silks, who needed no jewels, who held no fear. The woman who wielded a spear like a warrior, and won.

Andrés, the Arriero

This story has been adapted from a tale originally told by Charles F. Lummis in The Enchanted Burro And Other Stories As I Have Known Them From Maine To Chile And California, published in 1912 by A. C. McClurg & Co., Chicago.

I

"Hupa mula. What a family."

The command was fair enough, but the stubborn beast barely moved. Anyone who has ever dealt with mules would likely have echoed Andrés' exasperation. But few, if any, would have had the breath to say it here. By the time you reach 16,000 feet in the Andes, if you're not outright collapsing, you certainly don't have the energy to waste on words, not even enough to mutter, "This mouth is mine." Calling out to a pack mule to "get a move on" or trying to shame it by cursing its lineage? Impossible.

If someone were standing at the top of the pass offering a dollar per word for any remark, the odds are a hundred to one that you'd lack both the ambition and the lung capacity to earn even a nickel. The sheer altitude grips you like an iron vice, squeezing the breath from your lungs, turning your once-steady heartbeat into the weak fluttering of a wounded bird. Your vision fills with strange red threads, and your ears ring with a relentless tap-tap-tap, the dull drum of your own pulse. Worse still, it feels as if some sly trickster has quietly drained the last reserves of your strength before you even realised it was happening. If that were all, you'd count yourself lucky. Many suffer far worse.

A horrible nausea sets in, one far beyond seasickness, something so much worse than a mere stomach-ache that it defies comparison. Nearly everyone experiences it beyond a certain altitude. Then come the sudden haemorrhages, from the nose, mouth, ears, eyes, even fingertips. If you see these signs, they mean only one thing. Get down. Immediately. If you don't descend fast enough, you'll be carried down, but it will be too late. I've seen great, powerful men drop as if felled by an axe, never to rise again. Even at lower elevations, I've watched strong men perish within twenty-four hours with no ailment other than the altitude itself. Only recently, an acquaintance of mine visited a town at a mere 12,500 feet above sea level, went to bed in perfect health, and, as a mutual friend put it with sincere incredulity, "woke up dead in the morning."

The only certainty is that if you go high enough, you will pay the price. But no one can predict where that limit lies for any given individual, and even if you try to figure it out for yourself, you'll find the answer is never final. You might set out from one of Peru's inland towns at an already considerable altitude of 7,000 or 8,000 feet, where many people already struggle with the thin air. In your group, the strongest-looking traveller might suddenly become so sick at 10,000 feet that he has to be sent back immediately. The rest may press on to 12,000 feet before another succumbs, and so on.

You may even, though it's highly unlikely, reach 17,000 or 18,000 feet with little trouble, only to be struck down days later at a seemingly lesser altitude of 10,000 feet, requiring an urgent descent to save your life.

Personally, I've never felt the effects of altitude sickness. But then, my constitution is unreasonably stubborn. It seems to bash against obstacles without consequence. I've climbed and worked at elevations well over 19,000 feet, lived for long stretches between 12,000 and 15,000 feet, and never felt more than the nagging need for an extra pair of lungs in a world where the air is alarmingly scarce. Yet, I never took my good fortune for granted, warnings were all around me. I could never be sure my luck wouldn't change.

Of course, habit plays a role. You've all heard of the Irishman's horse that learned to live on shavings, though, tragically, it died just as it was becoming accustomed to the diet. Lungs, too, can adapt to surviving on the "shavings" of the upper air, that is, if they're strong enough and given enough time. Many die before they can fully adjust, but over centuries, a hardy type emerges.

And so it was with Andrés. For a thousand years, his ancestors had known no heavier air than that of the great Bolivian plateau. He was born in a village on the "small hills" near Lake Titicaca and raised in the rarefied atmosphere of the highlands. Leadville, the highest sizeable town in North America, is high enough to cause problems for many people, but Andrés had never in his life descended as low as 11,000 feet. If he were suddenly transported to New York, his lungs would struggle as much as yours would if you were yanked up to his mountain home. He might well demand an axe to break that dense air into breathable chunks. Meanwhile, you, gasping with bloodshot eyes and mouth agape, would wonder what this thin, useless atmosphere was, where ten minutes of desperate inhaling couldn't fill your lungs as easily as every casual breath does now.

The mule, too, was well-accustomed to altitude, born in Puno and never having set foot below 12,500 feet. True, it was now some 4,000 feet closer to the sky, and it crawled along the pass, struggling with every step. Every six or twelve paces, it would halt, heaving great sighs of despair, panting for five full minutes before gathering enough strength to move again. But this was a good mule. If you wanted to see what an ordinary mule did at this altitude, you needed only to look to either side of the trail. Hundreds of bleached skeletons lay where they had collapsed, their bones as white as the snow-capped peaks above. Here and there, even the remains of llamas, the highest-dwelling quadrupeds on earth, could be found. As for horses, they were utterly useless at such heights.

I've met people who seem to believe that mules ought to apologise for their very existence, as if nature was having an off day when she created them. But only the uninformed hold such foolish notions. Anyone with real experience of the world knows that the mule is the most versatile and invaluable beast ever to serve mankind. A horse may run faster, an elephant may carry heavier loads, and a llama may climb higher, but no other creature can match the mule for endurance, versatility, and sheer survival in extreme conditions. Wherever civilised man has ventured into the wilderness, the mule has been his greatest ally.

Such thoughts ran through the mind of the traveller sprawled beside the apacheta at the summit of the pass, watching his gasping saddle mule recover while the rest of his small caravan crept upward. He himself was breathing heavily, but otherwise, he showed no signs of exhaustion despite the hour-long climb. He had left Andrés behind with the pack mule, preferring to walk and drive his own beast rather than add to its burden.

"Yes," he mused to himself, "Old Tom Moore, Crook's chief packer, had it right when he used to say, 'God made mules for a reason.'" They've been the right hand of pioneers across the Americas. Well, Andrés, so you got him up at last."

Andrés doffed his weathered hat, revealing the long-peaked chullo of vicuña wool beneath. He removed the wad of coca leaves he had been chewing and flung it against the rough stone of the apacheta, which was already pocked with similar offerings. No Bolivian highlander would ever think of passing such a monument at the crest of a pass without making this small ritual sacrifice, just as you wouldn't enter a church without removing your hat.

"Si, viracocha," he answered with an easy smile, speaking in his usual mix of Spanish and Aymara. "You should chew coca, ps, viracocha, so the sorojchi won't catch you. We mountain folk do, and it gives us strength. Here, " he reached into his pouch and offered a pinch of the dried leaves along with a bit of lime.

The traveller shook his head with a polite smile, as if to say, "Thanks, but I have no need." Then he glanced up at the sky, noting the shifting clouds, and gestured for haste, pointing towards the descending trail ahead.

II

Andrés glanced over his shoulder and hesitated for just a moment before turning back. The thought of running flickered through his mind, he could make a dash down the rugged hillside where the carriage couldn't follow. But then he thought of the pack mule, sagging under the weight of those precious boxes that the viracocha

111

guarded so carefully. His thick lips pressed into a firm line, revealing his large, white teeth. No, he would stay.

The moment he stopped urging it forward, the weary mule halted as well, standing as still as a statue beside him. Together, they watched as the carriage rolled to a stop.

"So, the gringo is a hunter, is he?" one of the masked men said briskly, stepping down from the buggy. "A very expensive one, it seems, and not particularly friendly either. Well then, tell us, how much does he charge? I thought we had offered enough."

Andrés swallowed. "Who knows, Your Excellency?" he stammered. "I have been with him as an arriero for a month now, and so far, he has only taken pictures of the monuments. Even those, I have not yet seen, for he says he will finish them when we reach La Paz. As for people, he refuses, as Your Excellency saw. Except that once, in Copacabana, he took a picture of an old beggar at the gate. And for that, he did not even take payment."

"Ay, these gringos are all kinds of fools, but this one, all kinds." The masked man sneered. "Well then, these vistas he's taken must be in those boxes. Let's have a look at them."

His tone carried the authority of a man unaccustomed to defiance, so when the arriero hesitated, his expression darkened with surprise. Andrés, looking pale and uneasy, stammered, "P-pero, Excellency… I-I cannot."

The masked man scoffed. "¡Mira. Another one who 'cannot." Is it contagious, this no puedo? Oyez." His voice turned sharp, commanding. "Open those boxes for me, now."

Andrés took an involuntary step back. His brown cheeks had turned ashen, and his voice wavered as he pleaded, humble yet resolute.

"Do not shame me, Excellency. This viracocha hired me and treats me well. I am his arriero, yes, but he also entrusted me to guard his machine when he is not beside it. Many wish to look inside, but he says what is in these little flat boxes must only be opened at night, in a room without candles, not even a cigarette may be lit. He says even the slightest bit of light would ruin everything. And I have given my word that no one shall open or touch them. Please, Excellency, do not ask me."

"Ask you?" The masked man let out a harsh laugh. "A Jaúregui does not ask. Vaya. I order you, and quickly, before I teach you a lesson you won't forget."

With that, he snatched a short, lead-weighted whip from his driver.

Andrés stepped back further until his shoulders pressed against the pack of his exhausted mule, which stood motionless, as if frozen in place.

"No puedo, taita." he repeated, his eyes darting desperately.

The masked man's patience snapped. Reaching for the cinch rope, he prepared to unfasten the pack himself. Andrés instinctively threw out an arm to block him, his voice rising in alarm.

"Haniwa. Your Excellency must not."

That was the final straw. Furious, the man's masked face seemed to burn with rage. Without warning, he brought the whip slashing across Andrés's bare calves. A deep, angry welt rose immediately. Another strike. And another. Andrés flinched but barely made a sound, shifting his stance in discomfort.

"Haniwa, is it?" The man's eyes blazed behind his mask. "Then let's see if a few more lashes will knock some sense into that thick skull."

He adjusted his grip on the whip, readying the weighted end to club Andrés over the head. The young arriero raised his hands instinctively. He was strong, probably stronger than his tall assailant. And if it had been just the two of them, he might have fought back. But he wasn't thinking of his own strength or the men in the carriage. No, he was bound by something deeper. He had been raised in a land where respect still meant something. Even now, faced with cruelty, he couldn't bring himself to strike a don.

The leaden butt of the whip crashed down on his raised forearm. One hand dropped limply to his side, the other shielding his face.

"Now," the masked man growled, "will you open the boxes, or shall I crack that foolish skull of yours?"

Andrés stood firm. "Haniwa." he murmured again, eyes shut, bracing himself for the next blow.

But then, a voice called from the carriage.

"What's the point, brother? These people are no better than cattle. Beat one to death, and he will still refuse you. Let Pepe tie him up, then we can check the boxes ourselves."

The masked man hesitated. He was burning with rage, desperate to punish this arriero for his defiance. But after a moment, his hand fell away. With an irritated grunt, he muttered, "As you wish. Pepe, tie him up."

If Andrés had endured the nobleman's abuse in silence, it was another matter entirely when a man of his own blood laid hands on him. As Pepe stepped forward, rope in hand, Andrés moved.

With a sudden lunge, he doubled forward at the waist. His wild, tousled head struck Pepe square in the mouth, sending the henchman sprawling onto the road. Before the dazed man could react, Andrés was on him, raining down fistfuls of dirt into his face, shaking him like a terrier shaking a rat.

"Pig." Andrés spat, voice thick with fury. "Who gave you the right to interfere? Your master, I cannot fight. But you, barbarian, "

"¡Socorro." Pepe shrieked, thrashing beneath him. "Get him off me."

"I'll get him off." the masked man snarled. He surged forward, whip raised high, its heavy butt gleaming in the midday sun.

Andrés didn't see him coming. His focus was on Pepe, his hands tightening around the man's tunic.

Woe to you, Andrés, if that leaded whip finds its mark.

III

As the gringo and his weary mule tumbled down the steep side of a deep barranca, their target was still visible, a wounded vicuña, limping four or five hundred yards up the opposite hill. The rest of the herd had long since disappeared, already miles away, for these delicate creatures of the Andes, nature's tiniest camels, run almost like antelopes, as graceful as they are swift. But by the time the mule and its rider had clambered up the far bank, the wounded animal had vanished.

"Damn it. But I mustn't kill you in the process of trying to be merciful to him," the rider muttered as he sprang to the ground. It was just in time. The mule stood there, panting heavily, its head drooping, chin almost touching the earth, and its legs trembling violently. The traveller ran a remorseful but critical eye over the poor beast.

"You'll be fine with a rest. But I ought to apologise for making you suffer a fool for a rider. Right, this part is up to my legs. You stay here."

The stubborn creature responsible for all this trouble had been anything but considerate. Having had the misfortune of getting himself wounded, the least he could have done was wait to receive the Samaritan's mercy. But no, he had to go hobbling along, bleating pitifully, determined to rejoin his herd, even long after they had vanished from sight. It was astonishing how such a delicate, fawn-like animal could manage to run so far on a broken leg. And as his well-meaning pursuer soon discovered, it was more than astonishing, it was infuriating. Curse the little fool. He was making it as difficult as possible for someone to do him a kindness. It was strange how easily one could set out on a noble mission and yet slip into a thoroughly foul mood along the way.

By now, the hunter was undeniably angry, a dangerous luxury to indulge in at these high altitudes. His rising temper did nothing to slow his hammering heart, and any stranger looking up at the purpling face, the furrowed brow, and the tongue lolling with exhaustion would never have guessed he was on an errand of mercy.

"The condors might have to take you after all." he groaned inwardly. He could barely muster the breath to form the words aloud. "One more ridge. Just one more, and that's it."

But as he dragged himself up the final crest, there was a sudden, thunderous swoosh of wings. A great shadow plunged past him, and from the hollow beyond came a shriek, high, piercing, almost human in its agony.

Adrenaline surged through him. He launched himself forward, charging downhill with startling speed. The truth was, once he had started, he no longer had the strength to stop. The steep slope carried him forward, his feet barely keeping up, until he would either hit something or collapse. His vision blurred, his head roared, and his legs numbed. A strange, suffocating emptiness had taken the place of his heart. Still, he hurtled on.

Through the dizziness, he raised his revolver. The gun swung in his hand, wild and unsteady, but he fired three times in rapid succession, just before he stumbled headlong into a chaotic tangle of fur, feathers, and frantic movement. A tremendous blow from one of those vast wings slashed across his scalp, splitting the skin at the back of his head. The revolver barked again. Then, silence.

For several minutes, he lay there, staring in a dazed stupor. The mountain air, cold and sharp, combined with blood loss and exhaustion, began to clear his head. Slowly, he pushed himself upright, blinking at the aftermath of his reckless pursuit.

"Well," he muttered dryly, barely bothering to use what little breath he had left. "Next time I shoot before thinking, I won't." A wry ghost of a smile flickered on his lips. "Lucky I didn't drop dead from that chase. But if you start something, you finish it."

He looked down, satisfied. The little vicuña, whose soft flank he was leaning against, was now at peace. Not far away, sprawled lifeless on its back, was the enormous vulture, its great wings stretched wide, spanning nearly twelve feet, its talons frozen mid-clench in the empty air.

"He only managed to land one hit on you," the hunter murmured to the dead vicuña. "At least I arrived in time to give you a more merciful end. No point begrudging the effort, it's done now. But the least you can do to thank me is to part with that fine pelt."

Drawing his knife, he made quick work of skinning the animal, carefully removing the delicate, luxurious fleece. Then, casting an uneasy glance at the sky, those clouds were beginning to look unfriendly, he rose to his feet and set off once more, walking as briskly as his protesting lungs would allow.

Good. The mule was exactly where he had left it. It hadn't moved an inch. Though still standing in an attitude of utter dejection, it was no longer in any danger. The moment its master returned, the two set off again towards the trail, though at a sluggish, miserable pace.

Neither could have guessed what lay just beyond the rounded hill ahead. Had they known, they might have hurried, but hills, like fate, are rarely transparent. So, oblivious, they plodded on until, at last, they crested the ridge, where, without warning, the spurs dug sharply into the mule's sides, drumming an urgent, echoing rhythm against its ribs.

The poor beast, startled out of its exhaustion, forgot itself entirely. It took off at a full gallop, plunging recklessly down the hillside at a speed it hadn't managed in a month.

IV

Far down the trail, an old, battered buggy stood motionless, its team of horses shifting restlessly in their harnesses. Just ahead of it, at the heels of a weary pack mule, two men wrestled in the dust, locked in a desperate struggle. Over them, a hooded figure raised a heavy club, ready to strike.

At that moment, the mule, until now too exhausted to care, suddenly pricked up one ear while the other flicked back. Then, as if making a calculated decision, its hind leg coiled and lashed out. The long, linen-clad form at its rear folded in half before soaring through the air like a thrown spear. It crashed down a good distance away and did not stir.

Another hooded figure leapt from the buggy, charging towards the fight, but before he could reach them, he crumpled mid-stride, collapsing into the dirt as if struck by an invisible force.

From the ridge above, a lone rider had been watching. Now, with his heart hammering in his chest, he spurred his mount forward, whooping and urging it down the hillside. The horse, too slow for his liking, was quickly abandoned as the man leapt from the saddle and bounded down the slope like a rock dislodged from a cliff.

Andrés, seated atop his subdued foe, was breathing heavily but otherwise as calm and impassive as ever. His thick hands rested on his opponent's shoulders, though one finger hung at an awkward angle, clearly broken. Blood trickled from a gash on his forehead, running down the bridge of his nose.

"Mps, viracocha," he said with a sluggish nod as the breathless rider reached him. "These caballeros wanted to open your boxes, and when I refused, they beat me. But when this brute here grabbed me, well, that was a different matter. A gentleman's blow, perhaps, but not from a chuncho." He exhaled deeply, looking down at the man beneath him. "So, I measured him, like this."

His voice remained calm, matter-of-fact, as he continued, "And when the other one went to smash my head with his whip, Big-Ears here forgot his respect for the powerful and sent him flying." He nodded toward the mule, who now stood looking as disinterested as ever.

"And that one?" The viracocha pointed to the second hooded figure, still sprawled motionless in the road. "I saw him fall as he ran at you."

Andrés glanced at him without much concern. "Mps, probably sorojchi, the mountain sickness," he said. "See how the blood dribbles from his mouth? And you see, viracocha, how strong the coca is? Because I made an offering at the apacheta, as one should, to the spirits of the high places, all has turned out exactly as needed. Without that, well…" He shrugged. "They would have left me here, of no further use to you, and the magic boxes would have been emptied in the light."

That night, as darkness settled over the Quimca-Chata, a storm swept through the pass. Furious gusts of wind sent snow and hail spiralling through the canyons, shrieking like a beast denied its prey. But within the low, grimy tambo, laughter echoed against the stone walls.

The hut, a crude shelter wedged against the shoulder of a hill, was a typical Andean tambo, a lonely, inhospitable refuge for travellers caught in the harsh mountain wilderness. It had no windows, no chimney; just a heavy llama-wool poncho acting as a makeshift door. Inside, the smoke from a feeble taqui fire curled through the air, finding its way out through cracks in the walls, or else settling, thick and acrid, in the dimly lit space.

Five men sat along the rough stone benches. In the corner, six mules snuffled through a pile of discarded straw, searching for scraps. Two of the men were Indians, both with bandaged heads. The third, an American, sat with a handkerchief tied around his own bruised forehead. The last two were elegantly dressed men in fine vicuña ponchos, perched on their linen dusters. From their pockets peeked the tasselled ends of two white hoods.

One of the men kept glancing slyly at these. So, they weren't travelling performers after all. These were wealthy Bolivians. And those strange masks that had baffled him before? Simply a precaution against the harsh mountain air. Andrés had explained this with an air of patience, as if indulging the ignorance of a child. Considering their deep, sun-worn complexions, the idea that they needed protection from the sun had almost made the American laugh.

"Well," the American finally broke the silence, speaking in Spanish, the only language all five shared, "lucky for us the tambo was nearby. Not one of us was in any shape to keep travelling tonight, even without the storm. Ea. Listen to that wind, it howls like a beast that's been cheated."

"You speak wisely, caballero," the taller of the two Bolivians replied with courtesy. "And I am glad for the chance to make amends. In truth, we did not realise that opening your cases would ruin everything. We would not have taken the liberty, but we assumed you were a merchant, playing us for a higher price. But we were well answered." He glanced at Andrés with a wry smile. "Your stubborn arriero made me forget myself, and for that, I offer a caballero's apology. But that mule, ay de mí. I thought Illampu itself had collapsed onto me."

"Indeed, Señor. I saw it from the ridge. It was the most impressive thing I've ever seen. The way he sent you flying, like a pocketknife snapping shut."

The nobleman let out a faint chuckle, rubbing his ribs with a wince. "It was well deserved. I am ashamed of my temper. And I nearly broke your man's head for it." He turned to the American with a nod. "But since you hold no grudge, all is well."

"Oh, I understand both curiosity and temper," the American admitted. "Fortunately for me, it was Andrés's head and not mine that suffered." He clapped the arriero on the back. "But I'll make it up to him. I'm doubling his wages from today. A mule driver willing to take a beating to protect his employer's cargo, well, I haven't found many of those in Bolivia. Or anywhere else."

"You speak truly," the nobleman agreed. Then, after a moment's hesitation, he added, "And since we understand one another, pues, you know that Don Juan de Jaúregui cannot apologise to an arriero. But in truth, he is loyal, and I would be glad to offer him a well-paid position on my chacra."

The American turned to Andrés. "Well? The caballero offers you a fair deal. What do you say?"

Andrés's face lit up with a simple, honest pride. He twisted his cap in his hands as he rose, bowing clumsily.

"I would be glad," he said slowly. "But only if, until, when the viracocha no longer needs an arriero. While the magic boxes must still ride on the ribs of a mule, it is better that I be the driver. The viracocha has shown me, and I know how they must be handled. 'Gently. Gently. And for the love of God, let no light touch them.'"

How the Monkey Became a Trickster

This story has been adapted from a tale originally told by Elsie Spicer Eells in Fairy Tales from Brazil, published in 1917 by E. M. Hale and Company, Chicago.

Once upon a time there was a beautiful garden in which grew all sorts of fruits. Many beasts lived in the garden and they were permitted to eat of the fruits whenever they wished. But they were asked to observe one rule. They must make a low, polite bow to the fruit tree, call it by its name, and say, "Please give me a taste of your fruit." They had to be very careful to remember the tree's correct name and not to forget to say "please." It was also very important that they should remember not to be greedy. They must always leave plenty of fruit for the other beasts who might pass that way, and plenty to adorn the tree itself and to furnish seed so that other trees might grow. If they wished to eat figs they had to say, "Oh, fig tree, Oh, fig tree, please give me a taste of your fruit;" or, if they wished to eat oranges they had to say, "Oh, orange tree, Oh, orange tree, please give me a taste of your fruit."

In one corner of the garden grew the most splendid tree of all. It was tall and beautiful and the rosy-cheeked fruit upon its wide spreading branches looked wonderfully tempting. No beast had ever tasted of that fruit, for no beast could ever remember its name.

In a tiny house near the edge of the garden dwelt a little old woman who knew the names of all the fruit trees which grew in the garden. The beasts often went to her and asked the name of the wonderful fruit tree, but the tree was so far distant from the little old woman's tiny house that no beast could ever remember the long, hard name by the time he reached the fruit tree.

At last the monkey thought of a trick. Perhaps you do not know it, but the monkey can play the guitar. He always played when the beasts gathered together in the garden to dance. The monkey went to the tiny house, carrying his guitar under his arm. When she told him the long hard name of the wonderful fruit tree he made up a little tune to it, all his own, and sang it over and over again all the way from the tiny house to the corner of the garden where the wonderful fruit tree grew. When any of the other beasts met him and asked him what new song he was singing to his guitar, he said never a word. He marched straight on, playing his little tune over and over again on his guitar and singing softly the long hard name.

At last he reached the corner of the garden where the wonderful fruit tree grew. He had never seen it look so beautiful. The rosy-cheeked fruit glowed in the bright sunlight. The monkey could hardly wait to make his bow, say the long hard name over twice and ask for the fruit with a "please." What a beautiful colour and what a delicious odour that fruit had. The monkey had never in all his life been so near to anything which smelled so good. He took a big bite. What a face he made. That beautiful, sweet smelling fruit was bitter and sour, and it had a nasty taste. He threw it away from him as far as he could.

The monkey never forgot the tree's long hard name and the little tune he had sung. Nor did he forget how the fruit tasted. He never took a bite of it again; but, after that, his favourite trick was to treat the other beasts to the wonderful fruit just to see them make faces when they tasted it.

The Tale of Little Tenquita

This story has been adapted from a tale originally told by Ramón A. Laval in Folk Tales in Chile, originally a Spanish language title, and, published in 1923 by Cervantes Printing House, Santiago De Chile.

Once upon a time, in a land where winter wrapped the world in a thick, white blanket of snow, there lived a small bird called Tenquita. She had just become a mother to a nest full of tiny, fluffy chicks, whom she loved more than anything in the world.

One cold morning, Tenquita fluttered out of her nest to find food for her little ones. But as she hopped across the frozen ground, the snow burned her delicate foot with its icy touch.

With a chirp of pain, she looked up at the endless white all around her and cried, "Snow, why are you so cruel? Why did you burn my foot?"

The Snow, cold and indifferent, whispered back, "Do not blame me, little bird. It is the Sun who melts me, and it is I who must suffer under its power."

So, limping on her sore foot, Tenquita flew up into the sky, where the blazing Sun shone high above. "Sun," she called, "why are you so cruel? You melt the Snow, and the Snow has burned my foot."

But the Sun, proud and golden, merely sighed, "Do not blame me, little bird. It is the Clouds that hide me away, making the world colder still."

Determined to find the truth, Tenquita soared up to the great Clouds, thick and grey, who floated lazily across the sky. "Clouds," she chirped, "why are you so cruel? You hide the Sun, the Sun melts the Snow, and the Snow has burned my foot."

But the Clouds only rumbled, "Do not blame us, little bird. It is the Wind that pushes us wherever it pleases."

So, bracing against the gusts, Tenquita fought her way through the air until she found the roaring Wind, whistling fiercely across the land. "Wind," she cried, "why are you so cruel? You chase the Clouds, the Clouds hide the Sun, the Sun melts the Snow, and the Snow has burned my foot."

But the Wind howled in reply, "Do not blame me, little bird. It is the great Wall that stops me from running free."

And so, Tenquita fluttered down to the tall Wall, standing firm against the storm. "Wall," she chirped, "why are you so cruel? You stop the Wind, the Wind chases the Clouds, the Clouds hide the Sun, the Sun melts the Snow, and the Snow has burned my foot."

But the Wall rumbled in its deep voice, "Do not blame me, little bird. It is the Mouse who gnaws holes in my side, weakening me every day."

Determined to find an answer, Tenquita hopped along the ground until she found the Mouse, twitching its whiskers as it scurried about. "Mouse," she chirped, "why are you so cruel? You gnaw the Wall, the Wall stops the Wind, the Wind chases the Clouds, the Clouds hide the Sun, the Sun melts the Snow, and the Snow has burned my foot."

But the Mouse squeaked nervously, "Do not blame me, little bird. It is the Cat who hunts me, forcing me to dig holes in the Wall for safety."

Tenquita fluffed her feathers and flew off in search of the Cat, who sat licking its paws in the warm sun. "Cat," she asked, "why are you so cruel? You chase the Mouse, the Mouse gnaws the Wall, the Wall stops the Wind, the Wind chases the Clouds, the Clouds hide the Sun, the Sun melts the Snow, and the Snow has burned my foot."

The Cat yawned lazily and replied, "Do not blame me, little bird. It is the Dog that chases me, making me run for my life."

So Tenquita hopped over to the Dog, who was resting with its head on its paws. "Dog," she chirped, "why are you so cruel? You chase the Cat, the Cat hunts the Mouse, the Mouse gnaws the Wall, the Wall stops the Wind, the Wind chases the Clouds, the Clouds hide the Sun, the Sun melts the Snow, and the Snow has burned my foot."

The Dog lifted its ears and growled, "Do not blame me, little bird. It is the Stick that beats me, making me chase the Cat."

And so, little Tenquita found a Stick, lying forgotten on the ground. "Stick," she asked, "why are you so cruel? You beat the Dog, the Dog chases the Cat, the Cat hunts the Mouse, the Mouse gnaws the Wall, the Wall stops the Wind, the Wind chases the Clouds, the Clouds hide the Sun, the Sun melts the Snow, and the Snow has burned my foot."

But the Stick sighed, "Do not blame me, little bird. It is the Fire that burns me, making me hit the Dog."

Determined, Tenquita fluttered over to the Fire, glowing fiercely in the cold air. "Fire," she chirped, "why are you so cruel? You burn the Stick, the Stick beats the Dog, the Dog chases the Cat, the Cat hunts the Mouse, the Mouse gnaws the Wall, the Wall stops the Wind, the Wind chases the Clouds, the Clouds hide the Sun, the Sun melts the Snow, and the Snow has burned my foot."

But the Fire crackled and flickered, saying, "Do not blame me, little bird. It is the Water that puts me out."

So Tenquita flew to the Water, flowing gently through the land. "Water," she chirped, "why are you so cruel? You put out the Fire, the Fire burns the Stick, the Stick beats the Dog, the Dog chases the Cat, the Cat hunts the Mouse, the Mouse gnaws the Wall, the Wall stops the Wind, the Wind chases the Clouds, the Clouds hide the Sun, the Sun melts the Snow, and the Snow has burned my foot."

The Water bubbled softly and replied, "Do not blame me, little bird. It is the Ox that drinks me away."

So Tenquita fluttered to the Ox, grazing peacefully in the field. "Ox," she chirped, "why are you so cruel? You drink the Water, the Water puts out the Fire, the Fire burns the Stick, the Stick beats the Dog, the Dog chases the Cat, the Cat hunts the Mouse, the Mouse gnaws the Wall, the Wall stops the Wind, the Wind chases the Clouds, the Clouds hide the Sun, the Sun melts the Snow, and the Snow has burned my foot."

But the Ox shook its great head and replied, "Do not blame me, little bird. It is the Knife that slays me."

So, trembling, Tenquita went to the Knife, gleaming sharp and cold. "Knife," she whispered, "why are you so cruel? You slay the Ox, the Ox drinks the Water, the Water puts out the Fire, the Fire burns the Stick, the Stick beats the Dog, the Dog chases the Cat, the Cat hunts the Mouse, the Mouse gnaws the Wall, the Wall stops the Wind, the Wind chases the Clouds, the Clouds hide the Sun, the Sun melts the Snow, and the Snow has burned my foot."

The Knife answered, "Do not blame me, little bird. It is Man who made me."

And so, at last, Tenquita went to Man and asked, "Why are you so cruel?"

But Man only pointed to the sky.

Tenquita looked up, and there sat the Lord of all things, watching over the world with gentle eyes. And when He saw the little bird, He said softly, "Go home, Tenquita, to your little ones. They are cold and hungry and need their mother."

And so, Tenquita returned to her nest. And as she nestled her tiny chicks beneath her warm feathers, she realised something wonderful, her burnt foot had healed.

How the Monkey and the Goat Earned Their Reputations

This story has been adapted from a tale originally told by Elsie Spicer Eells in Fairy Tales from Brazil, published in 1917 by E. M. Hale and Company, Chicago.

Once upon a time the tiger sent an invitation to the goat asking the goat to accompany him on a visit. The goat promptly accepted the invitation and at the appointed day they started on their journey to the house of the tiger's friend. On the way there they came to a dangerous marsh. The tiger was afraid to cross it, but he pretended to be very brave. He said to the goat, "Friend Goat, how very pale you look when you think about crossing the marsh. Don't be afraid. Just go ahead."

The goat assured the tiger that he was no coward. He thrust out his chest and marched along toward the marsh like a brave soldier. As soon, however, as he stepped into the marsh, he fell into the mud and barely got through it alive. The tiger went around the marsh and walked on dry ground.

After the tiger and the goat had come together again they came to some banana trees. The tiger said to the goat, "Friend Goat, aren't you hungry? Let us stop here and eat some bananas. You climb up and pluck the bananas. Give me the ripe ones, and keep the green ones yourself." The goat climbed up and picked the bananas. He gave the ripe ones to the tiger and the tiger had a good meal. The goat went hungry.

The tiger and the goat walked along and after going for some distance they saw a cobra lying in the path. "Friend Goat," said the tiger, "here you have the opportunity to procure a beautiful necklace for your daughter, free of cost. Just pick it up and it is yours." The goat started forward to pick up the snake, but the tiger told him to let it alone if he did not want to be killed.

When the tiger and the goat arrived at the house of the tiger's friend it was very late. They soon went to bed in hammocks hung close together. At midnight the tiger rose quietly, walked on tip toe to the door, opened it, and went out. He hurried to the place where the sheep were kept, killed the fattest lamb of the flock, and had a feast. Then he went back to the hammock, wiped the blood on the goat, and went to sleep.

Early the next morning the host discovered that one of his lambs was missing. He hastened to the room where the tiger and the goat were sleeping and accused the tiger of having killed the lamb. The tiger looked up at him with an innocent expression and asked, "Do you see any blood on me?" There was no blood on the tiger, but the host looked into the next hammock and saw the goat all covered with blood. "I know now who killed my fattest lamb," he said, and he gave the goat such a beating that the poor goat barely escaped with his life. From that day to this when one speaks of a person who has been easily imposed upon he calls him "the goat."

Things happened very differently with the monkey. One day not long afterward the tiger invited the monkey to accompany him when he went to visit his friend. The monkey accepted, and the tiger and the monkey set out on the journey. When they came to the marsh the tiger said to the monkey, "Friend Monkey, how very pale you look when you think about crossing the marsh. Don't be afraid. Just go ahead."

"You go ahead yourself," replied the monkey. The tiger went through the marsh and fell into the mud so that he was barely able to get out again. The monkey went around the marsh and walked on dry ground.

After a while the tiger and the monkey came to the banana trees. "Friend Monkey," said the tiger, "aren't you hungry? Let us stop here and eat some bananas. You climb up and pluck the bananas. Give the ripe ones to me and you may keep the green ones for yourself." The monkey climbed up and picked the bananas but he ate all the ripe ones himself and threw the green ones down to the tiger. The tiger was forced to go hungry but the monkey had a good meal.

Finally the tiger and the monkey came to a cobra lying in the path. "Friend Monkey," said the tiger, "here you have the opportunity to procure a beautiful necklace for your daughter, free of cost. Pick it up and it is yours."

"Pick it up yourself," replied the monkey.

When the tiger and the monkey arrived at the house of the tiger's friend it was very late. They went to bed in hammocks hung up close together. The monkey had seen enough of the tiger that day to make him decide that he had better sleep with one eye open. Accordingly he pretended he was asleep, but he was really awake. At midnight he saw the tiger crawl quietly out of his hammock, walk on tip toe to the door, open it gently, and go out. The monkey decided to watch and see what happened when the tiger came back.

The tiger went to the place where the sheep were kept, killed the fattest lamb of the flock and had a feast. When he came back he tried to wipe the lamb's blood on the monkey. The monkey saw him and gave him a push so that he spilled the blood all over himself and his own hammock. Not a single drop went on the monkey.

Early the next morning when the host missed one of his lambs he came to the room where his guests were sleeping. He saw the tiger all covered with blood and he cried, "Oh ho, I have at last caught the one who kills my lambs." Then he gave the tiger such a beating that he barely escaped with his life. It was all he could do to crawl home again.

El Pombero

This story is my own telling of a traditional Argentinian folk tale based on various sources.

In the heart of the dense forests of Paraguay and northern Argentina, there lurked a mischievous and elusive creature known as El Pombero. He was said to be a small, gnome-like being with wild hair, glowing eyes, and the legs of a goat. Despite his diminutive size, El Pombero was known to possess great strength and magical powers.

According to legend, El Pombero was the guardian of the forests and all the creatures that dwelled within them. He was also known as a trickster, often playing pranks on unsuspecting humans who ventured too deep into his domain.

One of the most famous tales of El Pombero tells of a young hunter who wandered into the forest in search of game. As he roamed through the trees, he suddenly heard a voice calling his name. Startled, the hunter turned to see a small, hairy figure emerging from the shadows.

It was El Pombero, and he had a mischievous gleam in his eye. "What brings you to my forest, young hunter?" he asked in a voice that seemed to echo through the trees.

The hunter, knowing the reputation of El Pombero, replied cautiously, "I seek only to hunt for food to feed my family."

El Pombero chuckled, his laughter echoing through the forest. "Very well," he said, "but beware, for the creatures of the forest are under my protection. Harm them, and you will incur my wrath."

With that warning, El Pombero vanished into the undergrowth, leaving the hunter alone in the forest. For hours, the hunter searched for game, but every time he spotted an animal, it seemed to vanish before his eyes.

Frustrated and exhausted, the hunter eventually gave up and made his way back home empty-handed. From that day forward, he told everyone he met of his encounter with El Pombero, warning them to tread carefully in the forest and always show respect to the guardian of the woods.

And so, the legend of El Pombero lived on, serving as a reminder to all who entered the forest that they were guests in his domain and must treat the creatures of the wild with reverence and respect.

How the Monkey Got a Drink When He Was Thirsty

This story has been adapted from a tale originally told by Elsie Spicer Eells in Fairy Tales from Brazil, published in 1917 by E. M. Hale and Company, Chicago.

Once upon a time the monkey made the tiger very angry. This is how it happened. The monkey was seated high up among the leafy branches of a mango tree playing upon his guitar. The tiger passed that way and lay down under the tree to rest. Just to tease him the monkey played and sang this little song:

"Tango ti tar, tango ti tar,

The tiger's bones are in my guitar.

Tee hee, Tee hee."

The tiger was very angry. "Just wait until I catch you, Mr. Monkey," he said. "Then I'll show you a trick or two with bones."

The monkey leaped from one tree to another keeping himself so well hidden by the foliage that the tiger could not see him. Then he came down out of the trees and hid himself in a hole in the ground. When the tiger came near he again played and sang his little song:

"Tango ti tar, tango ti tar,

The tiger's bones are in my guitar.

Tee hee, Tee hee."

The tiger put his paw into the hole and caught the monkey's leg. "Oh, ho, Mr. Tiger." said the monkey. "You think that you have caught my leg but what you really have is just a little stick. Oh, ho. Oh, ho." Then the tiger let go of the monkey's leg.

The monkey crawled farther back into the hole in the ground where the tiger's paw could not reach him. Then he said, "Thank you so much, Mr. Tiger, for letting go of my leg. It really was my leg, you know." Again he played and sang his little song:

"Tango ti tar, tango ti tar,

The tiger's bones are in my guitar.

Tee hee, Tee hee."

The tiger was angrier than ever. He waited and waited for the monkey to come out of the hole in the ground but the monkey did not come. He had discovered another way out and once more from the high tree tops he sang down to the waiting tiger:

"Tango ti tar, tango ti tar,

The tiger's bones are in my guitar.

Tee hee, Tee hee."

There had been a great drought in the land and there was only one watering place where the beasts could drink. The tiger knew that the monkey would have to go there when he was thirsty so he decided to wait for him and catch him when he came to drink.

When the monkey went to the watering place to get a drink he found the tiger there waiting for him. He ran away as fast as the wind for he was really very much afraid of the tiger.

He waited and waited until he thought he should die of thirst, but the tiger did not go away from the watering place for a single minute. At last the monkey thought of a trick by which he would be able to get a drink.

He lay down by the side of the pathway as if he were dead. After a while an old woman came along the path carrying a dish of honey in a basket upon her head. She saw the monkey lying there by the path and, thinking that he was dead, she picked him up and put him into the basket with the dish of honey. When the monkey saw that it was honey in the dish he was very happy. He opened the dish and covered himself all over with the soft sticky honey. Then as the old woman walked under the trees he lightly sprang out of the basket into the trees. The old woman did not miss him until she got home and found only part of her dish of honey in the basket.

"Why, I thought I had brought home a dead monkey in my basket," she said to her children. "Now there is no monkey here and my dish is only half full of honey. The monkey must have been playing one of his tricks."

The monkey had, in the meantime, stuck leaves from the trees into the honey all over his body so that he was completely disguised. His own mother would never have recognised him. He looked something like a porcupine; but instead of sharp quills there were green leaves sticking out all over him. In this fashion he went to the drinking place and the tiger did not recognise him. He took a long, deep drink. He was so thirsty and the water tasted so good that he stayed in the drinking place too long. The leaves came out of the honey which had held them and the tiger saw that it was really the monkey. The monkey was barely able to escape.

He was so badly frightened that he waited and waited a long, long time before he went to the drinking place again. At last he got so thirsty that he couldn't wait any longer. He went to the resin tree and covered himself with resin. Then he stuck leaves into the resin and again went to the drinking place.

The tiger saw him, but as the tiger expected to see the leaves come off just as soon as the monkey got into the water, he thought he would wait and catch him in his bare skin. This time the leaves did not come off, for the resin held them fast and was not in the least affected by the water. The tiger thought that it was not the monkey and that he must have made a mistake. The monkey drank all he wished and then strolled away leisurely without the tiger attacking him. He used the resin and leaves every time he wanted a drink after that. He kept up the trick until the rainy season arrived and he could find plenty of water in other places than the big drinking place.

The King Has A Piece

This story has been adapted from a tale originally told by Ramón A. Laval in Folk Tales in Chile, originally a Spanish language title, and, published in 1923 by Cervantes Printing House, Santiago De Chile.

Once upon a time, in a grand and glittering kingdom, there was a mighty King who ruled with wisdom and power. But one day, the King was struck by a terrible headache, one so fierce that even his finest doctors, with their potions and herbs, could not cure it. Days turned to weeks, and the King remained in bed, unable to attend to his royal duties.

Finally, when he awoke, he felt different. He reached up to his head and, oh, horror., he discovered that a small horn had grown upon his forehead.

The King, being proud and mighty, was determined to keep this a secret. No one in the kingdom could ever know. But there was a problem, his hair grew so much that it had to be cut, and no matter how much he wanted to hide his strange new feature, he could not do it alone.

So, he summoned his Ministers. "Find me the most discreet barber in the land," he commanded. "One who speaks little and keeps secrets well."

The Ministers searched high and low, until they found a poor, quiet barber who barely had any customers, for he was a man of few words. "This one will do," they said. And so, the King appointed him as his Royal Barber.

On the first day of his new duty, the King made the barber swear an unbreakable oath.

"You must tell no one what you see upon my head," the King warned.

The barber, trembling, placed his hand upon his heart and swore, "Your Majesty, I shall never speak of it."

With that, he cut the King's hair, carefully working around the small, strange horn, and when his task was done, he left the palace. He was to return in a month's time to repeat the task.

But the moment the barber stepped outside, a terrible feeling washed over him. He had never held such a big secret before, and the weight of it pressed upon his chest like a great stone. He could not eat. He could not sleep. He could not work. The secret twisted and turned inside him, growing larger each day. His belly swelled like a balloon, and no matter what he did, he felt as if he might burst. Yet he had sworn never to tell a soul.

Desperate, and sure he would die if he did not release the secret, the barber came up with a clever plan. He ran to the countryside, far away from the city, and there he found a quiet little hill. He grabbed a wooden stake, drove it into the soft earth, and dug a deep hole. Then, lying flat on his stomach, he pressed his lips to the ground and whispered into the earth, "The King has a horn. The King has a horn."

He repeated it a hundred times, letting the words pour from his lips. And as he did, something miraculous happened, his belly began to shrink. With every whispered phrase, he felt lighter, freer, until at last, he had emptied the secret from his soul. With a sigh of relief, he covered the hole with fresh soil, patted it down, and walked home feeling like a new man.

That night, for the first time in weeks, the barber slept soundly, and when he awoke, he was filled with joy, humming and ready to work once more. Little did he know, the earth does not keep secrets for long.

Days passed, then weeks. One morning, a group of schoolchildren went out to play in the fields, laughing and tumbling through the grass. It was there that they found a strange bush of small, delicate flowers growing right where the barber had buried his secret. Curious, the children picked the flowers and, as they always did, squeezed them between their fingers to make them pop. But instead of a snap, the flowers spoke.

"The King has a horn." they cried.

The children gasped. They picked more flowers, squeezed them, and again,

"The King has a horn."

Word spread like wildfire. The children ran home, telling their parents, who told the shopkeepers, who told the merchants, who whispered it to the nobles, until, before long, the entire city knew the King's secret. And soon, the King himself heard the whispers.

The furious King summoned the barber at once.

"Betrayal." he thundered. "You shall pay with your life."

The barber, pale but determined, knelt before the King and spoke, "Your Majesty, I swore to tell no person your secret, and I have kept my oath. Not a single soul has heard it from my lips."

The King glared at him, sceptical. "Then how does the entire kingdom know?"

The barber swallowed hard. He dared not reveal what he had done, for it would surely sound mad. So he only said, "Sire, sometimes, the earth itself cannot hold a secret."

The King studied him long and hard. There were no witnesses, no proof that the barber had ever spoken the words aloud. At last, with a great sigh, the King let him go.

From that day on, the King no longer hid his horn. Instead, he wore a fine golden crown, shaped so that it rested naturally over his small but mysterious feature.

The people soon forgot their curiosity, for a King with a horn was still a King, and a good ruler was more important than an odd appearance.

As for the barber, he kept his job and his head, but never again did he take on a secret he could not bear.

And if you ever find yourself in a quiet meadow, surrounded by swaying wildflowers, be careful what you whisper to the earth, for secrets have a way of growing into stories.

How the Monkey Got Food When He Was Hungry

This story has been adapted from a tale originally told by Elsie Spicer Eells in Fairy Tales from Brazil, published in 1917 by E. M. Hale and Company, Chicago.

Once upon a time the monkey was hungry. He wanted to make some porridge, but he did not have any money to buy meal to make the porridge. So he went to the house of the hen to borrow some meal. The hen gave him some meal.

"Come to my house tomorrow at one o'clock," he said to the hen, "I'll pay back the meal then."

Then the monkey went to the house of the fox and said, "Oh, friend fox, please lend me some meal. Come to my house tomorrow at two o'clock and I'll pay you then." The fox gave him some meal.

Then the monkey went to the house of the dog and said, "Oh, friend dog, please lend me some meal. Come to my house tomorrow at three o'clock and I'll pay you back then." The dog gave him some meal.

Then the monkey went to the house of the tiger and said, "Oh, friend tiger, please lend me some meal. Come to my house tomorrow at four o'clock and I'll pay you back then." The tiger gave the monkey some meal.

The monkey went home and made a great pot of porridge. He feasted and feasted until he couldn't eat any more, but there was still plenty of porridge left in the pot. Then the monkey made his bed and took care to fix it high up from the floor.

The next day, at midday, he ate some more of the porridge. Then he bound a cloth about his head and went to bed pretending that he was sick.

At one o'clock the hen came and knocked at the door. The monkey in a low, weak voice asked her to enter. He told her how very sick he was and the hen was very sorry for him.

At two o'clock the fox came and knocked at the door. The hen was frightened almost to death. "Never mind," said the monkey, "you can hide here under my bed."

The hen hid under the monkey's bed and the monkey in a weak, low voice invited the fox to enter. The monkey told the fox how very ill he was and the fox was very sorry for him.

At three o'clock the dog came and knocked at the door. The fox was frightened almost to death. "Never mind," said the monkey, "hide here under my bed and everything will be all right."

The fox hid under the monkey's bed and the monkey, in a low, weak voice, invited the dog to enter. The monkey told the dog how very sick he was and the dog was very sorry for him.

At four the tiger came and knocked at the door. The dog was frightened almost to death. "Never mind," said the monkey. "Hide here under my bed and everything will be all right."

The dog hid under the monkey's bed. Then the monkey invited the tiger to enter. He told, the tiger how very sick he was but the tiger was not at all sorry for him. He sprang at the bed, demanding in a loud, fierce voice that the monkey pay back the meal at once, as he had promised to do. The monkey escaped to the treetops, but the bed broke down under the tiger's weight.

Then the fox ate up the hen and the dog ate up the fox and the tiger ate up the dog. The tiger is still trying to catch the monkey.

Why the Bananas Belong to the Monkey

This story has been adapted from a tale originally told by Elsie Spicer Eells in Fairy Tales from Brazil, published in 1917 by E. M. Hale and Company, Chicago.

Once upon a time when the world had just been made and there was only one kind of banana, but very many kinds of monkeys, there was a little old woman who had a big garden full of banana trees. It was very difficult for the old woman to gather the bananas herself, so she made a bargain with the largest monkey. She told him that if he would gather the bunches of bananas for her she would give him half of them. The monkey gathered the bananas. When he took his half he gave the little old woman the bananas which grow at the bottom of the bunch and are small and wrinkled. The nice big fat ones he kept for himself and carried them home to let them ripen in the dark.

The little old woman was very angry. She lay awake all night trying to think of some way by which she could get even with the monkey. At last she thought of a trick.

The next morning she made an image of wax which looked just like a little boy. Then she placed a large flat basket on the top of the image's head and in the basket she placed the best ripe bananas she could find. They certainly looked very tempting.

After a little while the biggest monkey passed that way. He saw the image of wax and thought that it was a boy peddling bananas. He had often pushed over boy banana peddlers, upset their baskets and then had run away with the bananas. This morning he was feeling very good-natured so he thought that he would first try asking politely for the bananas.

"Oh, peddler boy, peddler boy," he said to him, "please give me a banana." The image of wax answered never a word.

Again the monkey said, this time in a little louder voice, "Oh, peddler boy, peddler boy, please give me a banana, just one little, ripe little, sweet little banana." The image of wax answered never a word.

Then the monkey called out in his loudest voice, "Oh, peddler boy, peddler boy, if you don't give me a banana I'll give you such a push that it will upset all of your bananas." The image of wax was silent.

The monkey ran toward the image of wax and struck it hard with his hand. His hand remained firmly embedded in the wax.

"Oh, peddler boy, peddler boy, let go my hand," the monkey called out. "Let go my hand and give me a banana or else I'll give you a hard, hard blow with my other hand." The image of wax did not let go.

The monkey gave the image a hard, hard blow with his other hand. The other hand remained firmly embedded in the wax.

Then the monkey called out, "Oh, peddler boy, peddler boy, let go my two hands. Let go my two hands and give me a banana or else I will give you a kick with my foot." The image of wax did not let go.

The monkey gave the image a kick with his foot and his foot remained stuck fast in the wax.

"Oh, peddler boy, peddler boy," the monkey cried, "let go my foot. Let go my two hands and my foot and give me a banana or else I'll give you a kick with my other foot." The image of wax did not let go.

Then the monkey who was now very angry, gave the image of wax a kick with his foot and his foot remained stuck fast in the wax.

The monkey shouted, "Oh, peddler boy, peddler boy, let go my foot. Let go my two feet and my two hands and give me a banana or else I'll give you a push with my body." The image of wax did not let go.

The monkey gave the image of wax a push with his body. His body remained caught fast in the wax.

"Oh, peddler boy, peddler boy," the monkey shouted, "let go my body. Let go my body and my two feet and my two hands or I'll call all the other monkeys to help me." The image of wax did not let go.

Then the monkey made such an uproar with his cries and shouts that very soon monkeys came running from all directions. There were big monkeys and little monkeys and middle-sized monkeys. A whole army of monkeys had come to the aid of the biggest monkey.

It was the very littlest monkey who thought of a plan to help the biggest monkey out of his plight. The monkeys were to climb up into the biggest tree and pile themselves one on top of another until they made a pyramid of monkeys. The monkey with the very loudest voice of all was to be on top and he was to shout his very loudest to the sun and ask the sun to come and help the biggest monkey out of his dreadful difficulty.

This is what all the big-sized, little-sized, middle-sized monkeys did. The monkey with the loudest voice on top of the pyramid made the sun hear. The sun came at once.

The sun poured his hottest rays down upon the wax. After a while the wax began to melt. The monkey was at last able to pull out one of his hands. The sun poured down more of his hottest rays and soon the monkey was able to pull out his two hands. Then he could pull out one foot, then another, and in a little while his body, too. At last he was free.

When the little old woman saw what had happened she was very much discouraged about raising bananas. She decided to move to another part of the world where she raised cabbages instead of bananas. The monkeys were left in possession of the big garden full of banana trees. From that day to this the monkeys have thought that they own all the bananas.

The Huachita Lamb

This story has been adapted from a tale originally told by Ramón A. Laval in Folk Tales in Chile, originally a Spanish language title, and, published in 1923 by Cervantes Printing House, Santiago De Chile.

Once upon a time, in a small village nestled between rolling hills and verdant forests, there lived a poor man who had been widowed, leaving him with two young children, a little boy and his younger sister. Every day, before the first light of dawn, the father would set out to work, leaving his children in the care of a kind-hearted neighbour. She fed them, bathed them, and ensured they were warm at night.

One day, fortune smiled upon the father, and he married the neighbour, believing she would care for his children as her own. But once the wedding feast had ended, and the father left for work each morning, the woman's kindness vanished like smoke in the wind.

She forced the children to carry heavy buckets of water from the river, chop wood with hands too small for the task, and sweep floors until their little fingers ached. If they failed, she would strike them with whatever she could find.

One night, as they lay shivering in their beds, the boy whispered, "Little sister, let us run away. The world is wide, and somewhere, there must be kindness waiting for us."

And so, before the sun had risen, the two children fled into the unknown.

For days, they wandered through forests and fields, eating wild berries and sleeping beneath the stars. But as the days stretched on, thirst became their greatest enemy.

Finally, they stumbled upon a shimmering lagoon. Their hearts leapt with joy, and they rushed to drink. But just as they bent down, a deep voice rose from the water.

"Whoever drinks from this lagoon shall become a monster that devours their own sibling."

The boy pulled his sister back. "We must not drink. Let us keep going, no matter how much it hurts."

So, with aching throats, they walked on.

The next day, they found a well. Hope filled their eyes as they let down a bucket, but as they raised the water, a voice echoed from the depths, "Whoever drinks from this well shall turn into a serpent and consume their own flesh and blood."

Tears welled in the girl's eyes, but she obeyed her brother and stepped away.

By the third day, their strength had nearly left them when they found a clear, flowing stream. Cool, refreshing water sparkled before them, and as the girl bent down to drink, she heard the words, "Whoever drinks from this water shall become a lamb."

But thirst had stolen her senses, and before her brother could stop her, she drank. In an instant, her small hands and feet became hooves, her body was covered in soft, white wool, and her gentle face transformed into that of a lamb.

The boy cried out in despair, but the girl, though changed, could still speak. "Do not grieve, dear brother. I am still me."

And so, hand in hoof, they continued their journey together.

One day, as the boy sat weeping beside his lamb-sister, an old woman approached. "Why do you cry, child?" she asked.

Through his sobs, he told her their tale.

The old woman smiled kindly and placed a small wooden wand in the lamb's wool. "This is a wand of virtue," she said. "With it, she may return to her human form for three hours at a time. And one day, when a prince loves her truly, she shall be free forever."

And with that, the old woman vanished like mist in the morning sun.

From then on, the lamb was no longer sad. She would dance around her brother, bleating happily. When they were alone, she would transform into a girl for a few short hours, and the two would laugh and talk as they had before.

Years passed, and the boy grew into a strong young man. One day, he found work tending to the flocks of the King himself. The King, seeing the young man's loyalty, allowed him to keep his little lamb by his side.

But their arrival at the palace set fate into motion.

That very night, as the young shepherd and his lamb slept in the courtyard, the Prince of the kingdom passed by. From inside the shepherd's humble quarters, he heard a woman's voice. His eyes narrowed. No maidens were allowed in the servants' chambers. Who, then, could be speaking?

The next morning, the Prince told his mother, the Queen. That night, the shepherd was summoned.

"Who was in your chamber last night?" the Queen asked.

The shepherd bowed his head. "Only my lamb, Your Majesty. She is a clever little thing, and I have taught her a few words."

The Queen, intrigued, demanded to see the lamb.

The shepherd whispered to his sister, "Say only the words I have taught you."

And so, when the Queen saw the beautiful, snow-white lamb, she delighted in its intelligence. "Say something, little one," the Queen encouraged.

The lamb bleated sweetly, "Mama, Papa, Brother."

Enchanted, the Queen took the lamb as her own. From that day forward, she carried her everywhere, treating her as a beloved pet.

But fate had not yet finished its tale.

One day, the King declared a great festival, with three days of horse races to celebrate a victory in battle.

On the first day, as the royal family rode out in splendour, the lamb slipped away unseen and ran into the woods. Beside a thorn bush, she whispered, "Little wand of virtue, by the power you hold, make me a maiden dressed in the colours of the stars, and bring me a silver carriage drawn by two pairs of white horses."

And in an instant, she stood radiant and beautiful, dressed in a shimmering gown, and a grand carriage awaited her. Then, as she arrived at the festival, all eyes turned to her. The Prince was captivated.

"Who is she?" the people whispered.

The next day, she returned, dressed in moonlight and gold, and the Prince was even more enchanted.

By the third and final day, she arrived in a gown of sun, moon, and stars, riding in a chariot of diamonds.

But just as the Prince gathered his courage to ask her name, she disappeared into the night.

The Prince grew heartsick with longing for the mysterious maiden. He refused food and sleep, and no doctor could cure him. Then, one day, the little lamb turned to the Queen. "Mama, let me care for the Prince. Perhaps I can heal him."

What harm could it do? The Queen allowed it.

The moment they were alone, the lamb whispered to the wand, and the beautiful maiden appeared. The Prince's eyes fluttered open. "You." he gasped, reaching for her hand. "I thought you were lost forever."

They spoke for hours, and with every moment, his strength returned.

Then, as the wand's magic began to fade, the young woman whispered, "If you love me, truly love me, I shall never vanish again."

The Prince called for his parents. "I will marry her, and only her." he declared.

In that instant, the lamb's skin fell away, and she became human forevermore.

The wedding was grand, the kingdom rejoiced, and the young woman's brother, once a humble shepherd, was granted a noble title. And so, the Prince and his enchanted maiden lived in happiness, and not a single drop of cursed water ever touched their lips again.

Rere's Bell

This story is my own telling of a traditional Chilean folk tale based on various sources.

In the remote valleys of Chile, nestled amidst towering mountains and dense forests, there lies a small village where time seems to stand still. Here, the people live in harmony with nature, their lives intertwined with the rhythms of the land and the ancient legends that have been passed down through generations.

One such legend tells of a mystical creature known as Rere, a guardian spirit who watches over the village and its inhabitants. Rere is said to take the form of a majestic condor, with wings that span the sky and eyes that gleam with ancient wisdom.

But Rere is more than just a protector of the village, she is also the keeper of a sacred bell, a bell that holds the power to ward off evil and bring prosperity to those who hear its chime. For centuries, the bell has been hidden away in a secret chamber deep within the heart of the mountains, its location known only to Rere herself.

According to legend, Rere's Bell can only be rung in times of great need, when the village faces imminent danger or hardship. When the bell tolls, its melodic chime echoes throughout the valley, signalling to the people that help is on the way.

But the power of Rere's Bell comes with a price, for only those pure of heart and true of purpose are able to wield its magic. Many have sought to find the bell and harness its power for their own gain, but none have succeeded, thwarted by the watchful gaze of Rere and her unwavering dedication to protecting the village and its people.

Yet despite the dangers that lurk in the shadows, the villagers take comfort in knowing that Rere's Bell stands as a beacon of hope, a symbol of strength and resilience in the face of adversity. And though they may never lay eyes on the bell itself, they know that its presence is felt in every gust of wind, and every ray of sunlight that illuminates their mountain home.

For as long as Rere watches over the village and her bell remains hidden in its secret chamber, the people of the valley will continue to live in peace, secure in the knowledge that their guardian spirit will always be there to guide and protect them.

How the Monkey Escaped Being Eaten

This story has been adapted from a tale originally told by Elsie Spicer Eells in Fairy Tales from Brazil, published in 1917 by E. M. Hale and Company, Chicago.

Once upon a time, ages and ages ago, people ate fruits and nuts. Then there came a time when the fruits and nuts became scarce. People had to eat meat. So they began killing the various beasts to see which ones were the best to eat. They skinned them and cut them in pieces and cooked them over the fire. Some of the beasts were good to eat and others were not good at all.

The ox was found to be very good, and so was the sheep, and the armadillo. Then one day a man thought that he would try to eat the monkey.

The monkey was playing his guitar. "Lee, lee, lee, lee, lee lay, lee lay, lee ray, lee ray."

The man came close to him and said, "Come here, little monkey, and let me hear your music. I enjoy it very much."

All the time the man was coming closer and closer to the monkey. Just as he was about to stretch out his hand and seize the monkey, the monkey gave a sudden leap to the tree and hurried away to the tree top.

After that every time the man heard the monkey play the guitar he would come near and try to catch him. The monkey grew afraid of the man, so afraid that he gave up playing his guitar at all. For a long, long time he did not play upon it. One day he felt that he just must have some music. He hid in a hole in the ground and there he played upon his guitar. He did not think that the man would hear him, but the man had very sharp ears. When he got through playing he started to come out of the hole in the ground, and there was the man waiting for him. He crawled quickly back, so far back that the man could not catch him. The monkey waited and waited for the man to go away, but the man did not go away.

After a while the man became thirsty and went to get a drink. He left his little boy in his place to watch for the monkey. After the man had gone away the monkey called out to the little boy, "Oh, little boy, Oh, little boy, don't you wish that you could see the monkey dance?"

The little boy replied that he wished he could.

"Just put your eyes down to the door of my little cave, and I'll let you see the monkey dance, little boy," said the monkey.

The little boy put his eyes down close to the hole in the ground. No sooner had he done so than the monkey threw dirt into the little boy's eyes. When the little boy was rubbing his eyes to get the dirt out of them the monkey made a sudden dash out of the cave and escaped to the treetops. When the man returned the little boy did not dare to tell him that the monkey had escaped. The man waited and waited and waited there by the hole in the ground. At last he became tired of waiting and went away.

After that the man tried harder than ever to catch the monkey. If he had not had the good luck to catch the monkey napping one day there is no knowing when he would have got his hands upon him. One day, however, he caught the monkey napping. He shut him up in a box and carried him home to the children for supper.

The man put a big dish full of water over the fire ready to cook the monkey. Then he went away to collect more fuel for the fire. The monkey and his guitar were shut up in the box, and there, inside the box, the monkey played on his guitar. "Lee, lee, lee, lee, lee lay, lee lay, lee ray, lee ray." The children came crowding close to the box.

"Oh, children, Oh, children," said the monkey, "don't you wish that you could see the monkey dance?"

The children replied that they wished they could.

"This box is so small that there is not room enough for me to dance here," said the monkey. "Just let me out and I'll show you how well I can dance."

The children opened the box and let the monkey out into the room. The monkey played on his guitar, "Lee, lee, lee, lee, lee lay, lee lay, lee ray, lee ray," and he danced about the room. Then he said, "Oh, children. Oh, children. You have nothing at all cooking in that pot over the fire. Let us put something into the pot to cook."

The children thought that it would not be polite to tell the monkey what the pot of water was waiting for, so they let the monkey fill the pot as he liked. He put into it some little dry sticks and an empty cocoanut shell. Then he said, "Oh, children, Oh, children, I cannot dance any more. It is so hot here in this room."

The children begged him to dance some more.

"If you will open the door a little bit so that I can have more air to breathe I'll show you a new dance," said the monkey.

The children opened the door. The monkey danced over to the door and out of the door and away to the treetops. That was the last they ever saw of him. He moved to another part of the country after that experience.

When the man came home with fuel for the fire the children did not dare to tell him that the monkey had escaped. They let him think that the sticks and the cocoanut shell in the pot was the monkey. He built a big roaring fire under the pot and soon it was boiling merrily. After the pot had boiled a while he called the children to come to supper with him. The children let him taste first. He fished a hard stick out of the pot and bit into it. "This is not the monkey's leg. It is just a dry stick," he said, as he made a wry face. Then he fished the empty cocoanut shell out of the pot. "That is not the monkey's head," he said as he tasted it, "That is just an empty cocoanut shell." He couldn't find a single trace of the monkey in that monkey stew. He never wished to make a monkey stew again.

The Little One

This story has been adapted from a tale originally told by Ramón A. Laval in Folk Tales in Chile, originally a Spanish language title, and, published in 1923 by Cervantes Printing House, Santiago De Chile.

Long ago, in a quiet village where the streets shimmered with golden dust and the rivers whispered secrets to the trees, there lived an old couple, a humble water carrier and his washerwoman wife. No matter how hard they worked, they could barely earn enough to keep hunger from their door.

One night, as they sat beside their small fire, the old woman sighed. "If only we had a child," she whispered. "Even if he were no bigger than my finger, he could help us, and we would have someone to talk to in our old age."

Her husband nodded, but his voice was heavy. "Wishing will not fill our home," he said.

Just then, a voice echoed from the ceiling. "You shall have the child you desire."

The old couple stared at each other in shock, but the room was empty. Uneasy, they went to bed and soon fell into a deep sleep.

The next morning, the old man left for his daily work, carrying water through the village, while his wife began washing clothes in the river. As she scrubbed, she felt something stir inside her sleeve. Thinking it was a lizard, she shook her arm, and something small splashed into the water.

Then, a tiny voice cried out, "Mother, take me out. I'm drowning."

The old woman gasped and looked closer. There, barely the size of her little finger, was a baby. He waved his arms and kicked his legs, floating in the soapy water. Tears filled her eyes as she lifted him up, holding him close to her heart. When her husband returned, she showed him the child, and they named him Miñique, meaning Little One.

Though Miñique never grew taller, he possessed incredible strength and a voice so loud that it could shake the trees. The old couple, afraid that someone might steal him away, kept his existence a secret.

Years passed, and the couple grew older and weaker. One day, they realised they had only thirty coins left.

"Miñique," the old woman said, handing him a small coin. "Go to the butcher and buy us some meat."

The Little One took the coin and ran to the market. Reaching the butcher's shop, Miñique banged on the counter with his tiny fist.

The butcher looked around, but saw no one. "Who's there?" he called.

"It's me, Miñique. Sell me ten coins' worth of meat."

The butcher leaned over the counter and, after much squinting, finally spotted the tiny boy. He chuckled. "And how do you expect to carry ten coins' worth of meat, little one?"

"Why stop at ten?" Miñique boomed. "If you give me a whole ox, I'll carry that too."

The butcher laughed. "Alright then, take the ox hanging at the door."

To his utter shock, Miñique threw the massive ox over his shoulder and ran away. The butcher stood frozen, his mouth hanging open, as the villagers gasped in awe.

Back home, Miñique's parents were overjoyed. They roasted the meat and saved enough to last for days.

The next morning, Miñique ran to the baker. Bang. Bang. He knocked on the counter.

"Who's knocking?" the baker called.

"It's me, Miñique. Give me five coins' worth of bread."

The baker bent down, his eyes widening at the sight of the tiny boy. "And how will you carry that?" he asked.

"The same way as everyone else. If you give me that basket full of bread, I'll take it easily."

The baker, thinking this was a joke, placed the heavy basket on Miñique's shoulders. To his astonishment, the tiny boy dashed away, running faster than the wind. The villagers gasped as they saw a basket flying down the street, carried by an unseen force.

One day, Miñique was sent to buy onions. As he ran down the road, he spotted something shiny on the ground, a tiny knife. He picked it up, tucking it into his belt. Just then, he reached an onion seller on horseback, carrying two massive baskets of onions.

"Sell me five coins' worth of onions." Miñique called.

The onion seller searched for the voice, but saw no one. Just then, a cow passed by, munching on grass, and in one bite, it swallowed Miñique whole.

Inside the cow's belly, Miñique did not panic. He simply pulled out his knife and cut himself free, stepping out into the sunlight. The cow collapsed, and Miñique dragged it home by its tail.

His parents were stunned. They washed him clean and turned the cow into dried meat.

After all that, Miñique still remembered the onions. He found the seller and shouted, "Well? Are you going to sell me those onions or not?"

The onion seller, still looking around for his mysterious customer, nearly fainted when he saw the tiny boy standing there, safe and sound.

Miñique's legend spread across the land, until even the King heard of him.

"Bring him to the palace." the King declared.

The capital was far away, but Miñique had a clever idea. He tamed a tiny mouse and used a hairpin as a bridle, an old glove for a saddle, and a shoelace for reins. Strapping on his knife like a sword, he rode off to meet the King.

At the palace, the entire court marvelled at him. The King and Queen, princes and princesses, all gathered to admire the tiny warrior. They were amazed by his strength, voice, and courage.

"You must stay in the palace," the King said.

But Miñique bowed deeply. "I cannot, Your Majesty. My parents are old and sick. If I leave them, they will suffer."

The King, moved by Miñique's love for his family, brought his parents to live in the palace, giving them a home of comfort and joy.

When war came to the kingdom, Miñique saved the day. He alone carried the cannons when horses failed. His mighty voice carried orders across the battlefield. For his bravery and loyalty, the King knighted him and made him a captain in the royal army.

And so, Miñique, the Little One, lived the rest of his days honoured and beloved, proving that greatness is not measured in size, but in heart.

Why the Monkey Still Has a Tail

This story has been adapted from a tale originally told by Elsie Spicer Eells in Fairy Tales from Brazil, published in 1917 by E. M. Hale and Company, Chicago.

Once upon a time the monkey and the rabbit made a contract. The monkey was to kill all the butterflies and the rabbit was to kill all the snakes.

One day the rabbit was taking a nap when the monkey passed that way. The monkey thought that he would play a trick on the rabbit so he pulled the rabbit's ears, pretending that he thought they were butterflies. The rabbit awoke very angry at the monkey and he plotted how he might revenge himself on the monkey.

The rabbit and the armadillo are very good friends. The armadillo is very, very strong, you know, so it was he whom the rabbit asked to help him.

One day the rabbit caught the monkey napping. He had watched and waited a long, long time to catch the monkey napping, but at last he succeeded. Even the monkey sometimes takes a nap. The rabbit called the armadillo at once and together they rolled a big stone upon the monkey's tail. The monkey pulled so hard to get his tail out from under the stone that it broke off. The cat, who at that time had no tail of her own, spied the tail and ran away with it. The monkey was very angry at the rabbit. "Oh, we thought it was just a snake lying there," said the rabbit. "When you pulled my ears, you know, you thought they were butterflies."

That did not help the monkey to feel any better. How was he to live without his tail. How could he climb without it. He simply had to have it back so he at once set out to find the cat.

At last he found the cat and said to her, "Oh, kind cat, please give me back my tail."

"I will give it to you," replied the cat, "if you will get me some milk."

"Where shall I get the milk?" asked the monkey.

"Go ask the cow for some," replied the cat.

The monkey went to the cow and said, "Oh, kind cow, please give me some milk that I may give the milk to the cat so that the cat will give back my tail to me."

"I will give you the milk," replied the cow, "if you will get me some grass."

"Where shall I get the grass?" asked the monkey.

"Go ask the farmer," responded the cow.

The monkey went to the farmer and said, "Oh, kind farmer, please give me some grass that I may give the grass to the cow so that the cow will give me some milk so that I may give the milk to the cat so that the cat will give back my tail to me."

The farmer said, "I will give you some grass if you give me some rain."

"Where shall I get the rain?" asked the monkey.

"Go ask the clouds," responded the farmer.

The monkey went to the clouds and said, "Oh, kind clouds, please send me down some rain that I may give the rain to the farmer so that the farmer will give me some grass so that I may give the grass to the cow so that the cow will give me some milk so that I may give the milk to the cat so that the cat will give me back my tail."

"I will give you some rain," replied the clouds, "if you will get me some fog."

"Where shall I get the fog?" asked the monkey.

"Go ask the rivers," replied the clouds.

The monkey went to the river and said, "Oh, kind river, please give me a fog that I may give the fog to the clouds so that the clouds will give some rain so that I may give the rain to the farmer so that the farmer will give me some grass so that I may give the grass to the cow so that the cow will give me some milk so that I may give the milk to the cat so that the cat will give me back my tail."

"I will give you a fog," replied the river, "if you will find a new spring to feed me."

"Where shall I find a spring?" asked the monkey.

"Go search for one among the rocks upon the hillside," replied the river.

Then the monkey climbed up the steep hill and searched and searched among the rocks until he found a little spring to feed the river. He brought the spring to the river and the river gave him a fog.

He took the fog to the clouds and the clouds gave him rain. He took the rain to the farmer and the farmer gave him grass. He took the grass to the cow and the cow gave him milk. He took the milk to the cat and the cat gave him back his tail. The monkey was so glad to have his tail again that he danced and danced with glee. Ever since that time the monkey has been very careful to guard his tail. He still has one and he is still happy because of it.

The Fortune Parrot

This story has been adapted from a tale originally told by Ramón A. Laval in Folk Tales in Chile, originally a Spanish language title, and, published in 1923 by Cervantes Printing House, Santiago De Chile.

Once upon a time, in a kingdom bathed in golden sunlight, there lived a poor widow with three beautiful daughters. Their names were Rosa-Flor, Hortensia-Flor, and Maria-Flor. Though they had little wealth, they were honest, kind, and hardworking, and their beauty was known far and wide.

One evening, as they sat sewing by the fire, their laughter rang through the streets. It so happened that the King himself was passing by their home at that very moment. Curious, he stopped to listen.

They were speaking of marriage.

"If you could choose, Rosa-Flor," asked one sister, "who would you marry?"

"The King's pastry chef." Rosa-Flor declared. "So I could eat cakes and sweet puddings every day."

"And you, Hortensia-Flor?"

"I would marry the King's cook," she answered. "Then I would dine on the richest stews in the land."

Finally, they turned to Maria-Flor, the youngest.

She smiled dreamily and said, "I would marry the King himself and bear him two sons and a daughter, the most beautiful in the world. On their foreheads would shine the Sun, the Morning Star, and the Full Moon."

The King's heart stirred. The very next morning, he arrived at the widow's home with his ministers, his pastry chef, and his cook.

"I have come to grant your wishes," he said. "Rosa-Flor, you shall marry my pastry chef. Hortensia-Flor, you shall have my cook. And Maria-Flor… you shall be my Queen."

And so, the weddings were held, and Maria-Flor became the bride of the King.

For a time, all seemed well, but jealousy crept into the hearts of Rosa-Flor and Hortensia-Flor. Their sister was now a queen, while they remained mere wives of the palace servants.

One day, war broke out, and the King was forced to ride into battle. Before leaving, he entrusted his sisters-in-law with the care of his wife, who was expecting their royal children.

A few months later, the Queen gave birth to two sons and a daughter, just as she had foretold. Upon their tiny foreheads shone a golden Sun, a bright Morning Star, and a shimmering Full Moon.

But the wicked sisters-in-law saw their chance. They stole the newborns and replaced them with three tiny puppies, taken from Rosa-Flor's dog that very morning.

When the Queen woke and asked to see her children, they placed the little animals in her arms.

"What trickery is this?" they whispered amongst the palace courtiers. "A Queen who bears dogs instead of children? Surely, she is cursed."

The terrible news spread throughout the kingdom. From the battlefield, the King sent a command, "Wall up the Queen in the tower. Leave only a small window, through which she shall receive a loaf of bread and a cup of water each day. She shall remain there until God takes her."

Meanwhile, Rosa-Flor carried the three infants to a stream beneath the palace, placing them in a wooden trough and pushing them into the rushing waters.

Down the river lived a humble gardener and his wife. That very night, as the man bent to draw water from the stream, he saw something floating towards him, a trough, carrying three beautiful babies.

His wife, who had lost her own child at birth that same night, wept with joy. "It is a miracle." she cried. "We will raise them as our own."

And so, the children were named after the celestial signs upon their foreheads. The eldest was called Sol (Sun), the second Lucero (Morning Star), and the girl Luna (Moon).

Years passed, and the children grew into the most beautiful beings the kingdom had ever seen. Yet, they always wore handkerchiefs over their foreheads, never knowing of the royal marks hidden beneath.

One day, as the gardener lay dying, he called the children to his side and revealed the truth of their origins. Shocked but determined, Sol, the eldest, declared, "I will go and find our true parents."

And so, he set off into the wide world. After many days, he met an old woman on the road.

"A little charity, young man?" she pleaded.

Sol gave her bread and cheese, and in gratitude, the woman revealed, "To find your parents, you must seek the Singing Tree, the Water of Life, and the Fortune Parrot."

She handed him three balls of thread and told him to follow them until he reached the palace of a blind King, who would guide him further.

Sol followed the thread for seven days, until he stood before the blind King. The King gave him a magical horse, saying, "Let the horse guide you, but do not anger him. He will take you to the Singing Tree."

Sol rode through the night, but when the horse stopped in a meadow, he grew impatient and spurred the beast forward. The horse reared, throwing him to the ground, where he turned to stone.

Days passed. Lucero, the second brother, went in search of Sol, but he too failed the trial and was turned into stone.

Finally, Luna, the youngest, set out. When she met the old woman, she gave her half of all she carried, for Luna's heart was full of kindness.

Reaching the blind King's palace, she treated the magical horse with gentleness, allowing him to drink and rest. In return, the horse carried her safely to the Singing Tree.

The Tree, in a voice like the wind, said, "Take only my golden seed and seek the Water of Life."

At the sacred well, she waited patiently until the waters rose. Only then did she fill her jar. And just as she did, a brilliant Parrot fluttered onto her shoulder.

"You have succeeded, dear Luna." the Parrot chirped. "Now, sprinkle the Water of Life upon the stones and you shall see your brothers restored."

She did, and one by one, the men transformed back to flesh and blood. With the Parrot guiding them, the three siblings returned home, ready to claim justice.

The King, still mourning his lost children, was drawn to their magical Singing Tree, whose song echoed across the land. When he arrived, the Fortune Parrot spoke, saying, "Look upon these three children, Your Majesty. They are your own. The wicked sisters-in-law stole them and cast them away."

The truth struck like lightning. At once, the King ordered the wicked women tied to four horses and torn apart. Then, trembling with remorse, he rushed to the walled tower where Maria-Flor had suffered for twelve long years.

But she was too weak to even stand.

"Quickly. Give her the Water of Life." cried Luna.

As soon as the Queen drank, her youth and strength returned. She rose, radiant as ever, and at last embraced her long-lost children.

The King fell to his knees. "Forgive me," he whispered.

She smiled. "It is done."

That very week, Luna wed the handsome Prince, the son of the blind King. The kingdom rejoiced, and celebrations lasted for seven days and seven nights. And so, the rightful heirs ruled the land with wisdom and kindness, and the Parrot, perched atop the Singing Tree, sang of their happiness for all time.

The Curse of Luison

This story is my own telling of a traditional Argentinian folk tale based on various sources.

Once upon a time, in the vast expanse of the Argentine countryside, there lived a man named Diego. Diego was a simple farmer who toiled under the hot sun, tending to his crops and caring for his family with love and dedication. But Diego harboured a dark secret, a secret that would soon bring terror and despair to his life.

It was said that Diego had made a pact with the devil himself, trading his soul for riches and power beyond his wildest dreams. In exchange, he agreed to perform unspeakable deeds, sacrificing innocent lives to satisfy his insatiable thirst for wealth and influence.

For years, Diego revelled in his newfound prosperity, his fields abundant with crops and his coffers overflowing with gold. But deep down, he knew that his ill-gotten gains came at a terrible price, a price he would soon be forced to pay.

One fateful night, as Diego lay in bed, a shadowy figure appeared at his bedside. It was the devil, come to claim what was rightfully his.

With a wicked grin, he cursed Diego, condemning him to roam the earth as a monstrous creature known as Luison, a twisted blend of man and beast, consumed by rage and hunger for human flesh.

From that moment on, Diego's life was forever changed. Transformed into Luison, he prowled the countryside under the cover of darkness, his howls echoing through the night like a herald of doom. His once-human heart turned cold and merciless, his soul consumed by the darkness that now dwelled within him.

As Luison, Diego became a creature of nightmares, feared by all who crossed his path. He preyed upon the unsuspecting, hunting them down with relentless determination, his glowing eyes piercing the darkness like beacons of death.

But despite his monstrous appearance, there remained a glimmer of humanity within Luison, a faint echo of the man he once was. Deep down, he longed for redemption, yearning to break free from the curse that bound him to this wretched existence.

The legend of Luison lived is a cautionary tale of the dangers of greed and the consequences of selling one's soul to the devil. In the darkest of nights, when all hope seems lost, there remains the tantalising possibility of redemption, which is an unbearable and timeless torment.

How the Pigeon Became a Tame Bird

This story has been adapted from a tale originally told by Elsie Spicer Eells in Fairy Tales from Brazil, published in 1917 by E. M. Hale and Company, Chicago.

Once upon a time there was a father with three sons who had reached the age when they must go out into the world to earn their own living. When the time for parting came he gave to each of them a large melon with the advice that they open the melons only at a place where there was water nearby.

The three brothers set out from their father's house, each taking a different path. As soon as the eldest son was out of sight of the house he opened his melon. A beautiful maiden sprang out of the melon saying, "Give me water or give me milk." There was no water nearby and neither did the young man have any milk to give her. She fell down dead.

The second son left his father's house by a path which led over a steep hill. The large melon was heavy to carry and in a little while he became very tired and thirsty. He saw no water nearby and feared that there was no possibility of finding any soon, so he thought he would open the melon and use it to quench his thirst. Accordingly he opened his melon. To his great surprise, a beautiful maiden sprang forth saying, "Give me water or give me milk." Of course he had neither to give her and she fell down dead.

The third son also travelled by a path which led over a steep hill. He, too, became very tired and thirsty and he often thought how much he would like to open his melon. However, he remembered his father's advice to open it only where there was water nearby. So he travelled on and on hoping to find a spring of water on the hillside. He did not have the good fortune to pass near a spring either going up the hill or coming down on the opposite side. At the foot of the hill there was a town and in the centre of the town there was a fountain. The young man hurried straight to the fountain and took a long refreshing drink. Then he opened his melon. A beautiful maiden sprang forth saying, "Give me water or give me milk." The young man gave her a drink of water. Then he helped her to a hiding place among the thick branches of the tree which grew beside the fountain and went away in search of food.

Soon a little servant girl came to the fountain to fill a big water jar which she carried on her head. The maiden in the tree above the fountain peeped out through the branches. When the little servant girl bent over the water to fill her jar she saw the reflection of a charming face in the water. "How beautiful I have become," she said to herself. "How ridiculous that any one as beautiful as I should carry water on her head." She threw her water jar upon the ground in disdain and it broke into a thousand pieces.

When the little maid reached home with neither water nor water jar her mistress punished her severely and sent her again to the fountain with a new water jar to fill. This time the maiden in the tree gave a little silvery laugh when the servant girl bent over the water. The little maid looked up and spied her in the tree. "Oh, it is you, is it, who are responsible for my beating?" she said. She pulled a pin out of her camisa and, reaching up, she stuck it savagely into the beautiful maiden in the tree. Then a strange thing happened. There was no longer any beautiful maiden in the tree. There was just a pigeon there.

At that moment the young man came back to the tree with the food he had procured. When the little maid heard his footsteps she was frightened nearly to death. She hid herself quickly among the thick branches of the tree. The young man was very much surprised to find a little maid in the tree in the place of the beautiful maiden he had left there. "What has happened to you during my absence, " he asked in horror as soon as he saw her. "The sun has burned my complexion. That is all. It is nothing. I shall be myself again when I get away from this hot place," the little maid replied.

The young man married the little maid and took her away out of sunny places hoping that she would soon be again the beautiful maiden she was when he left her by the fountain in search of food. But she always remained as plain as plain can be.

Years passed and the young man became very rich. He lived in a beautiful mansion. All around the house there was a wonderful garden full of lovely flowers and splendid trees where birds loved to sing sweet songs and build their nests. In spite of his beautiful home the young man was not very happy. It was a great trial to have a wife who was so plain. He often walked up and down the paths in his garden at the close of the day and thought about how beautiful his wife had been the first time he ever saw her. As he walked in the garden there was always a pigeon which followed him about. It flew about his head in a way that annoyed him, so one day when his wife was sick and asked for a pigeon to be roasted for her dinner he commanded that this particular pigeon should be killed.

When the cook was preparing the pigeon for her mistress to eat for dinner she noticed a black speck on the pigeon's breast. She thought that it was a speck of dirt and tried to brush it away. To her surprise she could not brush it off easily because it was a pin firmly embedded in the pigeon's breast. She pulled and pulled but could not pull it out so she sent for her master to come and see what he could do to remove it. He at once pulled out the pin and then a wonderful thing happened. The pigeon was transformed into a beautiful maiden. He at once recognised her as the same lovely maiden who had sprung forth from his melon by the fountain and whom he had left hidden in the tree.

When the young man's wife learned that her husband had found the beautiful maiden again after all these years she confessed her deceit and soon died. The young man married the beautiful maiden who was still just as beautiful as she was the first time he saw her. They were very happy together but the wife never forgot about the time she had been a pigeon.

Up to that time pigeons had been wild birds who built their nests in the deep forest. The wife often wished that they would build their nests in her beautiful garden so she had little bird houses built and set up there.

One day a pigeon, bolder than the rest, flew through the garden and spied the little bird houses. He moved his family there at once and told the other pigeons that there were other houses there for them too. The other pigeons were timid and so they waited to see what terrible calamity might happen to the bold pigeon and his family, but not a single unpleasant thing occurred. They were just as happy as happy could be in their new home.

After a while other pigeon families moved into the garden and were happy too. Thus it came about that after years and years the pigeons no longer build their nests in the deep forest, but they always make their homes near the homes of men. The pigeons, themselves, do not know how it all came about, but the beautiful woman who was once a pigeon, when she had children of her own, told them about it, and they told their children. Thus it happens that the mothers in Brazil tell their children this story about the pigeon.

The Ship Of The Three Axe Blows

This story has been adapted from a tale originally told by Ramón A. Laval in Folk Tales in Chile, originally a Spanish language title, and, published in 1923 by Cervantes Printing House, Santiago De Chile.

Once upon a time, in a faraway kingdom, there stood a magnificent tree in the heart of the royal palace gardens. This was no ordinary tree, it was vast and ancient, with branches so thick they seemed to touch the sky. Yet, its secret was even greater than its beauty. By the will of a powerful witch, the tree could only be watered by the King's daughter, and it could never be touched by an axe without consequence. Any man who struck it on the wrong day would perish instantly.

The King, knowing of this enchantment, set forth a challenge to all his subjects. "Whoever can craft a ship from this tree with only three strikes of an axe shall have my daughter's hand in marriage."

Suitors came from across the land, eager to claim the Princess as their bride. Yet, each one fell dead the moment their axe touched the tree. Hope seemed lost.

In the kingdom there lived a young man named Antonio, a kind, hardworking, yet poor fellow who lived with his mother. One morning, he woke with a dream in his heart.

"Mother," he said, "I shall go to the palace and win the Princess's hand."

His mother, though fearful for him, blessed him and gave him three special thing. She gave him an axe for the trial, a marking iron, and a simple tortilla for his journey.

With nothing but courage, he set out on his way.

As Antonio travelled, he met an old beggar, who pleaded, "Please, kind sir, have you anything to share?"

Moved by compassion, Antonio handed him his only meal. The old man, smiling, gave him a small whistle and whispered, "Blow this when you are in danger, and help will come."

Before parting, the old man gave him another piece of advice. "Take as your companions the first four people you meet. They shall aid you in ways you cannot yet imagine."

With that, Antonio continued on his journey.

Before long, he met a man lying by a river, drinking deeply.

"What are you doing?" Antonio asked.

"Drinking the river dry," the man replied. "Yet my thirst remains unquenched."

Antonio, seeing his strength, invited him along. Next, they met a hunter, aiming his rifle at an unseen target.

"What are you shooting at?" Antonio asked.

"A mosquito, a league away," the hunter replied.

A gunshot rang out, and moments later, the mosquito fell at their feet, pierced cleanly through.

"Join me," Antonio said, "for I may have need of such skill."

Further along, they found a tall, wiry man gripping a tree for dear life.

"I must hold on, or I shall run faster than the wind and never stop." he cried.

Antonio and his new friends tied his legs with a rope and carried him along, just in case his speed proved useful.

Finally, they found a man pressing his ear to the ground.

"What do you hear?" Antonio asked.

"The Princess," the man said. "She waters the tree every time a suitor comes, so that no one can ever succeed."

Antonio's heart filled with determination. "Come with me," he said, "and together, we shall triumph."

And so, with his four strange companions, he reached the palace.

Before dawn, Antonio hid behind the bushes, watching the Princess. Just as she knelt to water the tree, he blew the whistle. A terrible, shrieking sound erupted, so loud and frightening that the Princess screamed and ran back to her chambers, forgetting to water the tree.

By midday, the royal court gathered in the garden to witness the trial. The King and Queen, the nobles, and the Princess herself watched as Antonio approached the tree.

He raised his axe. He struck the tree once, then twice, and finally a third time. With the third strike, the tree vanished, and in its place stood a golden ship with silver sails, floating in a shimmering pond filled with swans and golden fish. A thunderous cheer erupted from the crowd, and even the King and Queen could not help but applaud. Yet, despite the miracle, the King refused to let his daughter marry a mere commoner.

"Prove yourself further," he declared. "Complete these next tasks, and only then shall you wed my daughter."

Antonio, already smitten with the Princess, accepted without hesitation.

For the first trial, Antonio was led to a massive wine cellar, filled with barrels upon barrels of wine.

"You must drink it all by noon tomorrow," said the King, "or you shall die."

Antonio smiled and called for his first companion, the Drinker. By midnight, every barrel was dry.

For the second trial, the King gave two letters, one to a sorcerer, who transformed into a vulture, and one to Antonio. "The first to return with a reply wins," the King declared.

Antonio handed the letter to the Runner, who sped faster than the wind, beating the sorcerer before the vulture even reached its destination.

For the next trial the King gave Antonio twenty rabbits and ordered him to release them into the forest, but by nightfall, he must bring back every single one.

The Queen, determined to see Antonio fail, disguised herself and tried to buy two rabbits from him. Antonio pretended to agree but demanded a mark be placed on her in return. He branded her with a special ink, not knowing it was the Queen herself. Meanwhile, she rushed away with the rabbits, thinking Antonio had lost, but as soon as she left, Antonio blew his whistle, and all of the rabbits returned to him. When the Queen tried to show the stolen rabbits to the King, she found her hands empty.

The King then handed Antonio a sack and declared, "By noon, you must fill it with nothing, nothingness, three woes, and one truth, or you shall die."

At noon, he presented the king with the for items, saying, "This first is a piece of wood. This is nothing, for it floats in water. This second is a stone. This is nothingness, for it sinks This third is three nettle stings, which made the Princess's maid cry out in pain. These are three woes. And this last is the branding iron. This is the truth, for it marks the one who sought to deceive me."

The Queen turned pale, realising her secret was revealed before the court. The King, defeated, sighed and declared, "You have won."

Antonio married the Princess, and in time, he became King. He ruled wisely and justly, with his loyal companions by his side. And thus, a poor young man, armed with kindness, wit, and the help of friends, rose from humble beginnings to claim his happily ever after.

Tale of a Tortoise and of a Mischievous Monkey

This story has been adapted from a tale originally told by Andrew Lang in The Brown Fairy Book, published in 1904 by Longman Green and Company, London. The Brown Fairy Book contains a selection of fairy tales and folk stories from various countries and cultures, including Europe, Asia, Africa, and the Americas.

Once upon a time there was a country where the rivers were larger, and the forests deeper, than anywhere else. Hardly any men came there, and the wild creatures had it all to themselves, and used to play all sorts of strange games with each other. The great trees, chained one to the other by thick flowering plants with bright scarlet or yellow blossoms, were famous hiding-places for the monkeys, who could wait unseen, till a puma or an elephant passed by, and then jump on their backs and go for a ride, swinging themselves up by the creepers when they had had enough. Near the rivers huge tortoises were to be found, and though to our eyes a tortoise seems a dull, slow thing, it is wonderful to think how clever they were, and how often they outwitted many of their livelier friends.

There was one tortoise in particular that always managed to get the better of everybody, and many were the tales told in the forest of his great deeds. They began when he was quite young, and tired of staying at home with his father and mother. He left them one day, and walked off in search of adventures. In a wide open space surrounded by trees he met with an elephant, who was having his supper before taking his evening bath in the river which ran close by. "Let us see which of us two is strongest," said the young tortoise, marching up to the elephant. "Very well," replied the elephant, much amused at the impertinence of the little creature, "when would you like the trial to be?'

"In an hour's time; I have some business to do first," answered the tortoise. And he hastened away as fast as his short legs would carry him.

In a pool of the river a whale was resting, blowing water into the air and making a lovely fountain. The tortoise, however, was too young and too busy to admire such things, and he called to the whale to stop, as he wanted to speak to him. "Would you like to try which of us is the stronger?" said he. The whale looked at him, sent up another fountain, and answered, " Oh, yes; certainly. When do you wish to begin? I am quite ready."

"Then give me one of your longest bones, and I will fasten it to my leg. When I give the signal, you must pull, and we will see which can pull the hardest."

"Very good," replied the whale; and he took out one of his bones and passed it to the tortoise.

The tortoise picked up the end of the bone in his mouth and went back to the elephant. "I will fasten this to your leg," said he, "in the same way as it is fastened to mine, and we must both pull as hard as we can. We shall soon see which is the stronger." So he wound it carefully round the elephant's leg, and tied it in a firm knot. "Now." cried he, plunging into a thick bush behind him.

The whale tugged at one end, and the elephant tugged at the other, and neither had any idea that he had not the tortoise for his foe. When the whale pulled hardest the elephant was dragged into the water; and when the elephant pulled the hardest the whale was hauled on to the land. They were very evenly matched, and the battle was a hard one.

At last they were quite tired, and the tortoise, who was watching, saw that they could play no more. So he crept from his hiding-place, and dipping himself in the river, he went to the elephant and said, " I see that you really are stronger than I thought. Suppose we give it up for today?" Then he dried himself on some moss and went to the whale and said, " I see that you really are stronger than I thought. Suppose we give it up for today?"

The two adversaries were only too glad to be allowed to rest, and believed to the end of their days that, after all, the tortoise was stronger than either of them.

A day or two later the young tortoise was taking a stroll, when he met a fox, and stopped to speak to him. "Let us try," said he in a careless manner, "which of us can lie buried in the ground during seven years."

"I shall be delighted," answered the fox, "only I would rather that you began."

"It is all the same to me," replied the tortoise, "if you come round this way tomorrow you will see that I have fulfilled my part of the bargain."

So he looked about for a suitable place, and found a convenient hole at the foot of an orange tree. He crept into it, and the next morning the fox heaped up the earth round him, and promised to feed him every day with fresh fruit. The fox so far kept his word that each morning when the sun rose he appeared to ask how the tortoise was getting on. "Oh, very well; but I wish you would give me some fruit," replied he.

"Alas. the fruit is not ripe enough yet for you to eat," answered the fox, who hoped that the tortoise would die of hunger long before the seven years were over.

"Oh dear, oh dear. I am so hungry." cried the tortoise.

"I am sure you must be; but it will be all right tomorrow," said the fox, trotting off, not knowing that the oranges dropped down the hollow trunk, straight into the tortoise's hole, and that he had as many as he could possibly eat.

So the seven years went by; and when the tortoise came out of his hole he was as fat as ever.

Now it was the fox's turn, and he chose his hole, and the tortoise heaped the earth round, promising to return every day or two with a nice young bird for his dinner. "Well, how are you getting on?" he would ask cheerfully when he paid his visits.

"Oh, all right; only I wish you had brought a bird with you," answered the fox.

"I have been so unlucky, I have never been able to catch one," replied the tortoise. "However, I shall be more fortunate tomorrow, I am sure."

But not many tomorrows after, when the tortoise arrived with his usual question, " Well, how are you getting on?" he received no answer, for the fox was lying in his hole quite still, dead of hunger.

By this time the tortoise was grown up, and was looked up to throughout the forest as a person to be feared for his strength and wisdom. But he was not considered a very swift runner, until an adventure with a deer added to his fame.

One day, when he was basking in the sun, a stag passed by, and stopped for a little conversation. "Would you care to see which of us can run fastest?" asked the tortoise, after some talk. The stag thought the question so silly that he only shrugged his shoulders. "Of course, the victor would have the right to kill the other," went on the tortoise. "Oh, on that condition I agree," answered the deer, "but I am afraid you are a dead man."

"It is no use trying to frighten me," replied the tortoise. "But I should like three days for training; then I shall be ready to start when the sun strikes on the big tree at the edge of the great clearing."

The first thing the tortoise did was to call his brothers and his cousins together, and he posted them carefully under ferns all along the line of the great clearing, making a sort of ladder which stretched for many miles. This done to his satisfaction, he went back to the starting place.

The stag was quite punctual, and as soon as the sun's rays struck the trunk of the tree the stag started off, and was soon far out of the sight of the tortoise. Every now and then he would turn his head as he ran, and call out, "How are you getting on?" and the tortoise who happened to be nearest at that moment would answer, " All right, I am close up to you."

Full of astonishment, the stag would redouble his efforts, but it was no use. Each time he asked, " Are you there?" the answer would come, " Yes, of course, where else should I be?" And the stag ran, and ran, and ran, till he could run no more, and dropped down dead on the grass.

And the tortoise, when he thinks about it, laughs still.

But the tortoise was not the only creature of whose tricks stories were told in the forest. There was a famous monkey who was just as clever and more mischievous, because he was so much quicker on his feet and with his hands. It was quite impossible to catch him and give him the thrashing he so often deserved, for he just swung himself up into a tree and laughed at the angry victim who was sitting below. Sometimes, however, the inhabitants of the forest were so foolish as to provoke him, and then they got the worst of it. This was what happened to the barber, whom the monkey visited one morning, saying that he wished to be shaved. The barber bowed politely to his customer, and begging him to be seated, tied a large cloth round his neck, and rubbed his chin with soap; but instead of cutting off his beard, the barber made a snip at the end of his tail. It was only a very little bit and the monkey started up more in rage than in pain. "Give me back the end of my tail," he roared, "or I will take one of your razors." The barber refused to give back the missing piece, so the monkey caught up a razor from the table and ran away with it, and no one in the forest could be shaved for days, as there was not another to be got for miles and miles.

As he was making his way to his own particular palm-tree, where the cocoanuts grew, which were so useful for pelting passers-by, he met a woman who was scaling a fish with a bit of wood, for in this side of the forest a few people lived in huts near the river.

"That must be hard work," said the monkey, stopping to look, "try my knife, you will get on quicker." And he handed her the razor as he spoke. A few days later he came back and rapped at the door of the hut. "I have called for my razor," he said, when the woman appeared.

"I have lost it," answered she.

"If you don't give it to me at once I will take your sardine," replied the monkey, who did not believe her. The woman protested she had not got the knife, so he took the sardine and ran off.

A little further along he saw a baker who was standing at the door, eating one of his loaves. "That must be rather dry," said the monkey, "try my fish"; and the man did not need twice telling. A few days later the monkey stopped again at the baker's hut. "I've called for that fish," he said.

"That fish? But I have eaten it." exclaimed the baker in dismay.

"If you have eaten it I shall take this barrel of meal in exchange," replied the monkey; and he walked off with the barrel under his arm.

As he went he saw a woman with a group of little girls round her, teaching them how to dress hair. "Here is something to make cakes for the children," he said, putting down his barrel, which by this time he found rather heavy. The children were delighted, and ran directly to find some flat stones to bake their cakes on, and when they had made and eaten them, they thought they had never tasted anything so nice. Indeed, when they saw the monkey approaching not long after, they rushed to meet him, hoping that he was bringing them some more presents. But he took no notice of their questions, he only said to their mother, " I've called for my barrel of meal."

"Why, you gave it to me to make cakes of." cried the mother.

"If I can't get my barrel of meal, I shall take one of your children," answered the monkey. "I am in want of somebody who can bake my bread when I am tired of fruit, and who knows how to make cocoanut cakes.'

"Oh, leave me my child, and I will find you another barrel of meal," wept the mother.

"I don't WANT another barrel, I want THAT one," answered the monkey sternly. And as the woman stood wringing her hands, he caught up the little girl that he thought the prettiest and took her to his home in the palm tree.

She never went back to the hut, but on the whole she was not much to be pitied, for monkeys are nearly as good as children to play with, and they taught her how to swing, and to climb, and to fly from tree to tree, and everything else they knew, which was a great deal.

Now the monkey's tiresome tricks had made him many enemies in the forest, but no one hated him so much as the puma. The cause of their quarrel was known only to themselves, but everybody was aware of the fact, and took care to be out of the way when there was any chance of these two meeting. Often and often the puma had laid traps for the monkey, which he felt sure his foe could not escape; and the monkey would pretend that he saw nothing, and rejoice the hidden puma's heart by seeming to walk straight into the snare, when, lo. a loud laugh would be heard, and the monkey's grinning face would peer out of a mass of creepers and disappear before his foe could reach him.

This state of things had gone on for quite a long while, when at last there came a season such as the oldest parrot in the forest could never remember. Instead of two or three hundred inches of rain falling, which they were all accustomed to, month after month passed without a cloud, and the rivers and springs dried up, till there was only one small pool left for everyone to drink from. There was not an animal for miles round that did not grieve over this shocking condition of affairs, not one at least except the puma. His only thought for years had been how to get the monkey into his power, and this time he imagined his chance had really arrived. He would hide himself in a thicket, and when the monkey came down to drink, and come he must, the puma would spring out and seize him. Yes, on this occasion there could be no escape.

And no more there would have been if the puma had had greater patience; but in his excitement he moved a little too soon. The monkey, who was stooping to drink, heard a rustling, and turning caught the gleam of two yellow, murderous eyes. With a mighty spring he grasped a creeper which was hanging above him, and landed himself on the branch of a tree; feeling the breath of the puma on his feet as the animal bounded from is cover. Never had the monkey been so near death, and it was some time before he recovered enough courage to venture on the ground again.

Up there in the shelter of the trees, he began to turn over in his head plans for escaping the snares of the puma. And at length chance helped him. Peeping down to the earth, he saw a man coming along the path carrying on his head a large gourd filled with honey.

He waited till the man was just underneath the tree, then he hung from a bough, and caught the gourd while the man looked up wondering, for he was no tree-climber. Then the monkey rubbed the honey all over him, and a quantity of leaves from a creeper that was hanging close by; he stuck them all close together into the honey, so that he looked like a walking bush. This finished, he ran to the pool to see the result, and, quite pleased with himself, set out in search of adventures

Soon the report went through the forest that a new animal had appeared from no one knew where, and that when somebody had asked his name, the strange creature had answered that it was Jack-in-the-Green. Thanks to this, the monkey was allowed to drink at the pool as often as he liked, for neither beast nor bird had the faintest notion who he was. And if they made any inquiries the only answer they got was that the water of which he had drunk deeply had turned his hair into leaves, so that they all knew what would happen in case they became too greedy.

By-and-by the great rains began again. The rivers and streams filled up, and there was no need for him to go back to the pool, near the home of his enemy, the puma, as there was a large number of places for him to choose from. So one night, when everything was still and silent, and even the chattering parrots were asleep on one leg, the monkey stole down softly from his perch, and washed off the honey and the leaves, and came out from his bath in his own proper skin. On his way to breakfast he met a rabbit, and stopped for a little talk.

"I am feeling rather dull," he remarked, "I think it would do me good to hunt a while. What do you say?'

"Oh, I am quite willing," answered the rabbit, proud of being spoken to by such a large creature. "But the question is, what shall we hunt?'

"There is no credit in going after an elephant or a tiger," replied the monkey stroking his chin, "they are so big they could not possibly get out of your way. It shows much more skill to be able to catch a small thing that can hide itself in a moment behind a leaf. I'll tell you what. Suppose I hunt butterflies, and you, serpents.'

The rabbit, who was young and without experience, was delighted with this idea, and they both set out on their various ways.

The monkey quietly climbed up the nearest tree, and ate fruit most of the day, but the rabbit tired himself to death poking his nose into every heap of dried leaves he saw, hoping to find a serpent among them. Luckily for himself the serpents were all away for the afternoon, at a meeting of their own, for there is nothing a serpent likes so well for dinner as a nice plump rabbit. But, as it was, the dried leaves were all empty, and the rabbit at last fell asleep where he was. Then the monkey, who had been watching him, fell down and pulled his ears, to the rage of the rabbit, who vowed vengeance.

It was not easy to catch the monkey off his guard, and the rabbit waited long before an opportunity arrived. But one day Jack-in-the-Green was sitting on a stone, wondering what he should do next, when the rabbit crept softly behind him, and gave his tail a sharp pull. The monkey gave a shriek of pain, and darted up into a tree, but when he saw that it was only the rabbit who had dared to insult him so, he chattered so fast in his anger, and looked so fierce, that the rabbit fled into the nearest hole, and stayed there for several days, trembling with fright.

Soon after this adventure the monkey went away into another part of the country, right on the outskirts of the forest, where there was a beautiful garden full of oranges hanging ripe from the trees. This garden was a favourite place for birds of all kinds, each hoping to secure an orange for dinner, and in order to frighten the birds away and keep a little fruit for himself, the master had fastened a waxen figure on one of the boughs.

Now the monkey was as fond of oranges as any of the birds, and when he saw a man standing in the tree where the largest and sweetest oranges grew, he spoke to him at once. "You man," he said rudely, "throw me down that big orange up there, or I will throw a stone at you." The wax figure took no notice of this request, so the monkey, who was easily made angry, picked up a stone, and flung it with all his force. But instead of falling to the ground again, the stone stuck to the soft wax.

At this moment a breeze shook the tree, and the orange on which the monkey had set his heart dropped from the bough. He picked it up and ate it every bit, including the rind, and it was so good he thought he should like another. So he called again to the wax figure to throw him an orange, and as the figure did not move, he hurled another stone, which stuck to the wax as the first had done. Seeing that the man was quite indifferent to stones, the monkey grew angrier still, and climbing the tree hastily, gave the figure a violent kick. But like the two stones his leg remained stuck to the wax, and he was held fast. "Let me go at once, or I will give you another kick," he cried, suiting the action to the word, and this time also his foot remained in the grasp of the man. Not knowing what he did, the monkey hit out, first with one hand and then with the other, and when he found that he was literally bound hand and foot, he became so mad with anger and terror that in his struggles he fell to the ground, dragging the figure after him. This freed his hands and feet, but besides the shock of the fall, they had tumbled into a bed of thorns, and he limped away broken and bruised, and groaning loudly; for when monkeys ARE hurt, they take pains that everybody shall know it.

It was a long time before Jack was well enough to go about again; but when he did, he had an encounter with his old enemy the puma. And this was how it came about.

One day the puma invited his friend the stag to go with him and see a comrade, who was famous for the good milk he got from his cows. The stag loved milk, and gladly accepted the invitation, and when the sun began to get a little low the two started on their walk. On the way they arrived on the banks of a river, and as there were no bridges in those days it was necessary to swim across it. The stag was not fond of swimming, and began to say that he was tired, and thought that after all it was not worth going so far to get milk, and that he would return home. But the puma easily saw through these excuses, and laughed at him.

"The river is not deep at all," he said, "why, you will never be off your feet. Come, pluck up your courage and follow me.'

The stag was afraid of the river; still, he was much more afraid of being laughed at, and he plunged in after the puma; but in an instant the current had swept him away, and if it had not borne him by accident to a shallow place on the opposite side, where he managed to scramble up the bank, he would certainly have been drowned. As it was, he scrambled out, shaking with terror, and found the puma waiting for him. "You had a narrow escape that time," said the puma.

After resting for a few minutes, to let the stag recover from his fright, they went on their way till they came to a grove of bananas.

"They look very good," observed the puma with a longing glance, "and I am sure you must be hungry, friend stag? Suppose you were to climb the tree and get some. You shall eat the green ones, they are the best and sweetest; and you can throw the yellow ones down to me. I dare say they will do quite well." The stag did as he was bid, though, not being used to climbing, it gave him a deal of trouble and sore knees, and besides, his horns were continually getting entangled in the creepers. What was worse, when once he had tasted the bananas, he found them not at all to his liking, so he threw them all down, green and yellow alike, and let the puma take his choice. And what a dinner he made. When he had QUITE done, they set forth once more.

The path lay through a field of maize, where several men were working. As they came up to them, the puma whispered, " Go on in front, friend stag, and just say "Bad luck to all workers.""" The stag obeyed, but the men were hot and tired, and did not think this a good joke. So they set their dogs at him, and he was obliged to run away as fast as he could.

"I hope your industry will be rewarded as it deserves," said the puma as he passed along; and the men were pleased, and offered him some of their maize to eat.

By-and-by the puma saw a small snake with a beautiful shining skin, lying coiled up at the foot of a tree. "What a lovely bracelet that would make for your daughter, friend stag. said he. The stag stooped and picked up the snake, which bit him, and he turned angrily to the puma. "Why did you not tell me it would bite?" he asked.

"Is it my fault if you are an idiot?" replied the puma.

At last they reached their journey's end, but by this time it was late, and the puma's comrade was ready for bed, so they slung their hammocks in convenient places, and went to sleep. But in the middle of the night the puma rose softly and stole out of the door to the sheep-fold, where he killed and ate the fattest sheep he could find, and taking a bowl full of its blood, he sprinkled the sleeping stag with it. This done, he returned to bed.

In the morning the shepherd went as usual to let the sheep out of the fold, and found one of them missing. He thought directly of the puma, and ran to accuse him of having eaten the sheep. "I, my good man? What had put it into your head to think of such a thing? Have I got any blood about me? If anyone has eaten a sheep it must be my friend the stag." Then the shepherd went to examine the sleeping stag, and of course he saw the blood. "Ah. I will teach you how to steal." cried he, and he hit the stag such a blow on his skull that he died in a moment. The noise awakened the comrade above, and he came downstairs. The puma greeted him with joy, and begged he might have some of the famous milk as soon as possible, for he was very thirsty. A large bucket was set before the puma directly. He drank it to the last drop, and then took leave.

On his way home he met the monkey. "Are you fond of milk?" asked he. "I know a place where you get it very nice. I will show you it if you like." The monkey knew that the puma was not so good-natured for nothing, but he felt quite able to take care of himself, so he said he should have much pleasure in accompanying his friend

They soon reached the same river, and, as before, the puma remarked, " Friend monkey, you will find it very shallow; there is no cause for fear. Jump in and I will follow.'

"Do you think you have the stag to deal with?" asked the monkey, laughing. "I should prefer to follow; if not I shall go no further. The puma understood that it was useless trying to make the monkey do as he wished, so he chose a shallow place and began to swim across. The monkey waited till the puma had got to the middle, then he gave a great spring and jumped on his back, knowing quite well that the puma would be afraid to shake him off, lest he should be swept away into deep water. So in this manner they reached the bank.

The banana grove was not far distant, and here the puma thought he would pay the monkey out for forcing him to carry him over the river. "Friend monkey, look what fine bananas," cried he. "You are fond of climbing; suppose you run up and throw me down a few. You can eat the green ones, which are the nicest, and I will be content with the yellow.'

"Very well," answered the monkey, swinging himself up; but he ate all the yellow ones himself, and only threw down the green ones that were left. The puma was furious and cried out, " I will punch your head for that." But the monkey only answered, " If you are going to talk such nonsense I won't walk with you." And the puma was silent.

In a few minutes more they arrived at the field were the men were reaping the maize, and the puma remarked as he had done before, " Friend monkey, if you wish to please these men, just say as you go by, "Bad luck to all workers."

"Very well," replied the monkey; but, instead, he nodded and smiled, and said, " I hope your industry may be rewarded as it deserves." The men thanked him heartily, let him pass on, and the puma followed behind him.

Further along the path they saw the shining snake lying on the moss. "What a lovely necklace for your daughter," exclaimed the puma. "Pick it up and take it with you.'

"You are very kind, but I will leave it for you," answered the monkey, and nothing more was said about the snake.

Not long after this they reached the comrade's house, and found him just ready to go to bed. So, without stopping to talk, the guests slung their hammocks, the monkey taking care to place his so high that no one could get at him. Besides, he thought it would be more prudent not to fall asleep, so he only lay still and snored loudly. When it was quite dark and no sound was to be heard, the puma crept out to the sheep-fold, killed the sheep, and carried back a bowl full of its blood with which to sprinkle the monkey. But the monkey, who had been watching out of the corner of his eye, waited until the puma drew near, and with a violent kick upset the bowl all over the puma himself.

When the puma saw what had happened, he turned in a great hurry to leave the house, but before he could do so, he saw the shepherd coming, and hastily lay down again.

"This is the second time I have lost a sheep," the man said to the monkey, "it will be the worse for the thief when I catch him, I can tell you." The monkey did not answer, but silently pointed to the puma who was pretending to be asleep. The shepherd stooped and saw the blood, and cried out, " Ah. so it is you, is it? then take that." and with his stick he gave the puma such a blow on the head that he died then and there.

Then the monkey got up and went to the dairy, and drank all the milk he could find. Afterwards he returned home and married, and that is the last we heard of him.

The City of the Caesars

This story is my own telling of a traditional Chilean folk tale based on various sources.

In the vast and rugged terrain of the Andes mountains, there exists a legendary city shrouded in mystery and myth, the City of the Caesars. According to Chilean folklore, this city is said to be hidden deep within the remote valleys and towering peaks, its existence known only to a select few who have dared to venture into the uncharted wilderness.

The tale of the City of the Caesars begins centuries ago, during the time of the Inca Empire. As the story goes, the Inca ruler Pachacuti received a vision from the gods, revealing the location of a magnificent city filled with untold riches and treasures beyond imagination. Determined to find this fabled city, Pachacuti led a great expedition into the heart of the Andes, accompanied by his most trusted warriors and advisors.

For years, they journeyed through the treacherous mountain passes and dense jungles, facing fierce storms and hostile tribes along the way. But despite the hardships they encountered, they pressed on, driven by the promise of riches and glory that awaited them.

Finally, after many trials and tribulations, they reached their destination, a hidden valley nestled high in the mountains, where the City of the Caesars stood in all its splendour. The city was said to be built entirely of gold and precious gems, its streets lined with ornate palaces and temples dedicated to the gods.

But as they marvelled at the wonders before them, disaster struck. The earth shook violently, and the skies darkened with thunder and lightning. Pachacuti realized too late that the city was cursed, and that its riches came at a terrible price.

In a desperate bid to escape the wrath of the gods, Pachacuti and his men fled the city, leaving behind the treasures they had sought for so long. Legend has it that the City of the Caesars vanished into thin air, swallowed up by the mountains themselves, never to be seen again.

But despite its disappearance, the legend of the City of the Caesars lives on in the hearts and minds of the Chilean people, a reminder of the dangers of greed and the folly of seeking riches at any cost. And though the city may remain hidden from sight, its story continues to captivate adventurers and treasure hunters who dare to brave the untamed wilderness of the Andes in search of its elusive secrets.

Why the Sea Moans

This story has been adapted from a tale originally told by Elsie Spicer Eells in Fairy Tales from Brazil, published in 1917 by E. M. Hale and Company, Chicago.

Once upon a time there was a little princess who lived in a magnificent royal palace. All around the palace there was a beautiful garden full of lovely flowers and rare shrubs and trees. The part of the garden which the princess liked most of all was a corner of it which ran down to the sea. She was a very lonely little princess and she loved to sit and watch the changing beauty of the sea. The name of the little princess was Dionysia and it often seemed to her that the sea said, as it rushed against the shore, "Di-o-ny-si-a, Di-o-ny-si-a."

One day when the little princess was sitting all alone by the sea she said to herself, "O. I am so lonely. I do so wish that I had somebody to play with. When I ride out in the royal chariot I see little girls who have other little boys and girls to play with them. Because I am the royal princess I never have anybody to play with me. If I have to be the royal princess and not play with other children I do think I might have some sort of live thing to play with me."

Then a most remarkable thing happened. The sea said very slowly and distinctly and over and over again so there couldn't be any mistake about it, "Di-o-ny-si-a, Di-o-ny-si-a."

The little princess walked up close to the sea, just as close as she dared to go without danger of getting her royal shoes and stockings wet. Straight out of the biggest wave of all there came a sea serpent to meet her. She knew that it was a sea serpent from the pictures in her royal story books even though she had never seen a sea serpent before, but somehow this sea serpent looked different than the pictures. Instead of being a fierce monster it looked kind and gentle and good. She held out her arms to it right away.

"Come play with me," said Dionysia.

"I am Labismena and I have come to play with you," replied the sea serpent.

After that the little princess was very much happier. The sea serpent came out of the sea to play with her every day when she was alone. If anyone else came near Labismena would disappear into the sea so no one but Dionysia ever saw her.

The years passed rapidly and each year the little princess grew to be a larger and larger princess. At last she was sixteen years old and a very grown-up princess indeed. She still enjoyed her old playmate, Labismena, and they were often together on the seashore.

One day when they were walking up and down together beside the sea the sea serpent looked at Dionysia with sad eyes and said, "I too have been growing older all these years, dear Dionysia. Now the time has come that we can no longer play together. I shall never come out of the sea to play with you anymore, but I shall never forget you and I shall always be your friend. I hope that you will never have any trouble, but if you ever should, call my name and I will come to help you." Then the sea serpent disappeared into the sea.

About this time the wife of a neighbouring king died and as she lay upon her death bed she gave the king a jewelled ring. "When the time comes when you wish to wed again," she said, "I ask you to marry a princess upon whose finger this ring shall be neither too tight nor too loose."

After a while the king began to look about for a princess to be his bride. He visited many royal palaces and tried the ring upon the finger of many royal princesses. Upon some the ring was too tight and upon others it was too loose. There was no princess whose finger it fitted perfectly.

At last in his search the king came to the royal palace where the princess Dionysia lived. The princess had dreams of her own of a young and charming prince who would someday come to wed her, so she was not pleased at all. The king was old and no longer handsome, and when he tried the ring upon Dionysia's finger she hoped with all her heart that it would not fit. It fitted perfectly.

The princess Dionysia was frightened nearly to death. "Will I really have to marry him?" she asked her royal father. Her father told her what a very wealthy king he was with a great kingdom and a wonderful royal palace ever so much more wonderful and grander than the palace the princess Dionysia had always had for her home. Her father had no patience at all with her for not being happy about it. "You ought to consider yourself the most fortunate princess in all the world," he said.

Dionysia spent her days and nights weeping. Her father was afraid that she would grow so thin that the ring would no longer fit her finger, so he hastened the plans for the wedding.

One day Dionysia walked up and down beside the sea, crying as if her heart would break. All at once she stopped crying. "How stupid I have been," she said. "My old playmate Labismena told me that if ever I was in trouble she would come back and help me. With all my silly crying I had forgotten about it."

Dionysia walked up close to the sea and called softly, "Labismena, Labismena." Out of the sea came the sea serpent just as she used to come. The princess told the sea serpent all about the dreadful trouble which was threatening to spoil her life.

"Have no fear," said Labismena, "tell your father that you will marry the king when the king presents you with a dress the colour of the fields and all their flowers and that you will not marry him until he gives it to you." Then the sea serpent disappeared again into the sea.

Dionysia sent word through her father to her royal suitor that she would wed him only when he procured her a dress the colour of the fields and all their flowers. The king was very much in love with Dionysia, so he was secretly filled with joy at this request. He searched everywhere for a dress the colour of the fields and all their flowers. It was a very difficult thing to find but at last he procured one. He sent it to Dionysia at once.

When Dionysia saw that the king had really found the dress for her she was filled with grief. She thought that there was no escape and that she would have to marry the king after all. As soon as she could get away from the palace without being noticed she ran down to the sea and again called, "Labismena, Labismena."

The sea serpent at once came out of the sea. "Do not fear," she said to Dionysia. "Go back and say that you will not wed the king until he gives you a dress the colour of the sea and all its fishes."

When the king heard this new request of Dionysia's he was rather discouraged. However he searched for the dress and, at last, after expending a great sum of money, he procured such a gown.

When Dionysia saw that a dress the colour of the sea and all its fishes had been found for her she again went to seek counsel from her old playmate. "Do not be afraid," Labismena again said to her. "This time you must ask the king to get you a dress the colour of the sky and all its stars. You may also tell him that this is the last present you will ask him to make you."

When the king heard about the demand for a dress the colour of the sky and all its stars he was completely disheartened, but when he heard that Dionysia had promised that this would be the last present she would ask he decided that it might be a good investment after all. He set out to procure the dress with all possible speed. At last he found one.

When Dionysia saw the dress the colour of the sky and all its stars she thought that this time there was no escape from marrying the king. She called the sea serpent with an anxious heart for she was afraid that now even Labismena could do nothing to help her.

Labismena came out of the sea in answer to her call.

"Go home to the palace and get your dress the colour of the field and all its flowers," said the sea serpent, "and your dress the colour of the sea and all its fishes, and your dress the colour of the sky and all its stars. Then hurry back here to the sea for I have been preparing a surprise for you."

All the time the king had been procuring the wonderful gowns for Dionysia the sea serpent had been building a ship for her. When Dionysia returned from the royal palace with her lovely dresses all carefully packed in a box there was a queer little boat awaiting her. It was not at all like any other boat she had ever seen and she was almost afraid to get into it when Labismena asked her to try it. "This little ship which I have built for you," said Labismena, "will carry you far away over the sea to the kingdom of a prince who is the most charming prince in all the world. When you see him you will want to marry him above all others."

"Oh, Labismena. How can I ever thank you for all you have done for me?" cried Dionysia.

"You can do the greatest thing in the world for me," said Labismena, "though I have never told you and I do not believe that you have ever suspected it, I am really an enchanted princess. I shall have to remain in the form of a sea serpent until the happiest maiden in all the world, at the hour of her greatest happiness, calls my name three times. You will be the very happiest girl in all the world on the day of your marriage, and if you will remember to call my name three times then you will break my enchantment and I shall once more be a lovely princess instead of a sea serpent."

Dionysia promised her friend that she would remember to do this. The sea serpent asked her to promise three times to make sure. When Dionysia had promised three times and again embraced her old playmate and thanked her for all that she had done she sailed away in the little ship. The sea serpent disappeared into the sea.

Dionysia sailed and sailed in the little ship and it bore her to a lovely island. She thought that she had reached her destination, so she stepped out of the boat not forgetting to take her box of dresses with her. As soon as she was out of the boat it sailed away. "Now what shall I ever do?" said Dionysia. "The ship has gone away and left me and how shall I ever earn my living? I have never done anything useful in all my life."

Dionysia surely had to do something to earn her living immediately, so she at once set out to see what she could find to do. She went from house to house asking for food and work. At last she came to the royal palace. Here at the royal palace they told her that they had great need of a maid to take care of the hens. Dionysia thought that this was something which she could do, so she accepted the position at once. It was, of course, very different work from being a princess in a royal palace but it provided her with food and shelter, and when Dionysia thought of having to marry the old king she was never sorry that she had left home.

Time passed and at last there was a great feast day celebrated in the city. Everybody in the palace went except the little maid who minded the hens. After everybody had gone away Dionysia decided that she would go to the festa too. She combed her hair and put on her gown which was the colour of the fields and all their flowers. In this wonderful gown she was sure nobody would ever guess that she was the little maid who had been left at home to mind the hens. She did want to go to the festa. She hurried there as fast as she could and arrived just in time for the dances.

Everybody at the festa noticed the beautiful maiden in her gown the colour of the fields and all their flowers. The prince fell madly in love with her. Nobody had ever seen her before and nobody could find out who the beautiful stranger was or where she came from. Before the festa was over Dionysia slipped away, and, when the rest of the royal household returned home there was the little maid minding the hens just as they had left her.

The second day of the festa everybody went early except the little maid who looked after the hens. When the others had gone she put on her dress the colour of the sea and all its fishes and went to the festa. She attracted even more attention than she had the day before.

When the festa was over and the royal household had returned to the royal palace, the prince remarked to his mother, "Don't you think that the beautiful stranger at the festa looks like the little maid who minds our hens?"

"What nonsense," replied his mother. "How could the little maid who minds our hens ever get such wonderful gowns to wear?" Just to make sure, however, the prince told the royal councillor to find out if the little maid who minds the royal hens had been to the festa. All the servants told about leaving her at home with the hens and coming back and finding her just as they had left her.

"Whoever the beautiful stranger at the festa may be," said the prince, "she is the one above all others whom I want for my wife. I shall find her some way."

The third day of the festa Dionysia went attired in her gown the colour of the sky and all its stars. The prince fell more madly in love with her than ever. He could not get her to tell him who she was or where she lived but he gave her a beautiful jewel.

When the prince returned home he would not eat any food. He grew thin and pale. Everyone around the palace tried his best to invent some dish which would tempt the prince's appetite.

Finally the little maid who took care of the hens said that she thought she could prepare a dish which the prince would eat.

Accordingly she made a dish of broth for the prince and in the bottom of the dish she dropped the jewel which the prince had given her.

When the broth was set before the prince he was about to send it away untouched, just as he did everything else, but the sparkling jewel attracted his attention.

"Who made this dish of broth?" he asked as soon as he could speak.

"It was made by the maid who minds the hens," replied his mother.

"Send for the little maid to come to me at once," cried the prince. "I knew that the beautiful stranger at the festa looked like our little maid who minds the hens."

The prince married Dionysia the very next day and Dionysia was the very happiest girl in all the world, for from the first moment that she had seen the prince, she had known that he was the one above all others whom she wished to marry.

Alas. In Dionysia's excitement she forgot all about calling the name of her old playmate, Labismena, at the hour of her marriage as she had promised to do. She thought of nothing but the prince.

There was no escape for Labismena. She had to remain in the form of a sea serpent because of Dionysia's neglect. She had lost her chance to come out of the sea and become a lovely princess herself and find a charming prince of her own. For this reason her sad moan is heard in the sea until this very day. Perhaps you have noticed it.

You will often hear the call come from the sea as it breaks against the shore, "Dionysia, Di-o-ny-si-a." No wonder that the sea moans. It is enough to make a sea serpent sad to be forgotten by the very person one has done most to help.

The Compadrito Leon, Burnt Potato

This story has been adapted from a tale originally told by Ramón A. Laval in Folk Tales in Chile, originally a Spanish language title, and, published in 1923 by Cervantes Printing House, Santiago De Chile.

Once upon a time, in a grand kingdom ruled by a mighty King, there lived a thieving Monkey who had a taste for mischief and a love of stolen jerky. Every night, under the cover of darkness, he would sneak into the royal cellar, snatch up as much jerky as his little paws could carry, and scurry off to feast with his friends.

One day, the King decided to check on his precious supply, as he planned to sell it the next morning. But when he entered the cellar, he gasped in horror. The shelves were nearly empty. Furious, the King summoned his Steward.

"Have you sold my jerky?" he demanded.

"No, Your Majesty." the Steward stammered. "I haven't even stepped inside the cellar."

Suspicious and seething, the King ordered his guards to stand watch all night long. They shivered in the cold, their eyes darting in every direction. But the Monkey was far too clever, he never showed himself.

The next morning, the King stormed into the cellar, expecting to hear news of the thief's capture. Instead, his guards shrugged helplessly. Furious, the King counted his jerky again.

"More is missing." he bellowed. His gaze fell on the Steward. "I give you two days to catch the thief, or it is your head that will pay."

The poor Steward despaired. He had no idea who the thief was. Then he remembered the rumours about an old witch who lived deep in the woods, a woman said to have a pact with the Devil himself. Desperate, the Steward sought her out.

"Help me, wise one." he begged.

The old woman grinned. "Fear not," she said, "I have a plan…"

The witch instructed the Steward to build a great bonfire inside the cellar. "Watch carefully," she said, "for the smoke will reveal where the thief enters."

That very night, the Steward did as he was told. As the flames roared, black smoke curled through a tiny hidden door in the corner. Excited, the Steward rushed back to the witch.

"Aha." she cackled. "Now, set a trap. Place a garter monkey at a table inside the cellar, put a deck of cards in its hands, a pile of silver coins on one side, and a burning candle on the other. Lock the doors, and leave the rest to fate."

The Steward hurried back and prepared the strange setup. Then he locked the cellar tight. That night, the Monkey sneaked in through the little door, as usual. But this time, he stopped dead in his tracks.

There, sitting at the table, was another Monkey, a garter monkey, silent and motionless.

The real Monkey's eyes gleamed with excitement. "Tonight, I shall win all his money." he chuckled.

He sauntered up to the garter monkey, tossed a bean in the air, and said, "Heads or tails? Tails. You carve."

But the garter monkey said nothing.

"Oh, playing shy, are you?" sneered the Monkey. "If you don't play, I'll take your money and give you a thrashing."

Still, no response.

Frustrated, the Monkey snatched the deck and started the game himself. He placed two cards on the table and asked, "Which one do you choose?"

Silence.

"Fine, I choose. I bet a hundred pesos on the golden jack." He threw the cards and won.

"You still owe me more." he growled at the garter monkey.

But when his opponent refused to respond, the Monkey's temper exploded.

"You won't pay? Fine. I'll make you."

He swung a mighty punch, and his hand stuck fast.

"Let go of me, you wretched beast." he shouted, striking with his other hand, which also got stuck.

Terrified, he kicked out, only for his feet to stick too.

"No, no, no." he shrieked. He wriggled, struggled, and even bit the garter monkey's head, but now his mouth was stuck as well.

As dawn broke, the Steward arrived to find the thief trapped at last. Laughing in delight, he rushed to tell the King. The King, eager to see the culprit, strode into the cellar. When he saw his own Monkey caught red-handed, his fury knew no bounds.

"Take him outside." he roared. "Tie him to the chestnut trees and prepare the boiling water."

The Monkey sobbed and pleaded, but the King would not be swayed.

Just then, Compadre Lion happened to pass by.

"What are you doing there, Monkey?" he asked.

"Oh, my dear friend." the Monkey cried. "They think I ate an entire calf, but you are so much bigger. Wouldn't it be better if you took my place?"

Now, Compadre Lion was very hungry, so hungry that he hadn't eaten in days. The thought of a whole calf made his stomach growl.

"What must I do?" he asked.

"Just switch places with me." the Monkey grinned. "They will bring you the calf, and you will feast like a king."

The hungry and foolish Lion agreed.

As soon as the ropes were swapped, the Monkey darted away, calling, "Enjoy your meal, my dear friend."

Shortly after, the servants arrived, carrying boiling water and a red-hot iron rod.

"Ah. So you were a Monkey before, and now you've turned into a Lion? Well, it won't save you."

"Yes, yes, I will eat it. I will eat it all." the Lion roared eagerly.

SPLASH.

The boiling water scalded his fur.

SIZZLE.

The red-hot iron burned his tail.

With a howl of agony, the Lion broke free and ran for his life. He roared so loudly that the entire kingdom heard him. And from the safety of a treetop, the Monkey laughed.

"How was your meal, my dear friend?" he teased.

The Lion could barely speak from the pain, but he managed to growl, "You will pay for this, Monkey. Mark my words."

But the Monkey was already swinging away through the jungle, still chuckling at his own cleverness. And to this day, if you ever hear a Lion roaring deep in the wild, some say he is still searching for the trickster Monkey who made him a fool.

How the Brazilian Beetles Got Their Gorgeous Coats

This story has been adapted from a tale originally told by Elsie Spicer Eells in Fairy Tales from Brazil, published in 1917 by E. M. Hale and Company, Chicago. The book contains a selection of fairy tales and folk stories from Brazil, each brimming with vibrant characters, magical creatures, and moral lessons. These tales offer readers a glimpse into Brazilian culture, traditions, and beliefs, as well as the country's diverse landscapes and wildlife.

In Brazil the beetles have such beautifully coloured, hard-shelled coats upon their backs that they are often set in pins and necklaces like precious stones. Once upon a time, years and years ago, they had ordinary plain brown coats. This is how it happened that the Brazilian beetle earned a new coat.

One day a little brown beetle was crawling along a wall when a big grey rat ran out of a hole in the wall and looked down scornfully at the little beetle. "Oh ho." he said to the beetle, "how slowly you crawl along. You'll never get anywhere in the world. Just look at me and see how fast I can run."

The big grey rat ran to the end of the wall, wheeled around, and came back to the place where the little beetle was slowly crawling along at only a tiny distance from where the rat had left her.

"Don't you wish that you could run like that?" said the big grey rat to the little brown beetle.

"You are surely a fast runner," replied the little brown beetle politely. Her mother had taught her always to be polite and had often said to her that a really polite beetle never boasts about her own accomplishments. The little brown beetle never boasted a single boast about the things she could do. She just went on slowly crawling along the wall.

A bright green and gold parrot in the mango tree over the wall had heard the conversation. "How would you like to race with the beetle?" he asked the big grey rat. "I live next door to the tailor bird," he added, "and just to make the race exciting I'll offer a bright coloured coat as a prize to the one who wins the race. You may choose for it any colour you like and I'll have it made to order."

"I'd like a yellow coat with stripes like the tiger's," said the big grey rat, looking over his shoulder at his gaunt grey sides as if he were already admiring his new coat.

"I'd like a beautiful, bright coloured new coat, too," said the little brown beetle.

The big grey rat laughed long and loud until his gaunt grey sides were shaking. "Why, you talk just as if you thought you had a chance to win the race," he said, when he could speak.

The bright green and gold parrot set the royal palm tree at the top of the cliff as the goal of the race. He gave the signal to start and then he flew away to the royal palm tree to watch for the end of the race.

The big grey rat ran as fast as he could. Then he thought how very tired he was getting. "What's the use of hurrying?" he said to himself. "The little brown beetle cannot possibly win. If I were racing with somebody who could really run it would be very different." Then he started to run more slowly but every time his heart beat it said, "Hurry up. Hurry up." The big grey rat decided that it was best to obey the little voice in his heart so he hurried just as fast as he could.

When he reached the royal palm tree at the top of the cliff he could hardly believe his eyes. He thought he must be having a bad dream. There was the little brown beetle sitting quietly beside the bright green and gold parrot. The big grey rat had never been so surprised in all his life. "How did you ever manage to run fast enough to get here so soon?" he asked the little brown beetle as soon as he could catch his breath.

The little brown beetle drew out the tiny wings from her sides. "Nobody said anything about having to run to win the race," she replied, "so I flew instead."

"I did not know that you could fly," said the big grey rat in a subdued little voice.

"After this," said the bright green and gold parrot, "never judge any one by his looks alone. You never can tell how often or where you may find concealed wings. You have lost the prize."

Until this day, even in Brazil where the flowers and birds and beasts and insects have such gorgeous colouring, the rat wears a plain dull grey coat.

Then the parrot turned to the little brown beetle who was waiting quietly at his side. "What colour do you want your new coat to be?" he asked.

The little brown beetle looked up at the bright green and gold parrot, at the green and gold palm trees above their heads, at the green mangoes with golden flushes on their cheeks lying on the ground under the mango trees, at the golden sunshine upon the distant green hills. "I choose a coat of green and gold," she said.

From that day to this the Brazilian beetle has worn a coat of green with golden lights upon it.

For years and years the Brazilian beetles were all very proud to wear green and gold coats like that of the beetle who raced with the rat.

Then, once upon a time, it happened that there was a little beetle who grew discontented with her coat of green and gold. She looked up at the blue sky and out at the blue sea and wished that she had a blue coat instead. She talked about it so much that finally her mother took her to the parrot who lived next to the tailor bird.

"You may change your coat for a blue one," said the parrot, "but if you change you'll have to give up something."

"Oh, I'll gladly give up anything if only I may have a blue coat instead of a green and gold one," said the discontented little beetle.

When she received her new coat she thought it was very beautiful. It was a lovely shade of blue and it had silvery white lights upon it like the light of the stars. When she put it on, however, she discovered that it was not hard like the green and gold one. From that day to this the blue beetles' coats have not been hard and firm. That is the reason why the jewellers have difficulty in using them in pins and necklaces like other beetles.

From the moment that the little beetle put on her new blue coat she never grew again. From that day to this the blue beetles have been much smaller than the green and gold ones.

When the Brazilians made their flag they took for it a square of green the colour of the green beetle's coat. Within this square they placed a diamond of gold like the golden lights which play upon the green beetle's back. Then, within the diamond, they drew a circle to represent the round earth and they coloured it blue like the coat of the blue beetle. Upon the blue circle they placed stars of silvery white like the silvery white lights on the back of the blue beetle. About the blue circle of the earth which they thus pictured they drew a band of white, and upon this band they wrote the motto of their country, "Ordem e Progresso, order and progress."

The People From Stone

This story is my own telling of a traditional Peruvian folk tale based on various sources.

In the heart of the Peruvian Andes, nestled among the towering peaks and mist-shrouded valleys, there existed a mysterious village known as Pueblo de Piedra, the People From Stone. This ancient settlement was said to be inhabited by beings unlike any others in the world, creatures formed from rock.

Legend had it that long ago, when the earth was young and the mountains still took shape, a powerful sorcerer roamed the land. This sorcerer possessed great magic and wisdom, and he used his powers to shape the world around him according to his will.

One day, as he journeyed through the mountains, the sorcerer stumbled upon a hidden valley unlike any he had ever seen. In the centre of the valley stood a great rock formation, its surface gleaming in the sunlight like polished marble. Intrigued, the sorcerer approached the rock and placed his hands upon its surface.

To his astonishment, the rock began to shift and change, taking on the form of a man, a man made entirely of stone. And as the sorcerer watched in wonder, more and more stone beings emerged from the rock, until an entire village stood before him, its inhabitants fashioned from the earth itself.

The sorcerer was amazed by what he had witnessed, and he knew that he had discovered something truly extraordinary. Determined to learn more about these mysterious stone people, he remained in the valley, studying their ways and observing their customs.

Over time, the sorcerer grew to love the stone people as if they were his own kin. He taught them the secrets of magic and sorcery, passing down his knowledge from generation to generation. And in return, the stone people shared their wisdom with him, revealing the ancient mysteries of the earth and the mountains.

For centuries, the people of Pueblo de Piedra lived in harmony with the natural world, their village hidden away from the prying eyes of outsiders. But as the years passed and the world changed around them, they began to fade into legend, their existence known only to a select few who dared to seek out the secrets of the mountains.

Today, the ruins of Pueblo de Piedra still stand as a testament to the enduring power of nature and the magic that lies hidden within the earth. And though the stone people may have long since vanished from the world, their legacy lives on in the whispers of the wind and the echoes of the mountains. a reminder of a time when magic walked the earth and the boundaries between the natural and supernatural worlds were blurred.

Chilindrín, And Chilindrón

This story has been adapted from a tale originally told by Ramón A. Laval in Folk Tales in Chile, originally a Spanish language title, and, published in 1923 by Cervantes Printing House, Santiago De Chile.

Once upon a time, in a land of vast kingdoms and winding roads, there lived a master thief so cunning that no one had ever caught him. He was called Chilindrín, and his name alone struck fear into the hearts of noblemen and merchants alike.

But far away in the South, another thief's name was whispered in awe, Chilindrón, whose exploits were so daring that even the birds in the trees seemed to tell his stories.

Both thieves were legendary, each believing himself to be the finest in the land. Until, one day, news of each other's deeds reached their ears.

Intrigued, Chilindrón set off north to find this mysterious rival, hoping to become his ally, or, if the rumours were true, to challenge him.

At the very same time, Chilindrín heard of Chilindrón's brilliance and rode south, eager to meet the only thief who might be his equal.

Through mountains, forests, and treacherous paths they travelled, until fate led them both to the very same resting place, a quiet grove, just outside the capital.

Chilindrín sat under the shade of an ancient oak, resting against its thick trunk. As the afternoon heat shimmered in the air, the sound of hooves broke the silence. A stranger on horseback halted before him.

"Good day, my friend," the rider said. "Are you taking a nap?"

"No, just waiting for the heat to pass before continuing south," Chilindrín replied.

"Well, I'm travelling north," said the stranger. "Mind if I rest here with you? We can share a smoke and pass the time."

He slid from his horse and sat beside Chilindrín, the two strangers observing each other with interest.

"You know," the traveller said, "I've been riding for twenty days, searching for a man said to be the greatest thief alive, a rogue so clever that no one has ever caught him in the act."

Chilindrín smirked. "And who might this rogue be?"

The traveller lowered his voice to a whisper. "His name is Chilindrín."

Chilindrín chuckled. "Well, my friend, you've found him. And who, may I ask, are you?"

The stranger grinned. "I am Chilindrón."

For a moment, silence hung between them. And then, they burst into laughter, shaking hands like long-lost brothers.

Though both were master thieves, neither had ever witnessed the other's skills.

"I would love to see you in action," Chilindrón admitted.

"And I you," said Chilindrín. "Let's put our talents to the test."

Chilindrín pointed to an eagle's nest high in the oak tree above them. "Watch as I steal its eggs without the eagle noticing."

With the grace of a shadow, Chilindrín climbed the great tree, his hands moving as light as a whisper. When he reached the nest, he slid an egg into his pocket.

But Chilindrón, just as nimble, had secretly climbed behind him. As Chilindrín placed each egg in his pocket, Chilindrón took it without him noticing.

When Chilindrín climbed down, he proudly patted his pockets, only to find them empty.

"Looking for these?" Chilindrón laughed, revealing the stolen eggs.

Chilindrín's eyes widened, then he threw back his head and laughed. "You truly are my match, brother."

They swore a lifelong pact, agreeing to work together from that day forward.

Word soon reached the two thieves of the King's untold riches, locked away in a great tower. It was said the King loved his gold more than his own heart. Determined to test their skills against the greatest challenge of all, they devised a plan.

Under the cover of darkness, they crept across rooftops, slithering like serpents through the night. Reaching the tower, they climbed its walls like lizards, finding a single narrow loophole through which they could slip inside. One by one, they slid down a rope, their eyes gleaming as mountains of gold and jewels sparkled beneath the lantern light.

For nights, they returned, taking only what they could carry, until the King himself discovered his treasure had been plundered. His rage was boundless. Drawing his sword, he roared at his advisors, demanding an answer.

But the tower had only one entrance, locked with secret mechanisms known only to him. How had the thief entered?

An old, blind man, once a thief himself, stepped forward. "Set a trap, Your Majesty, and the thief will come to you."

The King agreed, and that night, a vat of boiling tar was placed beneath the very loophole the thieves used.

That night, as always, Chilindrín went first. But as he landed, he sank into thick, sticky tar, unable to move. Realising the trap, he called up to his friend.

"Don't let go, or you'll be caught too. Instead, swing far from the centre and drop down safely."

Chilindrón obeyed, landing just beyond the trap.

"Now, cut off my head," Chilindrín pleaded. "Take it far away and bury it where no one will ever find it, so they'll never know who I was, and you will not be caught."

Chilindrón hesitated, his heart heavy. But Chilindrín begged him. With great sorrow, Chilindrón granted his friend's final wish. He took the head, wrapped it in a cloth, and fled before dawn broke.

The next morning, the King and his court arrived to see the captured thief, only to find a headless body. The King raged once more, but the old blind man spoke again.

"The thief had an accomplice. To catch him, parade the body through the city. Wherever cries of mourning are heard, that is where the second thief hides."

And so, the dead man was carried through the streets, while soldiers in disguise listened for wailing from any house. Chilindrón, knowing the trick, warned Chilindrín's sister, his own kin, to remain silent. He locked her inside, but when the body passed, she broke into uncontrollable sobs.

A disguised soldier marked the house with a tarred cross. But Chilindrón saw the mark, and with unmatched cunning, he went out that night and painted the same cross on every door in the neighbourhood. The next day, the King's men found themselves helpless, every house bore the same sign.

The blind man sighed. "This thief is no ordinary man. We must try one last trick."

They left Chilindrín's body on a lonely hill, announcing that it would be left for the vultures. Hidden soldiers waited, hoping to catch the second thief when he came to claim the body. But Chilindrón, disguised as a monk, outwitted them all. With wine laced with poppy juice, he drugged the soldiers, shaved their heads, and dressed them in robes. Then, in the dead of night, he swapped the body for a bag of wine, setting fire to the soldiers' uniforms before escaping on horseback.

By dawn, the King's men awoke, dressed as monks, their real clothes burnt to ash. The King, realising he had been utterly humiliated, gave up the chase.

As for Chilindrón? He left the city with his sister, escaping to a faraway kingdom where no one knew their names. There, they lived like royalty, never stealing again. And so, the greatest thief in history vanished, his legend whispered in secret for years to come.

236

The Legend of Imaybé and Iniguazu Chiriguana

This story is my own telling of a traditional Bolivian folk tale based on various sources.

In the heart of the Bolivian Amazon, where the lush rainforest teems with life and the mighty rivers flow with untold secrets, there exists a tale as ancient as the land itself; the legend of Imaybé and Iniguazu Chiriguana.

Long ago, in a village nestled deep within the jungle, there lived a young maiden named Imaybé. She was known throughout the village for her beauty, her kindness, and her deep connection to the spirits of the forest. Imaybé spent her days wandering through the dense foliage, communing with the animals and plants that called the jungle home.

One day, while exploring the banks of the river, Imaybé encountered a mysterious stranger, a handsome young man named Iniguazu Chiriguana. He had travelled from a distant village, drawn by rumours of Imaybé's unparalleled beauty and her alleged ability to communicate with the spirits of the forest.

From the moment their eyes met, Imaybé and Iniguazu Chiriguana knew that they were destined to be together. They spent countless hours exploring the jungle together, sharing stories of their past and dreaming of their future.

But their happiness was short-lived, for jealousy lurked in the shadows, waiting to tear them apart. A rival suitor, envious of Iniguazu Chiriguana's affection for Imaybé, conspired to sabotage their love.

Under the cover of night, the rival suitor ventured into the jungle, armed with dark magic and malicious intent. Using powerful spells and incantations, he lured Imaybé away from Iniguazu Chiriguana, casting a spell that imprisoned her within the depths of the forest.

Desperate to rescue his beloved, Iniguazu Chiriguana embarked on a perilous journey into the heart of the jungle, braving treacherous terrain and fierce predators in his quest to find Imaybé. Guided by his love for her and his unwavering determination, he pressed on, refusing to be deterred by the dangers that lay ahead.

After days of searching, Iniguazu Chiriguana finally found Imaybé, trapped within a magical prison woven from vines and shadows. With tears in his eyes and love in his heart, he shattered the enchantment, setting Imaybé free from her captivity.

Together, Imaybé and Iniguazu Chiriguana emerged from the depths of the jungle, hand in hand, their love stronger than ever before. And as they returned to their village, they vowed to cherish each other for all eternity, knowing that their bond was unbreakable and their love was destined to endure.

To this day, the legend of Imaybé and Iniguazu Chiriguana lives on in the hearts of the Bolivian people, a testament to the power of love to overcome even the darkest of sorcery and the fiercest of trials.

And though time may pass and the world may change, their story will forever be woven into the fabric of the jungle, a timeless reminder of the enduring strength of true love.

239

The Story of the Yara

This story has been adapted from a tale originally told by Andrew Lang in The Brown Fairy Book, published in 1904 by Longman Green and Company, London. The Brown Fairy Book contains a selection of fairy tales and folk stories from various countries and cultures, including Europe, Asia, Africa, and the Americas.

Down in the south, where the sun shines so hotly that everything and everybody sleeps all day, and even the great forests seem silent, except early in the morning and late in the evening, down in this country there once lived a young man and a maiden. The girl had been born in the town, and had scarcely ever left it; but the young man was a native of another country, and had only come to the city near the great river because he could find no work to do where he was.

A few months after his arrival, when the days were cooler, and the people did not sleep so much as usual, a great feast was held a little way out of the town, and to this feast everyone flocked from thirty miles and more. Some walked and some rode, some came in beautiful golden coaches; but all had on splendid dresses of red or blue, while wreaths of flowers rested on their hair.

It was the first time that the youth had been present on such an occasion, and he stood silently aside watching the graceful dances and the pretty games played by the young people. And as he watched, he noticed one girl, dressed in white with scarlet pomegranates in her hair, who seemed to him lovelier than all the rest.

When the feast was over, and the young man returned home, his manner was so strange that it drew the attention of all his friends.

Through his work next day the youth continued to see the girl's face, throwing the ball to her companions, or threading her way between them as she danced. At night sleep fled from him, and after tossing for hours on his bed, he would get up and plunge into a deep pool that lay a little way in the forest.

This state of things went on for some weeks, then at last chance favoured him. One evening, as he was passing near the house where she lived, he saw her standing with her back to the wall, trying to beat off with her fan the attacks of a savage dog that was leaping at her throat. Alonzo, for such was his name, sprang forward, and with one blow of his fist stretched the creature dead upon the road. He then helped the frightened and half-fainting girl into the large cool verandah where her parents were sitting, and from that hour he was a welcome guest in the house, and it was not long before he was the promised husband of Julia.

Every day, when his work was done, he used to go up to the house, half hidden among flowering plants and brilliant creepers, where humming-birds darted from bush to bush, and parrots of all colours, red and green and grey, shrieked in chorus. There he would find the maiden waiting for him, and they would spend an hour or two under the stars, which looked so large and bright that you felt as if you could almost touch them.

"What did you do last night after you went home?" suddenly asked the girl one evening.

"Just the same as I always do," answered he. "It was too hot to sleep, so it was no use going to bed, and I walked straight to the forest and bathed in one of those deep dark pools at the edge of the river. I have been there constantly for several months, but last night a strange thing happened. I was taking my last plunge, when I heard, sometimes from one side, and sometimes from another, the sound of a voice singing more sweetly than any nightingale, though I could not catch any words. I left the pool, and, dressing myself as fast as I could, I searched every bush and tree round the water, as I fancied that perhaps it was my friend who was playing a trick on me, but there was not a creature to be seen; and when I reached home I found my friend fast asleep."

As Julia listened her face grew deadly white, and her whole body shivered as if with cold. From her childhood she had heard stories of the terrible beings that lived in the forests and were hidden under the banks of the rivers, and could only be kept off by powerful charms. Could the voice which had bewitched Alonzo have come from one of these? Perhaps, who knows, it might be the voice of the dreaded Yara herself, who sought young men on the eve of their marriage as her prey.

For a moment the girl sat choked with fear, as these thoughts rushed through her; then she said, " Alonzo, will you promise something?'

"What is that?" asked he.

"It is something that has to do with our future happiness."

"Oh. it is serious, then? Well, of course I promise. Now tell me."

"I want you to promise," she answered, lowering her voice to a whisper, "never to bathe in those pools again."

"But why not, queen of my soul, have I not gone there always, and nothing has harmed me, flower of my heart?"

"No; but perhaps something will. If you will not promise I shall go mad with fright. Promise me."

"Why, what is the matter? You look so pale. Tell me why you are so frightened?"

"Did you not hear the song?" she asked, trembling.

"Suppose I did, how could that hurt me? It was the loveliest song I ever heard."

"Yes, and after the song will come the apparition; and after that, after that, "

"I don't understand. Well, after that?"

"After that, death."

Alonzo stared at her. Had she really gone mad? Such talk was very unlike Julia; but before he could collect his senses the girl spoke again, "That is the reason why I implore you never to go there again; at any rate till after we are married."

"And what difference will our marriage make?"

"Oh, there will be no danger then. You can go to bathe as often as you like."

"But tell me why you are so afraid?"

"Because the voice you heard, I know you will laugh, but it is quite true, it was the voice of the Yara."

At these words Alonzo burst into a shout of laughter; but it sounded so harsh and loud that Julia shrank away shuddering. It seemed as if he could not stop himself, and the more he laughed the paler the poor girl became, murmuring to herself as she watched him, "Oh, heaven. you have seen her. you have seen her. what shall I do?"

Faint as was her whisper, it reached the ears of Alonzo, who, though he still could not speak for laughing, shook his head.

"You may not know it, but it is true. Nobody who has not seen the Yara laughs like that." And Julia flung herself on the ground weeping bitterly.

At this sight Alonzo became suddenly grave, and kneeling by her side, gently raised her up.

"Do not cry so, my angel," he said, "I will promise anything you please. Only let me see you smile again."

With a great effort Julia checked her sobs, and rose to her feet.

"Thank you," she answered. "My heart grows lighter as you say that. I know you will try to keep your word and to stay away from the forest. But, the power of the Yara is very strong, and the sound of her voice is apt to make men forget everything else in the world. Oh, I have seen it, and more than one betrothed maiden lives alone, broken-hearted. If ever you should return to the pool where you first heard the voice, promise me that you will at least take this with you." And opening a curiously carved box, she took out a sea-shell shot with many colours, and sang a song softly into it. "The moment you hear the Yara's voice," said she, "put this to your ear, and you will hear my song instead. Perhaps, I do not know for certain, but perhaps, I may be stronger than the Yara."

It was late that night when Alonzo returned home. The moon was shining on the distant river, which looked cool and inviting, and the trees of the forest seemed to stretch out their arms and beckon him near. But the young man steadily turned his face in the other direction, and went home to bed.

The struggle had been hard, but Alonzo had his reward next day in the joy and relief with which Julia greeted him. He assured her that having overcome the temptation once the danger was now over; but she, knowing better than he did the magic of the Yara's face and voice, did not fail to make him repeat his promise when he went away.

For three nights Alonzo kept his word, not because he believed in the Yara, for he thought that the tales about her were all nonsense, but because he could not bear the tears with which he knew that Julia would greet him, if he confessed that he had returned to the forest. But, in spite of this, the song rang in his ears, and daily grew louder.

On the fourth night the attraction of the forest grew so strong that neither the thought of Julia nor the promises he had made her could hold him back. At eleven o'clock he plunged into the cool darkness of the trees, and took the path that led straight to the river. Yet, for the first time, he found that Julia's warnings, though he had laughed at her at the moment, had remained in his memory, and he glanced at the bushes with a certain sense of fear which was quite new to him.

When he reached the river he paused and looked round for a moment to make sure that the strange feeling of someone watching him was fancy, and he was really alone. But the moon shone brightly on every tree, and nothing was to be seen but his own shadow; nothing was to be heard but the sound of the rippling stream.

He threw off his clothes, and was just about to dive in headlong, when something, he did not know what, suddenly caused him to look round. At the same instant the moon passed from behind a cloud, and its rays fell on a beautiful golden-haired woman standing half hidden by the ferns.

With one bound he caught up his mantle, and rushed headlong down the path he had come, fearing at each step to feel a hand laid on his shoulder. It was not till he had left the last trees behind him, and was standing in the open plain, that he dared to look round, and then he thought a figure in white was still standing there waving her arms to and fro. This was enough; he ran along the road harder than ever, and never paused till he was save in his own room.

With the earliest rays of dawn he went back to the forest to see whether he could find any traces of the Yara, but though he searched every clump of bushes, and looked up every tree, everything was empty, and the only voices he heard were those of parrots, which are so ugly that they only drive people away.

"I think I must be mad," he said to himself, "and have dreamt all that folly", and going back to the city he began his daily work. But either that was harder than usual, or he must be ill, for he could not fix his mind upon it, and everybody he came across during the day inquired if anything had happened to give him that white, frightened look.

"I must be feverish," he said to himself, "after all, it is rather dangerous to take a cold bath when one is feeling so hot." Yet he knew, while he said it, that he was counting the hours for night to come, that he might return to the forest.

In the evening he went as usual to the creeper-covered house. But he had better have stayed away, as his face was so pale and his manner so strange, that the poor girl saw that something terrible had occurred. Alonzo, however, refused to answer any of her questions, and all she could get was a promise to hear everything the next day.

On pretence of a violent headache, he left Julia much earlier than usual and hurried quickly home. Taking down a pistol, he loaded it and put it in his belt, and a little before midnight he stole out on the tips of his toes, so as to disturb nobody. Once outside he hastened down the road which led to the forest.

He did not stop till he had reached the river pool, when holding the pistol in his hand, he looked about him. At every little noise, the falling of a leaf, the rustle of an animal in the bushes, the cry of a night-bird, he sprang up and cocked his pistol in the direction of the sound. But though the moon still shone he saw nothing, and by and by a kind of dreamy state seemed to steal over him as he leant against a tree.

How long he remained in this condition he could not have told, but suddenly he awoke with a start, on hearing his name uttered softly.

"Who is that?" he cried, standing upright instantly; but only an echo answered him. Then his eyes grew fascinated with the dark waters of the pool close to his feet, and he looked at it as if he could never look away.

He gazed steadily into the depths for some minutes, when he became aware that down in the darkness was a bright spark, which got rapidly bigger and brighter. Again that feeling of awful fear took possession of him, and he tried to turn his eyes from the pool. But it was no use; something stronger than himself compelled him to keep them there.

At last the waters parted softly, and floating on the surface he saw the beautiful woman whom he had fled from only a few nights before. He turned to run, but his feet were glued to the spot.

She smiled at him and held out her arms, but as she did so there came over him the remembrance of Julia, as he had seen her a few hours earlier, and her warnings and fears for the very danger in which he now found himself.

Meanwhile the figure was always drawing nearer, nearer; but, with a violent effort, Alonzo shook off his stupor, and taking aim at her shoulder he pulled the trigger. The report awoke the sleeping echoes, and was repeated all through the forest, but the figure smiled still, and went on advancing. Again Alonzo fired, and a second time the bullet whistled through the air, and the figure advanced nearer. A moment more, and she would be at his side.

Then, his pistol being empty, he grasped the barrel with both hands, and stood ready to use it as a club should the Yara approach and closer. But now it seemed her turn to feel afraid, for she paused an instant while he pressed forward, still holding the pistol above his head, prepared to strike.

In his excitement he had forgotten the river, and it was not till the cold water touched his feet that he stood still by instinct. The Yara saw that he was wavering, and suffering herself to sway gently backwards and forwards on the surface of the river, she began to sing. The song floated through the trees, now far and now near; no one could tell whence it came, the whole air seemed full of it. Alonzo felt his senses going and his will failing. His arms dropped heavily to his side, but in falling struck against the seashell, which, as he had promised Julia, he had always carried in his coat.

His dimmed mind was just clear enough to remember what she had said, and with trembling fingers, that were almost powerless to grasp, he drew it out. As he did so the song grew sweeter and more tender than before, but he shut his ears to it and bent his head over the shell. Out of its depths arose the voice of Julia singing to him as she had sung when she gave him the shell, and though the notes sounded faint at first, they swelled louder and louder till the mist which had gathered about him was blown away.

Then he raised his head, feeling that he had been through strange places, where he could never wander anymore; and he held himself erect and strong, and looked about him. Nothing was to be seen but the shining of the river, and the dark shadows of the trees; nothing was to be heard but the hum of the insects, as they darted through the night.

The Princess Of The Springs

This story has been adapted from a tale originally told by Elsie Spicer Eells in Tales Of Giants from Brazil, published in 1918 by Dodd, Mead And Company, New York. Following the success of her previous work, Fairy Tales from Brazil,, this book focuses specifically on stories featuring giants, mythical beings of immense size and strength, from Brazilian folklore.

Once, long ago, the Moon Giant wooed the beautiful giantess who dwells in the Great River and won her love. He built for her a wonderful palace where the Great River runs into the sea. It was made of mother-of-pearl with rich carvings, and gold and silver and precious stones were used to adorn it. Never before in all the world had a giant or giantess possessed such a magnificent home.

When the baby daughter of the Moon Giant and the Giantess of the Great River was born it was decreed among the giants that she should be the Princess of all the Springs and should rule over all the rivers and lakes. The light of her eyes was like the moonbeams, and her smile was like moonlight on still waters. Her strength was as the strength of the Great River, and the fleetness of her foot was as the swiftness of the Great River.

As the beautiful Spring Princess grew older many suitors came to sing her praises beneath the palace windows, but she favoured none of them. She was so happy living in her own lovely palace with her own dear mother that she did not care at all for any suitor. No other daughter ever loved her mother as the Spring Princess loved the Giantess of the Great River.

At last the Sun Giant came to woo the Spring Princess. The strength of the Sun Giant was as the strength of ten of the other suitors of the fair princess. He was so powerful that he won her heart.

When he asked her to marry him, however, and go with him to his own palace, the Spring Princess shook her lovely head. "Oh Sun Giant, you are so wonderful and so powerful that I love you as I never before have loved a suitor who sang beneath my palace window," said she, "but I love my mother, too. I cannot go away with you and leave my own dear mother. It would break my heart."

The Sun Giant told the Spring Princess again and again of his great love for her, of his magnificent palace which would be her new home, of the happy life which awaited her as queen of the palace. At length she listened to his pleadings and decided that she could leave home and live with him for nine months of the year. For three months of every year, however, she would have to return to the wonderful palace of mother-of-pearl where the Great River runs into the sea and spend the time with her mother, the Giantess of the Great River.

The Sun Giant at last sorrowfully consented to this arrangement and the wedding feast was held. It lasted for seven days and seven nights.

Then the Spring Princess went away with the Sun Giant to his own home.

Every year the Spring Princess went to visit her mother for three months according to the agreement. For three months of every year she lived in the palace of mother-of-pearl where the Great River runs into the sea. For three months of every year the rivers sang once more as they rushed along their way. For three months the lakes sparkled in the bright sunlight as their hearts once more were brim-full of joy.

When at last the little son of the Spring Princess was born she wanted to take him with her when she went to visit her mother. The Sun Giant, however, did not approve of such a plan. He firmly refused to allow the child to leave home. After much pleading, all in vain, the Spring Princess set out upon her journey alone, with sorrow in her heart. She left her baby son with the best nurses she could procure.

Now it happened that the Giantess of the Great River had not expected that her daughter would be able to visit her that year. She had thought that all the rivers and lakes, the palace of mother-of-pearl, and her own mother heart would have to get along as best they could without a visit from the Spring Princess. The Giantess of the Great River had gone away to water the earth. One of the land giants had taken her prisoner and would not let her escape.

When the Spring Princess arrived at the beautiful palace of mother-of-pearl and gold and silver and precious stones, where the Great River runs into the sea, there was no one at home. She ran from room to room in the palace calling out, "Oh dear mother, Giantess of the Great River, dear, dear mother. Where are you? Where have you hidden yourself?"

There was no answer. Her own voice echoed back to her through the beautiful halls of mother-of-pearl with their rich carvings. The palace was entirely deserted.

She ran outside the palace and called to the fishes of the river, "Oh fishes of the river, have you seen my own dear mother?"

She called to the sands of the sea, "Oh sands of the sea, have you seen my darling mother?"

She called to the shells of the shore, "Oh shells of the shore, have you seen my precious mother?"

There was no answer. No one knew what had become of the Giantess of the Great River.

The Spring Princess was so worried that she thought her heart would break in its anguish. In her distress she ran over all the earth.

Then she went to the house of the Great Wind. The Giant of the Great Wind was away, but his old father was at home. He was very sorry for the Spring Princess when he heard her sad story. "I am sure my son can help you find your mother," he said as he comforted her. "He will soon get home from his day's work."

When the Giant of the Great Wind reached home he was in a terrible temper. He stormed and raged and gave harsh blows to everything he met. His father had hidden the Spring Princess in a closet out of the way, and it was fortunate indeed for her that he had done so.

After the Great Wind Giant had taken his bath and eaten his dinner he was better natured. Then his father said to him, "Oh my son, if a wandering princess had come this way on purpose to ask you a question, what would you do to her?"

"Why, I'd answer her question as best I could, of course," responded the Giant of the Great Wind.

His father straightway opened the closet door and the Spring Princess stepped out. In spite of her long wanderings and great anguish of mind she was still very lovely as she knelt before the Giant of the Great Wind in her soft silvery green garments embroidered with pearls and diamonds. The big heart of the Giant of the Great Wind was touched at her beauty and at her grief.

"Oh Giant of the Great Wind," said the Spring Princess, as he gently raised her from her knees before him, "I am the daughter of the Giantess of the Great River. I have lost my mother. I have searched for her through all the earth and now I have come to you for help. Can you tell me anything about where she is and how I can find her?"

The Giant of the Great Wind put on his thinking cap. He thought hard. "Your mother is in the power of a land giant who has imprisoned her," he said. "I happen to know all about the affair. I passed that way only yesterday. I'll gladly go with you and help you get her home. We'll start at once."

The Giant of the Great Wind took the Spring Princess back to earth on his swift horses. Then he stormed the castle of the land giant who had imprisoned the Giantess of the Great River. The Spring Princess dug quietly beneath the castle walls to the dungeon where her mother was confined. You may be sure that her mother was overjoyed to see her.

When the Spring Princess had led her mother safely outside the castle walls she thanked the Giant of the Great Wind for all he had done to help her. Then the Giantess of the Great River and the Spring Princess hastened back to the wonderful palace of mother-of-pearl set with gold and silver and precious stones, where the Great River runs into the Sea. As soon as she had safely reached there once more the Spring Princess suddenly remembered that she had stayed away from her home in the palace of the Sun Giant longer than the three months she was supposed to stay according to the agreement. She at once said good-bye to her mother and hastened to the home of the Sun Giant, her husband, and to her baby son.

Now the Sun Giant had been very much worried at first when the three months had passed and the Spring Princess had not come back to him and her little son. Then he became angry. He became so angry that he married another princess. The new wife discharged the nurses who were taking care of the tiny son of the Spring Princess and put him in the kitchen just as if he had been a little black slave baby.

When the Spring Princess arrived at the palace of the Sun Giant the very first person she saw was her own little son, so dirty and neglected that she hardly recognized him. Then she found out all that had happened in her absence.

The Spring Princess quickly seized her child and clasped him tight in her arms. Then she fled to the depths of the sea, and wept, and wept, and wept. The waters of the sea rose so high that they reached even to the palace of the Sun Giant. They covered the palace, and the Sun Giant, his new wife, and all the court entirely disappeared from view. For forty days the face of the Sun Giant was not seen upon the earth.

The little son of the Spring Princess grew up to be the Giant of the Rain. In the rainy season and the season of thunder showers he rules upon the earth. He sends upon the earth such tears as the Spring Princess shed in the depths of the seas.

The Myth of Manco Capac and Mama Ocllo

This story is my own telling of a traditional Bolivian folk tale based on various sources.

In the heart of the Andes Mountains, where the peaks reach towards the heavens and the valleys cradle the mysteries of the ancient world, there exists a tale as old as time itself; the myth of Manco Capac and Mama Ocllo, the legendary founders of the Inca Empire.

Long before the rise of the mighty Inca civilization, the land was ruled by chaos and strife. The people lived in fear, their villages constantly threatened by rival tribes and hostile forces. But amidst the turmoil, there arose a prophecy, a prophecy that spoke of two divine siblings who would descend from the heavens to bring order and prosperity to the land.

According to legend, Manco Capac and Mama Ocllo were born from the foam of Lake Titicaca, the sacred lake that lies at the heart of the Andes. Gifted with divine powers and guided by the will of the gods, they emerged from the waters to fulfil their destiny and lead their people to greatness.

As they journeyed across the land, Manco Capac and Mama Ocllo performed miracles and wonders, earning the admiration and devotion of all who crossed their path. They taught the people the arts of agriculture and irrigation, showing them how to tame the wild landscapes and cultivate the fertile soil.

But their greatest feat came when they reached the fertile valley of Cusco, where they decided to establish their capital city. With the help of the gods, they transformed the barren land into a thriving metropolis, laying the foundations for what would one day become the centre of the mighty Inca Empire.

As the years passed, Manco Capac and Mama Ocllo ruled wisely and justly, guiding their people with wisdom and compassion. Under their leadership, the Inca civilization flourished, expanding its borders and establishing itself as a powerful force in the region.

But even as they basked in the glory of their achievements, Manco Capac and Mama Ocllo knew that their time on earth was limited. As divine beings, they were bound to return to the heavens from where they came, leaving behind a legacy that would endure for eternity.

And so, on the day of their departure, the people of Cusco gathered to bid farewell to their beloved leaders. With tears in their eyes and gratitude in their hearts, they watched as Manco Capac and Mama Ocllo ascended into the sky, their spirits merging with the stars above.

Juan the Brave and the Stolen Heifer

This story has been adapted from a tale originally told by Ramón A. Laval in Folk Tales in Chile, originally a Spanish language title, and, published in 1923 by Cervantes Printing House, Santiago De Chile.

Once upon a time, in a kingdom of rolling meadows and golden fields, there lived a King and Queen who owned vast pastures filled with cattle. Their finest herds were watched over by Juan the Brave, a man of great strength and courage, who feared nothing and had fought in many battles.

One day, the King called for Juan. "Bring forth all the cows," he commanded. "We wish to see them milked."

Juan did as he was told, and the King and Queen marvelled at the fat, healthy cows, their rich milk filling buckets to the brim. But among them stood a small, scrawny heifer, thin as a twig.

The King turned to the Queen and said, "Let us give that one to Juan. He has served us well, and our herds have flourished under his care."

The Queen agreed, and so the little heifer became Juan's own.

Juan tended to his heifer with great care, feeding it the best grains and leading it to the freshest meadows. Before long, the little creature grew strong and fatter than any of the King's cows.

One day, the Queen saw the now-magnificent heifer and said, "Juan, kill that fine beast and make it into jerky for us."

Juan shook his head. "No, my Queen. She is mine, and I will not slaughter her unless I choose to."

The Queen fumed at his defiance. She demanded again, but Juan stood firm. Furious, the Queen went to the King, complaining that Juan had disrespected her.

The King sighed. "Juan, take your heifer and leave. The Queen is angered, and she will not rest until the creature is slain."

And so, with a heavy heart, Juan set off from the city, his beloved heifer following close behind.

As Juan passed through the forest, danger lurked in the shadows. A gang of bandits leapt from the trees and seized both Juan and his heifer. They dragged them to a hidden house deep within the woods.

At night, Juan crept into the hayloft to spy on them. But to his horror, he watched as the bandits butchered his heifer and roasted its meat over the fire. Tears filled Juan's eyes, but his sorrow quickly turned to rage.

"These villains will pay for this." he swore.

As the bandits drank and feasted, their captain silenced them. "Tomorrow," he announced, "we shall take to the high road and capture any young maidens who pass by."

Juan gritted his teeth. If these men were so wicked, he would deal with them himself. Juan slipped away under the cover of night and ran to a friend's house. There, he devised a plan. With his friend's help, he dressed in fine women's clothing, powdered his face, painted his lips, and hid a sharp sabre beneath his skirts. The next day, as the sun rose, Juan walked gracefully past the bandits' hideout, swaying like a noblewoman.

From their lookout, the bandits spotted him at once. "Look there." one of them called. "A fair maiden. Let us invite her in for a drink."

They rushed down and greeted Juan with smiles, offering him sweet wine and a guitar to entertain them. Juan played the role well, giggling and singing as if he had no care in the world. By afternoon, the captain of the bandits turned to his men.

"Go to the mountains," he ordered. "I will remain here… alone with our guest."

The bandits obeyed, leaving Juan face-to-face with their vile leader.

The captain, thinking himself alone, turned his back to pour more wine. At that moment, Juan lifted his skirts, drew his hidden sabre, and struck. The blade cut deep, and the captain screamed in agony. Juan quickly hid in the hayloft, watching as the wounded bandit howled so loudly that his men heard him from the mountains.

Believing the captain had killed the girl, the bandits rushed back to the hideout. But when they arrived, they found him lying on the ground, bleeding and gasping.

One of them cried, "We must find a healer at once."

Hearing their plan, Juan hurried back to his friend's house. There, he painted wrinkles upon his face, disguised himself in tattered rags, and dressed as a poor old herbalist.

At dawn, he hobbled past the bandits' house, pretending to gather herbs. The bandits spotted him at once.

"Good woman." one of them called. "Do you know how to treat wounds?"

Juan bowed his head and croaked in an old woman's voice, "I am the finest healer in all the land."

They rushed him inside and led him to the wounded captain.

Juan examined him carefully, then said, "This wound is grave. I need a rare ointment from the city. You must send all your men to different apothecaries to find it."

The bandits, desperate to save their leader, obeyed at once, scattering far and wide. Juan watched from the lookout, waiting until the last of them had disappeared over the hills. Then, with a triumphant smile, he drew his sabre and finished the job.

Now free to roam the hideout, Juan searched every chest and drawer. To his delight, he found gold, silver, rings, and precious jewels, all stolen from innocent travellers. He filled his pockets and returned to his friend's house, where he washed away his disguise and donned his true attire.

Meanwhile, the bandits returned to find their captain dead and their fortune gone. Fearing they would be hunted down, they fled to another town, never daring to return.

But Juan was not finished. Leading a band of men with carts, he returned to the hideout and broke down the doors. He and his allies took everything, every coin, every weapon, every last piece of treasure. And so, Juan and his family became richer than they had ever dreamed.

But the story does not end there.

Days later, the bandits learnt of Juan's newfound wealth and realised the truth. "That scoundrel tricked us." one of them cried. "He must have killed our captain and taken all we had."

Enraged, they plotted their revenge. One night, they returned to the city to ambush Juan. But Juan was ready. He stood at his door, sabre in hand, waiting for them. He had seen them coming from afar and had sent his father to summon the guards.

The battle was fierce. Juan fought bravely, cutting down one robber and gravely wounding another before the city's soldiers arrived. The remaining bandits were captured, judged, and sentenced. And so, justice was served.

From that day forward, Juan the Brave and his family lived in peace, wealth, and honour, knowing that courage and wit had made them richer than any treasure ever could. And that, dear friends, is the tale of Juan the Brave and the Stolen Heifer.

The Fountain Of Giant Land

This story has been adapted from a tale originally told by Elsie Spicer Eells in Tales Of Giants from Brazil, published in 1918 by Dodd, Mead And Company, New York. Following the success of her previous work, Fairy Tales from Brazil,, this book focuses specifically on stories featuring giants, mythical beings of immense size and strength, from Brazilian folklore.

Long ago there lived a king who was blind. He had employed all the wise physicians in the kingdom, but all to no avail. Not one of them did a single thing to restore his lost eyesight.

One day a little old woman came to the door of the palace begging alms. She said to the servant at the door, "I wish to say a word to the king who is blind. I know a sure cure for his blindness."

The servant led the little old woman into the king's presence. He was sitting upon the royal throne with his royal crown upon his head, but his blind eyes were bandaged and his royal face was sad because he could no longer see the bright sunlight shining upon the deep blue sea from the window of the palace, nor the lords and ladies of the court before him in their gorgeous garments of purple and cloth of silver and cloth of gold, nor of the face of the queen.

"Oh royal majesty," said the little old woman as she bowed low before him, "there is only one thing in the whole world which will restore your lost eyesight. It is the water of the fountain of Giantland. Bathe your eyes in that water and your lost eyesight will be restored at once."

"How can I obtain this wonderful water?" asked the king. "Giantland is a long distance from my kingdom and I do not know the way there." The king, the queen, and all the courtiers held their breaths to listen to the reply of the little old woman.

"Your Majesty will need to build a strong fleet to sail up the great river which leads to Giantland," she said. "The expedition will need as its leader a prince with a brave heart, for there will be many perils on the way to test his mettle. The fountain of Giantland is at the summit of a long steep rocky mountain, and it can be reached only by a prince who ascends the mountain looking neither to the right nor to the left. All along the way stand huge giants ready to enslave one the moment he stops looking straight ahead. If one should succeed in climbing the mountain the fountain is there at the summit, but it is guarded by a dragon. One can approach it only when the dragon is asleep. Many princes have tried this quest and all have failed. If you should be able to send a prince brave enough and wise enough to succeed, there at the top of the mountain he will find a little old woman who will tell him whether or not the dragon is asleep."

With these words the little old woman withdrew from the royal presence. The king pondered over her advice. Then he sent for the three princes and told them the story.

"Oh my father, I am brave and wise," said the eldest prince as soon as he had heard his father's words. "I will go upon this quest. I will bring you a bottle of the water of the fountain of Giantland that your sight may be restored."

The king ordered a great fleet to be prepared to sail up the river to Giantland. He collected an enormous sum of money to provide for the prince. The whole kingdom buzzed with preparation for the journey.

The prince planted an orange tree in the palace garden and said to his younger brother, "Keep close watch of this tree. If its leaves begin to wither you will know that some evil has befallen me. Come to my aid."

The eldest prince set out with a great fleet and his pockets lined with gold. He anchored in many harbours along the way. The prince was very fond of gaming and there were many opportunities to play. Before he had reached Giantland he had lost the golden linings from his pockets.

After the prince had sailed up the great river which leads to Giantland he saw the steep rocky mountain towering before him. He set a bottle for the water of the fountain of Giantland carefully upon his head and slowly ascended the steep path. He kept his eyes fixed straight ahead.

Soon, however, he heard giant voices shouting at him. From the corners of his eyes he could see giant forms along the pathway. He forgot that he must look neither to the right nor to the left.

The moment the prince turned his eyes a giant immediately seized him and made him his slave. "You shall be my slave for ever and a day," said the giant, "unless you have gold enough in your pockets to pay your ransom." The prince had no gold.

At home in the palace garden the leaves of the orange tree which the eldest prince had planted began to wither. His younger brother noticed it at once and went to the king. "Oh my father," said he, "I know that my brother has fallen into trouble. I must go to his aid."

The king at once prepared another great fleet. He provided the prince with even more gold than his brother had taken with him. Everyone in the whole kingdom did his best to hasten the preparations.

In the palace garden the prince planted a lemon tree and called the youngest prince into the garden. The youngest prince was playing with his dogs. He was a mere boy. "Keep close watch of this lemon tree while I am away," said the prince. "If its leaves begin to wither you will know that I am in trouble. Come to my aid."

The prince sailed up the great river which leads to Giantland. He anchored at many harbours and took part in many festas. By the time he had reached Giantland he had spent all his gold.

At home in the palace garden the youngest prince watched the lemon tree carefully every day. He watered it and pruned it. He took splendid care of it.

When at last the prince set out to climb the mountain which leads to the fountain of Giantland he felt very brave and very wise. He climbed steadily on and on, looking neither to the right nor to the left, even though he heard the voices of the giants shouting at him, and from the corners of his eyes could see the giant forms along the pathway.

Suddenly he heard the voice of his own brother, the eldest prince, weeping as the giant gave him blows. At that sound he forgot all about looking straight ahead.

The moment the prince turned his eyes from the pathway straight ahead of him a giant seized him and made him his slave. "You shall be my slave for ever and a day," said the giant, "unless you have gold enough to pay your ransom."

At home in the palace garden his little brother was watching the lemon tree. The very moment its leaves began to wither he noticed it and ran at once to the king. "Oh my father," he cried as soon as he was in the king's presence. "My brother is in trouble. I must go to his aid."

"You, my son, are only a lad," said the king. "How can you succeed when your two older brothers have failed? I cannot bear to let you go. You are all I have left. I prefer to remain blind the rest of my days. Oh, why did I ever listen to the story the little old woman told me about the water of the fountain of Giantland?"

The youngest prince begged so hard to go that at length his father granted his request and prepared a fleet for him. He gave him all the gold he could collect in the kingdom.

The prince set out with brave heart. He sailed on his way steadily although at every harbour there were voices which bade him linger. There were games and feasting and fair maidens.

Soon the youngest prince had reached Giantland. Above him rose the rough steep rocky mountain. Before he started to make the ascent he first stuffed cotton in his ears. Then he carefully placed upon his head a bottle to fill with the water of the fountain of Giantland.

He climbed up the steep mountain looking neither to the right nor to the left. Through the cotton in his ears he could faintly hear the giant voices calling him. From the corners of his eyes he could see the giant forms along the pathway. He resolutely kept his eyes fixed straight ahead and steadily climbed upward though the path was very rough and full of stones. The cotton in his ears prevented him from hearing the voices of his two brothers crying out when the giants beat them.

At length the lad was in sight of the fountain at the summit of the mountain. The little old woman was standing in the path, watching his ascent. As soon as he came near to her he took the cotton out of his ears so that he might hear what she had to say to him.

"You have arrived at a safe moment," the little old woman told him. "The dragon is asleep."

The little old woman helped the prince fill the bottle with water from the fountain. Then she said, "The dragon which guards the fountain is an enchanted princess. No prince has ever before been brave enough and wise enough to reach this spot. In a year and a day from this moment her enchantment will be broken. Come again and claim her as your bride."

The little old woman gave the prince a ring, and the prince drew a ring from his own finger and gave it to the little old woman. "When the enchantment is broken put my ring upon the finger of the princess," he said. "Expect me back in a year and a day. I'll be sure to come."

The prince made his way back down the steep slope of the mountain, guarding his bottle full of the water of the fountain of Giantland with the utmost care. When he was halfway down the mountain he saw his two brothers standing in his path.

"Viva," cried they. "You have been successful. You have a bottle full of the water from the fountain. Now if you also have your pockets full of gold you can pay our ransom and we will return with you to our father's kingdom."

"My pockets are still lined with gold which my father gave me," said the youngest prince. "Help yourselves. It is yours if it can serve you." There was more than enough money to pay the ransom of his two older brothers.

When they were sailing down the great river towards home the two older brothers plotted against the youngest prince. "Come," said one to the other. "How can we let our father know that it was our little brother who succeeded in this quest? Let us cast our brother ashore. Then we will go together to our father with the water from the fountain of Giantland. When his sight is restored we will share his blessing and the honours of the kingdom. We will claim no knowledge of our youngest brother."

This is what the two eldest princes did. The youngest prince was cast ashore when he was asleep. After many long weary wanderings he found refuge in the hut of a poor fisherman and hired out to work for him.

The king's eyesight was restored immediately when he had bathed his eyes in the water from the fountain of Giantland. The two princes were given all the honours of the kingdom. The whole kingdom, however, mourned the loss of the little prince. The king and queen never gave up hoping that he would come back to them. The queen carefully laid away all the clothes which had belonged to the youngest prince so that they would be ready for him if he should return to the palace. Every day she shook them out with loving care, so that the baratas and white ants would not eat holes in them.

A year and a day flew swiftly by. The huge dragon which had guarded the fountain of Giantland escaped from her enchantment and was restored to the form of a beautiful princess.

The little old woman and the princess watched and waited for the return of the prince according to his promise. "Some evil must surely have befallen the lad," said the little old woman. "Let us go in search of him. I know he was a lad who would not break his word."

The little old woman and the beautiful princess who wore the prince's own ring upon her finger came to the palace of the king. When the king had listened to the story they told, the guilty princes were called before him. They were forced to confess their evil deed. They were immediately thrown into prison. The anger of the whole kingdom was kindled against them.

Then the king and the queen and all the court sailed in their swiftest ships to the place where the little prince had been cast ashore. The little old woman and the beautiful princess who wore the prince's own ring upon her finger went with them. At length after much searching they found the fisherman's hut and the prince working for the fisherman.

The king and the queen and all the court wept tears of joy when they beheld the youngest prince alive and well. The queen wept again when she noticed the poor rough clothing which the prince was wearing. She had brought with her the prince's favourite suit of cloth of gold which she had laid away carefully. When the prince put it on it was a trifle tight and a little bit too short for him, as he had grown so much in the year. Nevertheless he looked very handsome in it when he stood before the beautiful princess and claimed her as his bride.

The fisherman was greatly astonished at all the proceedings, for he had never dreamed that it was the king's son who had been working for him all the year and sleeping on a mat at his side on the floor of his rude hut.

"He may be a prince, but he is the most faithful lad who ever worked for me," said the fisherman.

"He is indeed a prince," cried the courtiers, "and the bravest, most faithful prince which any land in all the world ever boasted of."

"His princely deeds have proven to all the world that he is fit to reign as king over our fair land when I no longer live," said the king as he gave the prince and the beautiful princess his royal blessing.

Go Out With Your Sunday Seven

This story has been adapted from a tale originally told by Ramón A. Laval in Folk Tales in Chile, originally a Spanish language title, and, published in 1923 by Cervantes Printing House, Santiago De Chile.

Once upon a time, in a quiet little village, there lived a kind and humble hunchback. Though burdened with a twisted back, he bore his fate with patience and good humour. Unlike some who let misfortune sour their hearts, he was never jealous nor cruel.

One evening, as he journeyed home from a nearby town, he lost track of time. Night had fallen, and the moon hung high and pale in the sky as he made his way through the whispering woods.

Just as he passed a darkened thicket, he heard a strange sound. Peering through the branches, he saw a circle of witches dancing beneath the ancient oak trees. Hand in hand, they spun round and round, their voices rising into the night as they chanted:

"Monday and Tuesday, Wednesday the third,"

Over and over, their eerie song rang out. The hunchback, though startled, was a quick-witted man with a lively imagination. Something about their song felt unfinished, as though it was missing something. Before he could stop himself, he called out from his hiding place, "Thursday and Friday, Saturday the sixth!"

At once, the witches froze. Then, their faces lit up with delight. "At last!" one cackled. "Someone has completed our song!"

They rushed to pull him into their circle, twirling him about with glee. "We must reward this clever man," declared the eldest witch. "What shall we give him?"

"A palace!" one suggested.

"All the gold he desires!" said another.

"A kingdom of his own!" a third offered.

But the hunchback, who had never been greedy, smiled and shook his head. "I ask for nothing more than for my hump to be taken away and to have enough to live a good life," he said.

The witches clapped their hands. "Granted!" they cried.

In an instant, his hump vanished, and he stood tall and straight for the first time in his life. They sent him on his way, and by morning, he was the handsomest man in the village.

The next day, as the newly transformed man walked through the streets, he bumped into an old friend, another hunchback, still stooped and burdened by his own twisted back. At first, the second hunchback barely recognised him.

"What happened to you?" he demanded, eyes wide with jealousy.

With a kind heart, the first hunchback shared the story of the witches and their magical reward. The second hunchback's mind whirled with envy. That very night, he set off for the enchanted clearing, determined to win the same fate. Hiding behind the same twisted thicket, he waited. Soon, the witches arrived, just as before, and began to dance in their ghostly ring.

Their song rang out:

"Monday and Tuesday, Wednesday the third,

Thursday and Friday, Saturday the sixth."

The second hunchback, eager to win their favour, stepped forward and boldly added, "Sunday the seventh!"

At once, the merry dance stopped. The witches stiffened, their eyes dark with fury. "Who dares ruin our perfect song?" hissed one.

"Find him!" screeched another.

It did not take them long to drag the trembling hunchback from his hiding place and into the circle.

"What shall we do with this fool?" asked the eldest witch, her eyes glowing like embers in the dark.

"Give him horns and a tail!" one cackled.

"Curse his mouth to spit out toads and snakes whenever he speaks!" suggested another.

"No," said a third, her smile wicked and sharp. "For his impertinence, let us give him another hump!"

"Yes! Yes!" the witches shrieked in agreement.

With a wave of their hands, the curse was cast. The second hunchback staggered back, feeling a terrible weight pressing down on him. Not only did his old hump remain, but now another had grown upon his chest! His heart sank as he realised his greedy mistake. With cruel cackles echoing behind him, the witches kicked him out of the circle and sent him stumbling home.

From that day forward, the second hunchback was known throughout the village, not only for his two great humps but for his foolishness. Meanwhile, the first hunchback lived happily ever after, his heart light, his back straight, and his days filled with comfort and ease. And so, the lesson was clear: A grateful heart earns reward, but greed brings only misfortune.

The Boy And The Violin

This story has been adapted from a tale originally told by Elsie Spicer Eells in Tales Of Giants from Brazil, published in 1918 by Dodd, Mead And Company, New York. Following the success of her previous work, Fairy Tales from Brazil,, this book focuses specifically on stories featuring giants, mythical beings of immense size and strength, from Brazilian folklore.

Once upon a time there was a man who had an only son. When the man died the son was left all alone in the world. There was not very much property--just a cat and a dog, a small piece of land, and a few orange trees. The boy gave the dog away to a neighbour and sold the land and the orange trees. Every bit of money he obtained from the sale he invested in a violin. He had longed for a violin all his life and now he wanted one more than ever. While his father had lived he could tell his thoughts to his father, but now there was none to tell them to except the violin. What his violin said back to him made the very sweetest music in the world.

The boy went to hire out as shepherd to care for the sheep of the king, but he was told that the king already had plenty of shepherds and had no need of another. The boy took his violin which he had brought with him and hid himself in the deep forest. There he made sweet music with the violin. The shepherds who were nearby guarding the king's sheep heard the sweet strains, but they could not find out who was playing. The sheep, too, heard the music. Several of them left the flock and followed the sound of the music into the forest. They followed it until they reached the boy and the cat and the violin.

The shepherds were greatly disturbed when they found out how their sheep were straying away into the forest. They went after them to bring them back, but they could find no trace of them. Sometimes it would seem that they were quite near to the place from which the music came, but when they hurried in that direction they would hear the strains of music coming from a distant point in the opposite direction. They were afraid of getting lost themselves so they gave up in despair.

When the boy saw how the sheep came to hear his music he was very happy. His music was no longer the sad sweet sound it had been when he was lonely. It became happier and happier. After a while it became so happy that the cat began to dance. When the sheep saw the cat dancing they began to dance, too.

Soon a company of monkeys passed that way and heard the sound of the music. They began dancing immediately. They made such a chattering that they almost drowned the music. The boy threatened to stop playing if they could not be happy without being so noisy. After that the monkeys chattered less.

After a while a tapir heard the jolly sound. Immediately his three toed hind feet and four toed front feet began to dance. He just couldn't keep them from dancing; so he, too, joined the procession of boy, cat, sheep, and monkeys.

Next the armadillo heard the music. In spite of his heavy armour he had to dance too. Then a herd of small deer joined the company. Then the anteater danced along with them. The wild cat and the tiger came, too. The sheep and the deer were terribly frightened, but they kept dancing on just the same. The tiger and wild cat were so happy dancing that they never noticed them at all. The big snakes curled their huge bodies about the tree trunks and wished that they, too, had feet with which to dance. The birds tried to dance, but they could not use their feet well enough and had to give it up and keep flying. Every beast of the forests and jungles which had feet with which to dance came and joined the happy procession.

The jolly company wandered on and on until finally they came to the high wall which surrounds the land of the giants. The enormous giant who stood on the wall as guard laughed so hard that he almost fell off the wall. He took them to the king at once. The king laughed so hard that he almost fell off his throne. His laugh shook the earth. The earth had never before been shaken at the laugh of the king of the giants, though it had often heard his angry voice in the thunder. The people did not know what to make of it.

Now it happened that the king of the land of giants had a beautiful giantess daughter who never laughed. She remained sad all the time. The king had offered half his kingdom to the one who could make her laugh, and all the giants had done their very funniest tricks for her. Never once had they brought even a tiny little smile to her lovely face. "If my daughter can keep from laughing when she sees this funny sight I'll give up in despair and eat my hat," said the king of the land of giants, as he saw the jolly little figure playing upon the violin and the assembly of cat, sheep, monkeys and everything else dancing to the happy music. If the giant king had known how to dance he would have danced himself, but it was fortunate for the people of the earth that he did not know how. If he had, there is no knowing what might have happened to the earth.

As it was, he took the little band into his daughter's palace where she sat surrounded by her servants. Her lovely face was as sad as sad could be. When she saw the funny sight her expression changed. The happy smile which the king of the land of giants had always wanted to see played about her beautiful lips. A happy laugh was heard for the first time in all her life. The king of the land of giants was so happy that he grew a league in height and nobody knows how much he gained in weight. "You shall have half my kingdom," he said to the boy, "just as I promised if anyone made my daughter laugh."

The boy from that time on reigned over half of the kingdom of giants as prince of the land. He never had the least bit of difficulty in preserving his authority, for the biggest giants would at once obey his slightest request if he played on his violin to them. The beasts stayed in the land of the giants so long that they grew into giant beasts, but the boy and his violin always remained just as they were when they entered the land.

The Devil And The Peasant

This story has been adapted from a tale originally told by Ramón A. Laval in Folk Tales in Chile, originally a Spanish language title, and, published in 1923 by Cervantes Printing House, Santiago De Chile.

Once upon a time, in a faraway land where the fields stretched as far as the eye could see, a cunning Devil approached a humble Peasant with an offer.

"Let us make a deal," the Devil proposed with a sly grin. "You will work the land, and I will provide the fields. We shall do this for three years, and when the time is up, the land shall be yours."

The Peasant, cautious but intrigued, asked, "And how shall we divide the harvest?"

The Devil chuckled, rubbing his hands together. "Simple! I shall take everything that grows above the ground, and you may keep everything that remains beneath it."

The Peasant nodded thoughtfully and agreed. The Devil, feeling smug and certain of victory, disappeared in a swirl of smoke, leaving the man to his work.

The Peasant, wise beyond his years, set to work and planted potatoes. The months passed, the seasons changed, and when the time came for the harvest, the Devil returned, eager to claim his prize. But when he stepped onto the field, he found himself staring at a disaster, for him, at least. All that remained above the soil were withered, worthless potato plants. But beneath the ground, the Peasant unearthed basket after basket of golden, plump potatoes.

"You tricked me!" the Devil howled, his tail twitching with fury.

"A deal is a deal," the Peasant said with a knowing smile.

The Devil stomped his feet, sending little clouds of smoke into the air. "This time, you will not make a fool of me," he growled. "Next year, I shall take everything that grows beneath the earth, and you shall keep what remains above it!"

"Agreed," the Peasant said with a twinkle in his eye.

And so, the Devil vanished, convinced that he had outwitted the clever farmer at last.

This time, the Peasant planted melons and watermelons, their thick vines curling across the ground. The sun rose and set, and the plants flourished, growing round and ripe under the open sky.

When the Devil arrived, eager to claim his reward, he dug deep into the soil, only to find nothing but roots. Meanwhile, the Peasant sat happily beside a mountain of juicy, sweet melons and plump, refreshing watermelons.

The Devil's face turned as red as fire. He clawed at his hair, sending sparks flying. "You cheated me again!" he bellowed.

The Peasant simply shrugged. "I only did as we agreed."

The Devil fumed, pacing in circles, his tail twitching like an angry snake. But he was not ready to admit defeat.

"This time, I will make sure there is no escape!" he hissed. "Next year, I shall take everything that grows above the ground AND everything that grows beneath it! You may only keep what grows in the middle."

"Agreed," the Peasant said without hesitation.

The Devil sneered, believing his victory was finally assured. With a puff of black smoke, he vanished into the night.

For the third and final year, the Peasant planted corn. As the months passed, the fields turned golden, and tall stalks swayed in the breeze, their ears of corn ripening perfectly in the middle.

The Devil arrived, grinning with wicked delight. He prepared to reap his victory, only to find himself defeated once more. Everything above the ground, the long stalks, belonged to him. Everything below, the tangled roots, also belonged to him. But the sweet, golden corn, the only thing of true worth, sat perfectly in the middle, rightfully belonging to the Peasant!

"You tricked me again!" the Devil roared, his voice shaking the earth.

The Peasant laughed, shouldering a basket of fresh corn. "A deal is a deal," he said one last time.

The Devil stomped his feet, shaking the fields with his rage. "You have beaten me," he admitted, scowling with fury. "Take your land, but mark my words, we shall meet again!"

And with that, he vanished in a cloud of fire and smoke, never to return.

With the cursed bargain broken, the Peasant claimed his land, which flourished for generations to come. And so, he proved a lesson that has echoed through time. "A man only loses to the Devil if he lets himself. But with a clever mind and a steady heart, even the greatest trickster can be outwitted."

And so, he lived happily ever after.

The Most Beautiful Princess

This story has been adapted from a tale originally told by Elsie Spicer Eells in Tales Of Giants from Brazil, published in 1918 by Dodd, Mead And Company, New York. Following the success of her previous work, Fairy Tales from Brazil,, this book focuses specifically on stories featuring giants, mythical beings of immense size and strength, from Brazilian folklore.

Once upon a time, in a distant kingdom, there lived a wise and noble king who had fallen gravely ill. His only hope for recovery, he believed, lay in a simple dish of hare broth. His devoted son, the young prince, determined to help his father, set out to the forest in search of a hare.

As he ventured along the woodland path, a delicate, golden-furred hare darted across his path from the hedge. Without hesitation, the prince gave chase. The hare, however, was no ordinary creature; it was incredibly swift, leading him deep into the heart of the forest. Just as he thought he might catch it, the hare disappeared into a hole beneath the roots of an ancient tree.

Driven by determination, the prince followed, only to find himself within a vast, dimly lit cave. At the far end of the cavern, seated upon a throne of bones, loomed the most monstrous giant he had ever seen.

"Oh ho!" rumbled the giant, his voice sending tremors through the cave. "You thought to catch my hare, did you? Well, now I have caught you instead!"

Before the prince could react, the giant snatched him up with a hand as large as a cartwheel and tossed him into a heavy iron chest. With a clang, the lid slammed shut and was locked with a massive key. Inside, the prince could barely breathe, only a tiny hole allowing him a sliver of air. Time passed in agony, his thoughts consumed with fear for his father and despair over his own fate.

At last, the lock turned, and the lid creaked open. To his astonishment, standing before him was the most beautiful maiden he had ever seen. Her eyes sparkled like the morning dew, and her smile was as warm as the sun.

"I am the hare you pursued," she said. "By day, I am cursed to take the form of a hare, but at night, I return to my true self. It was I who led you here, and I deeply regret that it has brought you such misfortune. But fear not, for I shall set you free."

The prince was mesmerized. "I would willingly remain here forever if only to gaze into your eyes," he declared.

She shook her head. "You would see nothing but a hare come sunrise. Besides, the giant is a merciless master. He has gone hunting, but should he return, you will surely be his supper. You must flee now, while you have the chance."

Reluctantly, the prince heeded her warning. He followed the escape path she pointed out and fled back to his father's palace. However, he was too late, his father had passed away, and the kingdom was draped in mourning.

Grief-stricken, the prince could not bear to remain in the palace. He left his title behind, disguising himself in the tattered clothes of a fisherman he met by the river. In exchange for his royal garments, the fisherman gave him a simple net, which, unknown to the prince, was enchanted, incapable of letting any fish escape.

As he wandered from kingdom to kingdom, catching his food with the magical net, he arrived in a grand city where a great festival was being held. The banners of the royal palace fluttered high, and each day a herald announced, " Our princess is the fairest in all the world!"

The prince scoffed. "I have seen a princess more beautiful," he muttered.

His words spread like wildfire. The king's guards seized him and dragged him before the throne. "You dare to claim my daughter is not the most beautiful in the world?" the king thundered. "You shall prove it. If you fail to present a princess fairer than mine within two weeks, you shall forfeit your life."

The prince agreed, certain of his quest. He retraced his steps to the enchanted forest, seeking the hidden entrance to the cave. However, a flood had reshaped the land, washing away all traces of his path. Desperate, he dug until he uncovered a great stone door. He knocked, and a tiny crack opened, revealing the wrinkled face of an elderly woman.

"I am the princess's caretaker," she said. "She has awaited your return."

Inside, the prince learned of the princess's plight. The enraged giant had imprisoned her in the iron chest in his fury, and at night, a great river encircled the cave, guarded by a monstrous fish that spewed vile curses.

The prince devised a plan. "Get into the chest with the princess," he told the old woman. "I'll swim out, and the wooden chest will float. Once you reach the surface, I will ensure your safe escape."

"But how will you defeat the guardian fish?" the woman asked.

"I have a net that no creature can break," he reassured her.

The moment he unbarred the door, the monstrous fish lunged at him. With skill and precision, he cast his enchanted net, capturing the beast. Dragging it to shore, he slew it and took its shimmering scales. As predicted, the chest floated to the surface, and he drew it safely to land. The princess emerged, her beauty more radiant than ever.

"You have freed me at last," she said. "I knew you would return."

Together, they travelled to the rival kingdom. As the prince presented the princess before the court, the nobles gasped, stunned into silence. The king himself looked at his daughter, then at the newcomer. "It is true," he admitted at last. "My daughter's nose is, ever so slightly, crooked."

He granted the prince his freedom, and the lovers returned to the prince's kingdom. There, they were wed with great rejoicing. From the moment the fish's scales fell upon the princess, her enchantment was broken, and she never again transformed into a hare. The giant, deprived of his prize, was never seen again.

And so, the prince and princess ruled with wisdom and love, never again daring to trespass in the giant's domain.

The Mystery of the Burnt Skeleton

This story is my own telling of a traditional Peruvian folk tale based on various sources.

Deep within the winding streets of Lima, Peru, there stood an old convent shrouded in mystery and intrigue. Tales of ghostly apparitions and unexplained phenomena had long surrounded the convent, sending shivers down the spines of all who heard them. But none were as chilling as the legend of the Burnt Skeleton.

It was said that many years ago, during the height of the Spanish Inquisition, the convent was home to a group of nuns who devoted their lives to prayer and penance. Among them was Sister Maria, a young novice known for her beauty and piety.

One fateful night, a fire broke out in the convent, its flames engulfing the building with terrifying speed. As the panicked nuns fled for their lives, Sister Maria remained behind, determined to save the sacred relics and artifacts housed within the convent's walls.

But as she reached the chapel, a sudden explosion rocked the building, sending debris flying in all directions. When the smoke cleared, all that remained was a pile of smouldering rubble, and the charred remains of Sister Maria.

In the days that followed, the convent was abandoned, its halls haunted by the ghostly apparition of Sister Maria. Locals whispered of strange happenings within its walls, of ghostly footsteps echoing in the night and mournful cries that pierced the darkness.

But it was not until years later that the truth behind Sister Maria's death was finally revealed. During renovations to the convent, workers stumbled upon a hidden chamber beneath the chapel, a chamber that contained a shocking discovery.

Beneath the rubble lay the burnt skeleton of a woman, her remains twisted and contorted by the heat of the fire. Beside her lay a rosary and a crucifix, their metal warped and melted by the flames.

As word of the discovery spread, so too did the legend of the Burnt Skeleton. Some believed that Sister Maria had been murdered, her death covered up by the convent's leaders. Others whispered of dark rituals and forbidden love, suggesting that Sister Maria had met her end at the hands of a jealous suitor.

But regardless of the truth, the legend of the Burnt Skeleton is a reminder of the dark secrets that lay hidden beneath the surface of the old convent, and of the tragic fate of Sister Maria, whose spirit still roams its halls, seeking justice for the injustice done to her in life.

The Little Sister Of The Giants

This story has been adapted from a tale originally told by Elsie Spicer Eells in Tales Of Giants from Brazil, published in 1918 by Dodd, Mead And Company, New York. Following the success of her previous work, Fairy Tales from Brazil,, this book focuses specifically on stories featuring giants, mythical beings of immense size and strength, from Brazilian folklore.

Once upon a time there was a little girl who was very beautiful. Her eyes were like the eyes of the gazelle; her hair hid in its soft waves the deep shadows of the night; her smile was like the sunrise. Each year as she grew older she grew also more and more beautiful. Her name was Angelita.

The little girl's mother was dead, and her father, the image-maker, had married a second time. The step-mother was a woman who was renowned in the city for her great beauty. As her little step-daughter grew more and more lovely each day of her life she soon became jealous of the child. Each night she asked the image-maker, "Who is more beautiful, your wife or your child?"

The image-maker was a wise man and knew all too well his wife's jealous disposition. He always responded, "You, my wife, are absolutely peerless."

One day the image-maker suddenly died, and the step-mother and step-daughter were left alone in the world. They both mourned deeply the passing of the kind image-maker.

One day as they were leaning over the balcony two passers-by observed them, and one said to the other, "Do you notice those beautiful women in the balcony? The mother is beautiful, but the daughter is far more beautiful." The step-mother had always been jealous of the daughter's loveliness, but now her jealousy was fanned into a burning flame. The wise image-maker was no longer there to tell her that she was peerless.

The next day the mother and daughter again leaned over the balcony. Two soldiers passed by and one said to the other, "Do you observe those two beautiful women in the balcony? The mother is beautiful, but the daughter is far more beautiful." The step-mother flew into a terrible rage. She now knew that it was true as she had long feared. The girl was more beautiful than she. Her jealousy knew no bounds. She seized her step-daughter roughly and shut her up in a little room in the attic.

The little room in the attic had just one tiny window high up in the wall. The window was shut, but Angelita climbed up to open it in order to get a little air. The next afternoon she grew weary of the confinement of the little room, so she dug a foothold in the wall where she could stand and look out of the window. Her step-mother was leaning over the balcony all alone when two cavalheiros passed by. One said to the other, "Do you observe the beautiful woman in the balcony?" "Yes," replied the other. "She is a beautiful woman, but the little maid who is kept a prisoner in the attic is far more beautiful."

The step-mother became desperate. She ordered the old servant to carry the girl into the jungle and kill her. "Be sure that you bring back the tip of Angelita's tongue, so that I may know that you have obeyed my order," she said.

Angelita was very happy to be taken out of the little attic room, and set out for a walk with the old servant with a light heart. They walked through the city streets and out into the open country. Soon they had reached the deep jungle. "Where are we going?" the girl asked in surprise.

"We are taking a walk for our health, yayazinha," replied the old servant.

Soon they were so far in the jungle that the path was entirely overgrown. No ray of light penetrated through the deep foliage. Angelita became frightened. "I'll not go another step if you do not tell me where you are taking me," she said as she stamped her little foot upon the ground.

The old servant burst into tears and told Angelita all that her step-mother had commanded. "I could not hurt one hair of your lovely head, much less cut off the tip of your little tongue, yayazinha," sobbed the old man.

Angelita stood still and thought. "Go back to my step-mother," she said to the old man. "On the way you will see plenty of dogs. Cut off the tip of a little dog's tongue and carry it home to my step-mother."

This is what the old servant did. The step-mother believed him and thought that he had slain her step-daughter according to her command.

Angelita, in the meantime, wandered on and on through the jungle. The big snakes glided swiftly out of her path. The monkeys and the parrots chattered to keep her from being lonely. She wandered on and on until finally she came to an enormous palace. The front door was wide open. She went from room to room, but the palace was entirely deserted. There was not a neat, orderly room in the entire palace.

"I can make these lovely rooms neat and clean," said Angelita. "They surely need someone to do it." She found a broom and went to work at once. Soon the whole palace was in order once more. Everything was clean and bright.

Just as Angelita was finishing her task she heard a great noise. She looked out of the door, and there were three enormous giants entering the house. She had never dreamed that giants could be so big. She was frightened nearly to death and scrambled under a chair as fast as she could.

When the giants came into the house they were amazed to find everything in such splendid order. "This is a different looking place from what we left," said the biggest giant.

"What dirty, disorderly giants we have been, living here all by ourselves," said the middle-sized giant. "I just realize it, now that I see what our house looks like when it is neat and clean."

"What kind fairy could have done all this work while we were away?" said the littlest giant, who was not little at all, but almost as big as his enormous brothers.

The three giants fell to discussing the question. They could not guess how their house could have been made so clean. Their voices were so very kind, in spite of being so loud and heavy, that Angelita decided she dare come out from under the chair and let them see who had done the work for them. She quickly crawled out from her hiding place.

"What lovely fairy is this?" asked the biggest giant, looking at her kindly. He thought that she really was a fairy.

"This is the loveliest fairy I ever saw in all my life," said the middle-sized giant.

"How did such a lovely fairy ever happen to find our dirty, disorderly palace?" asked the littlest giant who was not little at all.

Angelita told the three giants her story. Her beauty and her sweet ways completely entranced them.

"Please live with us always here in our palace in the jungle and be our little sister," said the biggest giant, and the middle-sized giant and the littlest giant, speaking all at once. Their three big deep voices all together made a noise like thunder.

Angelita lived in the palace with the three giants after that. Every day when they went out to hunt she would take the broom and make the palace neat and clean. They called her "little sister" and loved her with all their big giant hearts.

All was well until a little bird went and told Angelita's step-mother that she was alive and living in the depths of the jungle with the three giants. When the step-mother heard about it she was so angry that she thought she could never be happy as long as Angelita was living in the world. She consulted a wicked witch as soon as she could find her shawl.

The wicked witch gave the step-mother some poisoned slippers. "These will cause the immediate death of any person who puts them on," said the wicked witch. Then she showed the step-mother just how to reach the palace where Angelita lived in the depths of the jungle with the three giants.

Angelita's step-mother followed the directions which the witch had given her and easily found the giants' palace. Angelita was so happy living with the giants and keeping house for them that she had forgotten what fear was like. She was not frightened at all when she heard someone clap hands before the door one day when the giants were away. She went to the door; and, though she was very much surprised to see her step-mother, she invited her into the house. Her step-mother gave her a loving embrace and kissed her upon both cheeks. "Dear child, it is a long time since I have seen you," she said. "I have brought you a little gift to show you that I have not forgotten you. It is only a poor, mean little gift, but it is the best I could bring."

Angelita was touched at her step-mother's gift and accepted it with hearty thanks. As soon as her step-mother had gone she untied the red ribbon around the package and opened it. Inside was a pair of leather slippers. Angelita looked at the little slippers. They were like the slippers which her dear father, the image-maker, had once brought home to her. "How kind it was in my step-mother to bring these slippers to me," she said as she put them on.

As soon as the slippers were on Angelita's feet, she fell dead just as the wicked witch had promised the step-mother she would do. Her step-mother was watching through the window, and when she saw Angelita dead she hurried home in joy. "Now I, alone, am the peerless beauty," she said.

When the three giants came home to dinner they knew at once that there was something wrong. There were dirty tracks on the floor and dirty fingerprints upon the door. "Who made these dirty marks?" said the biggest giant.

"What has happened to our dear little sister that she has not cleaned them away?" asked the middle-sized giant.

"I am afraid there is something wrong with little sister," said the littlest giant who was not little at all.

They clapped their big hands before the door, but no smiling little sister ran to meet them. They entered the big hall of the palace with a bound. There in the middle of the floor lay Angelita, just as she had fallen when she put on the poisoned slippers which her step-mother had given her.

"What evil, has befallen our dear little sister?" said the biggest giant.

"Who could have slain our little sister whom we loved so much?" said the middle-sized giant.

"Who will keep house for us now that our dear little sister is dead?" asked the littlest giant.

Then the biggest giant and the middle-sized giant and the littlest giant all began to sob so loud that it shook the earth. "Our dear little sister is dead. What shall we do. What shall we do."

The giants could not go into the city to give their little sister Christian burial, but they built a beautiful casket out of silver and carried it to the path which led to the city. Then they hid themselves to watch and make sure that someone found it to carry to the burying place.

Soon a handsome prince passed by on horseback. He noticed the silver casket at once and opened it. The girl whose still form lay inside was the most beautiful maid he had ever gazed upon. "This dead maid is my own true love," he said and he carried the silver casket home to his own palace.

He commanded that no one should enter the room where he placed the silver casket, and this aroused the curiosity of his little sister at once. At the very first opportunity she slipped into the room. She opened the casket and was surprised to see the beautiful quiet maid. "You are very lovely," she said to the still form, "all except your slippers. I think they are very ugly." With these words she pulled off the leather slippers.

Angelita gave a deep sigh, opened her beautiful eyes, and asked for a drink of water.

The little sister called the prince at once. When he saw Angelita was really alive he could hardly believe the good fortune. He asked that the wedding night be celebrated immediately.

Angelita begged that she might go back into the deep jungle and invite the three giants to the wedding. The biggest giant, the middle-sized giant, and the littlest giant who was not little at all, came to the wedding feast. After that they visited their little sister often at her new home; and, when she had children of her own, it was the funniest sight one ever saw to see the biggest giant hold the tiny babes upon his knee.

The Forest Lad And The Wicked Giant

This story has been adapted from a tale originally told by Elsie Spicer Eells in Tales Of Giants from Brazil, published in 1918 by Dodd, Mead And Company, New York. Following the success of her previous work, Fairy Tales from Brazil,, this book focuses specifically on stories featuring giants, mythical beings of immense size and strength, from Brazilian folklore.

Once upon a time there was a man who took his wife and tiny baby son into the deep forest to make their home. With his own hands he built the house out of mud, and he made for it a thatched roof from the grass of the forest. For food they depended upon the fruits of the forest and the beasts which they killed in the hunt. They lived like hermits, seeing no one.

As the baby son grew into a large strong boy he learned from his father all the secrets of the forest. He grew wise as well as strong. From his mother he heard stories of their former life in the great city which had been their home before they went to live in the forest. These were the tales he loved to hear best of all. Very often when his father went out into the forest to hunt the boy would beg to remain at home with his mother. While his father was away she would sit on the ground before their hut and unfold to the boy all her memories of their old life.

"Father," said the lad one day after his father had returned from his hunting trip, "I am tired of living here in the forest all by ourselves. Let us return to the city to live."

"Your mother has been telling tales to you," replied his father. "I will see to it that she never mentions the city to you again. We left the city to save our lives. Let me never hear from you another word about returning to the city."

After that the lad was made to accompany his father when he went out hunting. There was no more opportunity to hear the tales he loved from his mother's lips. Nevertheless he hid away in his mind all that his mother had told him of their old life; and at night, when the fierce storms in the forest or the sound of the wild beasts would not let him sleep, he often lay awake upon his mat on the floor of the hut, pondering over the stories she had told.

At last the father grew sick of a fever and died. Now that the lad and his mother were left alone in the forest the lad said, "Come, let us return to our home in the city. Let us not stay here alone in the forest any longer. I must live in my own life the tales you have told me of the festas and the dancing, the great tournaments, and the songs at night under the balconies of the fair maidens."

The lad's request was so urgent that his mother could not have refused him, even if she, in her own heart, was not longing for a return to the life of the city. Accordingly, they took all their possessions, which consisted only of a horse and a sword, and set out for the city.

The lad and his mother reached the city at nightfall. They went from one street to another, but saw no living being. They knocked and clapped their hands before all the doors of the city, but no one responded. At last they reached the street where their old home had been. The lad was delighted to see what a big handsome house it was. "No wonder my mother longed to return to a home like this," he thought. "How could she ever have endured the rude hut in the depths of the forest?"

The doors of the beautiful house stood wide open. The lad and his mother entered, and passed from one room to another. His mother saw one room after another with everything unchanged. She recognized one object after another just as she had left it. There was one room in the house, which was securely barred on the inside, however.

The lad and his mother spent the night in their old home. In the morning they again walked about the deserted streets of the city. They saw no one and heard no living sound. It was like a city of the dead. They grew hungry at length; and the lad went outside the city to seek for food in the forest, according to the custom which he had known all his life.

The mother returned to her old home to await the coming of her son. As soon as she went upstairs she saw that the barred door was wide open. There in the hall stood the most enormous giant she had ever seen. The great halls of the house were high, but the giant could not stand up in them without stooping.

"Who are you and what are you doing in my house?" roared the giant in such a terrible voice that the house trembled.

The woman who had lived so many years in the forest was not easily frightened. "Who are you and what are you doing in my house?" she shouted at the giant in the loudest tones she could muster.

One might have expected that the giant would have killed her instantly, but on the contrary her bold answer pleased him exceedingly. He laughed so hard that he had to lean against the wall to keep from falling.

"So you think that this is your house, do you?" said the giant as soon as he could regain his voice. "Well, I'll tell you what we can do. I like you, and we can share this house if you will consent to be my wife."

"I am not alone," said the lad's mother as soon as she could recover from her surprise sufficiently to find words. "My son is with me and I am expecting him any moment to return from the forest whither he has gone to procure food for us."

"I can dispose of your son very quickly, just as I have destroyed all the inhabitants of this city," said the giant with a frown.

"You cannot dispose of my son so easily as you may think," replied his mother. "He has grown in the deep forest and is very strong, far stronger than the city dwellers. Besides his great strength, he is surrounded by the magic circle of his mother's love."

"I do not know what the magic circle of a mother's love is like," said the giant. "I don't remember having seen one anywhere. Nevertheless I like you, and because I like you I will endeavour to dispose of your son as painlessly as possible. I believe you say you are expecting him any moment. Just lie down here and pretend that you are sick. When the boy comes in tell him that you have a terrible pain in your eyes. As you have lived long in the forest you will know that the best remedy for a pain in your eyes is the oil of the deadly cobra of the jungle. Send the lad out into the jungle to obtain this oil for you, and I promise you he will never return alive. I'll go back into my room and bar the door so the boy will never see me, but I shall listen through the wall to know whether you carry out my command."

At that very moment they heard the lad's footsteps and his happy voice at the door. The giant went inside his room and barred the door. The lad's mother lay down with a cloth over her eyes, moaning in loud tones. "The giant little knows the strength and skill of the lad whose mother I am," she said to herself as she smiled amidst her moans and groans.

"Oh dear little mother, what evil has befallen you during my absence?" asked the boy as he entered the room.

His mother complained of the pain in her eyes just as the giant had instructed. "The only thing which will cure me of this terrible affliction is the oil of the cobra," she said.

The boy well knew the dangers which attended securing the oil from the deadly cobra of the jungle, but never in his life had he disregarded a request from his mother. He at once set out for the jungle; and, in spite of the perils of the deed, he succeeded in obtaining the oil which his mother had requested.

On the way back to the city, the boy met a little old woman carrying a pole over her shoulder from which there hung, head downward, several live fowls which she was taking to market. It was really the Holy Mother herself who had come to aid the lad in answer to his mother's prayer.

"Where are you going, my lad?" asked the old woman. The boy told his story and showed the precious oil which he had obtained from the cobra. "The day is coming, the day is coming, my lad, when you will, in truth, need the cobra's oil," said the little old woman. "But that day is not today. Today hen's oil will serve your purpose just as well. You may kill one of my hens and use the hen's oil, but leave the cobra's oil with me so that I may keep it safely for you until the day when you will require it."

The boy heeded the advice of the little old woman and killed one of her hens. He left the cobra's oil with her and took the hen's oil in its place to his mother. Because his mother had nothing at all the matter with her eyes, the hen's oil cured them just as well as the cobra's oil. There was no one who knew the difference, except the boy and the little old woman.

When the boy had gone out the giant came in from his own room and said, "In truth your son is a brave lad. I did not dream that he would have the courage to go in search of the oil of the deadly cobra, much less succeed in his quest."

"You do not know the great love we bear each other," said the lad's mother.

"I am going to demand a new proof of your son's strength and skill," said the giant. "Tomorrow you must complain of the pain in your back and send the boy in search of the oil of the porcupine to cure it. This is my command."

The next day the woman had to complain of a pain in her back just as the giant had commanded. There was nothing else which she could do. The boy at once went in search of a porcupine, and succeeded in slaying one and getting the oil.

On his way back to the city the lad again met the little old woman who was really Nossa Senhora. "Leave the oil of the porcupine with me, my son," said she when she had heard his story. "I will keep it for you until the morrow when you will have great need of it. Today hen's oil will serve your purpose just as well."

Because the boy's mother had nothing at all the matter with her back she was cured with the hen's oil which the boy brought, just as easily as if it had been the porcupine's oil. The giant came out of his room and said, "In truth, lad, you are a boy of great skill and strength."

The boy had not seen the giant before and he was very much surprised. Before he even had time to recover from his amazement the giant had seized him and bound him securely with a great rope. "If you are really a strong boy you will break this rope," said the giant. "If you are not strong enough to break it I shall cut you into five pieces with my sword."

The boy struggled with all his might to break the great rope. It was no use. He was not strong enough. The giant stood by laughing.

When the lad's mother saw that he could not break the rope she fell upon her knees before the giant and cried, "Do what you will to me, but spare my son."

The cruel giant laughed at her request. When she saw that she could not keep him from slaying the boy, she said, "If you will not grant my large request I beg that you will listen to just a tiny, tiny, little one. When you cut my son into five pieces do it with his father's sword which he has brought with him from the little hut in the forest where we used to live. Then bind his body upon the back of his father's horse which he brought with him out of the forest and turn the horse loose, so it may travel, perchance, back to the forest from which I brought my lad to meet this terrible death."

The giant did as she requested, and the horse bore the slain boy's body along the road to the forest. Outside the city they met the little old woman who was really Nossa Senhora. She took the parts of the lad's body and anointed them with the porcupine's oil. Then she held them tight together. They stayed securely joined. "Are you lacking anything," she asked the boy.

The boy felt of his legs, his arms, his ears, his nose, his hair. "I am all here except my eyesight," he said. The little old woman anointed his eyes with the cobra's oil. His sight was immediately restored. Then he knew that the little old woman was indeed the Holy Mother. She vanished as he knelt to receive her blessing.

The boy in his new strength quickly hastened back to the city. It was night and the giant was asleep. He seized his father's sword and plunged it into the giant's body. The giant turned over without awakening. "The mosquitoes are biting me," he muttered in his sleep.

The boy saw the giant's own enormous sword lying on the floor. It was so heavy he could barely lift it, but mustering all his strength he drove it into the giant's body. The giant died immediately.

"The magic circle of a mother's love, with the Holy Mother's help, will guard a lad against all perils," said the boy's mother when she heard her son's story and saw the giant lying dead.

The Three Brothers Who Went Out To Learn To Speak

This story has been adapted from a tale originally told by Ramón A. Laval in Folk Tales in Chile, originally a Spanish language title, and, published in 1923 by Cervantes Printing House, Santiago De Chile.

Once upon a time, in a land of rolling hills and golden fields, there lived a wealthy huaso, a proud farmer with vast lands and a fine estate. He had three sons, but, to his great despair, they were fools. They could barely string a proper sentence together, mumbling nonsense whenever they spoke. Determined to change this, the huaso called them before him.

"I cannot bear this any longer." he declared. "You must go out into the world and learn to speak properly, like true gentlemen! I will give you money for your journey, but you are not to return until you can hold a conversation with dignity."

And so, the three foolish brothers set off on their adventure, eager to return one day as fine, eloquent men.

Their travels took them far, and soon, they found themselves in a bustling town, filled with grand buildings and lively streets. Hungry from their journey, they entered a tavern, where the air was thick with the scent of roasting meat and the sound of dice clattering and dominoes clicking. As they ate, they listened closely to the well-dressed gentlemen at the table beside them, hoping to learn the art of conversation.

The eldest brother was captivated by a phrase spoken by one of the players. When asked who had won the game, the man casually replied, "We have won." The words sounded elegant and wise to the foolish brother. He repeated them under his breath, over and over, until they were etched into his memory.

The second brother's ears perked up when another player was asked why he was playing, to which he responded, "To win money."

"Ah! What a splendid phrase!" thought the second brother. He whispered it to himself a hundred times, determined never to forget it.

The youngest brother, not wanting to be left behind, seized upon another phrase spoken with great importance by one of the men, which was "For a very just cause."

He muttered it again and again, convinced he had learned something grand.

Feeling triumphant with their new knowledge, the brothers set off for home, eager to show their father the impressive words they had acquired.

As they journeyed across the countryside, they passed through a lonely field, where something horrifying caught their eye. Lying on the ground, motionless and covered in blood, was a dead man. He had been murdered, and fresh red stains soaked the earth beneath him. The three brothers stared in shock, their mouths hanging open, unable to comprehend what lay before them.

Before they could move, a mounted guard appeared, his eyes narrowing as he took in the scene. "You there!" he barked. "Who killed this man?"

The eldest brother, still proud of his newly learned phrase, puffed out his chest and declared confidently, "We have won."

The guard's face hardened. "What? So you admit to killing him?"

The second brother, eager to contribute, nodded enthusiastically. "To win money," he added.

The guard's eyes blazed with fury. "Thieves and murderers!" he roared. "You will all be thrown in prison!"

The youngest brother, not wanting to be left out, solemnly nodded and whispered, "For a very just cause."

And so, the three foolish brothers were dragged to the town prison, their wrists bound, as villagers muttered in horror at the terrible crime.

The next morning, they were taken before the great judge, who sat upon his high wooden chair, frowning down at them.

"These three men," the guard announced, "have confessed to murder! They must be punished!"

The judge, however, did not look convinced. He had heard of these three before, the sons of the rich huaso, known throughout the land for their utter foolishness. He studied them carefully. The eldest grinned like a fool. The second nodded eagerly. The youngest beamed with pride, as though he had won a prize.

With a deep sigh, the judge shook his head. "These men are not murderers," he said at last. "They are fools."

The court burst into laughter, and the three brothers were set free, much to the relief of their father. But from that day forward, no one ever trusted them to speak wisely again, and so, they never did.

How The Giantess Guimara Became Small

This story has been adapted from a tale originally told by Elsie Spicer Eells in Tales Of Giants from Brazil, published in 1918 by Dodd, Mead And Company, New York. Following the success of her previous work, Fairy Tales from Brazil,, this book focuses specifically on stories featuring giants, mythical beings of immense size and strength, from Brazilian folklore.

Once upon a time a prince called Don Joaõ went hunting with a number of companions. In the deep forest he became separated from his comrades and soon found out that he was lost. He wandered about for a long time, and at last he spied what looked like a mountain range in the distance. He journeyed toward it as fast as he could travel, and when he got near to it he was surprised to find out that it was really a high wall. It was the great wall which bounds the land of the giants. The ruler of the country was an enormous giant whose head reached almost to the clouds. The giant's wife was nearly as enormous as he was, and their only child was as tall as her mother. Her name was Guimara.

When the giant saw Don Joaõ he called out, "Oh, little man, what are you doing down there?" Don Joaõ narrated his adventures to the giant, and the giant said, "Your story of your wanderings interests me. It is not often that little men like you pass this way. If you like you may live in my palace and be my servant." Don Joaõ accepted the giant's offer and stayed at the palace.

The giant's daughter Guimara was very much pleased with Don Joaõ . He was the first little man she had ever seen. She fell deeply in love with him. Her father, however, was very much disgusted at her lack of good taste. He preferred to have a giant for a son-in-law. Accordingly he thought of a plot to get Don Joaõ into trouble.

The next day he sent for Don Joaõ to appear before him. "Oh little man," he said to him, "they tell me that you are very proud of yourself and that you are boasting among my servants that you are able to tear down my palace in a single night and set it up again as quickly as you tore it down."

"I never have made any such boast, your majesty," replied Don Joaõ.

He went to Guimara and told her about it. "I am an enchantress," said Guimara. "Leave it to me and we will surprise my father."

The very next night Guimara and Don Joaõ tore down the giant's palace and set it up again exactly as it was before. The giant was greatly surprised. He suspected that his daughter had meddled with the affair.

The next day he sent for Don Joaõ and said to him, "Oh little man, they tell me that you say that in a single night you are able to change the Isle of Wild Beasts into a beautiful garden full of all sorts of flowers and with a silvery fountain in the centre."

"I never said any such thing, your majesty," replied Don Joaõ .

He told Guimara about it and she said that it would be great fun to escape from her room that night and make over the Isle of the Wild Beasts into a lovely garden.

Accordingly Guimara worked hard all night long helping Don Joaõ to make the Isle of the Wild Beasts over into a garden full of all sorts of beautiful flowers and with a silvery fountain in the centre. The king was greatly surprised to see the garden in the morning and he was very angry at Guimara and Don Joaõ .

Guimara was so frightened at her father's terrible wrath that she decided to run away with Don Joaõ . She counselled him to procure the best horse from her father's stable for them to ride.

At midnight Guimara crept out of her room and ran to the place where Don Joaõ was waiting for her with the horse, which travelled one hundred leagues at each step. They mounted the horse and rode away.

Early the next morning the princess Guimara was missed from the royal palace. Soon it was discovered that Don Joaõ was gone too, and also the best horse from the stables. The giant talked over the matter with his wife. She told him to take another horse which could travel a hundred leagues a step and go after them as fast as he could. The giant followed his wife's advice, and soon he had nearly caught up with the fugitives, for they had grown tired and had stopped to rest.

Guimara spied her father coming and turned herself into a little river. She turned Don Joaõ into an old servant, the horse into a tree, the saddle into a bed of onions, and the musket they carried into a butterfly.

When the giant came to the river he called out to the old servant who was taking a bath, "Oh, my old servant, have you seen anything of a little man accompanied by a handsome young woman?"

The old servant did not say a single word to him, but dived into the water. When he came out he called the giant's attention to the bed of onions. "I planted these onions," he said. "Aren't they a good crop?"

The bed of onions smelled so strong that the giant did not like to stay near them. The butterfly flew at the giant's eyes and almost into them. He was disgusted and went home to talk it over with his wife.

"How silly you were," said the giant's wife. "Don't you see that Guimara had changed herself into a river and had changed Don Joaõ into an old servant, the horse into a tree, the saddle into a bed of onions, and the musket into a butterfly? Hurry after them at once."

The giant again went in pursuit, promising his wife that next time he would not let Guimara play any tricks on him. The next time that Guimara saw her father coming she thought of a new plan. She changed herself into a church. She turned Don Joaõ into a padre, the horse into a bell, the saddle into an altar and the musket into a mass-book.

When the giant approached the church he was completely deceived. "Oh, holy padre," he said to the priest, "have you seen anything of a little man, accompanied by a handsome young woman, passing this way?"

The padre went on with his mass and said:

"I am a hermit padre

Devoted to the Immaculate;

I do not hear what you say.

Dominus vobiscum. "

The giant could get no other response from him. At last he gave up in despair and went home to talk things over with his wife.

"Of all stupid fools you are the most stupid of all," said his wife when she had heard the tale. "Don't you see that Guimara has changed herself into a church, Don Joaõ into a priest, the horse into a bell, the saddle into the altar, and the musket into the mass-book? Hurry after them again as fast as you can. I am going with you, myself, this time, to see that Guimara does not play any more tricks on you."

This time the fugitives had travelled far when Guimara's parents overtook them. They had almost reached Don Joaõ 's own kingdom. Guimara threw a handful of dust into her parents' eyes, and it became so dark that they could not see. Guimara and Don Joaõ escaped safely into his own kingdom.

When they had started out on the journey, Guimara had said, "Oh, Don Joaõ , whatever happens, don't forget me for one single minute. Think of me all the time." He had promised and he had remembered her every instant on the journey. However, when they reached his own kingdom, he was so happy to see home once more after all his adventures that he thought he had never before been so happy in all his life. After one has been living in Giantland it is very pleasant to get home where things are a few sizes smaller and a bit more convenient. Then, too, it was very pleasant for him to see all his friends again. He was so happy at being home that, just for one little minute, he forgot all about Guimara.

When Don Joaõ remembered Guimara he turned around to look at her. When he saw her he could hardly believe his eyes. Instead of being a tall, tall giantess with her head up in the clouds, she reached just to Don Joaõ 's own shoulder. Don Joaõ was so surprised that he had to sit down in a chair and be fanned. He couldn't say a single word for eighteen minutes and a half--his breath had been so completely taken away.

"It is a good thing that you happened to think of me just as soon as you did," remarked Guimara. "I was getting smaller and smaller. If you had neglected to think of me for another minute I should have faded away entirely and you would have never known what had become of me."

When Guimara became small she lost her power as an enchantress entirely. Her lovely eyes were always a trifle sad because Don Joaõ had forgotten her that one little minute. She never went back to Giantland but reigned as queen of Don Joaõ 's kingdom for many years.

The Vision of Yupanqui

This story has been adapted from a tale originally told by Lewis Spence in The Myths of Mexico & Peru, published in 1913 by Thomas Y. Crowell of New York..

Long ago, in the golden age of the Incas, before he wore the crown of the empire, Prince Yupanqui journeyed through the sacred lands of his ancestors. He was on his way to visit his father, Viracocha Inca, the great ruler of the Andes.

His path took him deep into the mountains, where rivers sang to the stones and the winds whispered the secrets of the gods. As he wandered through the sacred valley, he came upon a fountain, nestled in the heart of the wilderness. The water was so clear it seemed like a piece of the sky had fallen to the earth. But as Yupanqui bent down to drink, something strange happened.

From the depths of the fountain, a shimmering crystal emerged, falling into his hands as if placed there by unseen forces. And as he peered into the crystal's heart, he saw a vision that stole his breath away.

Before him stood a warrior unlike any he had ever seen. The figure was mighty and radiant, his skin gleaming like burnished gold. Upon his forehead, he wore a royal fringe, the mark of an Inca ruler, yet his presence was not entirely human. From behind his head, three blazing rays shone like the very sun itself. Around his arms and shoulders, serpents coiled and slithered, their scales shimmering with power. His ears bore great golden discs, as only the lords of the Incas could wear. And yet, the most fearsome of all was the great lion's head resting between his legs, while another mighty puma draped over his shoulders like a cloak of the gods.

Yupanqui's heart thundered in his chest. This was no man. This was something beyond mortal understanding. Fear took hold of him, and he turned to flee. But before he could take another step, a voice filled the air, powerful and eternal.

"Do not run, Yupanqui."

The prince froze. The voice spoke his name, yet it was not the voice of a man, for it was like the wind and the fire, the mountains and the sky, all speaking as one.

"Do not fear me, for I am your father, the Sun."

Yupanqui fell to his knees, trembling. The Sun, the great and sacred Inti, had come to him!

"You will rise to be a mighty ruler," the voice continued. "You will conquer many nations, and your name will be sung in the temples long after you are gone. But you must remember this. All that you achieve, all that you build, must honour me. Your victories are my light made flesh. Raise temples in my name, offer me reverence, and your kingdom shall flourish like the golden fields beneath my gaze."

Then, as suddenly as it had appeared, the vision faded. The warrior was gone, the light dimmed, and the crystal in Yupanqui's hands fell still. But something had changed. The prince was no longer just a man, he was chosen.

When Yupanqui ascended to the throne, he never forgot the vision he had seen in the sacred fountain. He carried the crystal always, and through it, he could glimpse things beyond the sight of ordinary men, his enemies, his victories, and the will of the gods.

He ordered his finest artisans to craft a statue of the Sun, capturing the very likeness of the radiant warrior he had beheld in the crystal. Gold and jewels adorned its form, and it stood as a beacon to all his people.

And as he marched forth to conquer distant lands, he carried the name of Inti, the Sun, upon his lips. His enemies fell before him, for the Sun was at his back, and his destiny was carved in the light.

Across the empire, temples of gold rose in honour of the mighty Inti. No longer did the people worship the distant creator alone, they bowed before the Sun, the father of the Incas, the giver of life, the god who had spoken to Yupanqui himself.

And so, through the vision in the fountain, a new age dawned upon the land of the Incas, and the sun burned ever brighter upon its golden kingdom.

The Adventures Of A Fisherman's Son

This story has been adapted from a tale originally told by Elsie Spicer Eells in Tales Of Giants from Brazil, published in 1918 by Dodd, Mead And Company, New York. Following the success of her previous work, Fairy Tales from Brazil,, this book focuses specifically on stories featuring giants, mythical beings of immense size and strength, from Brazilian folklore.

Long ago there was a man and woman who lived in a little mud hut under the palm trees on the riverbank. They had so many children they did not know what to do. The little hut was altogether too crowded. The man had to work early and late to find food enough to feed so many. One day the seventh son said to his father, "Oh, father, I found a little puppy yesterday when I was playing on the bank of the river. Please let me bring it home to keep. I have always wanted one."

The father consented sadly. He did not know how to find food for the children, and an extra puppy to feed seemed an added burden. He went to the riverbank to fish that day with a heavy heart. He cast his net in vain. He did not catch a single fish. He cast his net from the other side with no better luck. He did not catch even one little piabinha.

Suddenly he heard a voice which seemed to come from the riverbed itself, it was so deep. This is what it said, "If you will give me whatever new you find in your house when you go home I will give you fisherman's luck. You will catch all the fish you wish."

The man remembered the request which his seventh son had made that morning. "The new thing I'll find in my house when I get home will be that puppy," said the man to himself. "This will be a splendid way to get rid of the puppy which I did not want to keep anyway."

Accordingly the man consented to the request which came from the strange voice in the depths of the river. "You must seal this covenant with your blood," said the voice.

The man cut his finger a tiny bit with his sharp knife and squeezed a few drops of blood from the wound into the river. "If you break this vow the curse of the river giant will be upon you and your children for ever and ever," said the deep voice solemnly.

The fisherman cast his net where the river giant commanded, and immediately it was so full of fish that the man could hardly draw it out of the water. Three times he drew out his net, so full that it was in danger of breaking. "Truly this was a fortunate bit of business," said the man. "Here I have fish enough to feed my family and all I can sell in addition."

As the fisherman approached his house with his enormous catch of fish one of the children came running to meet him. "Oh father, guess what we have at our house which we did not have when you went away," said the child.

"A new puppy," replied her father.

"Oh no, father," replied the child. "You have not guessed right at all. It is a new baby brother."

The poor fisherman burst into tears. "What shall I do. What shall I do." he sobbed. "I dare not break my vow to the river giant."

The fisherman's wife was heartbroken when she heard about the business which her husband had transacted with the river giant. However she could think of no way to escape from keeping the contract which he had made. She kissed the tiny babe good-bye and gave it her blessing. Then the fisherman took it down to the riverbank and threw it into the river at the exact spot from which the deep voice had come.

There in the depths of the river the river giant was waiting to receive the newborn babe. He took the little one into his palace of gold and silver and mother-of-pearl with ornaments of diamonds, and there the baby received excellent care.

Time passed and the little boy grew into a big boy. At last he was fifteen years old and a handsome lad indeed, tall and straight, with eyes which were dark and deep like the river itself, and hair as dark as the shades in the depths of the river. All his life he had been surrounded with every luxury, but he had never seen a single person. He had never seen even the river giant. All he knew of him was his deep voice which gave orders in the palace.

One day the voice of the river giant said, "I have to go away on a long journey. I will leave with you all the keys to all the doors in the palace, but do not meddle with anything. If you do you must forfeit your life."

Many days passed and the lad did not hear the voice of the river giant. He missed its sound in the palace. It was very still and very lonely. At last at the end of fifteen days he took one of the keys which the river giant had left and opened the door which it fitted. The door led into a room in the palace where the boy had never been. Inside the room was a huge lion. The lion was fat and well nourished, but there was nothing for it to eat except hay. The boy did not meddle with anything and shut the door.

Another fifteen days passed by, and again the lad took one of the keys. He opened another door in the palace which he had never entered. Inside the room he found three horses, one black, one white, and one chestnut. There was nothing in the room for the horses to eat except meat, but in spite of it they were fat and well nourished. The boy did not touch anything and when he went out he shut the door.

At the end of another fifteen days all alone without even the voice of the river giant for company, the lad tried another key in another door. This room opened into a room full of armour. There were daggers and knives and swords and muskets and all sorts of armour which the boy had never seen and did not know anything about. He was very much interested in what he saw, but he did not meddle with anything.

The next day he opened the room again where the horses were kept. This time one of the horses,--the black one,--spoke to him and said, "We like hay to eat very much better than this meat which was left to us by mistake. The lion must have our hay. Please give this meat to the lion and bring us back our hay. If you will do this as I ask I'll serve you for ever and ever."

The boy took the meat to the lion. The lion was very much pleased to exchange the hay for it. The lad then took the hay to the horses. All at once he remembered how he had been told not to meddle with anything. This had been meddling. The boy burst into tears. "I shall lose my life as the punishment for this deed," he sobbed.

The horses listened in amazement. "I got you into this trouble," said the black horse. "Now I'll get you out. Just trust me to find a way out."

The black horse advised the boy to take some extra clothes and a sword and musket and mount upon his back. "I have lived here in the depths of the river so long that my speed is greater than that of the river itself," said the horse. "If there was any doubt of it before, now that I have had some hay once more I am sure I can run faster than any river in the world."

It was true. When the river giant came back home and found that the boy had meddled he ran as fast as he could in pursuit of the lad. The black horse safely and surely carried the lad beyond his reach.

The black horse and his rider travelled on and on until finally they came to a kingdom which was ruled over by a king who had three beautiful daughters. The lad at once applied for a position in the service of this king. "I do not know what you can do," said the king. "You have such soft white hands. Perhaps you may serve to carry bouquets of flowers from my garden every morning to my three daughters."

The lad had eyes which were dark and deep like the depths of the river, and when he carried bouquets of flowers from the garden to the king's daughters the youngest princess fell in love with him at once. Her two sisters laughed at her. "I don't care what you say," said the youngest princess. "He is far handsomer than any of the princes who have ever sung of love beneath our balcony."

That very night two princes from neighbouring kingdoms came to sing in the palace garden beneath the balcony of the three princesses. The two oldest daughters of the king were proud and haughty, but the youngest princess had love in her heart and love in her eyes. For this reason she was one whom all the princes admired most.

The lad from the river listened to their songs. "I wish I looked like these two princes and knew songs like theirs," said he. Just then he caught sight of his own reflection in the fountain in the garden. He saw that he looked quite as well as they. "I too will sing a song before the balcony of the princesses," he decided.

He did not know that he could sing, but in truth his voice had in it all the music of the rushing of the river. When he sang even the two rival musicians stopped to listen to his song. The two older princesses did not know who was singing, but the youngest princess recognized him at once.

The next day a great tournament took place. The lad from the river had never seen a tournament, but after he had watched it for a moment he decided to enter. He went to get the black horse which had carried him out of the depths of the river and the arms he had brought with him from the palace of the river giant. With such a horse and such arms he carried off all the honours of the tournament. Everyone at the tournament wondered who the strange cavalheiro could be. No one recognized him except the youngest princess. She knew who it was the moment she saw him and gave him her ribbon to wear.

The next day all the cavalheiros who had taken part in the tournament set out to slay the wild beast which often came out of the jungle to attack the city. It was the lad from the river who killed the beast, as all the cavalheiros knew. When they returned to the palace with the news that the beast had been slain, the king said, "Tomorrow night we will hold the greatest festa which this palace has ever witnessed. Tomorrow let all the cavalheiros who are here assembled go forth to hunt for birds to grace our table."

The next day the cavalheiros went out to hunt the birds, and it was the lad from the river who succeeded in slaying the birds. None of the other cavalheiros were at all successful. The two neighbouring princes who were suitors for the hand of the youngest princess made a contract. "We cannot let this stranger carry off all the honours," said one to the other. "You say that you killed the beast, and I will say that it was I who killed the birds."

That night at the festa one prince stood up before the king and told his story of slaying the beast, and the other prince stood up and told how he had killed the birds. The other cavalheiros knew that it was false, but when they looked around for the cavalheiro who had done the valiant deeds they could not find him. The lad from the river had on his old clothes which he wore as a servant in the garden and stood at the lower part of the banquet hall among the servants.

When the king had heard the stories of the two princes he was greatly pleased with what they had done. "The one who killed the beast shall have a princess for a bride," said he, "and the one who killed the birds he too shall have a princess for his bride."

The youngest princess saw the lad from the river standing among the servants and smiled into his eyes. The lad came and threw himself before the king. "Oh my king," said he, "these stories to which you have listened are false, as all these assembled cavalheiros will prove.

It is I who killed the beast and all the birds. I claim a princess as my bride."

All the assembled cavalheiros recognized the lad in spite of his changed appearance in his gardening clothes. "Viva." they shouted. "He speaks the truth. He is the valiant one of us who killed the beast and the birds. To him belongs the reward."

The youngest princess had a heart filled with joy. The wedding feast was celebrated the very next day. The river giant found out about it and sent a necklace of pearls and diamonds as a wedding gift to the bride of the lad whom he had brought up in his palace. The fisherman and his wife, however, never knew the great good fortune which had come to their son.

The Legend of Viracocha

This story is my own telling of a traditional Peruvian folk tale based on various sources.

In the ancient land of the Incas, nestled amidst the towering peaks of the Andes, there lived a powerful deity known as Viracocha, the creator of all things. According to legend, Viracocha emerged from the depths of Lake Titicaca, the sacred waters giving birth to the world and all its wonders.

Viracocha was revered by the people of the Andes as the supreme god, the bringer of life and the architect of the universe. It was said that he possessed the power to shape the earth and the heavens, moulding the mountains and the valleys with his mighty hands.

But despite his divine status, Viracocha was a humble and benevolent deity, who walked among mortals in disguise, teaching them the ways of civilization and enlightenment. He travelled far and wide, wandering through the Andean highlands and the lush valleys, bestowing his wisdom upon those who were worthy.

One day, as Viracocha journeyed through the mountains, he came upon a barren wasteland, where the people lived in squalor and despair. Moved by their plight, Viracocha took pity on them and resolved to bring them prosperity and abundance.

With a wave of his hand, Viracocha transformed the desolate landscape into a fertile paradise, where fields of golden corn swayed in the breeze and crystal-clear rivers flowed through the valleys. He taught the people how to cultivate the land and harness its bountiful resources, imparting to them the knowledge they needed to thrive.

Under Viracocha's guidance, the people flourished, their villages growing into thriving communities, their hearts filled with gratitude for the divine gift they had received. They built temples and monuments in honour of Viracocha, offering prayers and sacrifices to express their eternal reverence for the god who had bestowed such blessings upon them.

But as time passed, the memory of Viracocha began to fade, his deeds becoming little more than myths and legends passed down through the generations. Yet still, his presence lingered in the hearts of the people. To this day, the legend of Viracocha lives on in the folklore of the Andes, a reminder of the ancient wisdom and boundless compassion of the creator god who shaped the destiny of a nation and left an indelible mark upon the land.

The Beast Slayer

This story has been adapted from a tale originally told by Elsie Spicer Eells in Tales Of Giants from Brazil, published in 1918 by Dodd, Mead And Company, New York. Following the success of her previous work, Fairy Tales from Brazil,, this book focuses specifically on stories featuring giants, mythical beings of immense size and strength, from Brazilian folklore.

Once upon a time there was a man and his wife who were very poor. The man earned his living making wooden bowls and platters to sell and worked early and late, but wooden bowls and platters were so very cheap that he could barely support his family no matter how hard he worked. The man and his wife were the parents of three lovely daughters. They were all exceedingly beautiful, and the man and his wife often lamented the fact that they did not have money enough to educate them and clothe them fittingly.

One day there came to the door of the poor man's house a handsome young man mounted on a beautiful horse. He asked to buy one of the poor man's daughters. The father was very much shocked at this request. "I may be poor," said he, "but I am not so poor that I have to sell my children."

The young man, however, threatened to kill him if he refused to do his bidding; so finally, after a short struggle, the father consented to part with his eldest daughter. He received a great sum of money in return.

The father was now a rich man and did not wish to make bowls and platters any longer. His wife, however, urged him to keep on with his former occupation. Accordingly he went on with his work. The very next day there came to his door another young man, even handsomer than the other, mounted upon even a finer horse. This young man made the same request that the other had done. He wanted to buy one of the daughters.

The father burst into tears and told all the dreadful happenings of the day before. The young man, however, showed no pity and continued to demand one of the daughters. He made fearful threats if the man would not yield to his request, and the father became so frightened that he at length parted with his second daughter. The first young man had paid a great sum of money, but this one paid even more.

Though he was now very rich the father still went on making bowls and platters to please his wife. The next day when he was at work the handsomest young man he had ever seen appeared riding upon a most beautiful steed. This young man demanded the third daughter. The poor father had to yield just as before, though it nearly broke his heart to part with his only remaining child. The price which the young man paid was so very great that the family was now as rich as it had once been poor.

Their home was not childless very long, for soon a baby son came to them. They brought up the boy in great luxury. One day when the child was at school he quarrelled with one of his playmates. This taunt was thrown in his face, "Ah, ha. You think your father was always rich, do you? He is a rich man now, it is true, but it is because he sold your three sisters." The words made the boy sad, but he said nothing about the matter at home. He hid it away in his mind until he had become a man. Then he went to his father and mother and demanded that they should tell him all about it.

His parents told the young man the whole story of the strange experiences through which they had obtained their wealth. "I am now a man," said the son. "I feel that it is right that I should go out into the world in search of my sisters. Perhaps I might be able to find them and aid them in some way. Give me your blessing and allow me to go."

His father and mother gave him their blessing, and the young man started out to make a search through all the world. Soon he came to a house where there were three brothers quarrelling over a boot, a cap, and a key. "What is the matter?" asked the young man. "Why are these things so valuable that you should quarrel over them?"

The brothers replied that if one said to the boot, "Oh Boot, put me somewhere," the boot would immediately put him anywhere he wished to go. If one said to the cap, "Oh Cap, hide me," immediately the cap would hide him so he could not be seen. The key could unlock any door in the whole world. The young man at once wanted to own these things himself, and he offered so much money for them that at last the three brothers decided to end their quarrel by selling the boot, the cap, and the key and dividing the money.

The young man put the three treasures in his saddle bag and went on his way. As soon as he was out of sight of the house he said to the boot, "Oh Boot, put me in the house of my eldest sister."

Immediately the young man found himself in the most magnificent palace he had ever seen in his life. He asked to speak with his sister, but the queen of the palace replied that she had no brother and did not wish to be bothered with the stranger. It took much urging for the young man to gain permission from her to relate his story; but, when she had once heard it, everything sounded so logical that she decided to receive him as her brother. She asked how he had ever found her home, and how he had come through the thicket which surrounded her palace. The young man told her about his magic boot.

In the afternoon the queen suddenly burst into tears. Her brother asked what the trouble was. "Oh dear. Oh dear. What shall we do. What shall we do." sobbed the queen. "My husband is King of the Fishes. When he comes home to dinner tonight he will be very angry to find a human in his palace." The young man told her about his magic cap and comforted her fears.

Soon the King of Fishes arrived, accompanied by all his retinue. He came into the palace in a very bad temper, giving kicks and blows to everything which came in his way, and saying in a fierce, savage voice, "Lee, low, lee, leer, I smell the blood of a human, here. I smell the blood of a human, here."

It took much persuasion on the part of the queen to get him to take a bath. After his bath he appeared in the form of a handsome man. He then ate his dinner, and when he had nearly finished the meal his wife said to him, "If you should see my brother here what would you do to him?"

"I would be kind to him, of course, just as I am to you," responded the King of the Fishes. "If he is here let him appear."

The young man then took off the magic cap by which he had hidden himself. The king treated him most kindly and courteously. He invited him to live for the rest of his life in the palace. The young man declined the invitation, saying that he had two other sisters to visit. He took his departure soon, and when he went away his brother-in-law gave him a scale with these words, "If you are ever in any danger in which I can help you, take this scale and say, 'Help me, Oh King of the Fishes.'"

The young man put the scale in his saddle bag. Then he took out his magic boot and said, "Oh Boot, put me in the home of my second sister." He found his second sister queen of even a more wonderful palace than his eldest sister. Her husband was King of Rams and treated the newly found brother of his queen with great consideration. When the young man had finished his visit there the King of Rams gave him a piece of wool saying, "If you are ever in any peril in which I can help you pull this wool and ask help of the King of Rams."

With the aid of his magic boot the young man went to visit the home of his youngest sister. He found her in the most magnificent palace of them all. Her husband was King of Pigeons. When the young man departed he gave him a feather telling him if he was ever in any danger that all he had to do was to pull the feather and say, "Help me, Oh King of the Pigeons."

All three of the young man's brothers-in-law had admired the power of his magic boot and they had all advised him to visit the land of the King of Giants by means of it. After having left each of his three sisters full of happiness in her costly palace he felt free to act upon this advice, so by means of his magic boot he again found himself in a new country.

He soon heard on the street that the King of the land of Giants had a beautiful giantess daughter whom he wished to give in marriage if she could be persuaded to choose a husband. She was such a famous beauty that no one could pass before her palace without eagerly gazing up in hopes of seeing her lovely face at the window. The giant princess had grown weary of being the object of so much attention, and she had made a vow that she would marry no one except a man who could pass before her without lifting his eyes.

The young man became interested when he heard this and at once rode past the palace with his eyes fixed steadily on the ground. He did not give a single glance upward in the direction of the window where the beautiful giant princess was watching him. The princess was overcome with joy at the sight of the handsome stranger who appeared as if in response to her vow. The king summoned him to the palace at once and ordered that the wedding should be celebrated immediately.

After the wedding the giant princess soon found out that her husband carried his choicest treasures in his saddle bags. She inquired their significance and her husband told her all about them. She was especially interested in the key. She said that there was a room in the palace which was never opened. In this room there was a fierce beast which always came to life again whenever it was killed. The giant princess had always been anxious to see the beast with her own eyes, and she suggested that they should use the key to unlock the door of the forbidden room and take a peep at the beast.

Her husband, however, gave her no encouragement to do this. He decided that it was too risky a bit of amusement; but one day when he had gone hunting with the king and court the princess was overjoyed to find that the magic key had been left behind. She at once picked it up and opened the forbidden door. The beast gave a great leap, roaring out at her, "You are the very one I have sought," as he seized her with his sharp claws.

When her husband and father returned from their hunting trip they were very much worried to find that the princess had disappeared. No one knew where she was. After searching through the palace and garden all in vain they went to the place where the beast was always kept. The prince recognized his magic key in the door, but the room was empty. The beast had fled with the giant princess.

Once more the young man made use of his magic boot and soon was by the side of the princess. The beast had hidden her in a cave by the sea and had gone away in search of food. The giant princess was delighted to find her husband whom she had never expected to see again and wanted to hasten away from the cave with him at once.

"You have got yourself into this affair," said her husband. "I can get you out again, I think, but I believe that it is your duty to at least make an effort to take the beast's life. Perhaps when he comes back to the cave you can extract from him the secret of his charmed life."

The princess awaited the return of the beast. Then she asked him to tell her the secret of his charmed life. The beast was very much flattered to have the giant princess so interested in him, and he told it to her at once. He never thought of a plot. This is what he said, "My life is in the sea. In the sea there is a chest. In the chest there is a stone. In the stone there is a pigeon. In the pigeon there is an egg. In the egg there is a candle. At the moment when that candle is extinguished I die."

All this time the prince had remained there, hiding under his magic cap. He heard every word the beast said. As soon as the beast had gone to sleep the prince stood on the seashore and said, "Help me, Oh King of the Fishes," as he took out the scale which his brother-in-law had given him. Immediately there appeared a great multitude of fishes asking what he wished them to do. He asked them to get the chest from the depths of the sea. They replied that they had never seen such a chest, but that probably the sword-fish would know about it.

They hastened to call the sword-fish and he came at once. He said that he had seen the chest only a moment before. All the fishes went with him to get it, and they soon brought the chest out of the sea. The prince opened the chest easily with the aid of his magic key, and inside he found a stone.

Then the prince pulled the piece of wool which his second brother-in-law had given him and said, "Help me, Oh King of the Rams." Immediately there appeared a great drove of rams, running to the seashore from all directions. They attacked the stone, giving it mighty blows with their hard heads and horns. Soon they broke open the stone, and from out of it there flew a pigeon.

The beast now awoke from his sleep and knew that he was very ill. He remembered all that he had told the princess and accused her of having made a plot against his life. He seized his great axe to kill the princess.

In the meantime the prince had pulled the feather which his third brother-in-law had given him and cried, "Help me, Oh King of the Pigeons." Immediately a great flock of pigeons appeared attacking the pigeon and tearing it to pieces.

Just as the beast had caught the princess and was about to slay her, the prince took the egg from within the slain pigeon. He at once broke the egg and blew out the candle. At that moment the beast fell dead, and the princess escaped unharmed.

The prince carried the giant princess home to her father's kingdom and the king made a great festa which lasted many days. There was rejoicing throughout the whole kingdom because of the death of the beast and because of the safety of the lovely princess. The prince was praised throughout the kingdom and there is talk of him even unto this very day.

The prince had cut off the head of the great beast and the tip of its tail. The head he had given to the king, but the tip of the tail he kept for himself. The beast was so enormous that just the tip of its tail made a great ring large enough to encircle the prince's body. One day, just in fun, he twined the tip of the beast's tail around his waist. He immediately grew and grew until he became a giant himself, almost as tall as the king of the land of giants, and several leagues taller than the princess. It is not strange that a man who became a giant among giants should be famous even until now.

The Bird Bride

This story has been adapted from a tale originally told by Lewis Spence in The Myths of Mexico & Peru, published in 1913 by Thomas Y. Crowell of New York..

Long ago, in the misty mountains of Canaribamba, where the clouds kissed the peaks and rivers wove silver paths through the valleys, there lived two brothers of the Canaris tribe.

The world was still young, and great floods had swept the land. When the deluge came, the brothers fled to the highest mountain, Huacaquan. As the waters rose, the mountain itself lifted higher, always keeping them safe from the hungry depths.

When at last the floodwaters receded, the brothers descended into the valleys below, where life had begun anew. They built a small house, surviving on herbs and roots, always watchful of the strange and powerful spirits that still roamed the land.

Then, one day, something extraordinary happened.

Returning home from a long day of foraging, the brothers found food waiting for them, perfectly prepared meals of roasted maize and steaming chicha to drink. Yet, neither of them had cooked. Bewildered but grateful, they ate in silence, unsure of who their mysterious benefactor might be.

The same thing happened again and again, for ten days, a feast appeared each evening, as if conjured by unseen hands. At last, the elder brother could bear the mystery no longer.

"I will hide," he whispered to his younger sibling, "and discover who brings us these gifts."

And so, as the sun set, he concealed himself within the shadows of their tiny home, waiting with bated breath.

As moonlight spilled over the valley, two birds swooped down from the sky, one shining blue like the Aqua, the other scarlet like the Torito. Yet, these were no ordinary birds.

They landed gently and, to the elder brother's astonishment, transformed before his eyes. Feathers melted into silk, talons became delicate hands, and the magnificent creatures turned into two breathtaking women, their long hair bound in the Canari fashion, their eyes gleaming like the stars above. Silently, they laid out food, working gracefully, their every movement like the dance of the wind.

The elder brother, entranced by their beauty, stepped from the shadows. At once, the bird-women gasped, their wings returning in a flash. The older sister seized her mantle and, in a flurry of feathers, flew into the night, her figure vanishing among the stars.

But the younger sister hesitated, her eyes locked on the man before her. Then, with a cry of sorrow, she, too, spread her wings and fled.

When the younger brother returned home and saw no food waiting, he grew angry. "You have frightened them away!" he accused.

Determined to right his brother's mistake, he hatched a clever plan. For ten nights, he waited in secret, just as his brother had done before. And on the tenth night, when the quacamayo sisters returned, he sprang from his hiding place, swift as a puma, and closed the door behind them.

The elder sister escaped, but the younger was trapped. She did not fight. She did not scream. Instead, she lowered her gaze and remained. And in time, she grew to love the man who had captured her.

Seasons passed, and the bird-woman became the brother's wife. She bore six children, daughters and sons as radiant as the dawn, with eyes that held the wisdom of the sky and laughter that carried like birdsong on the wind. From them, the Canaris people were born.

To this day, the Canaris honour the quacamayo birds, believing them to be their sacred ancestors. At every festival, their feathers adorn the dancers, shimmering in the sunlight, a tribute to the beautiful bird-bride, whose spirit still soars over the valleys of Canaribamba.

The Quest Of Cleverness

This story has been adapted from a tale originally told by Elsie Spicer Eells in Tales Of Giants from Brazil, published in 1918 by Dodd, Mead And Company, New York. Following the success of her previous work, Fairy Tales from Brazil,, this book focuses specifically on stories featuring giants, mythical beings of immense size and strength, from Brazilian folklore.

Once long ago there lived a king who had a stupid son. His father sent him to school for many years hoping that he might learn something there. His teachers all gave him up as hopelessly stupid, and with one accord they said, "It is no use trying to teach this lad out of books. It is just a waste of our valuable time."

At length the king called together all the wisest men of his kingdom to consult with them as to the best way to make the prince wise and clever. They talked the matter over for a year and a day. It was the unanimous opinion of the wise men of the kingdom that the lad should be sent on a journey through many lands. In this way he might learn many of the things which his teachers had not been able to teach him out of books.

Accordingly the prince was equipped for his journey. He was given fine raiment, a splendid black horse upon which to ride, and a great bag full of money. Thus prepared, he started forth from the palace one bright morning with the blessing of the king, his father, and of all the wise men of the kingdom.

The prince journeyed through many lands. In one country he learned one thing, and in another country he learned another thing. There was no country or kingdom so small or poor that it did not have something to teach the prince. And the prince, though he had been so insufferably stupid at his books, learned the lessons of his journey with an open mind.

After long wanderings the prince arrived at a city where there was an auction going on. A singing bird was being offered for sale.

"What is the special advantage of this singing bird?" asked the prince.

"This bird, at the command of its owner, will sing a song which will put to sleep anyone who listens to it," was the reply.

The prince decided that the bird was worth purchasing.

The next thing which was offered for sale was a beetle. "What is the special advantage of this beetle?" asked the prince.

"This beetle will gnaw its way through any wall in the world," was the reply.

The prince purchased the beetle.

Then a butterfly was offered for sale. "What is the special advantage of owning this butterfly?" asked the prince.

"This butterfly is strong enough to bear upon its wings any weight which is put upon them," was the answer.

The prince bought the butterfly. With his bird and beetle and butterfly he travelled on and on until he became lost in the jungle. The foliage was so dense that he could not see his way, so he climbed to the top of the tallest tree he could see. From its summit he spied in the distance what looked like a mountain; but, when he had journeyed near to it, he saw that it was really the wall which surrounds the land of the giants.

A great giant whose head reached to the clouds stood on the wall as guard. A song from the singing bird put this guard to sleep immediately. The beetle soon had gnawed an entrance through the wall. Through this opening the prince entered the land of the giants.

The very first person whom the prince saw in the land of the giants was a lovely captive princess. The opening which the beetle had made in the wall led directly to the dungeon in which she was confined.

The prince had learned many things on his journey, and among the lessons he had learned was this one, "Always rescue a fair maiden in distress." He immediately asked what he could do to rescue the beautiful captive princess.

"You can never succeed in rescuing me, I fear," replied the princess. "At the door of this palace there is a giant on guard who never sleeps."

"Never mind," replied the prince. "I'll put him to sleep."

Just at that moment the giant himself strode into the dungeon. He had heard voices there. "Sing, my little bird, sing," commanded the prince to his singing bird.

At the first burst of melody the giant went to sleep there in the dungeon, though he had never before taken a wink of sleep in all his life.

"This beetle of mine has gnawed an entrance through the great wall which surrounds the land of the giants," said the prince to the captive princess. "To escape we'll not have to climb the high wall."

"What of the guard who stands on top of the wall with his head reaching up to the clouds?" asked the princess. "Will he not spy us?"

"My singing bird has put him to sleep, too," replied the prince. "If we hurry out he will not yet be awake."

"I have been confined here in this dungeon so long that I fear I have forgotten how to walk," said the princess.

"Never mind," replied the prince. "My butterfly will bear you upon his wings."

With the lovely princess borne safely upon the butterfly's wings the prince swiftly escaped from the land of the giants. The giant on the wall yawned in his sleep as they looked up at him. "He is good for another hour's nap," remarked the prince.

The prince returned to his father's kingdom as soon as he could find the way back. He took with him the lovely princess, and the singing bird, and the gnawing beetle, and the strong-winged butterfly.

His father and all the people of the kingdom received him with great joy. "Never again will the prince of our kingdom be called stupid," said the wise men when they heard the account of his adventures. "With his singing bird and his gnawing beetle and his strong-winged butterfly he has become the cleverest youth in the land."

The Myth of Alicanto

This story is my own telling of a traditional Chilean folk tale based on various sources.

In the rugged and majestic landscapes of Chile, where the Andes Mountains stretch towards the sky and the Atacama Desert extends to the horizon, there exists a mythical creature known as the Alicanto, a creature of legend and mystery.

According to Chilean folklore, the Alicanto is a magnificent bird that dwells deep within the heart of the mountains, hidden away in caverns and crevices far from the prying eyes of humans. Its feathers shimmer with the colours of precious metals, gold and silver, copper and bronze, casting a radiant glow that illuminates the darkness of the underground world.

But what truly sets the Alicanto apart is its diet, for legend has it that this extraordinary bird feeds exclusively on precious minerals and metals. As it flies through the labyrinthine tunnels of the mountains, it seeks out veins of gold and silver, devouring them with a voracious appetite.

As a result, the Alicanto's feathers are said to change colour depending on the minerals it consumes. If it feasts on gold, its plumage gleams with a brilliant golden hue, casting a warm and inviting light wherever it goes. But if it indulges in silver, its feathers shimmer with a cool and ethereal glow, lighting up the darkness with a silvery luminescence.

Throughout the ages, countless treasure hunters and adventurers have sought to capture the elusive Alicanto, hoping to uncover the secrets of its miraculous powers. But the bird is a master of evasion, vanishing into the depths of the earth at the first sign of danger, leaving only the echo of its melodic song lingering in the air.

The Giant's Pupil

This story has been adapted from a tale originally told by Elsie Spicer Eells in Tales Of Giants from Brazil, published in 1918 by Dodd, Mead And Company, New York. Following the success of her previous work, Fairy Tales from Brazil,, this book focuses specifically on stories featuring giants, mythical beings of immense size and strength, from Brazilian folklore.

Long years ago there lived a little boy whose name was Manoel. His father and mother were so very poor that they could not afford to send him to school. Because he did not go to school he played all day in the fields on the edge of the forest where the giant lived.

One day Manoel met the giant. The giant lived all alone in the forest, so he was very lonely and wished he had a little boy like Manoel. He loved little Manoel as soon as he saw him, and after that they were together every day. The giant taught Manoel all the secrets of the forests and jungles. He taught him all the secrets of the wind and the rain and the thunder and the lightning. He taught him all the secrets of the beasts and the birds and the serpents. Manoel grew up a wise lad indeed. His father and mother were very proud of him and so was his kind teacher, the giant.

One day the king's messenger rode up and down the kingdom with a message from the king's daughter. The king's daughter, the beautiful princess of the land, had promised to wed the man who could tell her a riddle she could not guess. All the princes who had sung of love beneath the palace window had been very stupid. The princess wished to marry a man who knew more than she did.

When Manoel heard the messenger's words he said to his father and mother, "I am going to the palace to tell a riddle to the princess. I am sure I can give her one which she cannot guess."

"You are an exceedingly clever lad, I know, my son," replied his mother, "but there will be many princes and handsome cavalheiros at the palace to tell riddles to the princess. What if she will not listen to a lad in shabby clothing."

"I will make the princess listen to my riddle," replied Manoel.

"What riddle are you going to ask the princess?" asked Manoel's father.

"I do not know yet," replied the lad. "I will make up a riddle on the way to the palace. I am going to start at once."

The kind giant who had been the lad's friend gave him his blessing and wished him luck. The lad's mother prepared a lunch for him to carry with him. His father sat before the door and boasted to all the neighbours that his son was going to wed the king's daughter. Manoel took his dog with him when he went on his journey, because he wanted someone for company.

Manoel journeyed on and on through the forests and jungles and after a time he had eaten all the lunch his mother had given him when he went from home. When he became hungry he spent his last vintem for some bread from a little venda in the town he passed through. He went on to the forest to eat the bread, and before he tasted it himself he gave a piece to his dog. The dog died immediately. The bread was poisoned.

Even as Manoel stood by weeping for his faithful dog, three big black buzzards flew down and devoured the dead beast. They fell dead immediately. Just then the lad heard voices, and soon he saw seven horsemen approaching. The men were robbers, and though they had much gold in their pockets they had no food. "I am hungry enough to eat a dead buzzard," said the captain of the robbers. The robbers greedily seized the three buzzards and devoured them at once. The seven men immediately died from the poison.

"The buzzards stole the body of my dog, so they became mine," said Manoel. "The seven robbers stole my three buzzards, so they became mine, too." He took all the gold from the pockets of the seven robbers and dressed himself in the garments of the captain of the robbers because they were finest. He mounted the horse of the captain of the robbers because that was the best horse.

The lad rode on toward the palace of the king. After a time he became thirsty and pushed the horse into a gallop. The horse became covered with sweat, and with the horse's sweat he quenched his thirst. Soon he arrived at the royal palace.

Dressed in the robber's fine garments and mounted upon the robber's fine horse, Manoel had no difficulty in being admitted to the palace. He was taken at once before the princess to tell his riddle.

The princess saw in Manoel's eyes all the secrets of the forests and jungles which the kind giant had taught him. "Here is a youth who will tell me a riddle which will be worth listening to," said the princess to herself. All the princes and cavalheiros from all the neighbouring kingdoms had told her such stupid riddles that she had been bored nearly to death. She could always guess the answers, even before she had heard the end of the riddle.

This is the riddle which Manoel told the princess:

"I went away from home with a pocket full;

Soon it became empty;

Again it became full.

I went away from home with a companion;

My pocket-full killed my companion;

My dead companion was the slayer of three;

The three killed seven.

From the seven I chose the best;

I drank water which did not fall from heaven.

And here I stand

Before the loveliest princess in the land."

The princess listened to the riddle carefully. Then she asked Manoel to say it all over again. The princess thought and thought, but she did not have a good enough guess as to the answer to the riddle.

No one in all the palace could understand Manoel's riddle. "You have won my daughter as your bride," said the king, after he had used all his royal wits to solve the riddle and could not do it.

When Manoel explained his riddle to the princess, she said, "Nossa Senhora herself must have sent you to me. I never could have endured a stupid husband."

351

Thonapa

This story has been adapted from a tale originally told by Lewis Spence in The Myths of Mexico & Peru, published in 1913 by Thomas Y. Crowell of New York..

Long ago, before the mountains whispered secrets and the rivers carved their way through the land, there walked a divine traveller named Thonapa. He was no ordinary man, for he carried the wisdom of the heavens and the power of the gods. Some say he was a god of the sun, others that he was a great teacher, but all who crossed his path felt the weight of his presence.

He wore only a long white robe and a mantle, and in his hands, he carried a book of knowledge. From village to village, from valley to valley, he travelled, preaching to the people, teaching them the ways of wisdom and righteousness.

But not all were willing to listen.

One day, Thonapa arrived in the village of Yamquisupa, weary from his long journey. He stood in the village square and spoke to the people about the balance of the earth and sky, the respect owed to the gods, and the virtues of kindness and wisdom. But the villagers only mocked him. They laughed at his ragged clothes, jeered at his words, and refused to offer him food or shelter.

Thonapa did not grow angry, but his heart was heavy with sorrow. That night, he lay beneath the open sky, his only companions the stars. A single tear fell from his eye and touched the earth. And then, as the sun rose, Yamquisupa was gone. The village had vanished beneath the waves, swallowed by a great lake. The people, their homes, their mocking voices, all lost forever beneath the water.

Beyond the lake stood a mighty hill called Cachapucara, where the people worshipped a golden idol in the form of a woman. Upon this sacred peak, they made sacrifices, believing the statue had the power to bring them prosperity and rain.

When Thonapa climbed the hill and saw the idol gleaming in the sun, he was filled with righteous fury. "This is not the way of the gods," he declared.

He set fire to the idol, its golden form melting into the earth. And as the flames roared, the very hill crumbled, its mighty stones tumbling down the mountainside. Where once had stood a place of false worship, now there was only ruin and silence.

Not long after, Thonapa came upon a great feast, a grand wedding celebration where hundreds had gathered. The air was filled with the scent of roasting meats and the sound of flutes and laughter.

Thonapa stepped forward, his voice rising above the revelry. "Hear me, people of this land! Turn your hearts to wisdom, for the gods watch over all!"

But the people ignored him, lost in their wine and merriment. Anguish filled Thonapa's heart. He raised his hand, and in that instant, the sky darkened. A great silence fell over the feast. And then, they turned to stone. The dancers, the musicians, the bride and groom, all frozen in place, their revelry preserved for eternity. To this day, their stone figures remain, scattered across the land, a silent warning to those who refuse to heed wisdom when it is given.

Thonapa wandered far and wide, reaching the mighty mountain of Caravaya. There, he raised a great cross, its shadow stretching far across the valley. He climbed the hill of Carapucu, and with such fervour did he preach, that tears streamed from his eyes. A chieftain's daughter, standing nearby, felt a single drop of Thonapa's tears land upon her head.

The people, seeing this, cried out in horror. "He washes his head before us!" they shouted, outraged, for among them, it was forbidden for a man to cleanse himself in the presence of others. They seized Thonapa, dragging him down the mountainside, declaring him a criminal.

That night, as he lay bound in a darkened prison, a brilliant light filled the room. A radiant youth stood before him, his face glowing like the morning sun. "Fear not, Thonapa, for I have been sent to free you," the youth whispered.

In an instant, Thonapa's bonds fell away, and the doors swung open. He fled into the night, pursued by his captors. Reaching the shores of Lake Carapucu, he stepped onto the water. His mantle billowed around him, lifting him as if upon the wings of the wind. Before the astonished eyes of his pursuers, he glided across the lake, untouched by the waves, and disappeared into the mist.

From there, Thonapa journeyed to Tiahuanaco, where once again, he found people too lost in their own pleasures to hear his words. He cursed them, as he had before, and they too turned to stone, their forms still standing to this day.

He followed the great river Chacamarca, his feet never tiring, until at last, he reached the sea. And there, like Quetzalcoatl, like the gods of old, he walked into the waves and was never seen again.

Some say he returned to the House of the Sun, where his father awaited him among the stars. Others whisper that he still walks the earth, appearing in the hour of greatest need, when wisdom must once again be spoken to those who would listen.

But all agree on one thing: The name of Thonapa will never be forgotten.

The Poet Viceroy and the Pirate's Curse

This story has been adapted from a tale originally told by Ricardo Palma in Peruvian Traditions, A Spanish language book originally, and published in 1872 by Imprenta del Estado, Lima.

Once upon a time, in the grand city of Madrid, there was a young nobleman named Don Francisco de Borja y Aragón. Born into a family of great lineage, descended from both a saint and a pope, he was raised in glittering palaces, where golden chandeliers cast light upon his poetry, and velvet-draped balconies whispered of his duels and courtly romances.

Now, Don Francisco was not known for his battles or his wisdom in ruling. He spent his days composing verses, serenading ladies, and weaving words into golden tapestries of rhyme. But fate had other plans for him.

One day, King Philip III summoned him to the royal court. "Francisco," the king declared, "I am sending you across the great ocean to rule over a kingdom vast and troubled, the Viceroyalty of Peru."

The courtiers gasped. "But Your Majesty," they whispered among themselves, "he has never governed anything but his own heart."

Philip III, overhearing their murmurs, smiled. "He may be the youngest viceroy ever sent to the Indies, but he has both a fine mind and a strong arm."

And so, with a heavy heart and a ship full of books, Don Francisco set sail across the sea, bound for the fabled land of gold.

As his ship neared the coast of Peru, a shadow fell over the waves. A fleet of dark-sailed ships emerged from the mist, and at their helm stood the fearsome pirate captain George Spilberg. It was said that Spilberg had struck a terrible bargain with the spirits of the sea, so long as he plundered without mercy, the waves would never betray him.

"Seize the viceroy." the pirate captain bellowed.

But just as the pirates closed in, a strange wind rose from the east, howling through the sails like the voices of malevolent ghosts. The sky darkened, and the sea churned as if the spirits themselves were angered. Suddenly, the viceroy's ship was swallowed by a veil of mist, and when it cleared, Spilberg's fleet had been cast far off course.

When Don Francisco reached the safety of Lima's shores, the people rejoiced. "It is a miracle." they cried. "The Virgin of Lima has protected him."

But the new viceroy, ever the poet, merely smiled. "Perhaps it was fate," he mused. "Or perhaps the sea wished to hear my verses another day."

Though the viceroy had arrived safely, Peru was far from peaceful. The City of Kings, Lima, lay trembling under the shadow of pirates.

The streets, once filled with music and laughter, were now lined with locked doors and silent prayers.

The old viceroy, the weary Marquis of Montesclaros, stood at the walls of Callao, watching the horizon darken with approaching sails. "We have but a thousand men," he whispered. "And the people hide in churches instead of taking up arms. We are doomed."

But Don Francisco was no ordinary ruler. He was a poet, and he knew that courage was sometimes found not in swords, but in stories.

He gathered the people of Lima and told them a tale of the old Inca kings, of warriors who fought not for gold, but for honour. He reminded them that their city was not built by cowards, but by men and women who defied even the gods. And as he spoke, the fear in their eyes flickered, replaced by the light of courage.

And then, just as Spilberg's ships drew close to the shore, a storm unlike any other swept across the land. Lightning split the sky, and waves rose like mountains, swallowing the pirate fleet whole.

When the storm cleared, the ships were gone.

"The Virgin has saved us once more," the people whispered.

But Don Francisco, looking out at the sea, only said, "Perhaps even the waves have no love for thieves."

With the pirate threat behind them, Don Francisco turned his mind to the kingdom entrusted to him.

He built walls to protect Callao from future raids, secured the mines of Potosí and Huancavelica, and filled the royal treasury with wisdom as well as gold.

Yet his greatest love was for learning. He founded a school for the children of chieftains, ensuring that the wisdom of the old world and the new would walk hand in hand. He gathered scholars, poets, and dreamers in his palace, where they spoke of ideas as grand as the Andes and as deep as the ocean.

Every Saturday, he held a secret gathering in a candlelit hall. Only twelve guests could attend, lawyers, theologians, poets, and soldiers, brought together not by birth, but by the power of words. They sipped chocolate and ate biscuits as they recited verses, debating philosophy and destiny beneath the golden glow of lanterns.

It was said that the viceroy's library held books so rare that the words themselves whispered to those who dared to read them.

Years passed, and the poet-viceroy knew that his time in Peru was coming to an end. When the king called him back to Spain in 1622, the people of Lima lined the streets, weeping at his departure.

"Do not mourn," he told them, smiling. "For every poem, no matter how beautiful, must have an ending."

He returned to Spain, where he was received with honour. He lived many more years, writing poetry and stories, until at last, in 1658, he left the world behind, perhaps to join the spirits of the sea, or perhaps to find a new kingdom where words ruled above all else.

And so, the legend of the Poet Viceroy lived on, carried in the pages of books and whispered among dreamers who still believe that poetry can shape the world. And if you ever find yourself in an old library, where the candlelight flickers without a breeze or a draught, you might hear a voice among the bookshelves, reciting verses, forever weaving words into history.

Domingo's Cat

This story has been adapted from a tale originally told by Elsie Spicer Eells in Tales Of Giants from Brazil, published in 1918 by Dodd, Mead And Company, New York. Following the success of her previous work, Fairy Tales from Brazil,, this book focuses specifically on stories featuring giants, mythical beings of immense size and strength, from Brazilian folklore.

Once upon a time there was a man who was very poor. He was so poor that he had to sell one thing after another to get food to keep from starving. After a while there was nothing left except the cat. He was very fond of his cat, and he said, "Oh, Cat, let come what will, I'll never part with you. I would rather starve."

The cat replied, "Oh good master Domingo, rest in peace. You will never starve as long as you have me. I am going out into the world to make a fortune for us both."

The cat went out into the jungle and dug and dug. Every time he dug he turned up silver pieces. The cat took a number of these home to his master so that he could purchase food. The rest of the pieces of silver the cat carried to the king.

The next day the cat dug up pieces of gold and carried them to the king. The next day he carried pieces of diamonds.

"Where do you get these rich gifts? Who is sending me such wonderful presents?" asked the king.

The cat replied, "It is my master, Domingo."

Now the king had a beautiful daughter. He thought that this man Domingo must be the richest man in the whole kingdom. He decided that his daughter should marry him at once. He made arrangements for the wedding through the cat.

"I haven't any clothes to wear at the wedding," said Domingo when the cat told him that he was to marry the daughter of the king.

"Never mind about that. Just leave it to me," replied the cat.

The cat went to the king and said, "Oh King, there has been a terrible fire in the tailor shop where they were making the wedding garments of my master, Domingo. The tailor and all of his assistants were burned to death, and the entire outfit of my master Domingo was destroyed. Hasn't your majesty something which you could lend him to wear at the wedding?" The king sent the richest garments which his wardrobe afforded. Domingo was clothed in state ready for the wedding.

"I have no palace to which to take my bride," said Domingo to the cat.

"Never mind. I'll see about it at once," replied the cat.

The cat went into the forest to the great castle where the giant dwelt. He marched straight up to the big giant and said, "Oh Giant, I wish to borrow your castle for my master Domingo. Will you not be so kind as to lend it to me a little while?"

The giant was very much insulted. "No, indeed, I'll not lend my castle to you or your master Domingo or anybody else," he shouted in his most terrible voice.

"Very well, then," replied the cat. He changed the giant into a piece of bacon in the twinkling of an eye and devoured him on the spot.

The giant's palace was a very wonderful palace. There was one room decked with silver, and one room decked with gold, and one room decked with diamonds. A beautiful river flowed by the garden gate.

As Domingo and his bride sailed down the river to the garden gate in the royal barge, they saw the cat sitting in the window singing. After that they never saw him again. He disappeared in the jungle and went to make some other poor man rich. Perhaps he will come your way some day. Who knows?

"Quem sabe?" as they say in Brazil.

Historical Notes

This section contains some brief biographical notes about the original collectors and their books featured in this collection. These notes have been adapted from various digital sources along with other supporting written sources and notes.

Ricardo Palma

Ricardo Palma (1833–1919) was a distinguished Peruvian author, scholar, and librarian, celebrated for his unique contributions to Latin American literature. Born in Lima, he began his literary journey at a young age, publishing his initial verses and editing a satirical newsletter, *El Diablo*, by the age of 15.

Palma's most renowned work is the *Tradiciones Peruanas* ("Peruvian Traditions"), a series of short stories that blend history and fiction to depict Peru's colonial and early republican eras. These narratives, written to both entertain and educate, draw from folklore, legends, and archival research, offering readers a rich tapestry of Peruvian culture and history. The *Tradiciones* were published between 1872 and 1910 and have since become a cornerstone of Peruvian literature.

Beyond his literary achievements, Palma played a pivotal role in preserving Peru's cultural heritage. Following the War of the Pacific, he was instrumental in reconstructing the National Library of Peru, which had suffered extensive damage. His dedication to this cause ensured the preservation of countless historical documents and books, safeguarding them for future generations.

Palma's influence extended beyond his writings; he was a prominent figure in Peruvian society, engaging in politics, journalism, and cultural preservation. His legacy endures, with his works continuing to be studied and celebrated for their contribution to Latin American literary traditions.

Select bibliography:

- "El hijo del sol" (1849): An early work showcasing Palma's literary beginnings.
- "Rodil: Drama en tres actos y un prólogo, escrito en prosa y verso" (1851): A drama blending prose and verse.
- "Anales de la Inquisición de Lima: Estudio histórico" (1863): A historical study on the activities of the Spanish Inquisition in Lima.
- "Tradiciones Peruanas" (First series published in 1872): A collection of short stories that mix history and fiction, depicting Peru's colonial and early republican eras.
- "Monteagudo y Sánchez Carrión: Páginas de la historia de la independencia" (1877): Essays on figures from Peru's independence movement.

- "Neologismos y americanismos" (1896): A work focusing on linguistic studies, particularly neologisms and Americanisms in the Spanish language.
- "Tradiciones en Salsa Verde" (Published posthumously in 1973): Similar to his "Tradiciones Peruanas" but with a more risqué tone; these were not published during his lifetime to avoid shocking the conservative Lima society.

Ramón A. Laval

Ramón Arminio Laval Alvial (1862–1929) was a distinguished Chilean writer, bibliographer, and folklorist, renowned for his dedication to preserving Chile's cultural heritage through meticulous documentation of its folklore and oral traditions.

Born on March 14, 1862, in San Fernando, Chile, Laval was one of six children of French immigrant Ramón Eduardo Laval Anglade and Chilean María del Socorro Alvial Díaz. At the age of three, his family relocated to Santiago's Recoleta district, where his father worked as an engineer. Laval received his early education at the Recoleta Dominica school, later studying theology and calligraphy. At 21, he began his career at Correos de Chile (Chilean Postal Service), and subsequently, in 1892, he joined the Biblioteca Nacional de Chile (National Library of Chile), where he served for over three decades, eventually becoming its subdirector and secretary in 1913.

Laval's tenure at the National Library deepened his interest in bibliography. In 1911, he curated the *Bibliografía de la Semana* ("Bibliography of the Week") section in the newspaper El Ferrocarril, providing 183 bibliographic reviews, primarily of Chilean and Latin American works. His seminal work, *Bibliografía de bibliografías chilenas* (1915), is acclaimed for its comprehensive cataloguing of Chilean bibliographies, including catalogues and indexes of magazines, as well as bibliographies of Chilean authors and subjects published abroad.

Laval was a pivotal figure in Chilean folklore studies. In 1909, he co-founded the Sociedad del Folklore Chileno (Chilean Folklore Society), which, despite its brief existence, played a crucial role in consolidating the study of popular cultures in Chile. Laval's meticulous fieldwork in rural areas, such as Carahue in southern Chile, led to the collection of a vast array of oral narratives, including tales, proverbs, and traditional expressions.

Laval's dedication to documenting Chile's folklore has been instrumental in preserving the nation's intangible cultural heritage. His works continue to serve as valuable resources for understanding Chilean identity and cultural expressions. Ramón Laval passed away on October 14, 1929, in Santiago, at the age of 67, leaving behind a legacy of scholarly contributions that continue to influence Chilean cultural studies.

Selected Bibliography:

- "Cuentos chilenos de nunca acabar" (1910): A collection of traditional Chilean endless tales.
- "Oraciones, ensalmos y conjuros del pueblo chileno comparados con los que se dicen en España" (1910): A study comparing Chilean prayers, charms, and incantations with their Spanish counterparts.
- "Contribución al folklore de Carahue" (1916): An exploration of the folklore from the Carahue region in southern Chile.
- "Tradiciones, leyendas y cuentos recogidos de la tradición oral de Carahue" (1920): A compilation of traditions, legends, and stories gathered from the oral traditions of Carahue.
- "Paremiología chilena" (1923): A work focusing on Chilean proverbs and sayings.
- "Cuentos populares en Chile" (1923): A collection of popular Chilean folk tales.

- "Cuentos de Pedro Urdemales" (1925): Stories centred around the trickster figure Pedro Urdemales in Chilean folklore

M. Rigoberto Paredes

Manuel Rigoberto Paredes Iturri (1870–1951) was a distinguished Bolivian folklorist, ethnographer, historian, essayist, and politician, renowned for his pioneering contributions to the study of Andean folklore and cultural anthropology in Bolivia.

Born on April 17, 1870, in Puerto Carabuco, a small town in the Eliodoro Camacho province of the La Paz Department, Paredes was deeply rooted in Bolivian heritage. His father, Manuel Silvestre Paredes, was a lawyer, and his mother, Ubaldina Iturri de Miranda, was the daughter of physician and writer Pedro José Iturri. Paredes pursued legal studies and graduated with a law degree from the Universidad Mayor de San Andrés (UMSA) in 1894.

Paredes held several significant positions throughout his career, including serving as a deputy in various legislative sessions and as President of the Chamber of Deputies between 1921 and 1922. He was also a member of the Supreme Court of Justice (1936–1941) and served as Minister of Development and Communications (1929–1930). His active involvement in the Sociedad Geográfica de La Paz and the Academia Boliviana de Historia underscored his commitment to Bolivian cultural and historical studies.

As an essayist, Paredes was among the most important sociological writers of his generation and a precursor in the study of Andean folklore. His seminal work, *Mitos, supersticiones y supervivencias populares de Bolivia* (1920), is a comprehensive compilation of indigenous expressions related to dances, music, popular poetry, and customs of his time. This work aimed to preserve these cultural manifestations, especially as contemporary societies began to favour the exotic and overlook native traditions.

Paredes married twice; his second marriage to Haydeé Candia Torrico in 1914 resulted in several children, including Hernán Paredes Candia, Antonio Paredes Candia, Elsa Paredes Candia, Orestes Paredes Candia, Mercedes Paredes Candia, and Rigoberto Paredes Candia. He passed away on May 17, 1951, in La Paz, Bolivia, due to uremia. Paredes' extensive body of work continues to serve as a foundational reference for scholars and enthusiasts of Bolivian folklore and cultural studies.

Selected Bibliography

- Datos para la historia del arte tipográfico en la Paz (1898)
- Monografía de la Provincia de Muñecas (1898)
- Provincia de Inquisivi: Estudios geográficos, estadísticos y sociales (1906)
- El arte en la Altiplanicie (1913)
- La Altiplanicie: Descripción de la Provincia Omasuyus (1914)
- El Kollasuyo: Estudios históricos y tradicionales (1916)
- Relaciones históricas: Régimen colonial en el Distrito de la Audiencia de los Charcas (1917)
- Mitos, supersticiones y supervivencias populares de Bolivia (1920)
- El arte folklórico de Bolivia (1949, posthumous)

Lewis Spence

James Lewis Thomas Chalmers Spence (25 November 1874 – 3 March 1955) was a Scottish journalist, poet, author, folklorist, and scholar of the occult. Born in Monifieth, Angus, Scotland, Spence pursued studies at Edinburgh University before embarking on a career in journalism. He served as an editor at The Scotsman from 1899 to 1906, and later at The British Weekly between 1906 and 1909.

Spence's scholarly interests encompassed a broad spectrum, including Scottish folklore, ancient mythologies, and the study of Atlantis. His extensive body of work includes titles such as *The Mythologies of Ancient Mexico and Peru* (1907), *Myths and Legends of Ancient Egypt* (1915), and *The Problem of Atlantis* (1924). In these works, Spence explored connections between ancient civilizations, often drawing parallels between the Old and New Worlds.

An ardent Scottish nationalist, Spence founded the Scottish National Movement, which later merged to form the National Party of Scotland, a precursor to the modern Scottish National Party. His passion for Scottish culture also found expression in his poetry, notably in collections like *The Phoenix* (1923) and *Weirds and Vanities* (1927), where he employed a style reminiscent of 16th-century Scottish makars.

Spence's fascination with the esoteric led him to delve into occult studies, culminating in works like *An Encyclopaedia of Occultism* (1920). He was also involved with the Ancient Druid Order, serving as its Presider, a group instrumental in the revival of modern Druidry and from which the Order of Bards, Ovates & Druids evolved.

Throughout his career, Spence authored over forty books, reflecting his diverse interests and contributions to the study of folklore, mythology, and the occult. He passed away in Edinburgh in 1955 at the age of 80 and is interred alongside his wife, Helen S. Bruce, in Dean Cemetery, Edinburgh.

Selected Bibliography:

- Mythology and Folklore
    - "The Mythologies of Ancient Mexico and Peru" (1907): An exploration of the myths and legends from ancient Mesoamerican civilizations.
    - "The Popol Vuh: The Mythic and Heroic Sagas of the Kichés of Central America" (1908): A translation and analysis of the sacred text of the K'iche' Maya people.
    - "Myths and Legends of Ancient Egypt" (1915): A comprehensive collection of Egyptian mythology.
    - "The Myths of the North American Indians" (1914): A compilation of Native American myths and legends.
    - "Legends and Romances of Brittany" (1917): A study of Breton folklore and romantic tales.
    - "Legends and Romances of Spain" (1920): An examination of Spanish myths and romantic stories.
    - "An Introduction to Mythology" (1921): A foundational text introducing various mythological systems.
- Atlantis and Lost Continents
    - "The Problem of Atlantis" (1924): An investigation into the legend of the lost continent of Atlantis.
    - "Atlantis in America" (1925): Proposing connections between Atlantis and ancient American civilizations.

- o "The History of Atlantis" (1927): A historical analysis of the Atlantis narrative.
  - o "The Problem of Lemuria: The Sunken Continent of the Pacific" (1932): An exploration of the Lemuria hypothesis.
- Occult and Esoteric Studies
  - o "An Encyclopaedia of Occultism" (1920): A reference on occult sciences and personalities.
  - o "The Occult Sciences in Atlantis" (1925): A study of esoteric practices in the context of Atlantis.
  - o "Occult Causes of the Present War" (1940): An analysis of the esoteric influences behind contemporary conflicts.
- Celtic and British Traditions
  - o "The Mysteries of Britain: Secret Rites and Traditions of Ancient Britain" (1905): An examination of ancient British secret rites and traditions.
  - o "The Magic Arts in Celtic Britain" (1949): A study of magical practices in Celtic Britain.
  - o "British Fairy Origins: The Genesis and Development of Fairy Legends in British Tradition" (1946): An analysis of the origins and evolution of British fairy legends.
  - o "The Fairy Tradition in Britain" (1948): A comprehensive study of fairy lore in British culture.
- Poetry
  - o "The Phoenix" (1923): A collection of poems reflecting Spence's interest in Scottish heritage.
  - o "Plumes of Time" (1926): A poetry collection delving into themes of time and tradition.
  - o "Weirds and Vanities" (1927): Poems exploring Scottish folklore and mysticism.
  - o "Collected Poems of Lewis Spence" (1953).

Charles F. Lummis

Charles Fletcher Lummis (1859–1928) was an American journalist, author, photographer, ethnographer, and preservationist known for his contributions to the preservation of Southwestern American culture and his advocacy for Native American rights. Here's a detailed biography of Charles F. Lummis:

Charles Fletcher Lummis was born on March 1, 1859, in Lynn, Massachusetts, USA. He was the eldest child of Henry Swift Lummis, a clergyman, and Harriet B. Lummis. Lummis showed a keen interest in literature, history, and culture from an early age, and he pursued his passion for writing throughout his life.

After attending Harvard University for two years, Lummis left without graduating to pursue a career in journalism. In 1884, he began working as a reporter for the "Los Angeles Times" in California. Lummis quickly gained recognition for his colourful and evocative writing style, which captured the spirit of the American Southwest.

Lummis embarked on a remarkable journey in 1884, walking over 3,500 miles from Cincinnati, Ohio, to Los Angeles, California, in what he called a "tramp across the continent." This adventure, which took him over a year to complete, provided him with firsthand experience of the diverse landscapes, cultures, and peoples of the American West.

Throughout his career, Lummis developed a deep appreciation for the culture, history, and traditions of the American Southwest. He became a passionate advocate for the preservation of Southwestern American culture and heritage, particularly the traditions of Native American communities.

Lummis documented his experiences and observations through writing, photography, and ethnographic research. He founded the Southwest Museum in Los Angeles in 1907, which became a leading institution for the study and preservation of Native American artifacts and art.

In addition to his journalistic and ethnographic work, Lummis was a prolific author and poet. He wrote numerous books, articles, and essays on a wide range of topics, including Southwestern American history, Native American culture, and the Spanish missions of California.

One of Lummis's most famous works is his autobiography, "A Tramp Across the Continent" (1892), which chronicles his epic journey from Cincinnati to Los Angeles. The book became a bestseller and established Lummis as a prominent literary figure.

Charles F. Lummis continued to be actively involved in journalism, cultural preservation, and advocacy throughout his life. He remained dedicated to promoting awareness and appreciation for the cultural heritage of the American Southwest until his death.

Lummis passed away on November 24, 1928, in Los Angeles, California, leaving behind a lasting legacy as a pioneering journalist, author, ethnographer, and cultural preservationist.

Selected Bibliography:

- "Birch Bark Poems" (1882): A collection of poems printed on thin sheets of birch bark, showcasing Lummis's early literary creativity.

- "A New Mexico David and Other Stories & Sketches of The Southwest" (1891): A compilation of stories highlighting the unique narratives of the Southwest.
- "Some Strange Corners of Our Country: The Wonderland of the Southwest" (1892): An exploration of the lesser-known regions and tales of the American Southwest.
- "A Tramp Across The Continent" (1892): Lummis's account of his 3,507-mile journey on foot from Cincinnati to Los Angeles, providing insights into the landscapes and cultures he encountered.
- "The Land of Poco Tiempo" (1893): A reflection on the cultures and environments of the Southwest, emphasizing the region's timelessness.
- "The Spanish Pioneers" (1893): A historical examination of the contributions and legacies of Spanish explorers and settlers in the Americas.
- "The Man Who Married the Moon and Other Pueblo Indian Folk Tales" (1894): A collection of Pueblo Indian folklore, preserving indigenous narratives.
- "My Friend Will" (1894): A personal narrative or story reflecting Lummis's experiences or observations.
- "The Gold Fish of Gran Chimu: A Novel" (1896): A novel set against the backdrop of South American history and culture.
- "The Awakening of a Nation: Mexico of To-day" (1898): An analysis of contemporary Mexico, exploring its culture, politics, and society.
- "Pueblo Indian Folk-Stories" (1910): Further exploration into the rich oral traditions of the Pueblo people.

- "The King Of The Broncos and Other Stories of New Mexico" (1915): Stories capturing the spirit and challenges of life in New Mexico.
- "A Bronco Pegasus: Poems" (1928): A collection of poems reflecting Lummis's deep connection to the Southwest.
- "Flowers of Our Lost Romance" (1929): A poetic work delving into themes of nostalgia and cultural loss.

Tales From South America

Elsie Spicer Eells

Elsie Spicer Eells (1880–1963) was an American author, journalist, and folklorist, best known for her significant contributions to children's literature and her works on folklore and mythology. Here is a detailed biography of her life:

Elsie Spicer Eells was born on February 19, 1880, in Lansing, Michigan, United States. Not much is known about her early life and upbringing, including details about her family background and childhood.

Eells embarked on her writing career during the early 20th century, focusing primarily on children's literature and folklore. She wrote numerous short stories, articles, and books aimed at young readers, often drawing inspiration from myths, legends, and folktales from around the world.

Elsie Spicer Eells gained recognition for her ability to retell traditional folktales and myths in a captivating and accessible manner for children. Her works often featured themes of adventure, heroism, and moral lessons, making them popular among young readers and educators alike.

Some of her most notable works include "Indian Myths, Legends, and Folk Tales" (1917), "The Hungarian Fairy Book" (1913), and "Japanese Fairy Tales" (1920). These collections brought stories from diverse cultures to Western audiences, helping to preserve and share the rich oral traditions of various peoples.

Eells was also a dedicated folklorist, with a keen interest in exploring and documenting the oral traditions of different cultures. Through her research and writings, she aimed to introduce readers to the diverse folklore and mythology of various regions, shedding light on the beliefs, customs, and values of different societies.

Her works often featured detailed introductions and annotations, providing valuable context and insights into the cultural significance of the stories she presented. Eells' contributions to the field of folklore studies helped to promote cross-cultural understanding and appreciation for the world's diverse heritage of myths and legends.

Elsie Spicer Eells' writings continue to be cherished by readers of all ages for their enchanting storytelling, cultural richness, and educational value. Her books remain popular choices in schools, libraries, and homes, where they inspire imagination, curiosity, and a love for world folklore.

Although much of her life remains shrouded in obscurity, Eells' enduring legacy as a storyteller and folklorist endures through her timeless literary works, which continue to captivate and entertain readers around the globe.

Selected Bibliography:

- Fairy Tales from Brazil: How and Why Tales from Brazilian Folk-Lore (1917): This collection presents a series of Brazilian folk tales, offering readers insight into the rich storytelling traditions of Brazil.
- Tales of Giants from Brazil (1918): Focusing on Brazilian legends, this book compiles stories centred around giants, reflecting the country's vibrant mythological heritage.
- The Islands of Magic: Legends, Folk and Fairy Tales from the Azores (1922): Eells explores the folklore of the Azores in this compilation, bringing to light the enchanting tales from these Portuguese islands.
- The Magic Tooth and Other Tales from the Amazon (1927): This work features stories from the Amazon region,

highlighting the diverse cultural narratives found within the Amazonian communities.

- South America's Story (1931): Eells provides a broader perspective on South American folklore and history through this publication, encompassing various tales and cultural insights from across the continent.
- Tales of Enchantment from Spain (1950): In this collection, Eells delves into Spanish folklore, presenting a series of enchanting tales that reflect Spain's rich cultural heritage.

Andrew Lang

Andrew Lang (1844–1912) was a Scottish poet, novelist, literary critic, and anthropologist, best known for his prolific literary output and his contributions to the field of folklore studies. Here is a detailed biography of his life:

Andrew Lang was born on March 31, 1844, in Selkirk, Scotland, to John Lang, a town clerk, and Jane Plenderleath Sellar Lang. He was the eldest of eight siblings. Lang received his early education at the Selkirk Grammar School before attending the Edinburgh Academy and later the University of St. Andrews, where he studied classics and modern literature.

Lang began his literary career as a journalist and editor, contributing articles, essays, and reviews to various newspapers and magazines. He gained recognition for his literary criticism, demonstrating a keen intellect and a deep understanding of literature, folklore, and mythology.

Lang's interests were diverse, and he wrote extensively on a wide range of subjects, including poetry, fiction, history, anthropology, and psychology. He was a prolific author, producing numerous works across multiple genres throughout his lifetime.

One of Lang's most significant contributions to scholarship was his work in the field of folklore studies. He was deeply fascinated by the oral traditions and folk beliefs of different cultures, and he devoted much of his career to collecting, researching, and analysing folktales, myths, and legends from around the world.

Lang's "Fairy Books" series, which included collections such as "The Blue Fairy Book" (1889), "The Red Fairy Book" (1890), and "The Green Fairy Book" (1892), among others, became immensely popular and influential. These collections featured fairy tales from various cultural traditions, translated and adapted for English-speaking audiences, and helped to preserve and popularize many classic folk stories.

In addition to his contributions to folklore studies, Lang wrote numerous other books on diverse subjects. He authored poetry collections, such as "Ballads and Lyrics of Old France, " (1872) and "Rhymes à la Mode, " (1884), which showcased his talent for verse.

Lang also wrote historical works, biographies, literary histories, and novels, including "The Monk of Fife, " (1895), a historical novel set in the time of Joan of Arc. He was a versatile writer, capable of tackling both fiction and non-fiction with equal skill and enthusiasm.

In 1875, Andrew Lang married Leonora Blanche Alleyne, with whom he had four children. Blanche, as she was commonly known, was a talented author and translator in her own right, and she often collaborated with Lang on his literary projects.

Andrew Lang's legacy as a writer, folklorist, and scholar endures through his extensive body of work, which continues to be studied, admired, and enjoyed by readers around the world. His contributions to folklore studies helped to popularize the study of folk traditions and fairy tales, shaping the way these stories are understood and appreciated to this day. Lang's influence on literature, anthropology, and cultural studies remains significant, and his works remain important sources for scholars and enthusiasts interested in the rich tapestry of human culture and imagination.

Selected Bibliography:

- Fairy Books - Lang's "Coloured Fairy Books" are among his most celebrated works, each named after a different colour:
  - The Blue Fairy Book (1889)
  - The Red Fairy Book (1890)
  - The Green Fairy Book (1892
  - The Yellow Fairy Book (1894)
  - The Pink Fairy Book (1897)
  - The Grey Fairy Book (1900)
  - The Violet Fairy Book (1901)
  - The Crimson Fairy Book (1903
  - The Brown Fairy Book (1904)
  - The Orange Fairy Book (1906)
  - The Olive Fairy Book (1907)
  - The Lilac Fairy Book (1910)
- Other Notable Works:
  - The Blue Poetry Book (1891): A collection of poems suitable for children.
  - The True Story Book (1893): A compilation of historical narratives presented in a storytelling format.
  - The Red True Story Book (1895): Continuation of historical tales aimed at younger readers.
  - The Animal Story Book (1896): Stories centred around animals, blending fact and fiction.
  - The Arabian Nights Entertainments (1898): Lang's rendition of the classic Middle Eastern tales.
  - The Book of Romance (1902): A collection of romantic tales from various traditions.
  - The Red Book of Animal Stories (1899): Further animal-centric tales for children.

- Scholarly and Literary Criticism:
  - Custom and Myth (1884): Essays exploring the origins of various customs and myths.
  - Myth, Ritual and Religion (1887): A two-volume work examining the connections between mythology, rituals, and religious practices.
  - Books and Bookmen (1886): Essays on literary topics and book collecting.
  - Letters to Dead Authors (1886): Imaginary letters addressed to famous authors of the past.
  - Homer and the Epic (1893): A study of Homer's works and their place in epic literature.
- Translations:
  - The Odyssey of Homer (1879): Prose translation in collaboration with S.H. Butcher.
  - The Iliad of Homer (1883): Prose translation with Walter Leaf and Ernest Myers.

About The Editor

Clive Gilson was born in 1962 into a household steeped in sport and rhythm. His father was a senior amateur and lower-league professional footballer, while his mother, equally formidable, was an award-winning ballroom dancer. Their spirited household didn't just hum with ambition, it danced to it.

After earning a degree in History from Leeds University, Clive took an unexpected turn into the then-nascent world of information technology in the late 1980s. Yet, the call of story and stage never left him. Alongside a thriving tech career, he freelanced as a journalist and book reviewer, earning one small by-line in the national press, and also spent over a decade performing in village halls and professional theatres across the south of England.

A true inheritor of his family's sporting zeal, Clive later pivoted into live sports broadcasting. In the 1990s, he became a trusted rugby 'stato' for the BBC, ITV, EuroSport, and TVNZ, bringing insight and analysis to major tournaments including the Heineken Cup, Six Nations, World Sevens, and Rugby World Cups.

As a writer, Clive has made his mark across genres. His debut novel, *Songs of Bliss*, was published in 2017, followed by *A Solitude of Stars* in 2019. Since then, he has released three acclaimed short story collections, *The Mechanic's Curse*, *The Insomniac Booth*, and, in 2025, *Melodies in Black Ink*.

He is also an award-winning poet and the author of a biography detailing the life of a former professional footballer, namely his father. Since 2018, Clive has served as Managing Editor of the Firesides Tales Project, a global storytelling initiative that has published over 30 collections of folktales, fairy tales, myths, and legends from around the world.

Today, Clive continues to write fiction rich in folklore, memory, and quiet transformation, combining his deep love of narrative with a lifelong fascination with the human spirit.

For more about his work, visit clivegilson.com, where stories are always waiting to be found.

ORIGINAL FICTION BY CLIVE GILSON

- *Songs of Bliss*
- *Out of the Walled Garden*
- *The Mechanic's Curse*
- *The Insomniac Booth*
- *A Solitude of Stars*
- *Melodies In Black Ink*

AS EDITOR – *FIRESIDE TALES – Western Europe*

- *Tales From the Land of Dragons* – Welsh Folk & Fairy Tales
- *Tales From the Land of The Brave* – Scottish Folk & Fairy Tales
- *Tales From the Land of Saints And Scholars* – Irish Folk & Fairy Tales
- *Tales From the Land of Hope And Glory* – English Folk & Fairy Tales
- *Tales from Gallia* – French Folk & Fairy Tales

AS EDITOR – *FIRESIDE TALES – Northern Europe*

- *Tales From Lands of Snow and Ice* – Scandinavian Folk & Fairy Tales
- *Tales From the Viking Isles* – Icelandic Folk & Fairy Tales
- *Tales From the Forest Lands* – Finnish Folk & Fairy Tales
- *Tales From the Old Norse* – Scandinavian Folk & Fairy Tales
- *Tales from Germania* – German Folk & Fairy Tales

AS EDITOR – *FIRESIDE TALES – Southern Europe*

- *Tales From the Land of Rabbits* – Spanish & Portuguese Folk & Fairy Tales
- *Tales Told by Bulls and Wolves* – Italian Folk & Fairy Tales
- *Tales of Fire and Bronze* – Greek Folk & Fairy Tales

AS EDITOR – *FIRESIDE TALES – Eastern Europe*

- *Tales From The Samodivi* – Balkan Folk & Fairy Tales
- *Tales From the Land of the Strigoi* – Romanian Folk & Fairy Tales
- *Tales Told by the Wind Mother*– Hungarian Folk & Fairy Tales

AS EDITOR – *FIRESIDE TALES* – *North America*

- *Okaraxta* - Tales from The Great Plains
- *Tibik-Kìzis* – Tales from The Great Lakes & Canada
- *Jóhonaa'éí* –Tales from America's Southwest
- *Qugaaĝi^* - First Nation Tales from Alaska & The Arctic
- *Karahkwa* - First Nation Tales from America's Eastern States
- *Pot-Likker* - Folklore, Fairy Tales, and Settler Stories from America

AS EDITOR – *FIRESIDE TALES* – *Africa*

- *Arokin Tales* – Folklore & Fairy Tales from West Africa
- *Hadithi Tales* – Folklore & Fairy Tales from East Africa
- *Inkathaso Tales* – Folklore & Fairy Tales from Southern Africa
- *Tarubadur Tales* – Folklore & Fairy Tales from North Africa
- *Elephant And Frog* – Folklore from Central Africa

AS EDITOR – *FIRESIDE TALES* – *Middle East*

- *Tales From The Meddahs* – Turkish Folk & Fairy Tales
- *Tales From The Hakawati* – Arabic Folk & Fairy Tales
- *Tales Told By Balebos & Gusan* – Jewish & Armenian Folk & Fairy Tales

AS EDITOR – *FIRESIDE TALES* – *Asia & The Far East*

- *Tales Told By The Kathaakaar* – Folk & Fairy Tales from India
- *Tales Of The Gùshì Yuan* – Chinese Folk & Fairy Tales

AS EDITOR – *FIRESIDE TALES* – *Animal Tales*

- *Dog Tails* – Folk & Fairy Tales featuring our canine chums
- *Cat Tails* – Folk & Fairy Tales featuring our feline friends

AS EDITOR – *FIRESIDE TALES* – *South & Central America*

- *Tales From The Caribbean* – Folk & Fairy Tales from Caribbean islands
- *Tales From Central America* – Central American Folk & Fairy Tales
- *Tales Told From South America* – South American Folk & Fairy Tales